"Now, sweetie, I knew you'd be mad."

"Mom, I'm not mad. Really. It's just that I feel terrible. I mean, Mom, I didn't tell you to buy that stock. I didn't say anything like that. I just thought you'd think it was funny. About Ernie, I mean."

"I know, sweetie. I know you didn't tell me. And I know you *never* tell me. I know it's your rule. That's why I didn't say anything. But you said you were pretty sure you'd make a nice chunk on this one, that's what you said. That's *exactly* what you said." Her voice dropped to a whisper. "And after I got off the phone with Roddy, I called Clarissa."

"Oh, Mom."

"And she called her stock guy and bought some, too."

"Oh, *Mom*." It was a virus. It was spreading. And I had started it.

"And...and now it's gone down quite a lot and Roddy says I should sell, but I thought...I thought I'd better call you."

It was difficult for me to talk, what with my forehead pressed to my desk while I studied the floor. My neck was rapidly cricking up and all the blood was rushing into the top of my head. But, for the moment, the pain was good. I wanted pain. Because of a casual remark I had made, my mom was currently down five thousand bucks on the day. My *mom*: the woman who spent sixteen hours in difficult labor bringing me into the world, but who is too sweetly tempered to ever bring that up at a time like this.

*Watch for the next Madeline Carter novel
from LINDA L. RICHARDS*

FIVE

Coming December 2005

LINDA L. RICHARDS

Mad MONEY

MIRA

ISBN 0-7783-2103-7

MAD MONEY

Copyright © 2004 by Linda Richards.

www.MIRABooks.com

Printed in U.S.A.

ACKNOWLEDGMENTS

Nothing in my life has ever gone as smoothly as the birth of Madeline Carter. Every aspect of the midwifing up to this point has gone with the sort of clocklike precision generally only found in fiction. It seems that Madeline—like Brie and marzipan and ice wine—was simply meant to be. Sometimes I'm not even sure I had a lot to do with it. One day, Madeline simply *was*.

Many thanks to my agent, Loretta Barrett of Loretta Barrett Books in New York, for her wisdom, grace and for being instrumental in helping Madeline find her place in the world. Loretta is agent, but also cheerleader, guide and teacher.

The novelist M. J. Rose has been a special friend and mentor through this process. She helped open doors I didn't even realize were there. Read her books: they're wonderful, and so is she.

Thanks to my life partner, David Middleton. David is always my first reader, and without him Madeline would be a much duller girl. David has the sharpest eye for detail and continuity imaginable and, as everyone says: David knows everything. A very good trait for a first reader. Also—and of course—thanks to David for fostering the bubble of creativity that shelters and inspires us wherever we go. And for the lattes. We've discovered it takes a *lot* of caffeine to write a book.

My son, the actor Michael Karl Richards, has shown me some of the most salient secrets to creative success. I'll share the most important of these with you now: Want it with every fiber, then give it all you've got. Thank you, Mike. You inspire me. Always.

Thanks to my special sister-daughter, Carrie Wheeler, for her unshakable faith, unwavering encouragement and a pile of very good advice.

Thanks to Madeline's Goddess of Compliance,
Mary Beck, and her consort/husband, Lang Evans,
for their expert and loving reading of the manuscript.
Mary and Lang helped make sure that my representations
of Madeline's trading in particular and of the stock market
in general were accurate. If there are errors in this regard,
they are mine, but Mary and Lang helped make the good
stuff better.

Thanks to Murray Baker, Todd Clarke and Andrew Heard
for putting up with—and answering—endless questions
about everything to do with the stock market when I first
found this passion. Who knew?

Thank you to Madeline's earliest readers, my dear friends
Michelé Denis, Laura-Jean Kelly and Debbie Warmerdam.
Your support was more appreciated than you know,
your enthusiasm a happy wave that carried me through
the home stretch. Thanks also to Patricia McLean,
Betty Middleton, Jackie Leidl, Tami Adams and
Carolyn Withers. Where would I be without you guys?

Thanks to my brother, Dr. Peter Huber, whose belief in
me has been unshakable, always, even at times when I've
had my own doubts. Your support and input always mean
so much. Not to mention, of course, having inadvertently
supplied many of the locations in *Mad Money*. Thanks
doesn't even begin to cover it.

Thanks to the *JanuaryMagazine.com* team for
their support, understanding and encouragement,
especially J. Kingston Pierce, crime fiction editor,
and Pamela Patterson, associate editor. Thanks
also to the *January Magazine* Novel Support Society:
Margaret Gunning, Tony Buschbaum and David Abrams.
You guys rock.

The fact is, nothing comes; at least nothing good.
All has to be fetched.
—Charles Buxton

One

No one accused me of killing Jackson Shoenberger. The hand on the weapon wasn't mine. I didn't pull the trigger or point the gun. After Jack was dead, no one looked at me and said, "She did it. Madeline Carter widowed that woman, orphaned those kids."

Yet I felt responsible. Responsible and, at the same time, I felt how easily it could have been me. Those things might sound mutually exclusive, but they're not.

I wasn't a junior broker. Neither was Jack. We'd both been with the company ten years when Sal came to us and offered to pull us out of the bullpen—give us offices of our own. Jack looked as if he thought it was a good idea, but I wouldn't bite. I loved the electric crackle in the pen on bullish mornings when the room hummed with possibilities—the phones, the yells, the excited high fives. It was all a part of it for me. I loved being a broker. Becoming an investment manager didn't feel like a step up.

I wouldn't have blamed Jack for accepting Sal's

offer. Jack had a wife, kids and a house in Jersey. I didn't even have a cat. But when I declined, Jack looked at me with those heavy-lidded eyes of his and grinned. "What she can hack, I can hack." It could have meant a lot of things, but I took it at face value.

We never got a clear answer on how the shooter made it past security and into the bullpen. He looked normal enough. Fortyish, short dark hair, well-pressed chinos and a good wool coat, not out of keeping with the season. In retrospect I think that when he said, "Jackson Shoenberger?" to confirm Jack's identity, there was a quaver in his voice. A hesitation. But maybe that's just my mind filling things in after the fact.

The rest isn't filled in.

Initial surprise. Then a smile. An extended hand. "Yeah, I'm Jack. What can I do you for?" A coat flung aside, a flash of chrome, a crack of sound, then Jack on the floor in a cascade of blood. I can't forget the smell: metallic and burnt all at once. The smell of the firearm discharging. Cordite. But something else. Not the smell of death, but of dying.

Before any of us had time to react, another crack sounded and the shooter was down. So little space separated the two men that the shooter's ruined face came to rest on Jack's left foot. More blood. Then a cone of silence you could hold in your hand. The world stopped. No one said anything. No one screamed. No one even seemed to breathe. Ten seconds. Maybe thirty. It was the blood on my hand that woke me from my daze. Moved me. Blood cooled by its flight through the air.

Then chaos: we all moved at once. It didn't matter;

we could have stayed there for an hour. Forever. Jack was dead. Jackson Shoenberger—thirty-five-year-old husband of Sarah, father of Nigel and Rose, the man who never missed the first-Thursday-night-of-the-month meetings of his gourmet club—was dead before he hit the floor.

And it was stupid. Pointless. Without sense. The shooter had been a client. Not an important one. He'd made a bit of money when the bull was raging and had started investing heavily just as the bear pulled up. The worse the market got, the more money he plugged in. I know Jack wouldn't have asked his client where the cash was coming from. That wasn't part of our job.

Once the blood was mopped up, we followed the paper trail. Jack had been trying to steer the guy right, but he hadn't listened, hadn't trusted and had said, "Buy," when Jack had told him, "Sell."

It had only been a couple of hundred grand but, as it turned out, it belonged to the shooter's mom. According to the pieces the police and the old woman's boyfriend put together, the lady asked for her cash back to buy a condo in Florida and her son just snapped. Killed her pretty much the way he'd killed Jack—at close range with the same small gun—then hauled his ass to Manhattan from Long Island and did the double deed, Jack and then himself, all in the space of a couple of hours.

The funeral was in New Jersey—in Lawrenceville, where the Shoenbergers lived. I was pleased to see Sarah's delicate face light up when she saw me, and surprised to see Nigel and Rose standing somberly on either side of their mother.

"They're little, I know," Sarah said when she saw me notice. "But I wanted them to be part of this. Funerals are about completion for those that are left behind." She said it like a mantra, smoothing Nigel's pale hair absently as she spoke. "They deserved the chance to say goodbye, too."

Sarah was, in all ways, the opposite of her husband. *Late husband,* I corrected myself. Sarah was a tiny bundle of energy, where Jack had been big and rangy and, for a broker, laid-back. Sarah was dark where Jack had been fair. Each had been given a child: at nine, Nigel, with fine wheat-colored hair and pale eyes, was the image of his father. Today it hurt to look at him. Rose, just six, was dark and composed, a jade-green ribbon bringing out the red highlights in her hair.

"I was afraid you wouldn't come," Sarah said, grasping my hand tightly when she saw me after the funeral.

"Of course I'd come, Sarah. How could I not?"

"I was worried when you didn't return my calls."

"Sarah, I'm so sorry. I…I didn't know what to say." I glanced down at the kids, lowered my voice. "I was…I was there."

"Oh, honey, I know you were." She reached out and squeezed my hand. "That must have been so hard."

The touch undid me. On the surface of things, I'd been managing fine. Not thinking too much about anything, just moving. But the touch, from someone so close to Jack, someone with whom I shared a link to my old friend, was like a flame to wax on the place I'd been protecting. I could feel my face cloud, tears threatening, something I couldn't bear the thought of Sarah seeing.

Her pain, I thought, was enough. She didn't need the added weight of mine. She didn't see it that way.

"After all of this—" she indicated the crowds of people filing through, both Jack and her families, co-workers and friends "—just a few people are coming by the house. I'd like you to be one of them."

I nodded, quickly kissed her on the cheek and went to move on, to let other mourners pay their respects, but Sarah didn't let me slip away. She grasped my hand firmly and pulled me back. "Don't even think about bailing, Carter," she said firmly. "I *need* you there. Jack would have wanted you there."

"Yes'm," I said, smiling for what felt like the first time in days. "That does not sound like an invitation that can be turned down."

"It's not."

"I get that, already. When?"

"Anytime, really. My parents headed back to the house to make coffee and prepare food."

I didn't head straight for the house. I drove around Lawrenceville in my rental, mentally placing Jackson everywhere I looked. In a ball cap and jeans, on the weekend, scooting into the hardware store for whatever gunk he needed to fix a leaky faucet in the kids' bathroom. Taking Sarah out for Italian food on their anniversary. Running the kids to day care and, later, to school. When I cruised past the high school and thought about how he wouldn't get to see his kids go there, let alone graduate, I made myself stop. None of this, clearly, was going to bring Jackson back. And none of it was making me feel any better, either.

Sarah and the kids were already back at the house when I pulled up, a strudel purchased from a local bakery in my arms.

"I was afraid you weren't going to come," Sarah said. She was outwardly composed, but I knew her well enough to see the strain around the edges: the reddened eyes, the line above her brow that didn't seem to go away even when her expression was relaxed. That hadn't been there a month ago.

"Naw." I showed her the strudel. "Couldn't come empty-handed."

"Right," she said sarcastically, taking it and indicating I should follow her to the kitchen. "I know what a stickler you are for tradition."

I stuck my tongue out at her tone, a childish gesture, and we both started to laugh, the laughter turning to tears in a heartbeat.

Jack and Sarah's kitchen was bright and modern. The hand-painted milk jugs from the 1940s and 50s that Sarah had collected over the course of her marriage brought happy splashes of color to the room. I had watched the collection grow over the years, exclaimed at new acquisitions when I'd joined them for family dinners. It felt odd being here now, knowing that Jack wouldn't be joining us. Wrong.

Sarah was crying like someone for whom tears are no longer an effort, the way oil moves through a well-made machine: smoothly and with grace. "Everything is just the same. Nothing will ever be the same." She shrugged, leaning on the counter. "I'm a widow now, Madeline. A *widow*. I can't get my mind around that.

And I keep expecting him to come back. To walk through that door." She looked out to the backyard as though she was, indeed, expecting him to walk in, bags of groceries in his arms, yelling, "Sarah, did you forget to pay the goddamn Visa bill?"

It was me, I wanted to say. *It's all because of me and what I wanted, what I said.* I didn't, though. "Is everything going to be okay, Sarah? Financially, I mean? You wouldn't need that on top of…"

"No, no. Everything is great that way. And the company has been terrific. More than terrific. They've sent out a grief counselor and therapists for the kids and you name it. You're lucky to work for such a great company."

"I'm thinking of quitting," I said quietly, surprising myself. It was the first time the thought had entered my head, but it suddenly seemed my obvious next move.

Sarah just looked at me.

"I'm thinking of leaving Merriwether Bailey," I said with more confidence.

"You are not."

I just nodded.

"Oh, Madeline. Why?"

"I can't go back there. I mean, not to work, like, every day."

"What'll you do?"

It felt terrible, taking sympathy from the newly bereaved widow, but it also felt good, allowing my pain to ease away a little bit. As if the blending of our pain would somehow open it to the light for sharing. Or maybe it was just good to air some of the stuff that had been rocking around in my head since Jack died.

"I'm not sure. I feel so...bad, Sarah. I feel..."

"Responsible?"

I looked at her sharply. How had she known?

"There was nothing Jack didn't tell me, Madeline. Nothing. That's one of the reasons I could love you as much as I did—do—because no matter what some people thought, I knew that the love you shared with Jack was different than the love I needed from him. Part of the reason I *could* love him so deeply was because he was a man who could have a woman as his best friend. Other women might not have understood that. I did." She smiled at me through a thin cloud of tears. "And you got to be my friend, too.

"Jack told me he was up for a promotion. And then it came and he told me what happened. Told me what both of you had said."

I crumpled then. I felt diminished, reduced. I had wanted to tell Sarah. Yet at the same time I hadn't wanted her to know.

"But, Madeline, you said what you said and Jack did what he wanted. That was his way. Once you've thought about it, you'll know what I'm saying is true. He loved the market. He *lived* for the market. And he made a good living as a broker. A very good living. He didn't need the extra salary moving into an office would have given him. He told me, 'I'd miss the sweat and the Maalox.' Those were his exact words. And I know he would have missed you."

And that was just it. What if—more what-ifs—what if there *hadn't* been a me? Or if I'd never joined Merriwether Bailey? It was clear to me that Jack would still be alive.

I didn't say this to Sarah. I figured she'd been through enough. "Thank you, sweetie," I said, hugging her quickly. "It's been so hard for me. And you're his *wife*. I feel like such a loser feeling as bad as I do and knowing how much harder it must be for you."

"That's the thing about grief, hon. It's not a contest. No one gets to win." She smiled bitterly and I knew that bitterness wasn't directed at me. "I have felt..." She searched for a word. "Flatlined. I've felt flatlined since it happened. I go through the motions, but none of it matters." She shrugged. "So that's my big plan, for now. For the kids. Just keep the motions going and maybe sometime it'll surprise me. Maybe someday it won't be pretend."

The idea of the flatline got into my head. It covered precisely how I felt. Entirely flat, not quite alive. I was someone who had always thought of herself as buoyant. *Vibrant.* And suddenly I was anything but. For the first time in my life it was possible for me to spend a whole day in bed, doing nothing. I'd drag myself up to go to the bathroom, maybe make some toast with peanut butter or a soft-boiled egg, and then try to throw myself back into sleep.

I didn't quit my job right away. Unlike Jack, who got taken out with a bullet, I went with a whimper. I took a leave of absence—a week that stretched into two then four—and contemplated basic things. The meaning of life, for me. How I fit into the pattern that I'd created. On good days I was able to leave my apartment and I didn't cry. On bad ones, I'd encounter Jack's face at every turn: in the antique mirror over my armoire, in the dull gloss of the tiles behind the stove, through the window when I tried to imagine what was in the world beyond my door.

Jack and I had never been lovers, though I'm sure people in the office had their doubts. In the time we worked together, both of us got married, one (me) got divorced, one (him) had children, and in between were all the challenges of lives being lived, both in the markets and out of them. I loved Jack. Not as a wife loves a husband, yet not quite as a sister loves a brother, either. I'd always felt that what we shared transcended all those things. That we'd be together always, each forever the emergency other in our lives. And now...

My world was full of what-ifs. What if Jack had taken Sal's offer and had been safely working with corporate clients behind a closed office door? What if I had said yes to Sal and Jack had followed my lead? But the world can be too full of questions. Stack them all together and you end up a dollar store cashier in Bend, Oregon, or a gas station attendant in New Hampshire. You end up spending your life looking for low risk gigs. What did low risk look like, anyway? No one had ever warned me about the physical dangers involved with being a stockbroker.

Before Jack died, I'd already been having thoughts about changing my life. I'd spent the last few years coasting on high tech, just like everybody else. It's hard to think now about, what it was like being a broker during the boom, but it was...delicious. Touch anything and it goes gold. Pick some crappy little Web-based company with a happy idea and a slick annual report trading at six and a half dollars, trade it, promote it, and within two weeks it's trading at twenty bucks. By the end of the boom I was working with scores of securities just like that, trading at twenty, forty, sixty dollars a share. For some of them, two hundred wasn't even a reach.

I saw and felt it coming. I was crunching Advil like candy. Do I even *have* a stomach lining anymore? And Maalox. I never drank it right out of the bottle like some of the guys did, but that's what was in the coffee mug on my desk anytime after lunch.

I had a nice little co-op apartment—stand on a chair and look out the bathroom window and see Central Park—that I'd paid mostly cash for. My own trading had never been on the margin. I lost the bazillion or so dollars I'd been worth on paper. But I was a broker; I'd never been convinced it was real money, anyway. I had my apartment. I had a Chagall etching I'd bought with some pretend money I'd converted into real money. I thought, I'm gonna be okay. I'm gonna coast through this. I still had a job. Not everyone did.

Then Jack.

I thought briefly about not doing something with stocks. I wanted to make a new life. I could do *anything*. I could wait tables. Become a real estate agent. Be a film director. Open a dress shop. Or a café. But the reality was that the stock market was the only thing I knew. Except I also knew I didn't want to be a broker anymore. I didn't want to invest other people's money. And I realized I was tired of having to stand on a chair to see a slice of green. My apartment was worth enough to buy a whole house in most cities that weren't New York. It was certainly enough for a stake.

I had a lot of questions, was shy on answers, but there was one thing I knew: my days at Merriwether Bailey—or any other brokerage—were over. And it wasn't just that the new economy was looking like it was going to suck so badly there'd be too many of us. I was good. I could have kept my job. I just didn't want it anymore.

"What are you gonna do?" Sal asked when I went into the office to clean out my desk.

As I loaded the cardboard box that was proving to be too large for my few personal possessions, I had been trying to impress details on my mind so I wouldn't forget: the wood-grain laminate that seemed to coat every hard surface in the office (active traders can be messy), the dumb, dippy bird on Jamal Henderson's desk (bright red with a real feather on his head and always dipping toward water but never making it), the viral hum of the air conditioner (noiseless noise, white noise). My eyes stopped on Jack's desk, catty-corner from mine. Empty now, his family pictures gone. Had Sarah come in for everything? Or was there a box somewhere in one of the back offices with "Shoenberger" scrawled across it in big, black letters? I figured I didn't really want to know.

It was 4:30 p.m. on a trading day. The markets were closed, the bullpen in the post-coital lull that follows the closing bell: brokers cleaning up their desks, doing paperwork, chatting softly, amicably; traders horsing around like the self-satisfied adolescents they seem to pride themselves on being. All of this activity, all in anticipation of tomorrow's opening bell, while still riding the ebbing high of the day's trading. I knew this was one of the things I'd miss.

"Carter?"

"Sorry, Sal. I was just thinking."

"I asked what you're going to do." I noticed that the corner of Sal's mouth was twitching, as it does when he's worried about something. I wondered if I might be the cause.

Sal was my boss, but he was more, as well. My father died when I'd only been at Merriwether Bailey a couple of years. Sal hadn't tried to be a father to me after my Dad was gone, but he'd slid into the senior-male-figure in my life position comfortably. Watching me closely through heartbreaks and workaholic periods. Prodding me when I seemed to spend too much time at the office or forgot to eat. He worried about me. I could see it on him now.

"I don't know," I told him honestly.

"Just not this, huh?"

I nodded.

"Jack," he said. It wasn't a question.

"I guess." I looked again at the empty desk, allowing my eyes to scan the place where Jack had fallen. Self-indulgent, self-punishing. I made myself stop. "And it just doesn't make sense to me anymore. Not so much."

He hugged me then. I hadn't expected a hug, not from Sal. But we both needed it—the touch of another human. The world was changing. Jack's death was the grand finale for me, but Sal and I had both seen the changes coming for a long time. You don't get to be an old racehorse without learning to recognize the sound of the starting gate. Or, for that matter, the feel of the finish wire.

Sal pulled a strand of hair away from my eyes, tucked it behind my ear. "We're gonna miss your smiling mug, kiddo. I always said you were too pretty to be a broker."

I made a shooing motion with my hands, though I couldn't stop the grin that slid over my face. It was an old line with us. Lady brokers were seldom slender, five-foot-eleven blondes with lots of unruly hair. I've never thought of myself as gorgeous—attractive, sure— but in the early days, the guys gave me a fairly hard time. After a while, once I'd earned my stripes, it turned into good-natured ribbing. These days it was all about Barbie. If I made the company a lot of money, they'd call me Vacation Barbie, as in I'd earned a vacation. Or if word leaked out that I was in a relationship, the guys would ask, "How's Ken?"

The Barbie stuff didn't irritate me perhaps as much as it should have. The trading floor is always tense. As a result brokers get their laughs as cheaply and easily as possible, there's no time or energy for sophisticated humor, not during working hours.

Now Sal said, "Good luck, Barbie," and, despite the teeny inside joke, I could see the sentiment was sincere. "You always know where I am."

And I did.

I was disappointed when, a couple of weeks after I'd quit my job, I still didn't feel any better. I started getting seriously worried about myself. Was this what had happened to those crazy ladies you saw pushing shopping carts filled with all their possessions? Did it start with some sharp, personal tragedy they never recovered from? The moment that possibility seemed like an achingly clear forecast of my future, I pulled myself out of bed and made a conscious effort to do something. *Anything.* And in those first few days of stumbling recovery, a walk around a couple of blocks chased my breath away. But it helped. It was like there was a light ahead somewhere, if only I squinted diligently enough.

My timing on choosing to return to what was left of my life was flawless. Around the time I could manage a whole meal, cared enough to shower every day, and felt strong enough to catch up on my laundry, my co-op sold and I knew that the time for introspection was over. In thirty days new people would be moving into my apartment and would expect me not to be living there. I had to do *something.* I just wasn't quite sure what.

Two

I felt apprehensive until my lungs took in the air outside the terminal. Inside, it hadn't felt very different from the plane or JFK before that. But standing right outside the building, as I searched for a cab, it hit me in an amazing wave. The smog, almost dense enough to cut with scissors. The moist heat after the air-conditioned neutrality of the airport. The smell of the sea and, inexplicably and faintly, the scent of something vaguely tropical and sweet... This, to me, is the smell of Los Angeles—thick and moist and slightly mysterious beneath the dirt, though the dirt is real. I smiled as I hailed a cab. The cabbie smiled back as he stopped for me. I'd never been in the city before, but I knew I was home.

Before I'd decided on Los Angeles I'd considered Seattle, but that would have meant going back. I wasn't sure what I wanted, but I knew that retracing my steps wasn't it. I'd had a brief fling with the idea of Canada—cool and clean—but even though a lot of Canadians speak English, it's a different culture and I didn't feel up to that. I saw some program on television about Sedona, Arizona. It looked so pretty, so new. But I wasn't sure I'd be able to get a high-speed Internet connection out there and, if I decided to stay involved with the markets, that would be key.

By then I knew I wanted west and warm and *new*. It wasn't that big of a leap to think of L.A. I'd heard so much about the place. Not all of it had been good, but I'd been living in New York City for over ten years, so adversity didn't daunt me. Especially not at a steady seventy degrees.

"Where to?" the driver asked, still smiling, when my stuff was stored in the trunk and I was settled in the cab.

Where to, indeed? Sal had given me a lead on an apartment in a friend's house in Malibu, but I felt the need to touch the earth and regroup a little bit.

"The Beverly Hills Hotel, please." It was cliché and would probably be expensive, but I was *here* and I needed somewhere to land while I scouted a course of action. What better place than that famous landmark? More, from what I knew about it, like a museum than a hotel.

I didn't have a reservation, but it was midweek in March. I knew they'd find something for me. And when they did, it was all about airy lightness and so exactly as I'd imagined—right down to the pool and the palm trees I could see out my window—that I pulled off my clothes, flung myself onto the canopied bed and slept off my six hour flight. Welcome to L.A.

Giving Los Angeles six months had felt like a good idea. If I hated it, there were other places; my life was portable now. Before I'd left New York I'd sold practically all my stuff. Everything that wouldn't fit easily into a box or suitcase, including my Chagall. I hadn't had that much to begin with, but it felt good and *right* when it was mostly all gone, and my life was very light. And when Jack's face would pop into my mind I'd push it away and move on to the next aspect of my big, new project: my newly revamped life. A work in progress.

I needed a place to live. The hotel was wonderful, the perfect respite, but staying there for more than a week or so wouldn't be a good idea. I had enough money, but I wouldn't for long at four hundred a night. And I needed to think more about what I was going to do for gainful employment. But this was L.A. For the first time in my adult life, I needed a car.

My second day in Los Angeles I asked another cab driver to take me to where "a lot of car lots" could be found.

"What kind of car?" he asked.

I shrugged. I knew I didn't want an old car, and I wanted it silver and not terribly expensive. Beyond that, I wasn't fussy.

I bought the first new silver, domestically priced automobile I plunked my eyes on, quietly delighted at the power that buying a new car without a lot of fuss made me feel. My own magic carpet. And it was easy to rationalize the purchase: I kept thinking that part of my Chagall had paid for the whole vehicle. Viewed in that light, it was a good swap.

Driving myself back to the hotel wrapped in the scent of new car, I felt positively *Californian*. Even when I took a wrong turn off the freeway and ended up lost, I still felt exhilarated. When you're not in a hurry to get anywhere, even being lost can feel like sightseeing. It's all in the way your mind frames a situation.

A few days later, this same frame of mind carried me out to Malibu to meet Sal's friend and look at the apartment he had for rent. He'd actually called it a "guest house" on the telephone, which I took to be localese for "really, really cramped and small." But he also said it had a view and privacy, and both of those things sounded good to me—as did the price—so we set a time and I headed out to see it.

I fell in love with Malibu before I got there. The Santa Monica Freeway very abruptly becomes the Pacific Coast Highway, and as you head north, the city falls away. The closer I got to my destination, the more peaceful things became until, when I started driving up Las Flores Canyon as directed, I found myself on twisty mountain-style roads. After crowded Beverly Hills, it was like a beautiful moonscape.

I saw the address I'd been given, but couldn't see a house, just sort of a widening in the road and a post with the street address on it. I pulled over, got out. Sure enough, there was a house there—a big one—down the cliff. Precarious stairs led me downward.

Sal had told me his friend with the Malibu house was named Tyler and that they went "way, way back." Nothing more. And nothing Tyler said on the phone when we set up the appointment prepared me. But when he opened the door, I recognized him instantly. There are very few film directors that the average person can identify on sight. Tyler Beckett—director of *Spirit of the*

Flame and *Thanks for Midnight* and I don't know how many other movies—is one of them. I would have recognized the inky hair, cheerful single eyebrow and assertively stooped shoulders anywhere.

If he noticed me trying not to ogle him, he was cool about it. "You'll be Madeline." He smiled as he took my hand. "Sal told me to keep an eye on you out here on the big, bad Coast."

"That's Sal." I smiled back. "My self-appointed guardian. He's the sweetest guy. How do you two know each other?"

"We were at Neighborhood Playhouse together. About a million years ago, I guess."

"Neighborhood Playhouse in New York? The *acting* school?"

Tyler laughed at my obvious amazement. Nodded.

"Sal was an *actor*?"

"Well..." Tyler was grinning widely now "...let's just say that, as an actor, he was a pretty good stockbroker."

"Wow. Sal an actor. Bizarre."

"I guess that's what some of our coaches thought, too. Poor old Sal." He shrugged. "I shouldn't talk, though. I wasn't so great on that end of things myself."

"And you guys have stayed in touch?"

"He handles a lot of my investments. And we're old friends. Which is why he figured this would work out. He knew the guest house was empty and that we have plenty of room in the house for actual guests. Let me show you the place."

The apartment was teeny. And perfect. Tucked under the big deck we walked over to get to the stairs down to it, the guest house was so impossibly private you would have missed it if you didn't know it was there.

"This used to be the governess's apartment. My daughter is seventeen now. No governess. It's been empty for the last couple of years and my wife suggested we rent it if we could find the right person. We're gone a lot and it seemed like a good idea to have someone around. Keep an eye on things, you know."

I did. With a seventeen-year-old daughter around, you could have problems that your security company wouldn't be able to handle. Having once been a seventeen-year-old girl myself, I knew the game. I smiled at Tyler. "I get it—you're hoping for a deterrent."

"She's a good kid, really." He spread his hands helplessly. "Just some of her friends... With someone—an adult—down here, it might keep things from getting out of hand."

The apartment charmed me. Four small rooms—counting the bathroom and the closet—led off the guest house's own deck, big enough for a barbecue or a lounge chair, but not both. The front door brought you into a tiny living room, the kitchen little more than an alcove in one corner, which opened into the bedroom, which opened into a closet. The rooms were small, but the view was huge. Each room, even the closet, had floor-to-ceiling windows. The house was perched above Las Flores Canyon and what you saw from the apartment was—literally—a bird's-eye view. It made you feel as if you were soaring.

"I love it," I said, drinking in the sight.

Tyler smiled. "And you haven't even seen the bathroom."

"There's a bathroom?" I joked, following him. It was right next to the entrance. When the door to the apartment was open, the bathroom door was hidden, which was how I'd missed it. Though as small as the rest of the place, the bathroom was charming, with a clawfoot tub and a pedestal sink. I could imagine candles lit around the room, a glass of wine balanced on the edge of the tub and me looking like a glamourpuss from an old movie, bubbles up to my armpits and a satisfied smirk on my face.

"Now I love it even more. And I'd like to take it but, to be honest with you, I'm not anything like a baby-sitter. I like kids okay, but I haven't spent a lot of time around them."

"Oh, no," he assured me. "We're not looking for anything that…" He hesitated, searching for a word. "Pro-active. We were just hoping to find someone responsible—someone we know something about, obviously—to be around. Like you said—" he grinned engagingly "—a deterrent."

I grinned back. "That I can do."

"Sal told me you worked with him until recently. He didn't tell me how."

"I'm… I'm in stocks." The hesitation surprised me, though it shouldn't have. I was in the middle of redefining myself.

"A stockbroker?" he asked.

"I was. Until recently. I'm not anymore."

Tyler looked at me speculatively. He had kind eyes, so it wasn't an uncomfortable feeling. "You're a day trader?" he asked, as though this would be the most natural thing in the world. I shook my head—no—but I could feel something inside me taking root, growing.

"The stuff about being a deterrent didn't scare you?"

"Naw," I replied. "Seems like a good idea, actually. And it seems to me that you're hunting for someone who looks grown-up enough that they won't party with your offspring, but who also looks as though they can stand up for themselves." It had occurred to me that, since the deck was above me, any partying that went on would be directly above my head. I mentioned this, as well.

Tyler smiled. "I think you'll fit the bill pretty well. So, if none of what I've said scares you..." He hesitated and I shook my head. "I think you've found yourself a room with a view."

Tyler had me fill out a rental agreement, I wrote him a check and, even though it was more than a week until the end of the month, he said I could move right in. "It's empty, anyway." And so I did. Right after I did some shopping.

The nice thing about living in a small place is that you don't need a lot to fill it. The bed was built into an alcove along one wall, so I only needed a mattress. I bought a dresser. A small wood dining table and two chairs filled the kitchen and overflowed into the living room. A couple of tall stools at the back of the kitchen counter would give me a place to have breakfast or make phone calls. I bought a Metropolitan Opera poster for *Die Zoberflötte* featuring a reproduction of *The Magic Flute* by Marc Chagall. I had always loved this image: an angel playing music for, perhaps, all of the animals in Eden. It was peaceful, colorful, cheerful.

And since, beautifully framed and matted, it cost me less than two hundred bucks, it was a bit of a personal joke. The rare and beautiful early etching had brought me $25,000, but reflected something no longer real to me. Same artist, different phase. For both of us. I liked the way that felt as much as I enjoyed the color the poster added to the room.

I got a big desk and placed it in front of the living room window; I'd be able to watch the world while I worked. I got a big computer to put on the desk. And a comfy office chair. All these purchases made something clear to me: though I had yet to acknowledge a plan to myself, it certainly seemed to include some serious work.

I had just taken delivery of the last piece of furniture—the dresser—and was celebrating how nice everything looked by stretching out on the bed and alternately glancing around the apartment and gazing at the view, when I heard a loud snuffling. It sounded to me like a badger closing in on its prey. I pulled my duvet over me and listened. And didn't hear it again, though I listened hard. I relaxed; it must have been my imagination. And just as I felt the tension begin to drain out of my body, I heard it again. Not imagination. And louder this time. Closer. Inside my apartment, I was sure.

Instinct squeezed my eyes shut, accelerated the pounding of my heart. I was going to die here in my new apartment, with my books and my clothes still unpacked. My phone wasn't even connected yet.

The snuffling got louder. Closer. Fetid breath touched my face.

I chided myself for my cowardice. If I was going to

die here, eaten by some strange and exotic beast, the least I could do was fight back or, better still, make an attempt to run. I opened my eyes to find another set of eyes looking back at me. Kind, amber canine eyes. And the opening of my eyes caused a tail to wag.

And then a feminine voice, outside. "Tycho? Tycho! Get back here."

"He's in here," I croaked, relief still flooding my body, but not quite relinquishing its hold. A dog. Only a dog.

A girl poked her head into my room just as I managed to pull myself to a sitting position. She looked fifteen going on twenty-four—smooth pale-mahogany hair, well-cut chin, carefully tweezed eyebrows and familiar blue eyes. I had no trouble guessing her identity.

"Ohmigawd! Tycho, you bad boy." To me, she added, "He knows he's not supposed to be in here. You big goof." She petted his head affectionately. "I'm Jennifer Beckett. Tyler is my dad."

"Hi, Jennifer, I'm Madeline."

"I know. What a welcome. Did he scare you?"

I nodded, reddening slightly.

"Sorry. He likes it in here for some reason. And I don't think anyone that's ever lived here has liked him. He's a little scary looking."

I studied him more closely now that I knew he wasn't a feral animal. I saw that the girl was right: the dog *was* a little scary looking. And big. Very big. About a hundred and twenty pounds, with a coat like an abused Brillo pad and ears that looked as if they wanted to be erect, but couldn't quite make it.

"I guess he *does* look sorta scary," I admitted aloud,

less embarrassed in the face of Jennifer's friendliness. "I thought…I thought he was a badger. Before I saw him, I mean. I heard him."

Jennifer scratched the dog's back and he snuffled again, appreciably this time, then shook his back leg comically. "He's just a big silly, but he's harmless. Unless you're a rock lizard."

"What's a rock lizard?"

"Oh, I don't know," Jennifer replied, absently petting the dog's head. "I don't think they're actually called rock lizards. But they're little lizards and they live in the rocks on the cliffs next to the house. When it's warm, they come out and sun themselves. And then doofus here catches them, if he's quick and they're old."

"Yuck."

She nodded in agreement. "Pretty much."

"Why Tycho?"

Jennifer rolled her eyes. "Because my dad thinks he's *so* funny. The whole story is just too, too Dad. You'll have to ask him about it because I don't tell it right. See, he's named for some philosopher guy who exploded at a dinner party."

I laughed. "Astronomer, actually. Sixteenth century." Did I see Jennifer's eyes glaze over as I gave this information? Maybe a little. But it's fun to haul out bits of knowledge you never thought you'd have a use for and show them to the light. It makes you feel as though all those books you read getting your degree weren't a total waste of time. "Tycho Brahe. And, man, that *is* a funny name for a dog but it totally makes sense, in a weird sort of way."

Jennifer shrugged in the completely dismissive way that only teenage girls can pull off properly. "That's *so* my father. Weird!" The story about Brahe was actually pretty good, though it was clear Jennifer didn't want to hear it. She'd moved on to topics of greater interest to her than her father's weirdness. "Dad tells me you're a friend of Uncle Sal's and you just moved here from New York."

"Last week."

She looked interested. "No kidding? Where did you live?"

"Manhattan."

"Cool. That's where I'm going to live. When I'm eighteen. I'm an actress. Or I will be. Dad said you're a stockbroker."

I shook my head. "I was. I'm not anymore."

"But you were?" she insisted.

"Yeah. I was. For a long time."

"How'd you get into it?"

The question made me think about my Dad, Burton Carter. He'd been dead for quite a while. I didn't think about him every day anymore, but I always thought of him with a grateful fondness. My mother continued to provide the safest, most loving zones in my life. But my father had given my adulthood its shape, even if that shaping hadn't always been intentional.

Jennifer's question brought a strong image to my mind. Me: a little girl out for a special day with her father which ended up including an illicit trip to Seattle's local stock exchange. Illicit because, when I was a kid, the trading floor was no place for a child, my mother had made that clear. I remember the feeling of being adrift in a sea of wool-clad knees, all of them male. The huge room was filled with cigarette smoke and excited shouts and important yells. It was as though the air in the room had its own life: a life different and more exciting than the more mundane air that might be found outside. I never forgot the feeling and, even though the electronic world I was part of had changed the physical aspects of the stock market beyond recognition, the tension and excitement I'd felt that day had never really diminished.

"My Dad," I said to Jennifer now. "He taught me about the stock market when I was a little kid."

"He was a stockbroker?"

"Naw," I said. "He was an insurance agent. He just liked the stock market. A lot."

"Why'd you stop?"

People change careers all the time. There were a lot of things I could have told her. But, as I went to answer, the sight of Jack just before he went down flitted in front of my eyes. I saw his big, friendly face, the welcome on it giving way to recognition of the inevitable. I shook my head, pushing the image away.

"Sorry, Jennifer. It's not something I feel I can talk about right now."

I could see by her look—smug understanding—that she figured some affair had ended painfully, and I decided this wasn't a bad conclusion for her to draw. Easier for me than the truth. At least for the time being.

"Sorry," she said in turn, sounding as if she meant it, at least a little. "I get too curious sometimes. None of my beeswax. But the stock thing got my dad's attention," she admitted. "I think he hopes you'll rub off on me."

I laughed. "That's funny. I've never been cast as a role model before."

"That's my dad, always casting. Goes with the territory."

I looked at her thoughtfully. "I guess it would."

"And he hates that I want to be an actress, which is also funny. Considering."

"Considering…?"

"Well, the business he's in, for one. And the fact that his wife is an actress."

"Your mom is an actress?"

"No, my mom makes pots. She's a potter," she clarified. "In Taos. His wife—" she jerked a thumb at my ceiling, toward her own part of the house "—is Tasya Saranova."

"I saw her in *Wings of Dawn*. She was wonderful." I thought of something. "Oh…she's…"

"Not much older than me. Well, she's twenty-seven, so she's a lot older than me, but that's what my mom said when she found out."

"She nice? Tasya, I mean."

"I guess. And her and my dad are crazy about each other." The way she said it came out sounding like "kar-ay-zee."

"That's important."

She shrugged. "They're gone a lot, though. You know, moving and shaking and stuff." Her voice was nonchalant.

"That rough?"

"Not really. It means I get the place to myself." She pulled affectionately at Tycho's head. "Me and lizard boy here, that is."

"Not anymore," I said.

"True." She had a new thought. "Did Dad remember to show you the pool?"

He hadn't, and the existence of the pool was a nice surprise, so off we went to check it out.

Three

My mom, who lives in Seattle, seemed mixed about my new situation. She's worked hard all her life, for not much return. To her the money I was making in New York was beyond the moon, my lifestyle fabulous outside comparison and I was safe, as far as she could see. Set. Even without a husband. Leaving my job before I had a plan or another position seemed like insanity to her. And since there were moments when it seemed like insanity to me, it wasn't hard to see things from her point of view.

On the other hand, the fact that I was now renting an apartment from her "favorite director in the world!" was of considerable interest to her and would earn her some bragging rights with her pals. I'd never heard her mention Tyler until I told her about renting his guest house, but this didn't minimize her claim.

"Is he incredibly good-looking?" she asked on the phone.

It was one of the first calls from my new nest. Saturday night around eight o'clock, I was snuggled into the built-in bed, the Pacific Ocean at night a velvet curtain outside my window.

"Mom, you *know* what he looks like."

"But in person. Does he have, you know, charisma?"

"He's married."

"Oh. Well. Are you going to be okay for money? What are you going to do?"

That was a question I was trying not to stress about, though this wasn't something I wanted to tell my mother. "I'll be okay, Mom. I need to take some time and reevaluate, you know? I…I need to heal a bit. I feel very raw."

"I wish you would have come home." Other mothers might have made this sound sullen. Needy. Mine made it sound factual. It *was* what she would have wished. On one level, it was even what I would have wished.

"I thought about it. But it would have felt like coming back with my tail between my legs."

She laughed, a cheerful sound. "I understand. But sometimes that's okay."

After I'd said goodbye, I thought about what she'd said. "Home" was a carefully preserved Victorian in the Greenwood neighborhood of Seattle. From "home" I could walk to my old high school and poke around and look at the latest crop of kids doing early preparation for their lives. I could go a couple of blocks up the street and grab a fish taco or a well-made espresso—never tough to find in that city—or travel another block to the friendly little tavern where they poured a lovely ale and the bartender/owner knew you by name. "Home" was a pair of well-worn slippers, comfortable with long use. And thinking about it all now made me wonder if my mother wasn't right. In New York I'd had a career, friends, a neighborhood I knew and understood. In Seattle I had history and a support system. In L.A. I had…possibilities. Which was more than nothing, but would it be enough?

A soft knock on my door broke through my thoughts.

"Open!" I called, while I swung my feet out of bed.

"Is open a good idea?" It was Jennifer, smooth in well-made jeans and a cutaway blouse, bringing the scents of evening and barbecue with her. Tycho padded in behind her, making amazingly little noise for a dog so large.

I grinned. "Do you mean, is leaving the door unlocked a good idea?"

She nodded.

"Sure. I don't think anyone could even find me down here. It's like my little secret sky-cave."

Jennifer hopped up onto one of the kitchen stools uninvited, and Tycho plopped himself down at my feet with a bit of a grunt. The place suddenly felt even smaller, but in a nice way. "You thinking about getting, like, a couch or anything?"

"Not really. I think I'll get a TV for the bedroom, but I guess the living room is going to be about work," I said, indicating the oversize desk.

"You're a day trader?"

I blinked at her. "Do you even know what that is?"

"Not exactly. It sounds cool, though. Dad explained it."

"Well, I'm not one," I said, then qualified it. "Yet. I'm not one yet. But I'm thinking on it."

"Great! If you decide, you can tell me what it is. Meanwhile, Dad sent me down here to tell you to come upstairs."

"I'm being summoned?"

She laughed. "No. Sorry. I didn't say it right. Dad and Tasya are having some people over and he sent me down here to *invite* you."

"You going?" I asked, curious about who might be there.

"For a while. Corby is coming to pick me up soon, though."

"Corby?"

"Boyfriend person." She looked me over carefully. "The party—it'll be casual but nice, you know?"

I looked at my track pants and sweatshirt with a grin. "This *is* casual."

Jennifer laughed. "No, that's undressed. There'll be, like, boys and everything. You know, boys your age. Half an hour or so, 'k?" She pushed herself off the chair. "See ya."

I stressed ridiculously over what to wear, which was, in itself, a happy diversion. I knew what to wear to a gallery opening in Soho or for dinner at Balthazar. I could put together a wardrobe for a weekend in the Hamptons quite easily—not that I'd done it so often, but I would have known what to wear. But a barbecue at the Malibu home of a famous director? This was new territory.

I decided to follow Jennifer's lead: good jeans and a cutaway top, though not as cutaway as hers had been.

Some things are best left to seventeen-year-olds. Soft little sandals on my feet and my hair loose around my shoulders. L.A. enough, I decided when I surveyed myself in the full-length mirror on the back of the bathroom door.

The big deck above my apartment had been transformed since I had crossed it earlier in the day. Lit torches illuminated strategic corners, bringing the velvety night alive with golden light. Music echoed from the house and filled the air. People had already begun arriving and were arranged around the deck in little groups, standing and chatting, or sitting on various types of comfortable-looking patio furniture, drinks in hand. Even though it was early spring, the night was mild. I settled in to enjoy my first Malibu party.

Tyler was holding court from the center of a big-ass barbecue. The barbecue itself would have done well by a professional chef: huge, stainless steel and commanding. But Tyler's barbecue was an entertainer's special. It had a conversation pit built around it, where people could sit and chat with the chef, sip their drinks and taste any newly prepared tidbits he saw fit to offer. With Tyler at the barbecue, you had the impression that the place where he stood was a stage, the seats around him a little amphitheater—the director where you might expect to find an actor.

"Madeline!" he said when he saw me, sounding genuinely pleased that I'd joined them. "Glad you could come."

"Thanks for inviting me. That's an amazing barbecue, Tyler. I've never seen anything like it."

"I had it custom made a few years ago," he said,

looking pleased and faintly self-conscious at the same time. "It's the same old story. When I was growing up in Colorado, everybody had a better barbecue than my family did. Ours was rusty and old-fashioned and terrible. But I *loved* barbecue. And I resolved…" He spread his hands out, indicating the barbecuing beast at his disposal.

"You've arrived," I said firmly with a smile. Understanding.

He grinned, at once sheepish and proud. "I have. And now you have, too. Let me introduce you around."

I was the new kid, and there were a lot of guests, so the names soon melded together. By the time we'd done the rounds, more people had arrived and mixed themselves up with the ones whose names I was trying hard to remember. I saw a few familiar faces, but they looked smaller to me. Diminished in person—looking oddly normal—when I'd gotten to know them on the big screen.

Tyler's wife, Tasya, stood out from the crowd. This was partly because of her position as hostess, but also through the sheer force of her presence. Calling her beautiful was too obvious, plus an understatement: she's an international actress. A *movie star.* Beauty is self-evident. But it's more than that. Her look is dark, smoky and sublime. Audrey Hepburn with an exotic edge. Her voice is also smoky, her accent pleasingly esoteric—Eastern European with an overlay of dialect coach—and her cheekbones look as though they could seriously slice anything that ventured too close.

She brought me a glass of wine. "I'm so glad to meet

you, Madeline." It sounded like "Mad-eh-leen" when she said it. "Jennifer can't stop talking about you."

"Really?" I was oddly touched. "She seems like a sweet kid."

"She can be, but she's seventeen." She shrugged, as though the age alone spoke volumes. I refrained from reminding her she was just a decade older. "I think you will have a good influence on her," she added.

I proceeded with caution. "I'm not sure I'll be in any position to have an influence."

Tasya shrugged again, a *we'll see* kind of gesture. "It's a difficult time for her, I think. It's not so easy to be that age under any circumstances, but she has also had many changes over the last little while." She indicated herself as part of the change.

"How long have you and Tyler been married?"

"Just since Christmas. Tyler and I met in Ibiza. I was in his last movie." This would, I know, be *Dream a Dream,* a remake of a Roberto Rossolini film that was yet to be released. The entertainment press was rabid about it, though. At times crucifying Tyler for being pretentious enough to try and remake a European classic, at others shouting that it was going to be brilliant and that in Tasya he'd discovered his Ingrid Bergman.

"Ibiza. I've never been." I smiled. "But it sounds like it's the place to fall in love."

"It is, though I think it wouldn't have mattered where we were. We wrapped just ahead of Christmas and Tyler proposed. We were married in Barcelona in a small and beautiful ceremony." Her eyes had taken on a faraway look, remembering.

"Jennifer flew out there for the wedding," I ventured.

Tasya smiled. "No, we surprised her when we came back to Los Angeles." Her smile faltered. "She was very surprised."

I could imagine. And I could also now understand the way Jennifer's jaw tightened slightly at the mention of Tasya's name. Poor kid. Not the thing to surprise a teenager with.

When Tasya excused herself to resume her hostessing duties, I moved to the edge of the deck, putting my elbows on the railing and straining to see the ocean through the dark. I couldn't. But, faintly, I could hear it, even above the party noises and music. The night was clear and pleasantly cool, the scent of eucalyptus and salt drifting through the air.

I thought about what Tasya had said, about my having a possible influence on Jennifer. It alarmed me a bit, made me feel responsible in a way I hadn't signed on for. Tyler had admitted he'd hoped his new tenant would provide a deterrent for possible shenanigans in the house in his absence. Perhaps Tasya had indicated a deeper hope. I wasn't sure how I felt about it.

As though thinking about her had conjured her up, Jennifer was suddenly at my elbow, a solid-looking dark-haired woman about my own age in tow. "Excellent! You came," Jennifer said to me before beginning introductions. "Madeline, this is Emily." The woman had a good-humored smile and I liked her instantly. We exchanged greetings and Jennifer went on.

"This is a secret..." The teen looked pleased to not be keeping it. "But Emily is *completely* not supposed to be here. She's not invited." her voice dropped to a whisper. "She *crashed*."

"Okay. Well." I wasn't sure how to respond. "That's nice, I guess. Good to meet you, Emily."

"Madeline," Jennifer explained to Emily, "rents our guest house." She pointed under the deck. "She's a day trader and stock market *expert*. And my dad is hoping I'll grow up to be her."

"Yikes, Jennifer. I wouldn't have put it *that* way," I demurred.

"Hmm. Wait until you get to know him better." She said it with a smile, but I heard the bite.

"Stock market expert, huh?" Emily asked. "Sounds like a good thing to know about. I'm in this business, myself." She spread her hands to encompass the show biz types ranged around the deck.

"Why'd you have to crash, then?" Jennifer asked the question, but I wanted to know myself.

"Not the same league at all," she said candidly. "Present company—myself excluded, of course—are on the A list. The movies I work on are somewhere below the B list. Lately I've been thinking that, if you want to change lists, it would be a good idea to hang with people from the list you aspire to be on." She snagged a scallop wrapped in bacon from a tray as it went past. "The food's better up here, too. We do a party at my level, you're lucky to get pizza."

This was something I hadn't thought about before: the possibility of a Hollywood echelon in the twenty-first century. I either liked a movie or I didn't, and for me, the two things were seldom related to budget. But it made sense. In my world, there were firms that dealt with big money clients and there were smaller, lower profile firms that didn't. Having always worked with the former, I'd never spent much time thinking about the latter.

Emily told us she was currently a first A.D.—I had to stop her so she could explain to me that meant first assistant director—but that she aspired to being "the big D, myself." She hoped, one day, to direct. Though the way things worked, if she managed to get involved with the production of an important film—say the kind that Tyler Beckett directed—she'd slide back down the side of the well a bit. "But to be a second—hell, even a *second* second—A.D. on one of your dad's movies would be a big enough deal for my career to make it worth the drop." The drop would, in effect, be a rise. It all sounded pretty complicated to me, but Jennifer looked fascinated, as though this were an aspect of her father's life she'd never thought about before.

"I'm…I'm going to be an actress," she confided to us. Then, with a glance at me, "That's why I'm moving to New York next year. I'm going to study acting."

"Why New York?" Emily asked. "There are a lot of great coaches right here in L.A."

I saw Jennifer's eyes skim to the other side of the deck, where her father was happily flipping burgers and other edible meat products. When she spoke, her voice had dropped to a lower level. "Dad hates the idea of my being in the business. And, anyway, I don't want to just be Tyler Beckett's daughter. And I don't think I would be anything but that in L.A."

"That's why the crack," I said. Jennifer looked mystified, so I added, "You know, when you said your dad was hoping you'd grow up to be me."

She reddened slightly, but murmured, "I guess. He's got the idea that I want to be an actor because of him, because that's all he's exposed me to, and he suddenly wants to round me out or something."

"So I'm part of some campaign to add diversity to your life?"

Jennifer looked even more embarrassed. "Something like that I guess. Are you mad?"

I laughed. "Far from it. It got me an excellent apartment at a price I could afford, and invitations to parties that are apparently difficult to get into." I looked meaningfully at Emily.

Emily and I both saw Jennifer's attention diverted, and followed her glance and smile to a young man who was headed toward us. He was tall, lanky and looked to me to be at least five years too old for Jennifer. He looked, I thought uncharitably, more like he should be dating Tasya than Tyler's teenage daughter. Not that Tasya would have deigned to let him wash her car.

"Hey." He greeted Jennifer, not kissing her but putting his hand possessively at the small of her back.

"Corby, this is Madeline and Emily."

He nodded to us in turn. "Hey," he said by way of greeting, running his free hand through spiky red hair.

"Corby is a surfing instructor," Jennifer informed us. I bit back a laugh just in time when I realized she was serious. Was there really such a thing? I looked him over and decided that, if there was, it would look like this.

"We outta here?" he asked Jennifer. I was relieved to discover he could say more than, "Hey."

"'K," she said to him. "I'll meet you in the van, all right?"

"Ai't." He contracted the words "all right" so far down they were almost unrecognizable, then took his leave.

"Does he always talk that much?" I asked Jennifer once he was out of earshot.

I was pleased when she laughed. "Hey! He's very sweet, okay? Though maybe not the world's greatest conversationalist," she admitted with a smile. "Well, obviously, I gotta go."

"Obviously," said Emily. "Your chariot awaits, madam. But, listen, this has been altogether too much fun. You guys want to catch a movie or something next week?"

Jennifer looked delighted to be included, and in my present newly relocated condition, I needed all the friends I could get. "Sounds great," Jennifer said. "You guys work out the details, okay? I can make it work any night next week. Just let me know." And she was gone.

Emily and I exchanged phone numbers and said we'd call each other early in the week. "But now Emily," I said, "you ought to go mingle. You've got some serious networking to do. No sense wasting a perfectly good crash."

"Good point." She laughed, though she insisted on dragging me deep into the party as cover on her early networking forays.

From my perspective, the party was a crashing bore. I was in the center of what might have been a headline story on *Entertainment Tonight*—if they could have gotten access—and after a while, all I could do was stifle yawns. I'd always assumed that the clichés were just that: the bubbleheaded starlet, the hungry agent, the ambitious young actor. And while, as with most clichés, there are probably exceptions, I didn't see any on that night.

Emily didn't seem to care about any of that. She worked the room, even though it was a deck and not a room at all. She seemed adept—a creature in her own element—walking the walk and talking incessantly. It was obvious that, if networking was the way to go, Emily would achieve her goals before much time had passed.

After a while I knew that if one more person flashed me a supernaturally whitened smile, I'd theatrically clutch my head and scream, "My eyes, oh God, my eyes! I'm blind!" Knowing that was too great a risk, I took myself out of the networking loop and stood again by the railing, enjoying the party more from a distance than I had at its center.

"I agree with you." The voice was slightly accented and it surprised me, coming as it did from the shadows.

"Excuse me?"

The man who came and stood beside me was the other side of fifty, but was nonetheless *fine*. Up here at a barbecue in ever-casual Malibu, he wore well-pressed chinos and a golf shirt the way other men wear a tux: like they mean it. He looked as though he'd given up lunch appointments for tennis dates a decade ago and like someone who could clearly afford Cartier but had opted for Tag-Hauer.

"It becomes intense after a while, I find. These parties. These..." he seemed to search for the right word "...these competitions. In your business, it is all about competition—who gets the best scripts, who has the best agent, the best manager, hairstylist. It goes on and on and on. No offense, but it can be a bit overwhelming, don't you think?"

My business. I struggled for understanding, then realized he assumed I was one of Tyler's Hollywood connections. "I'm not in the business," I told him. "I rent Tyler's guest house. I'm his tenant."

He looked slightly relieved. "I am not alone then. It is good to meet you. My name is Alejandro Montoya, but please call me Alex. Almost everyone does."

I introduced myself and asked what he'd meant about not being alone. He told me he was a clinical psychologist. No longer in private practice, he did research work and taught some grad classes at UCLA. Tyler had met him when he'd brought Alex in to consult on *Generation Gone,* a movie about a midlevel executive who loses it and ends up wreaking havoc on his company and his family. At the end of the movie, this anti-hero offs himself. That had been the best moment in the film. I'd loathed the movie. Having worked in a big brokerage, I'd seen more than my share of corporate crazies. Fully half of the guys I'd worked with had been, at various times, certifiable. *Generation Gone* had just seemed like yesterday's news. The world hadn't agreed; the film had done well and had been nominated for a couple of Golden Globes, though no Oscars.

None of this was attributable to Alex, who'd merely

acted as a consultant. But he and Tyler had formed a connection and now included each other on their guest lists. "Though, to be honest, he's had few invitations from me since my ex-wife and I split up. I don't entertain much by myself. Too much trouble."

I realized that he'd included the tidbit about his marital status for my benefit and, truly, I didn't mind. It had been awhile since I'd put myself in a position where a man might recognize me as potential mating material. It was a nice feeling to be looked at that way again.

Alex secured drinks for us and steered me to a table that I hadn't noticed before near the corner of the deck. The torchlight didn't quite touch it, though candles illuminated the immediate vicinity and, with a vine-covered cliff wall behind us and the other guests fanned out over the outer regions of the deck, it was a quiet place to chat.

We talked initially, the way single adults most often do, about our work. That meant that, truly, my end of that conversation was fairly brief. I was transitional. For the moment I didn't know what I wanted to do when I grew up. Anyway, I was more interested in what Alex did. His area of specialization—and the reason Tyler had brought him in for *Generation Gone*—was in something Alex referred to as "corporate psychopaths." The term alone was intriguing.

"Do you really think there are a lot of them?"

"My research in that area remains inconclusive. I just haven't been able to test a large enough field of subjects."

He had, however, been given access to many prison inmates, and there he'd found a large percentage of the population to be, by his definition, psychopathic.

"As high as twenty-five percent. That's no surprise, of course. Our system is set up to flag psychopaths with an everyday sort of criminal bent. A psychopath, you see, has no loyalty to anyone or anything besides themselves. They are all about ego, incredibly self-centered. And some even seem to believe that everything they do is right, because what else is there besides them. Do you see?"

I glanced around theatrically at the people sitting near us, lowered my voice, and, with a smile, said, "By that definition, a lot of these people—film people— would be psychopaths."

He laughed, a good, clear sound. "You're right, if that's all there was. But there's so much more. We are not talking about psychotic individuals. These are not people who are dull-witted or give the appearance of such. The most successful psychopaths—those that stay undetected throughout most of their lives—are highly intelligent. They are most often very charming and have a knack for manipulating others, getting them to do what they want and blaming them for their actions. Perhaps even getting those others to believe that the psychopath is right."

"And they eat people." This came out of my mouth before I even thought about it. And it earned another bout of healthy laughter.

Alex nodded. "That is the common misconception. Born, I think, of fiction. Fiction and films. But, no, there is no evidence that psychopaths exhibit any more cannibalistic tendencies than the rest of us. There are many misconceptions around what constitutes psychopathic behavior. Some of my colleagues go so far as to insist that, in our enlightened day, we can no longer even use the term. That psychopaths are, in some way, learning or behavior deficient and should be treated as such. I don't agree. In my experience, the psychopath—the *true* psychopath—is untreatable. There is something deficient in their makeup that can not simply be installed, like a computer program. True psychopaths have no conscience. They are incapable of feeling remorse or regret. They are predators and, as such, they predate."

I reached out absently toward the rockwork and plucked a yellow flower from a nearby vine. It was small and tenacious looking, as well it must be to not only survive but to thrive under such unlikely circumstances. When I crushed it slightly in the palm of my hand I was surprised at the strong fragrance the little flower released. It occurred to me that things are not always what they seem. "How would you spot a psychopath?" I asked as I opened my palm and let what was left of the flower drop to the deck.

If Alex had noticed my wandering attention, he didn't comment. "Most likely, you wouldn't. Not in casual acquaintance or conversation, such as you and I are having now. As I've said, such a person is charming, sometimes even charismatic. The functioning psychopath will often be married or have other types of relationships, though they mostly won't last. And though they might give the appearance of outward calm, their personal lives are often on the brink of collapse."

My attention was beginning to wander, but I struggled not to let it show. Alex went on. "He's often a pathological liar and, to make matters worse, he's often easily bored—with his relationships, with his life. It's not uncommon to see the individual psychopath's style change drastically over the years, due to that boredom factor, I believe. In a psychopath with a criminal bent we'll see that manifest itself in a sort of career arc—perhaps stealing from the corner store when he's a child, then stealing from department stores as an adolescent, perhaps moving to cars or other large-ticket items when he's a teenager and then up to various types of grand larceny as an adult."

"But you said you specialize in corporate psychopaths. How would they differ?"

"Well, they're in corporations, for one." This was a joke, but I could see it was also the truth. "In general, psychopaths appear in society more readily at times of turmoil and upheaval. This is true in corporate structures as well as political ones. In times of crisis, for instance, or when a company is undergoing great change, that's when the corporate psychopaths come to the fore, for fairly obvious reasons."

We talked a bit longer, but after a while the good food and the wonderful wine did their work and I began to get dangerously tired. I told Alex how pleased I'd been to meet him. He gave me two of his business cards; I wrote my number on the back of one of them and handed it back. We said a warm and polite good-night, and then I went off to take my leave of Tyler, Tasya, Emily and the few people with normally colored teeth I'd met and made a connection with.

In my little house I delighted in the relative quiet— the footsteps overhead were understandable and couldn't, in any case, be helped. I'd brought a full glass of a lovely red wine downstairs with me, reasoning I could return the glass at any time. And the wine had been flowing freely enough that I was sure no one would care.

I cracked the new box of candles I'd bought and placed them strategically around the bathroom, ran myself a pleasantly stinky bubble bath and sank into the tub with my red wine and a sigh. I thought about the evening. This bath, sans the wine, had been my original Saturday night plan, but for the interruption of several interesting hours of party-going.

All things considered, I'd had a pretty good time. As odd as they were, Tyler and Tasya were very nice, not to mention model landlords. It had been sweet of them to invite me to one of their shindigs. Jennifer seemed to be rapidly forming herself to some sort of little-sister mode, and I had a feeling I had made a new friend in Emily, with whom, though we didn't have a lot in common, I seemed to share a biting sense of humor and a respect for the ridiculous. I found myself looking forward to a sort of girls' night out with her and Jennifer, and the possibility of an evening with Alex flitted through my mind, as well.

As I settled back in the tub, I realized something else. The feelings of guilt, apprehension and impending doom that had been following me since the moment that shooter pulled out his gun weren't gone. Not even close. But for the first time since that awful day, I felt the faintest glimmer of hope. As if maybe a time *could* come when dark thoughts wouldn't bring in every new day or chase out every night. It was an encouraging thought.

Four

No matter what they tell you, it rains in California. Of course it does. Just not very often. And when it does, it doesn't come down in the delicate but consistent sprinkle I'd grown up with in the Pacific Northwest, or even the persistent but polite downpour that occasionally overtakes New York. Rain in Southern California can be traffic stopping. It's like movie rain, as if from a hose in the sky. It tends not to last long, this opening up of the heavens, but while it does, it's intense, and if you can avoid going out in it, you do.

On the morning following Tyler and Tasya's barbecue, I got to experience my first serious Southern California rainfall. It woke me just before 6:30 a.m., slapping enthusiastically against my big windows, reverberating off the decks, pouring down the cliffsides. For a few minutes, I just snuggled in bed, wide awake and listening to the weather manifest itself on my little world. It was oddly comforting and frightening at the same time, the coziness of my little apartment, the anger of the passing storm.

By 6:30 on the nose I was fully awake and realizing that, in another and recent life, the opening bell would have just sounded and I'd be settling in for the trading day—it was 9:30 in New York.

For the first time since my little exodus, I felt curiosity about some of the securities I'd been tracking, and sensed a small pang in the place where my adult identity lived. I realized that I missed the feeling of being connected to the larger-than-life presence of the stock exchange. I felt the way a weatherman at the top of his game might feel if denied access to meteorological reports, or a farmer blinded to the condition of the crops. As I popped out of bed and headed toward my computer, I told myself that I just wanted to know.

That was how it started, anyway—that rainy Malibu morning. A day when I'd thought to take a jog up the canyon, but the weather closed off the option.

It took some time, bringing myself up to speed, a while even before I encountered enough information to make me realize it was Sunday and the domestic markets were closed. But by the end of the day—a day filled with instant soup and steaming cups of tea—I'd given myself an in-depth course on the stock market as viewed from a private home, as opposed to the millions of dollars worth of connectivity, hardware and source reports that had always been available to me as part of the trading team at a big brokerage.

It was a different world, it was true. If I wanted to get the kind of Level II quotes and market executions I was used to, I'd have to spend more money than I was currently willing to part with.

I opted instead to use a reliable discount broker. My trades wouldn't be executed as quickly as they would have had I been in New York. I told myself this probably wouldn't matter; that was the price of not *being* in New York. And, anyway, the kind of trading I was planning on doing—and that was the first time I acknowledged it in that way, as a plan—that kind of trading wouldn't require the split-second timing necessary on some of the larger deals I'd made on behalf of clients in days gone by.

By the end of the day a full-scale plan—complete with account application forms filled out and ready to be mailed, and pads scribbled with calculations—had emerged. Even after the car and my sojourn at the Beverly Hills Hotel and my furniture and computer shopping forays, I still had close to $150,000 cash on hand. That might sound like a lot—and in many ways, it is— but if you're just taking from it and not adding to it, I knew it could dwindle pretty quickly. Sure, if I budgeted for five years, I could live on thirty grand a year before all that money would be gone. And five years is a long time. But it wouldn't just be the money pouring out when it should have been seeping in, it would be the panic I suspected would descend as I watched my options—and my cash—dwindling.

The scribbles on the pad told me that, if I was careful and mindful and watchful, I *should* be able to make five grand a month easily—or $60,000 a year. I knew as well as anyone that "should" and "could" and even "would" as used in relation to the stock market can be completely dangerous words. Especially since all of your plans and schemes and calculations about the market must always be based on past performance. But if it was easy, mindless and obvious, everyone would be doing it. I was, in effect, planning on investing in my training, acumen and over ten years experience as a broker for one of the top firms in the world. The investment was my life savings and my time. The stakes were, in one way, my peace of mind. The worst-case scenario? I'd lose all my money and be forced to get a job.

I determined to put it all into motion quickly, before I had a chance to change my mind. In addition to an online trading account, I still needed to research various channels of information to get me to a speed that was in any way comparable to the things I'd always taken for granted at Merriwether Bailey. But by the end of that rainy Sunday I knew that Tyler and Jennifer's comments had either been prescient or inspiring: I was going to be a day trader.

This news seemed momentous enough to demand sharing, but I realized I didn't have anyone to tell, which left me feeling pathetic again. I saw Jack's face—jovial, welcoming, laughing, as I'd so often seen it. I thought of calling my mother in Seattle, but since I'd just talked to her the evening before, I ruled this out; she was astute enough that a phone call like that would have made her realize how sad and needy I currently was. That meant contacting my sisters was out, as well. A call to either of them would get back to Mom, which would put her on the alert. And, anyway, though I loved my sisters, it had been years since we'd had the type of telephone closeness that some siblings share.

I was sitting there, feeling sorry for myself, when the phone rang, nearly causing me to jump out of my chair.

"Carter," I fairly shouted into the phone, reverting to habit in my uncertainty.

"Madeline?" It was a woman's voice, and I recognized it instantly. Realistically, there weren't a lot of people it could be.

"Hey, Emily, yeah it's me."

"Funny way to answer the phone on a Sunday night," she said pleasantly.

"Old habits die hard."

"You in work mode?"

"I guess. Yeah, I am." What the hell, I thought. I'd been wanting to tell someone. "I've decided to do it. I'm going to be a day trader."

"Ah…cool." Which reminded me how the whole stock market scene is *so* not a chick thing. It's why I've had so few friends outside the industry over the years. A lot of people can't align what I do with what I project. Like I should have lesbian hair and wear lumpy pinstriped suits because I trade. "Anyway," she continued, "work is not what I was calling about."

"Unless you were hoping for a hot stock tip, I didn't think so," I grinned.

I could hear her smile back as she said, "So you and the kid want to do a movie next week?"

"Completely. Jennifer told me just to let her know when. I have virtually nothing scheduled in my life right now—" which was amazingly true "—and as far as I know, Jennifer has no essential business meetings in the evening, so you can pretty much name a day and time."

"Cool. I'm in pre-production on my next project right now, so I have a bit of flex time. I was thinking Thursday night. That new space movie is playing at Mann's. Since you're the new kid in town, I thought you might appreciate the chance to play tourist."

Mann's Chinese Theater! I was enough of an American kid at heart to actually feel somewhat thrilled at the thought. "That sounds like a lot of fun."

"You guys want to go for dinner first? There are about a million options right in that area. Well, half a million, since the kid is underage."

"Sure. Name the spot."

We agreed to meet the following Thursday at seven o'clock at a restaurant walking distance from Mann's that Emily felt sure Jennifer would know. "If not, it's in the book."

I found myself looking forward to the evening, a shot at playing tourist and the opportunity to deepen my relationship with my first California friends. It felt as though, since I'd lost Jack, I'd been looking in the wrong end of a kaleidoscope and, despite the fact that I was doing everything I could to turn it around, I had seen my world protracted in a way that was out of my control.

And now? Well, I couldn't quite see all of the bright colors I'd once seen, but with the rough sketch of a career plan, and an upcoming outing with friends, I felt a little bit closer. Something in my heart opened slightly. It eased.

Five

By Thursday morning I was five days into a new routine. I woke each day at five forty-five, put on the coffee and went for a run. Invariably, Tycho—an earlier riser than his family—joined me as we pounded up and down the canyons, the fresh sea air putting a lie to the dirty metropolis just a few miles down the coast.

By six-fifteen, Tycho and I were back at my place. He had started spending so much time there that I had food and water bowls for him, so after a run, I'd replenish his water. While he drank noisily I poured my coffee. By six-twenty we were in position: me at my computer, after a while so focused on my screen I barely noticed the beautiful drama unfolding outside my window; Tycho stretched flat in the middle of the living room, the occasional snore the only thing reminding me of his presence.

I wasn't trading yet. Not really. I was preparing. And preparations were going well. I'd established what I was now calling my "pretend portfolio," tracking an increasing number of securities, marking purchases in as buys and sells on a special program I'd installed for the purpose, calculating in brokerage fees and all fluctuations just as though I were actually trading. Only I wasn't. There was no money behind these trades. So far. That, I'd told myself, would change the following Monday, which would coincide with the activation of my online trading account. The trading I was doing at present was a trial run. And if the trial was any indicator, my plan for solvency was going to go pretty well. I was delighted to note that, based on what I'd done so far, it would be a piece of cake to exceed my expectations. I mentally splashed cold water on my face, though; the best laid plans were likely to go to hell where the stock market was concerned.

Just before the closing bell—4:30 p.m. New York time—I "sold" a couple of securities that netted me what would amount to a half year's wages in my new world. Or, rather, would have had the trades been real. I knew that, once I started trading with real money, I was likely to be a little more conservative than I was being with my pretend portfolio. But I also knew that I was ready. I'd spend Friday at my computer for good measure, but Monday was D day. I was going live.

One of the things I'd been doing during market hours this week—aside from continuously refreshing my quotes to see how the stocks I was watching were doing—was to evaluate various news sources in order to keep my finger on the market's pulse.

It's not enough to track your own securities or those that catch your interest. You also have to keep a close eye on what's happening in the world at large. Especially financial news: what the Federal Reserve is up to, what's happening with consumer spending and so on. Even things that might seem unrelated to the stock market can affect it quite deeply. Keeping up with it all means a lot of reading.

So I'd been scouting for sources of reliable newsfeeds, some of which I then set up to come to me directly by e-mail. Others were at Web sites I'd determined deserved various degrees of watching. I knew from experience that how much of this stuff I actually read on a daily basis would depend on how hectic the rest of my day was and how much I needed new blood in the form of securities I hadn't looked closely at before. But having the source of it all in place was important.

By the closing bell I felt as if I'd done a good day's work, and I looked forward to unwinding with Emily and Jennifer. This, I told myself, was going to be a whole new chapter for me. A lifestyle, not just a life. Like millions of disenchanted Americans before me, I'd come to California to find myself and—though it was early to say—I was perhaps on the path to succeeding.

After the bell, I showered in preparation for my evening out, and was just pulling on black pants, a light sweater with a deep v neck and black boots when the phone rang.

"Hey Madeline." It was Jennifer's voice. "I'm in Santa Monica. I hooked up with friends this afternoon and ended up going shopping. Can I meet you guys for dinner?" The plan had been for the two of us to drive in together, but I told her I'd find my way. And with a few basic directions, I was set.

Dinner was fun. For me it was a little like coming home; having grown up with two sisters, the company of women is easy and welcoming for me. The banter that erupted naturally among the three of us reminded me of being with Miranda and Meagan, we always had a lot to say to each other, even if it wasn't about anything that anyone else would find remotely interesting. Jennifer, Emily and I had a lot to say, as well, and each of us seemed to find the other two vastly amusing.

Emily said she had chosen a place she felt would appeal to all three of us, and she was right. The restaurant was cheerful without being chipper, and colorful without the strain that can go with that. And the company was good. Emily told a lot of amusing stories about the almost-famous people she works with on the fairly low rent movies she's worked on. I could see that her stories enchanted Jennifer, the would-be actress, because the girl seemed to hang on Emily's every word.

I found myself watching Jennifer as she raptly listened to Emily's stories. The teenager was a pile of contradictions. Not that this was especially surprising. The condition seems to arrive with puberty and not disappear altogether until around the time you get your first apartment. But it was interesting seeing it this way, from an intimate distance.

Over the course of the last week I'd seen Jennifer speak rudely to her father and deliberately walk away from him while he was in midsentence. I'd seen her ignore Tasya altogether. Yet to me she was unfailingly sweet and polite, and she always seemed to have time to give Tycho a tummy scratch, even when she was running off to be with her friends. It was obvious she had issues with her father and stepmother, though from what I could see, the problems weren't overlapping into the rest of her life.

Tonight she was enjoying the company of adult women as equals rather than from the position of a child, something that a girl who'd had a governess and other adult caretakers throughout her life would have been used to. She seemed to glow in our presence and I liked the way that felt: the big sister in me stretching to accommodate this newest sibling. And I loved the food.

"This is just so *good*," I declared, enthusing over my veggie burger and sweet potato fries.

Emily commented, "Don't they feed you up at your beach?"

But I was hungry. During this last week of being back in the market I'd fallen into old habits. Between following newsfeeds and watching securities rise and fall, there wasn't enough time left over to eat. Tycho had watched me down a lot of coffee and the occasional rice cake or piece of toast, but food preparation? Forget it. And the markets drain you. After a day of trading—even pretend trading—I just didn't feel up to cooking. I'd been ready for a night out.

The movie was banal, predictable and completely enjoyable. The plot flew out of my head the moment we left the theater, but the joy at actually sitting in a building that was practically a national landmark, rubbernecking in case I saw anyone famous—though Emily and Jennifer assured me I wouldn't—and just enjoying the uncomplicated company of my own gender was enough to put me in a great mood. Afterward Emily suggested we go for coffee, and I enthusiastically agreed.

"Not me. I've got school in the morning," Jennifer said, wrinkling her nose distastefully. "I think I'd better head home. Madeline, you stay and have fun. Great evening, you guys! Thanks."

"You still want to do coffee?" I said to Emily after Jennifer had left us.

"Are you kidding? Coffee can wait, age is no longer a consideration. I'll show you the town."

Los Angeles has clubs and bars the way other towns have gas stations and fast-food restaurants. L.A. has those, as well, but clubbing is a serious Angeleno activity and, that evening, Emily seemed determined to show me a lot of them.

The first three places we went to reminded me that Southern California is the center of the musical universe. No matter where we went, if there was live music, it was awe-inspiring, regardless of what genre was being played. The result, Emily told me, of the area being a Mecca for bands from all over the world. And while those bands waited to be discovered, they still had to pay rent. L.A. nightlife is the richer for it.

There was no live band at the fourth and final club we went to. Club Zanzibar had an air of caution about it. Hesitation. And exclusivity. You practically had to know someone—or at least, know someone who knows someone—to get in. Emily knew someone, and so we went.

Of the stops we made that night, Club Zanzibar was my least favorite, though that might just be because of the later association. The only part of Club Z I really liked was the ladies' room. The attendant was warm and helpful, not judgmental or threatening. And the bathroom was beautiful, with a sort of museumlike quality to it—antiques and marble everything—plus linen hand towels and a big vase of lilies, stargazers, on the counter next to the sink. The scent was wonderful. Inviting. I think it quite likely that heaven smells just like the stargazer lilies at Club Z. The rest of the club was just as posh, but not as much fun. And if smelling lilies and drying your hands on linen is as good a time as it gets, you have to rethink your attendance at that particular club.

Emily liked it a lot—*adored* was the word she used the moment we walked in. She said she loved the leather banquettes and the attractive, well-dressed waiters and the music—a bit like dance with a touch of jazz. Ambient. Tonal. I agreed about the music, but found the atmosphere edgy enough to slice you.

We had barely found seats and ordered drinks when Emily hooked up with a guy she'd worked with on a recent film. He was tall but stout and wore his good suit badly, though the fact that I was already feeling out of sorts with the place probably didn't help my assessment of him. It wasn't that I minded Emily dancing, but I did feel suddenly and oddly alien and alone. And uncomfortable. Like a flashback to high school, waiting apprehensively to be asked to dance.

I tried not to appear self-conscious. And it wasn't simple nonchalance. I hoped my look of bored disinterest really came across that way and didn't just make me look like I was smelling something bad.

The hands on my shoulders startled me. And the voice. Deep and male. Too close and disturbingly familiar.

"Madeline." I would have bolted from my seat at the touch, but he squeezed my shoulders—gently but firmly—and held me in place before he swung into the chair opposite me. His face held wonder but no real surprise. "Madeline Carter," he said. "In L.A. With me. How did this happen?"

I couldn't say anything. I was surprised to see him, sure. But also—and maybe more—I was surprised at my reaction to him. I wanted to feel *anything* but what I felt. I wanted to feel revulsion, annoyance, even fear. Fear can be a healthy emotion. Fear keeps us safe. But I felt none of the predictable things I might have hoped for.

There had always been something compelling about Ernest Carmichael Billings. A charisma, even when he was still in the process of shedding his callow youth. I had too often been a rabbit to his snake, mesmerized into submission. Exposing my throat when it would have been far safer to flee.

I hadn't seen him since our senior year at Harvard, almost twelve years before. There were changes to note now. He seemed larger. And sleek, like an eel. He owned the well-fed look that men in their mid-thirties can acquire if their lives have gone pretty much as planned. His features were more clearly drawn now, though I noticed his eyes hadn't changed; they were still as cold and flat as stones.

College Ernie might have been an early sketch;

today I was looking at the finished product. That finished product reminded me of what I'd run from. His presence now compelled and revolted me at the same time. While he dropped into the vacant seat opposite me, I touched my wrist surreptitiously under the table. I could feel the galloping of my pulse and a faint glow of perspiration. I hoped none of this showed in my face.

A waiter came by quietly and Ernie ordered a couple of drinks—a single malt Scotch for himself, neat, and a gin and tonic for me. I shook my head, fighting the wave of anger that welled up at him for assuming I'd still favor the same thing I'd been drinking over a dozen years ago, and ordered cranberry and soda. I would be driving shortly and, anyway, I suddenly felt the need to keep my wits about me.

"It's a very small world, Madeline. Who would have thought I'd run into you in a club in L.A.?"

I shrugged. What was there, really, to say? I chose the obvious. "Are you here on business?"

"Moved here about a month ago. New gig," he said airily, like a rock star. "You'll want to check it out." He ran two fingers down my forearm as he spoke, as though it were a natural gesture. I didn't try to pretend I was doing anything but avoiding his touch when I sat back out of his reach, simultaneously wishing I'd opted to wear something with a neckline that didn't plunge.

"Small world, Mandy." I'd always hated that: Mandy. No one else ever called me that. It isn't a proper diminutive for Madeline, even if I was someone who diminutives stuck to, and I'm not. "I was talking to Benson in New York," he said. "Not three days ago. He told me you'd left Merriwether Bailey. You gone renegade?"

Another shrug. "That's just silly."

Ernie smiled which, for me, produced an odd effect. The same smile in a face that was similar but not quite the same. Time had changed it, though I could see the Ernie I knew beneath the crags and weathering. "No? Well, you'll want to watch for this one, anyway, Mandy. Langton Regional Group. LRG on the Exchange." He grinned in a manner which was meant to be self-deprecating, but which, on his polished face, had quite the opposite effect. And he didn't need to tell me that when he said "Exchange" he meant New York Stock Exchange. To both of us, it could only mean one thing. "I'm the new CEO," Ernie continued. "They're making the announcement on Monday, but it's a secret until then. Don't tell anyone."

"Who would I tell?" I said it pleasantly, though I didn't feel pleasant. If anything I felt slightly sick. I just wished Emily would get her butt back to the table and then, hopefully, Ernie would go away.

"Are you here alone?" he asked, as though he'd read my thoughts.

"No. I'm with my friend. Emily." I looked toward the dance floor, thinking to point her out and perhaps somehow signal that her presence was urgently required, but there was no one there. The dance floor was suddenly empty. Which meant she was either smelling the lilies and chatting to the attendant, or she'd decided to sit down somewhere to talk to her friend with the nice suit.

"You?" I found I didn't really care, but I had to say something, and that seemed as good as anything.

"I'm here with my lovely wife, Arianna." He'd pitched his voice oddly, so I looked at him and saw I was right—the words had been for someone else's benefit. I followed his glance.

Watching her come toward us was entirely filmic—you could almost hear music and maybe a voice-over. The air moved through her hair and her conservatively slit skirt as though created in CGI. She was beyond beautiful. Tall, blond, slender, perfectly coifed, perfectly turned out.

"I wondered where you'd gotten to." Her voice was perfect, as well. Attractively modulated, educated. In another context, she would have been an easy woman to loathe. But she was Ernie's wife. Knowing what I did about him, I could almost feel pity.

"Arianna." He held out a hand, inviting her to join us. "Come meet an old friend, Madeline Carter. Madeline, this is Arianna Billings. My wife."

I'm sure I must have smiled at her, taken the hand she extended to me quite graciously. I don't remember precisely. The only thing I could really think about was putting as much space as possible between me and Ernie.

For her part, Arianna seemed to mull my name over—as though running it through some internal Rolodex—until she came up with a match. "Madeline, it's delicious to meet you after all this time. Ernie has told me so much about you."

This surprised me. I was pretty sure I hadn't mentioned *him* to anyone other than my mother in more than a decade. I'd read about him from time to time, whenever some business magazine sporting his smiling face on the cover would end up on my desk. Wunderkind, they'd call him. Golden Boy. I would read as much as I could without retching and then practice my aim at the recycling bin. But *speak* about him? Never. What we'd shared was so long ago now. It had just seemed better to bury it. The year we'd spent together had certainly given me very few moments I'd contemplate cherishing. "Well rid of him," was how my mother had put it.

"Madeline, it was *so* nice to finally meet you," Arianna repeated, rising, the rustling of some silky fabric following her. "But we really have to go." To Ernie she added, "The Gunnarsons were expecting us fifteen minutes ago."

Ernie nodded, threw back the remainder of his Scotch, dropped a twenty on the table to cover our drinks, then rose, all in a single smooth motion. "It was wonderful seeing you again, Mandy." And I wondered if I was right in thinking that he'd angled his body between me and his wife intentionally in order to cover the fingers he ran once more down my arm. He couldn't have missed how abruptly I pulled back, but he didn't react. "And remember what I told you—LRG. It's a good tip."

When they'd gone I just sat there for a while thinking about stuff. When Emily reappeared I couldn't wait to get out of there. I found I didn't want to see any more clubs. I got home as quickly as I could and hit the shower. And, inexplicably, afterward I still didn't feel clean.

Six

I spent Friday in much the same way I had the previous four days: at my computer preparing for the following week and my new occupation as a day trader. And I spent some time reassuring myself. Sure, it was a crap market, but things were still moving. And if IBM was down it was really only a problem if you owned a lot of IBM. I was a pro; I knew the market. I knew when movement meant something real was afoot or whether it was just the hysterical reaction of an increasingly inexperienced phalanx of traders—most of them at home in Helena, Montana, or Tulsa, Oklahoma, or some other not-stock-connected place, trading on their little PCs. And, in going kinda cowboy, I could take advantage of that with my own money for my own gain. That was the theory, anyway.

As much as I tried to not think about it, the vision of Ernie and his "good tip" kept sneaking into my head. The information he'd given me—if I acted on it—could be considered only the most borderline kind of insider trading. I wasn't a broker anymore; no one cared very much about what I did with my own money. And if you meet someone you used to know in a bar and they tell you they have a new job…well, is that any more insider trading than acting on something you read in the newspaper? Well, it is. But it's pretty easy to rationalize around. Especially if you think no one will be paying attention. So I went in for a peek. What would be the harm?

As it turned out, the Langton Regional Group was typical of the kind of company I'd been watching during the previous week, now that I had no clients to service, and quick action on my mind. Langton's fifty-two week high was over fifteen dollars, and they'd been trading around the six dollar mark for a couple of months. Nothing exciting in either direction, just a solid and long-term slide into the land of the not interesting. I knew an announcement could change all of that quickly, news that would show that their prospects were up. They seemed that kind of ripe.

To most people, LRG would have been an uninspiring little security. The Langton Regional Group made those little glass jars that companies order by the truckload for stuffing jams into and sending out to supermarkets. Nothing mysterious. No shaky high-tech and—heaven forbid—no tricky resources where an oil well can dry up or an engineer's report can bollocks everything, or people can just decide they no longer want whatever mineral is being raped from the ground. Just little glass jars.

At the height of the boom, LRG had been trading over twenty bucks, but that was then. After a while, analysts frowned at all of the money they weren't making and suggested this wasn't a very collectable stock. And, let's face it, glass jars are not sexy, by anyone's standard.

Langton's financials weren't bad, but they weren't especially great, either. LRG had a lot of employees, a lot of overhead and—from the looks of things—fairly complacent management. The current CEO was seriously old and was the grandson of the guy who had founded the company back in the 1930s. The family was prominent—what passes for old money in Southern California—and they lived pretty well. The fact that the company couldn't always support their familial excesses didn't seem to really matter to anyone besides, of course, the stockholders, and an increasing number of grumpy analysts. And when enough stock analysts get sufficiently grumpy, things start to change.

From what Ernie had told me, the change they'd decided on was him. And, as he'd implied, it was a change that could make all the difference for this particular company. He'd said they were set to make an announcement Monday—my first independent trading day.

Over the weekend I wrestled with the insider trading thing, but—to be perfectly honest—not too mightily. It was a day trader's wet dream. A teensy bit of unasked for information could potentially make me a lot of money. All of my instincts said, This is it. And in my business you listen to your instincts. At least, if your instincts have, over the years, instructed you that they're worth listening to. Mine always had.

Monday dawned clear and bright. Tycho and I pounded through the hills, but today I barely noticed the eucalyptus and the palm trees and I ignored the ocean vistas altogether. My mind was on other things.

Back at my computer, I scanned the early notices. Nothing on LRG, which meant it would probably come around 9:00 a.m. Pacific time—my time in L.A.—which made sense, as that's when, since they were based in the city, their office would be open.

Regardless of when the office opened, the stock, of course, was already trading. I checked it the way a moth checks a flame. As I'd expected, even prior to the announcement it was starting to happen. Most of the time, just before the breaking of some significant piece of news, a narrow column of insiders will hop on board, causing the stock to give a little jump before anything really happens. I realized with a start that I was now lining up to be part of that crowd.

And so I moved. While LRG hovered between $5.88 and $6.00, I put in a buy order for twenty thousand shares. To a lot of people, a hundred twenty grand is hardly worth getting out of bed for, but at this stage, it was a big chunk of my liquid wad. I tried to ignore the sweat on my palms.

I kept my eyes on my newsfeed and when an hour after my buy on LRG an announcement was made, I read the whole thing: Langton Regional Group Announces the Appointment of New CEO.

It was the usual company PR material—lots of forward face and future optimism—but it was the announcement that, essentially, Ernie had told me to expect. Between refreshing my screen to watch how the announcement would hit the market, I read the news release. Basically, LRG said that their old CEO, William Gunnarson III, had opted for an early retirement (yeah, right!) and that the company was—blah, blah, blah— pleased to announce his replacement, one Ernest Carmichael Billings late of NeanderTek.

It tickled me that two-timing, double-dealing Ernie should have been the one to give me this tip. I had no doubt he'd be able to turn the company around. Ernie was tough as a garden slug and he had this incredible killer instinct, even back in college. Sometimes being with Ernie then had been like sharing a nest with a baby vulture. Baby vultures are cute in a kind of repulsive way, and though, essentially, they are helpless, at some base level they understand what they've been put on this earth to do. Back then Ernie was like that. A baby vulture waiting for his big break. It was not so easy to be around.

And, in fact, the vulture analogy isn't even a very good one. Despite their revolting habits and the low opinion society holds of them, vultures are innocents. They're creatures of instinct and evolution. They can't help what they are, they just are. There was something more calculating about Ernie. And controlled. On first contact, it came off as a kind of burning intensity, something that my twenty-two-year-old self had found incredibly sexy and somehow reassuring.

From the beginning, he was emotionally and sexually demanding. When we were in public together, he'd stand very close—later I'd find it oppressively close—

and across a table or a room his eyes would always search for mine, ultimately find them and hold them. He was intense in all ways. He took my breath away. After a while, it felt like he was squeezing it out of me.

To say that Ernie was arrogant sounds like ridiculous understatement but, again at first, it struck me as an arrogance he owned, not something borrowed, or some hollow pretense. That arrogance seemed balanced by a bold impulsiveness that, in my youth, I took to be something pretty and romantic. Everything about Ernie was big. His dreams, his ambitions, his ego. And none of that was a problem for me. At first. Once it became a problem, I didn't stick around.

The little bit I knew about him since then had come from the trades. It was all about his growing reputation as a corporate whiz kid who was making a career out of bailing out public companies that were on the pale side of successful.

It interested me that Ernie was doing exactly what he'd set out to do: he was in the business of running stuff and bossing people around. You don't do an MBA at Harvard to be a stockbroker. Sometimes life just happens, as it had to me. I was betting the market would respond to the news of his appointment.

I checked the stock price; it was already at $6.07, and climbing. So I put in another buy order—a market buy this time—for an additional forty-five hundred shares. I was sweating, but it was happy sweat. I had a good feeling about it. It was practically all of my working capital—the cash I needed to make my living—but Ernie knew his stuff.

The electronic purr of the telephone nearly caused me to push my keyboard onto the floor as my hand sought out the handset in order to make the ringing cease.

"Hi, Maddy!" The voice was cheery. Bright. A post-breakfast daughter salute.

"Hey, Mom. How's Seattle?"

"Incredibly dry, sweetie. How's your life?"

Broad questions are my mother's specialty. And no matter how many times I hear it, "How's your life?" always floors me. Like I should start cataloging stuff: I'm trying to eat more bran and whole grains; I think my body will thank me for the consideration when I'm forty. I'm regular. So is my period. Which reminds me, no, in case you're thinking of asking, I'm not seeing anyone and am therefore not getting laid.

I didn't say any of that.

"Great, Mom. You?"

"Oh, you know. Clarisa Meyers and I are thinking of going to Vegas in November. On a bus. And I thought wouldn't it be fun if Madeline joined us? In Vegas. Do you think you could?"

"Geez, maybe, Mom. November isn't for a while yet."

"But if you *planned,* sweetie. If you planned. Then maybe you could go. You're so close now. Not like when you were in New York."

"It's true. Okay. It's only about a four-hour drive for me from here. It might be fun. But listen, remind me in October, okay?"

"Great! That would be so great. So is anything new?"

Now this was a question I could actually handle. I even had a bit of news.

"Well, guess who I ran into last week."

"Am I really supposed to guess?"

"Ernie Billings."

"No!"

"Yes."

"Where?"

"At a club in Santa Monica. He was there with his *wife.*"

"His wife? Oh Madeline, I'm sorry, honey. Did it hurt?"

I thought for a second before answering, but only for a second. "You know, Mom, it didn't. Not at all. But it's been a long time, hasn't it? And so much has happened. I was pleased to discover I was relatively fine with it all." And I was pleased, now, to discover that what I was saying was true. The romantic aspects—if you could call what Ernie and I had shared a romance—had not phased me. When I saw him I had been revolted by his touch and intrigued by potential stock announcements, but there had been nothing that felt like pain.

"What was she like? The wife, I mean."

"She was beautiful. Perfect. Tall—probably as tall as I am—and blond."

"She looks like you." It wasn't a question.

"Oh, no, Mom. She's beautiful. Like, magazine beautiful, you know? But with a Martha's Vineyard edge."

"She looks like you." Whatever. This was obviously not an argument I was going to win. Not with my completely unbiased mother.

"Well, anyway, I maybe did a bad thing," I said cheerily. "He's out here to be the CEO of another company, the Langton Regional Group. They're based in Culver

City. Last week he told me they were making the announcement today. And…I feel kind of embarrassed admitting this, but…well, I bought a whack of them today."

"A whack of what?"

"His stock. LRG."

"How is that a bad thing?"

"Well, I acted on knowledge that I didn't get through conventional sources. Which is insider trading. And if everything goes the way I think it will, I stand to make a fair amount of money. So I'm feeling, you know, kind of guilty."

"Don't be silly." Which is maybe why I'd told my mother all of this in the first place. If you couldn't trust your mom to make pooh-poohing sounds in a situation like this… "I mean, he was your *boyfriend* back when. It's not like he told you so you *could* make money. Knowing Ernie, he was just bragging. But to make a lot of money, I know that means you had to invest a lot. Will it be all right? This *is* Ernie we're talking about."

"He was the world's worst boyfriend, it's true. But since then he's made a whole career out of turning little struggling companies into little successful companies, so I'm actually pretty excited. And it's not like I have to talk to him or anything. I'm pretty sure I'll make a nice chunk on this one."

"That's wonderful, Madeline."

I love my mom. More, I *like* her. No, really. She's a supernice person, everyone loves her and she never has a bad word to say about anyone. But she has only the vaguest idea of what I do for a living, even after all this time. Which is only fair. She's been working at a golf course for over twenty years, is now the manager, and I'm never really sure exactly what it is that she does, either. Except whenever I'm in town she manages to parade a large number of men around my age in front of me. Predictably, they all play golf.

After I hung up, I quickly checked LRG. It was really starting to happen now—an hour after the announcement and the stock was trading at $6.25. And trading was brisk. It was a stock that usually had a daily volume of a couple of million max, and they'd already hit that mark and passed it. I looked at the clock: nine-thirty. Twelve-thirty NYC time. My gut said the stock would hit at least $6.80 by the East Coast's 1:00 p.m. *If* it happened that way, I could happily sell a big chunk of my early purchase. That would mean a profit of just under twenty thousand dollars—less brokerage fees, which would be inconsequential, a few hundred bucks. I grinned. I felt good. Not bad for my first day's work. Later, of course, I'd wonder at my smugness.

I put in a sell order for all 24,500 shares at $6.80, with no special instructions attached. That meant that if LRG reached $6.80 at any time during the trading day, my sell order would be waiting whether I was looking or not. If LRG went over $6.80 while I wasn't looking, I'd beat myself up, but I'd do it with a smile on my face; a quick twenty grand is nothing to get too upset over. But having watched the intraday trading chart carefully for a while and, as a result, feeling confident I knew how this was going to go, I figured LRG would be peaking out a couple of hours before the end of the trading day. I had plenty of time.

I found that the constant watching was getting to me. This playing with my own money was costing me more emotionally than I'd thought it would. So I took a shower. A *shower,* for crying out loud. Such was my confidence, such was my nervosity. I wanted to return to my computer to see a delicious fait accompli, with my stock at its high of the day and at least some of the securities safely sold and the money, so to speak, back in the bank. So I didn't hurry. In fact, I did the opposite of hurry—I made my mundane tasks drag out beyond the time I usually spent on them.

I scratched Tycho's tummy and stroked his glossless gray coat.

I brushed my hair—a hundred strokes—and put moisturizer on my face.

I made myself a little sandwich: sliced Haas avocado and cream cheese on this really beautiful bread I'd bought on the weekend at a bakery in Santa Monica. Soy and buttermilk bread with funny little nuts in it.

I felt celebratory, so I opened a bottle of San Pelegrino and enjoyed the fizzy way the water settled into the glass.

I carried my little repast over to my computer, set it down, then—with a satisfying feeling of anticipation— brought up my trading screen.

There was a hugely disconcerting "N/A" where the LRG quote should have been, and the even more disconcerting message: "Trading is halted pending announcement."

Now, trading halts happen all the time. And, as I used to be obliged to tell my clients, they're not necessarily something to be concerned about. Yes, it means that the funds you have tied up in the stock stay that way until trading is resumed. And true, coming so soon after a happy announcement, it seemed fairly certain that this particular trading halt would mean something less happy. But they really aren't something to get upset about.

I didn't want my sandwich anymore.

I checked to see what the stock had been trading at before the trading halt: $5.86. Which was entirely the wrong direction. This was not good. This was not good at all.

I watched the bubbles in my water erupt on the surface and dissipate. It felt like a metaphor. I poured the San Pelegrino into the potted palm next to my desk. Here. *You* drink it.

I contemplated the vastness of what I had done. All of my cash. All of my liquid wad. I'd told myself I wouldn't do that no matter what. It didn't feel good. *I* didn't feel good. In fact, I felt ridiculous, if you can feel ridiculous and queasy at the same time. When had I ever put this much of my own money—or someone else's, for that matter—into a stock based on little more than a strong hunch? Exactly never, that was when. Hindsight is always 20-20, but now that I had the luxury of having it—because it was behind me—I wondered what I could have been thinking, what point I'd been trying to make, by playing it all on one lousy stock? "Stupid, stupid, stupid!" I said aloud.

I had read, prior to this moment, novels where, at some point or another, the hero says something like, "I felt as if invisible hands were squeezing my throat, choking off the air and my very life." Cheesy beyond belief. And yet, right that moment, that's exactly how I felt. The air was coming to me less easily than usual and the pressure around my throat was almost tangible. I knew I wasn't about to fall down with some type of attack or anything, but I felt…beyond words.

And it wasn't simply fear of financial loss—though that could be devastating enough. I've always believed that there's nothing about the stock market that's a sure thing; every time you make a trade, you have to be willing to take the associated risk—so it wasn't just that. It was also the feeling that I'd lost some professional edge that I'd believed in my whole career. Is this what happened at age thirty-five? Did your senses get dulled by time? Did your eye and your instincts become less sharp? Were your hunches, intuitions and gut feelings less reliable? That was a frightening thought to me. As frightening, in some ways, as an earthquake. You *believe* in the ground under your feet. You trust it will remain solid, remain steady. And I believed in my abilities— my talents—the ones I'd honed for more than a decade as a professional trader. You learn to do things a certain way. You learn what works. You know what you're *supposed* to do. That was just it, though, wasn't it? I hadn't done what I was supposed to do. That's the double-edged sword of insider trading. If you make a bundle, it's indictable, people point fingers. If you lose your shirt, people snicker into their fists.

And how can you *not* act on information that comes from somewhere inside? Especially if, like me, you are somewhere on the farthest edge of the inside? I suddenly remembered something my father had told me when I was sixteen and he was teaching me to drive. He'd said that if you're driving fast and your palms are sweating, it means you're going too fast, you should slow down.

I pushed my palms across my desk. They left a glossy trail.

After about fifteen minutes of self-pity and self-loathing—and with no change in LRG's status—I kicked my somewhat sorry butt into gear. Dashing off an e-mail with the details, then dialing the Merriwether Bailey number felt like action. I'd sent Sal a postcard once I'd rented the guest house, but I hadn't spoken to him since I left New York. He'd be trading right now, but he'd take my call—he'd know that *I'd* know when to pipe down and let him do his stuff.

"Hey, hey," he said when he heard my voice. "How's Malibu Barbie?"

"Skating, Sal. Until today. D'you get my e-mail?"

"Naw. Lemme see." I could hear computerish clacking over the line. "LRG. What are you peeking at a stinky little stock like that for?"

"You know me, Sal," I said by way of an answer.

Sal had always liked playing with the big, solid stuff. Blue chip and related cousins. He'd teased that he'd leave the flyers for "cowboys" like me. He'd always said it with a smile and you could tell he liked this cowboy joke, but underlying his jest was the fact that he knew what he knew and believed what he believed. If there were happier surprises to be had from the sometimes risky securities I tended to like, so be it. The risk attached to those stocks was always greater, as well. I was thankful that there would be no lecture. His voice told me that he still believed all that he'd ever believed, but I could tell he was too busy with his own trades to worry much about my style today.

"Give me a sec and let me run it." A pause. More computerish clicking. And then a not very encouraging, "Ouch. You buy?"

"Yeah." My voice was quiet. I would have paid money to be able to deny it. If I'd had any left.

"Not today, though, right?"

"Yeah. Today."

"When?"

"Maybe 9:45." When talking with New York traders, you always use their time. After all, New York time is everyone's time. During the trading day, at least.

"Like I said, ouch. What were you thinking?"

Fortunately, I was spared answering by a spate of activity on Sal's end, activity that didn't involve me or LRG. I stayed on the line, listening to the familiar hubbub without even the faintest twinge of longing or nostalgia. Funny.

Sal was off the line a long time—maybe ten minutes—but when he came back, he had some news. "I asked a guy, who asked a guy. You know?"

I did.

"He says the dude is missing. The Billings dude. And not missing friendly."

"No way."

"Way."

"What do you think that means, missing?"

"Dunno. That's all I've got."

I knew better than to ask how he knew or from whom

he'd heard. In fact, Sal had only told me this much be-cause he knew I *wouldn't* ask. I wanted to, but I saved it.

"Well, thanks, Sal. I guess that explains the halt."

"Yeah, but there's more on your scummy security. You looked at the intradays? Seems to me like LRG had some serious short action this morning."

I suddenly felt, if possible, even stupider than I had before. And with my stomach plummeting to the region of my knees, I felt sicker, as well.

"You can't *know* it was short action, Sal," I said, while I brought the charts up on my own screen. "Not from the intradays."

"Of course not, Carter. I can't *know*. But look at them. Study them. And tell me what you see."

And, of course, he was right. It wasn't, at this point, verifiable. But the large blocks of stock that had traded together, and the prices they'd traded at, indicated pretty clearly that's what it was. To anyone who was looking carefully enough and who knew what they were look-ing at.

How had I missed this? Or rather, why hadn't I checked? After Sal and I said a quick goodbye—he was working and I felt the need to indulge in some serious self-flagellation along with the self-pity and self-loath-ing—I spent some more time with the intraday chart. As I had suspected, the possible short action Sal was talk-ing about had come at 10:00 a.m. eastern time. So, in Madeline time, I'd probably been someplace between a shampoo and a condition when the first big whack of stocks hit the market and started a gentle plummet. By the time I was slicing my Haas, the plummet had gone as far as it could go because the trading halt had been called. And who knows? If there had been no halt, LRG might have ridden the hump and continued the upward trend I'd spotted this morning. But, seeing what I was seeing, I doubted it. A lot.

The invisible hands tightened their grasp on my throat. And I felt like an idiot.

Short-selling is an odd phenomenon, something exclusively in the domain of the stock market. I've tried to come up with real world parallels and I can't. It's completely counterintuitive; it goes against everything you've ever been taught about how monetary interaction works...outside of the stock market.

A short-sell is when people sell stocks they don't own in anticipation of the price going down. When that happens, the sellers can cover their position by buying the stock they've already sold at a much lower price than they bought at, pocketing the difference. There's the potential to make a lot of money in between. Sell at two dollars. Stocks you don't own. Buy later at one dollar to replace the stocks you already sold. You keep the buck in the middle. The hitch is, in order for this to work—in order for you to make money—the stock *has* to go down. It simply must.

In a short-sell the risk is huge. There's only a certain amount a stock can drop; if you've bought in the traditional way, once you get to zero, you've lost it all and you can just write it off. But there's really no top on how high a stock can go. In a short-sell that backfires you can lose an infinite amount of money, because the stock could just keep rising forever.

There had been times in the past when I'd been so confident a stock was going to tank that I'd seriously considered short-selling it. But in the end, I couldn't make myself do it. There's nothing actually wrong with short-selling, from a legal perspective or otherwise. I just can't get my head around the part where you have to wish for a stock to go *down* instead of *up*. As I said, it's counterintuitive, and intuition plays a larger part in my schtick than I tend to admit in public.

But now, obviously, someone without my particular hang-ups was playing it large with LRG. From my perspective, the timing pretty much sucked. And then there was the whole "missing" thing. What the hell did that mean, exactly? Sal had said Ernie was "not missing friendly," which could be taken in a number of ways, but *had* to mean Ernie was not missing by choice. Which meant…nothing. Was he missing because of the short-sell? Was the short-sell due to Ernie being missing? Or were the two completely not connected?

A sharp knock on the door interrupted my self-flagellation. "It's open," I called, figuring I knew who it was. I knew I was right when I saw Tycho's tail wag, though he didn't bother getting up at the approach of his young mistress.

I swiveled around in my chair, but didn't get up, either. "Hey, Jen."

"Madeline do you have a few minutes to talk?"

I looked at her closely. Her hair was pulled back in a messy ponytail and she looked a little agitated, but otherwise all right.

"Listen, kiddo, I'm having a helluva day. Can it

wait until after 1:00 p.m.? My mind just isn't here right now."

If Jennifer was disappointed, she covered it well. "Sure, Madeline. No problem," she said as she headed for the door. "Later."

I forgot about Jennifer the moment the door closed behind her and the reality of my situation came back. It just seemed so flat and bleak—feelings I'd told myself I'd never have again. I didn't have any Maalox in the house, but my insides were suddenly crying for it. It was like needing a fix.

What I know after spending practically all of my adult life trading is that the market is like an ocean. It can seem unpredictable but, within limits, it isn't really. At least, that's how a successful trader feels—just like a successful mariner. That with all the right tools and all the right study, she can get herself around the world. If you followed the curve of the waves rather than fighting them, in the end it would all come right. Sometimes it's just hard to see the end. That's how I felt right now. But the trouble with that analogy is that ships sometimes sink, no matter what quality gear the crew has. If captains thought about it like that, they'd never leave the harbor. And brokers would all be herbologists.

I scanned my newsfeed. Nothing from LRG. I nibbled at my sandwich, but even if I had felt like eating, which I no longer did, the avocado was starting to look distressingly like some sort of extremely ripe, brownish-green cheese.

When the phone rang again, I jumped. It was starting to feel like Grand Central.

"Hi, sweetheart, just me again."

"Hey, Mom." She calls me every few days, but never twice in the same day. I knew something had to be up.

"Madeline, I'm going to tell you something, but you have to promise not to be mad at me."

Agreement is easiest in these cases. I know that. And your loved one will always forgive you if you renege. It's just not my nature, though. "How can I promise that, Mom? I don't even know what it is."

A sigh. A pause. Another sigh. "I love you, you know that?"

"Mom!"

"Okay, the thing is, right after I got off the phone with you earlier I called Roddy." Something that was already low in me sank lower. Roddy was my father's best friend and best golfing chum. Since Roddy was a financial consultant, after my father died it just made sense for him to take over my parents'—my mom's—investment portfolio. And Roddy was a good enough guy. He cared about my dad, in some ways loved my mom and so was certainly trustworthy. And *I* sure didn't want to do it. Bad enough being responsible for other people's money, but your *mother's?* No, thank you.

"Do I want to know this, Mom?"

She continued as though I hadn't spoken. "I told him what you told me about Ernie—"

"Oh, Mom, you didn't do it. Tell me you didn't."

"—and I told him to buy a *lot* of that stock for me."

"How much is a lot, Mom?" My voice was a monotone. But I was still a little hopeful. A lot could be anything to my mom. It could be a few thousand bucks. Nothing serious.

"Well, Roddy had sold some tech stocks I was holding awhile back and he hadn't found anything for me that he liked well enough to reinvest the money into…."

"How much, Mom?"

"Eight thousand shares."

"At how much?" It was already worse than I thought.

"A little over six dollars."

I did a quick calculation. "Are you saying you bought about fifty thousand dollars of LRG? This morning? *After* we talked?"

"Now, sweetie, I knew you'd be mad."

"Mom, I'm not mad. Really. It's just that I feel terrible. I mean, Mom, I didn't tell you to buy that stock. I didn't say anything like that. I just thought you'd think it was funny. About Ernie, I mean."

"I know, sweetie. I know you didn't tell me. And I know you *never* tell me. I know it's your rule. That's why I didn't say anything. But you said you were pretty sure you'd make a nice chunk on this one—that's what you said. That's *exactly* what you said." Her voice dropped to a whisper. "And after I got off the phone with Roddy, I called Clarisa."

"Oh, Mom."

"And she called her stock guy and bought some, too."

"Oh, *Mom*." It was a virus. It was spreading. And I had started it.

"And…and now it's gone down quite a lot and Roddy says I should sell but I thought…I thought I'd better call you."

It was difficult for me to talk, what with my forehead pressed to my desk while I studied the floor. My neck was rapidly cricking up and all the blood was rushing into the top of my head. But, for the moment, the pain was good. I wanted pain. Because of a casual remark I had made, my mom was currently down five thousand bucks on the day. My *mom*—the woman who'd spent sixteen hours in difficult labor bringing me into the world, but who is too sweet-tempered to ever bring that up at a time like this. And, needless to say, managing a par-three golf course with a snack bar—not a restaurant—outside of Seattle is not the most lucrative of occupations. Five thousand bucks was serious change to her. And her friend Clarisa—who, by the way, is also a widow—how much had she "invested"? I didn't even want to know. I had fleeting thoughts about karma, about what happens when you make the wrong choice. About how you pay. Was I paying now? With my mother's—and my mother's best friend's—security?

"Mom, I *can't* tell you what to do. I'm not your broker." I thought about it for a moment. "I'm not even a broker at all anymore. I can't give you advice."

"Madeline Carter, I'm your *mother,* not a client."

"I know, Mom. That's what I mean."

"So what should I do?"

"Well..." I checked my screen to confirm what was happening "...right now there's a trading halt. You can't do anything."

"I can't?"

"Roddy didn't tell you that part?"

"Oh, he might have. Yes, maybe he did. But I didn't

think it meant I couldn't actually sell if I wanted to. I didn't think that could happen."

I sighed. My forehead was beginning to sweat. It was now stuck to the desk. "It can. It does." I sighed again. "It did."

"When will it stop?"

"Stop being stopped? I'm not sure. Maybe before the end of the trading day." There was a time when I'd had a spiel for situations like this: Don't worry, everything will be fine, it's all—ahem—par for the course. But that was then. And never for the woman who, when I was five, had been able to tell I was up to something if I was too quiet, even when I was in another room. It had made me think she was magic. "And, Mom, I really can't tell you what to do. I just can't. Ask Roddy. He's your broker. It's his *job*."

She was very quiet. "But I'm not his mother."

"Mom, I'm sorry. I'm sorry about the whole thing. I should never have mentioned Ernie or anything. I was excited, I didn't think. But please don't ask me what to do, not about this. And...I'll make it up to you somehow. I promise."

It was that promise that did it. Or maybe just her childlike acceptance of it. Just as she'd accepted my news about Ernie and his stupid stock with the same trust. My mother *believed* in me. She always had. And I—inadvertently, sure, and indirectly—had let her down. I loathed how it made me feel. And the load it added to a day that had been careening downhill almost since I'd placed the first cup of coffee on my desk.

I needed action. I wiped the sweat off my forehead

and applied myself to my computer. I consulted several of the databases I'd signed up for, scanning for information on the Langton Regional Group. I was looking for, I don't know, a hint, I guess. Some clue about whatever was suddenly going on with LRG, whatever nasty thing I'd inadvertently stumbled into. It was all information I'd gone over expertly on Friday and during the weekend: financials, rundowns on LRG's corporate structure, press releases and news items going back the last couple of years. I'd looked at all this stuff before, but even reading through it again now, with my newly jaundiced eye, it presented the picture I'd come to prior to this morning's disaster: a quiet little company ripe for good things. Except that wasn't what was happening. Not today.

Before I thought about it too much, I picked up the phone and dialed the number on the bottom of one of the press releases.

"Langton Regional, how can I direct your call?" It was one of those bright, slightly nasal voices that, as far as I know, answer telephones at large corporations worldwide, though in different accents and appropriate languages.

"Martin Hewitt, please," I said, reading the public relations flack's name from the release.

I was on hold for a mercifully brief time before a youthful male voice burst onto the line. "Hewitt!" he said briskly, practically shouting it.

"Hi, Martin," I started brightly. "My name is Madeline Carter. I'm an LRG shareholder." It was a recent event, my becoming a stockholder. But it was still true.

And I didn't feel the need to mention my mom or Clarisa. "Did you know that there is a trading halt on Langton's stock?"

"I did… I do know that. Yes. It's true. There is." It occurred to me right away that he was talking too much. Of course, there are times when such a piece of information can be useful. In a business negotiation, for example, when you're trying to pay less for something that costs more. If the other guy starts prattling, you know you've got him on the run. Right here and now, though, having figured that out wasn't helping me much. Public relations guys often spend their whole careers on the run, or a reasonable facsimile. Prattling goes with that territory. In the second place, unless I asked the right questions, I knew I probably wouldn't get Hewitt to volunteer anything. PR guys just aren't built to blab. Probably part of the whole careers-on-the-run thing.

I thought I'd try, anyway. "Can you tell me the reason for the halt?"

"Well, um, Miss…"

"Carter," I said again helpfully.

"Well, Miss Carter, as you, um, can imagine, these things can be fairly sensitive in nature, and…"

"And?"

"Well, no, sorry. I'm not at liberty to say. At the moment. Right now. Maybe I will be later. But not now. No."

"Well, perhaps someone else can help me? Mr. Carmichael Billings, maybe? Will you please forward me to his extension?"

"No! That is to say, I'm sorry, I won't be able to do it. Our phone system doesn't have that capacity."

"But he'd probably be able to answer my question?"

"Well, no, maybe not. That is, he might also not be at liberty to say. As well. But…but if you can be patient, we are confident that the matter will resolve itself. Quickly."

"Well now, see," I said being ultrareasonable, "I don't want to wait for the matter to resolve itself. I want to know now. So who do you suggest I talk to to get some answers?"

"I really couldn't say, Miss…"

"Carter."

"Miss Carter. But we currently feel confident that the matter will resolve itself prior to the end of trading today. By tomorrow morning, at the latest."

"Mr. Hewitt…" My voice was honey sweet, innocent. "Is it true that Mr. Billings is missing?"

There was a longish pause before he answered. I presumed he was collecting himself while wishing that it wasn't so darn easy for shareholders to get his name and number. "I can't comment on that," he said carefully. After another pause, he added, "Where did you hear that?"

"It's true then?"

"I didn't say that." But there was the teensiest note of wheedling in his voice.

"But you're obviously concerned that—"

He cut me off. "As I said, we are confident that the matter of the trading halt will be resolved shortly. Have a nice day." Then he hung up.

After I got off the phone, I sat and pondered for a bit. I felt as if I'd discovered something, but wasn't sure what. Sal had said Ernie was missing, and Hewitt hadn't denied it, but missing could mean a lot of things. He could be missing work. He could have missed his off ramp on the freeway. He might have dumped LRG at the last minute—before he even started—for a better job offer. Somehow I doubted all of these things, and the doubt—combined with my continued self-recriminations, my sudden questioning of my own abilities, the very real fear of losing all of my working capital and the thought of my mother's face—made me, to put it mildly, a little squirrelly. It's not a feeling I can take sitting down, especially with the knowledge that the company in question was headquartered less than an hour down the road from me.

I looked back over that morning's first LRG news release and the name "Ernest Carmichael Billings" jumped out at me again. A little, half-baked plan was starting to form, and I contemplated the intelligence of what I was thinking. But then, what the hell? What are ex-lovers for if not to answer questions? And, anyway, I *did* have a valid reason to call him. More or less. There had been that less than idyllic year back at school and the drink last week and his "good tip." Besides, if my information from Sal and my gut reaction about what Hewitt had said were true, it wasn't likely I'd get Ernie on the telephone, anyway. But how would I feel about myself if I didn't even try? My mom's face floated in front of my eyes again and I punched the redial button on my phone before I could stop myself.

"Langton Regional, how can I direct your call?" It sounded like a recording of the voice I'd heard when I called the PR guy, Hewitt.

"Ernest Carmichael Billings, please."

Was I getting paranoid? Jumping at shadows? It seemed to me that the receptionist's voice got a little more distant, if that were possible. Sort of evasive, without evasiveness being required. "I'm sorry, Mr. Billings isn't in the office at the moment. Can I have him return your call?"

Not in the office? I wanted to shout it. How could he not be in the office? They'd just made an announcement. It was his first official day on the job. Not exactly the right day for a three martini lunch or a nooner, was it? I, of course, said none of this. "When do you expect him?" I asked instead.

And here again, I imagined I heard a hedge. "I'm not precisely certain."

"He didn't leave word?"

"No. Sorry. But I can take a message and—"

"Wait, though. It's his first day on the job and you're telling me you don't know where he is?" I said it calmly, but there was a cut to it.

"No, but a message…"

"I'm an old friend. From Boston. Is he reachable by cell phone?" Did I even have the teensiest idea that this line—true though it may be—would work? No. I did not. Any receptionist who gave me that information should be fired on the spot. Shot, even. This one was in no danger. In fact, having recovered from the hard line I was taking, she was having no more of me. I couldn't blame her—I would have put up with less of me than she did.

"I'm sorry, Miss," and I could tell she wasn't. "If

you're not going to leave a message, I'm going to have to terminate this call."

Telephones are so safe, aren't they? So pleasingly anonymous? "So now you're the Terminator?" I quipped before I hung up, feeling pleased with myself for about forty-two seconds. Because all of that had gotten me exactly...nowhere. And anyway, really, what was so weird about him *not* being in the office? Sure, Sal had said he was missing and Hewitt had sounded— to my prejudiced ear—somewhat cagey, but there were any number of places Ernie could be that had nothing to do with being missing. He could be at home changing his children's diapers—because, of course, there seemed no possibility that Ernest Carmichael Billings wouldn't have children by now. (Though the diaper part was probably stretching it. He'd have *people* to do that.) Or he could be on the golf course. Or in a boardroom. Driving to a meeting. And yet none of this really made sense. Sure, he might be "in a meeting" or "unable to come to the telephone" or "not taking calls, can I direct you to someone else in the company" (with the words "someone less important" left silent). But the day that a publicly traded company with a less than sterling recent record chose to announce a new CEO, you'd think that said new CEO would be somewhere on the premises, holding court or rolling heads or otherwise making his presence felt so that the damn stock would go up. That was how it was supposed to work. That's what he'd implied to me at Club Zanzibar that night. That's what I wanted him doing now.

But here, on the heels of their big announcement,

came a trading halt. Which could mean any number of things, most of them not good. The most obvious possibility—and the least likely, considering the nature of this company—was that they'd somehow and suddenly run afoul of the Securities and Exchange Commission. But it just didn't seem like that kind of company. Or they might have botched some sort of official paperwork. And here again, it didn't seem likely. For one thing, the Ernest Carmichael Billings that I knew wouldn't have gotten himself mixed up with an operation that wasn't doing things the right way. For him, even wrong things had to be done the right way. He would have done his own sort of due diligence before signing on.

The most frequent non-SEC reason for a halt to trading was that something was going down that would effect the stock price one way or the other and, in order to keep insiders out before the announcement could be made, trading was stopped. And, to be honest, at this point I would have almost preferred some lost-paperwork scenario to this last possibility. Because that sort of trading halt at this stage in the game likely meant a plummet would happen when the halt came off.

Back to the phones. Ernie had told me he'd moved into the area the month before. I might be able to get a new residential listing from information. But even as I dialed, I knew this was just me trying to make myself feel like I was doing *something*. Ernie was as likely to have a listed phone number as he was to live in Reseda. And I was right. No listings anywhere in the greater Los Angeles area—including Reseda—for an Ernest Carmichael Billings or any corruption thereof. Back to square one.

By now the markets were closed and I could safely leave my terminal without all hell breaking loose. Except, somewhere inside, I was planning hell breaking loose without even being completely aware of it.

First I called Emily, who, as luck would have it, was home. I told her I was planning on being in town this afternoon and did she feel like meeting somewhere in West L.A. for dinner? We agreed to meet at a Mexican place on La Cienega that I'd heard about and that Emily liked a lot.

Now, just under the freeway and a little bit west is Culver City—a coincidence that I had created. I put on a camel-colored business suit—trousers, not a skirt—a black turtleneck and my best Italian pumps. Did I know I was going to Culver City as I dressed? Maybe. It's a possibility. It could happen. But it's a kick-ass suit: Prada, left over from my trading days, but still chic and shapely. At least, enough for L.A.

For me, part of all of this had to do with my mom. That trust. Her unwavering—albeit in this case unasked for—faith in me. That I knew what I was doing. That I'd always do the right thing. But another part of me was running on pure instinct. This is also part of the whole stock thing. It's like you're a jungle animal and there's nothing in the world you can rely on besides your instinct. Like you're a big cat and you have to be prepared to pounce at the first sign of movement to make sure you don't miss dinner. Other times it's like you're some pathetic rodent—or a bird or a rabbit or something else highly edible—and you just trust your gut and run in order to avoid being another creature's dinner. I have been a successful broker for over ten years. In me these instincts are so highly honed sometimes it feels as though I don't control them. I don't always think; I just act, or react, as the situation dictates. And then I deal with the consequences, one way or another.

So, at this point, what was I thinking? Drinks, dinner and maybe clubs with Emily. But somewhere in the back of my mind was Culver City to find out if Ernie was missing, and if he wasn't, to have a one-on-one with him, just to answer some questions. And, anyway, if rationalized correctly, Culver City was *precisely* on my way to meet Emily.

Remembering I had told Jennifer I'd talk to her after the closing bell, I called upstairs. Tasya told me the girl had gone out. I left a message. I figured that whatever girlish crisis Jennifer had been in a couple of hours ago had probably passed, but I could catch up with her later.

I took another swipe at my unruly, pale mop, gave it up for tousled, pushed Tycho onto the deck and followed my instincts out the door.

Seven

My canyon sweeps you majestically seaward, but it's peaceful. Quiet. It affords you the illusion of living in some perfect rural setting. And it's true—my part of Las Flores Canyon is delightfully barren of houses. However, the fact is that both Los Angeles County and the district of Malibu have declared my neighborhood to be an earthquake zone. Call it living dangerously and definitely on the edge. If a house slides down the cliff, it cannot be replaced. If an owner wants to tear down his house and rebuild anew, he won't get a permit; Las Flores Canyon, say the geologists, will see a finite amount of time on this earth in its present form. Those who live here take their chances. And so it's a fairly deserted canyon, but those who take that chance assure themselves that's the cost of the exclusivity they enjoy. To a certain degree they're right. And I'm right, because I rent. But owning a two million dollar house in the neighborhood would not be my idea of a good time, especially since insurance that will protect you—fi-

nancially—from earthquakes is expensive and somewhat prickly. And anyway, two million would buy a *lot*
of stocks.

And here's what I love about living in Malibu: the
street that I would logically take to get down the canyon is called Rambla Pacifico. It's the most direct route
to the Pacific Coast Highway. But you can't take that
street, because a mudslide wrecked it more than ten
years ago and so a big chunk of it has been closed ever
since. In most communities in the country this would
be an outrage, unthinkable. In Malibu, where a lot of
people's house taxes are more than most American
homeowners' annual incomes, the road repair is not encouraged. It's pretty much an added deterrent to
wannabe star searchers if there is no road to get to their
favorite movie or rock star's house. It also, of course,
makes it tougher for those same movie and rock stars
to get home, but there's a price for everything, or so
everyone keeps saying. At some point you just have to
start wondering if they're right.

So, because Rambla was not available I took Las
Flores Canyon Drive, which swoops you down to the
Pacific Coast Highway in a sort of roundabout fashion.
Not the most direct route, but supremely beautiful. On
this day, however, I didn't look at the gnarled eucalyptus trees that line the road. I didn't pay attention to the
cotton-candy clouds floating over the horizon or the
sun-tipped sea. Nor did I marvel at the lovely homes
along PCH as I headed down the coast, or the occasional
glimpses I caught of surfers or sailboaters or even the
happy visual cacophony that is Santa Monica Pier once

I got to where PCH joins the Santa Monica Freeway. I saw an internal stock ticker—not such a news flash, I guess—and I kept seeing Ernie's face. As it was then, and as I'd seen it at Club Zanzibar.

Taking the Santa Monica Freeway there's actually an off ramp where if you go left—north—you head toward Beverly Hills. Turn right and you're in Culver City. Guess which direction I chose? As I drove, I struggled with my bag, looking for the printout of the press release that just happened to have the Langton Group's Culver City address on it. Quite the coincidence. At least I have a subconscious mind that believes in being prepared.

By L.A. standards, it didn't take me long to find what I was looking for. A couple of false starts, a stop at a gas station to consult my *Thomas Guide*—the seriously thick book of maps that I'd quickly discovered is the secret to finding anything in L.A.—and I located the Langton Building, way down at the end of Arizona Crescent, which is off Arizona Avenue, which is off Centinela. The route was so convoluted, by the time I found the building there was absolutely no way I could convince myself that I was just planning on cruising by to take a look from the car. Although, had I been doing only that, the look from the car would have been impressive. From the vantage point of the single undergrad architecture course I'd taken, I recognized the Langton Building as having been designed in the zigzag moderne style. Probably built in the early 1930s, it looked like a friendly art deco fortress and, together with its parking lot, it occupied most of a city block. It looked as though the Gunnarson family had been doing things up in style for a very long time.

From the driver's seat of my nondescript sedan I could see, along with the usual corporate array of late model cars, a couple of even more nondescript vehicles than mine parked haphazardly in the lot, the telltale Mickey Mouse ears—you know, those flat, black plastic discs on the car roof—fairly shouting, *high-tech equipment inside.* I knew from watching television that this was likely to mean some sort of coplike creatures were lurking in the vicinity. Something really *was* happening here.

Part of me had been thinking—hoping?—that, as I drove by, I'd see Ernie walking from his car to the building and I'd ever so casually cruise into the parking lot, have a repulsive little reunion and say, I was in the neighborhood so, now tell me, what the hell is up? And, of course, he'd tell me. It's a funny fact that every time you picture something like that—something complicated going smoothly—when actually faced with the reality you always say to yourself, Just what the hell was I thinking?

So that's what I did now—I berated myself for my recent naiveté. Then, still without anything that could be called a goal or a plan, and with Ernie nowhere in sight, I cruised into the parking lot as casually as possible, slid into a spot marked Visitors and sauntered determinedly to the entrance.

In my work, I've often had the opportunity to meet people on the telephone prior to meeting them in person: clients, co-workers, even office drones. In my experience, when you finally get around to seeing them face-to-face, telephone-met people never look like the pictures their voices have drawn. I remember, for instance, a guy I dated briefly a few years ago, a broker who also worked at Merriwether Bailey. We'd had reason to have telephone conversations a couple of times before our conversations started getting warmer and more familiar.

His voice seduced me. I don't know what it was, but it held all of the right cadences to push my buttons. Maybe the feeling was mutual and, despite company policy to the contrary, we exchanged home phone numbers, each eager to take what had blossomed into an odd little telephone romance to more personal levels. Which we did. Nothing too weird. Just first-date-type conversations, but all on the telephone.

It didn't seem strange to me. That location of our company alone occupied four floors of an office tower, and he worked on a different floor than I did and in a different department. There was virtually no chance we'd meet at the water cooler or in a photocopy room. And even if they'd had company picnics at Merriwether Bailey, I probably wouldn't have bothered going.

Considering the business we were in, neither of us was in a big hurry to take our relationship from virtual to reality. If you're working sixty to eighty hours a week, a romance that requires no more maintenance than a pleasant half hour chat in the evening can look pretty good. After a while, though, we were ready for some face-to-face conversations. To be honest, I was pretty curious to see the man behind supervoice.

I don't want to say I was disappointed when I finally met him. It wasn't that he was gross, or anything. He was actually, when I think about it, reasonably attractive. He just wasn't at all what I was expecting.

What was I expecting? Once I'd met him, I wasn't sure anymore. I just knew he wasn't it. But, what the hell, I let it ride. And he let it ride, or whatever, because we kept seeing each other for a while. Which was pretty weird. Every time I didn't see him—on the telephone or in the dark—in my head, he'd go back to looking like the guy he'd been before I met him. It was startling, because when the lights came back on, it would always give me this teeny jolt. Like, what the...? Oh, yeah. It was disconcerting.

Who knows, if we'd kept seeing each other, maybe my mental image of him would have aligned with reality, but we didn't. And I don't even know who ended it. I just noticed one day that he hadn't called me and I hadn't called him. And, more importantly, I didn't care. I guess that's what they call fizzling out.

Here and now, standing in the really-quite-impressive lobby of the Langton Building and trying to catch the eye of the receptionist, I was startled. She looked *exactly* as I'd pictured her. Right down to the tired-looking mauve twinset (okay, maybe I hadn't imagined it mauve) and the well-cut but overprocessed hair. It was remarkable. Nor was it a pleasant surprise, because her voice hadn't painted a particularly pleasant picture and, what with that Terminator crack, I hadn't left things on the best footing.

Right now she was a picture in studied busyness. It

was getting to be late afternoon—maybe fourish—but there was no sign of people leaving the office and the phones looked pretty lit up. Abnormally busy for this time of the day? I wondered. Or maybe I was just being paranoid again.

As I entered the office, she fixed me with a quelling glance, held up an imperious hand that told me she'd be with me when it was appropriate, and kept saying, "Langton Regional, how may I direct your call?" into her headset. It was the nasal voice that I remembered from earlier, so there was no mistaking her. I tried to compose my face in a pleasant and patient mask until she freed up a moment to talk to me.

Being patient was made easier by the fact that, while I waited, I kept my whole being tuned to—I don't know—possibilities, I guess. Or at least a hint at the reason I'd come. I listened for an oddness, a wrongness, something off. I listened to her side of curt conversations, and I listened to—forgive me for sounding New Age, but I'd just moved to Southern California, so I guess I felt entitled—the *vibe* of the office. And, really, I heard a whole lot of nothing. Nothing interesting, anyway. And the reception area was constructed in such a way that the rest of building with its—presumably—teeming offices filled with busy workers might as well not have existed.

After a while I quite simply got bored. I did the thing I knew would get her instant attention and, if not, get me closer to what I wanted anyway. Without telegraphing my intent in any way, I calmly walked toward the opening that separated the airlock of reception from the rest of the office. That did it. Before I could even see what was beyond, she'd whipped off her headset and was on her feet to, it seemed, physically stop me if need be.

"Excuse me." The same nasal voice. And she didn't say it like she actually wanted to be excused from anything. "Just where do you think you're going?"

I smiled brightly in the face of her obvious disapproval. "I could see how busy you were," I said sweetly, "so I just thought I'd make my own way."

"And you are…?" She did not say it sweetly.

"I'm here to see Mr. Billings." Again, I'm a *broker*. Or at least I was one recently enough that I knew how to get things without giving anything back. Emotionally, physically, whatever. It goes with the territory.

I once again got the feeling that this request produced the slightest hesitation, as though she was a bit unsure of what to do under the circumstances. And I noticed she cleared her throat before she answered, something that struck me as being based on nervousness, though I might have been jumping at shadows again. "He's in…he's in a meeting," she said.

"He's here then?"

She made a sound that could be taken for assent, but was not entirely clear.

"Well, call him then, please. He won't want to have missed me." I tried to look directly into her eyes.

"I can't." That throat clearing again. "I can't call him. In the meeting." She didn't look back into mine.

"Fine," I said, and turning away from her, I headed for the inner sanctum. "I'll go find him myself."

"You can't. Okay. I'll. Call. Him." She did not physically stop me, but the effect was the same.

I turned toward her, arms crossed. "Okay then. Call him." It came out sounding like a challenge. And, really, I wanted her *not* to be lying. I wanted Sal's information and all of my hunches put to rest. I *wanted* Ernie to be back there somewhere, doing CEO-appropriate stuff. But I didn't think he was.

She was back at her desk, putting on her headset. "What did you say your name was?"

"I don't believe I did."

"And you're with…?"

"I'm an old friend."

This last was a mistake. She was rude and possibly underpowered, but she wasn't dumb, and I could see something click into place as I said the words.

"You called earlier." It wasn't a question. And I noticed the headset was back on the desk.

"That's right."

"I told you then that he's unavailable. Why are you here?"

"So he isn't here?"

"I didn't say that!"

"You did. You said it when I called earlier."

"But I didn't say it now."

"Look, if he's here, just call him and tell him I've come to see him. He *will* see me. And I happen to know he'll be quite annoyed with you if you don't." This last was an overstatement, but I thought the situation warranted it.

"What kind of game do you think you're playing?" She said it coldly. I had the feeling that she suddenly felt she understood something that I was completely in the dark about. At a loss, I shot for the same tone I'd started with.

"I guess you're telling me he's not here?" I asked less than politely.

"You'd better show me some identification," she said, surprising me. This was, to the best of my knowledge, outside the realm of a receptionist's duties. Though, if nothing else, this incredibly odd request confirmed that things were not all they seemed to be at the Langton Regional Group. When receptionists start asking for identification from perfectly innocent (!) visitors, you know they've gotten orders from someone to do so. Someone not at all corporate who probably carries a gun.

"Excuse me?" It was all I could think to say.

"You heard me. If you are who you say you are—or who you *aren't* saying you are—you won't mind showing me your driver's license."

"This is ridiculous," I told her. "I'm not going to show you my driver's license. That's crazy."

She was adamant. "If you don't show me your driver's license, I'm calling security." Which, any way you sliced it, was weird and getting weirder. And the weirdness was catching, I guess. Because, as she continued in this vein, it gave me my answer: Ernie wasn't on the premises, or why wouldn't she have just called him?

In any case, I wasn't hanging around. I wasn't even really sure why I didn't want to give her my driver's license. Part of it was principle, sure. It was an invasive request. But a larger part had to do with not giving too much away. And that, again, was instinct. Pure instinct. At the moment I was a rabbit (or a deer or an elk or something else made of meat) and I had to get out of the forest.

I left the building and got back to my car without any real idea of what I was going to do next, but there were still two hours left between now and when I was meeting Emily for dinner. I left the parking lot, turning left instead of right and thinking I'd circumnavigate the building and see what I could see. See what? Ernie out back locked in a cage that the killer receptionist had constructed? A neon sign flashing the words *Something Fishy?* Ernie in an office window waving a sign that read Help Me? Really, none of the above, but I did the circumnavigation, anyway.

As I turned the corner, almost the first thing I noticed gave me a new idea. A fairly dangerous idea, but what the hell? I was apparently in that sort of mood.

Near a side door was that necessity of the modern workplace: an outdoor smoking area. At the moment, Langton's had half a dozen well-dressed workers ranged around a cylindrical chrome object, no doubt some sort of ashtray.

I parked in the next block, in front of a fast-food place, went in, ordered coffee and a bagel to go, then sauntered toward the smokers—different ones by now, no doubt—with my take-out food providing a badge of belonging. If I had, indeed, worked at that office, it would be weird to go for a coffee and a snack so close to the end of the day, but it probably wouldn't be the kind of weird anyone would comment on. These days enough people work funny shifts and extra time that food and coffee can happen whenever. So I headed over with my goodies and made like I was mingling or thinking about smoking.

This was a scary moment for me. Scary even though I'd spent enough time working in large offices to know that not everyone knows everyone. Also, I knew that even if I was found out, the worst that was likely to happen would be I'd be given the bum's rush. Or carded again. Whichever came first. Still, it's moments like these that make you realize that anthropologists are dead wrong about the history of humankind. At one point, no matter what they all tell us, we were herd animals. We all live with the fear of being discovered as not quite fitting in with the group. We're afraid that, should the leaders discover this, they'll turn and kill us. With their bare hands or teeth or hooves or other sharp, pointy animal bits. This is a fairly universal human fear. And it's one I've experienced periodically throughout my life—high school springs immediately to mind. But I've never had the feeling so strongly as when I was standing outside the Langton Building with a bunch of smokers I'd never met before, praying desperately to fit into their clique while I figured out if I'd need some sort of key to get in the side door they'd all evidently come out of.

And, of course, they were all busy with their own lives and conversations, so barely noticed me. I relaxed against a stone bench and sipped my coffee, hoping I looked like I was enjoying a stolen moment in the afternoon sun and that I wouldn't seem *too* conspicuous not smoking.

"I haven't seen you around here before." The owner of the voice was tall, maybe twenty-five and good-looking in that cookie cutter corporate way. Well-trimmed hair, closely shaven, strong features, well-pressed suit. What he had said was so cliché I wasn't sure if I should laugh or act chagrined. Since it was also true, I settled on the former.

"Well, I haven't seen you, either." Also true.

"I work out of the sales office down at the factory in Orange," he said by way of introduction.

I nodded knowledgeably and decided to make a stab in the dark. "You just came up for the...stuff today?" I asked airily. But it stood to reason that the announcement of a new CEO would provide the sales department with a lot of...stuff. Even so, I didn't breathe again until he nodded.

"Yeah. And look how *that* turned out. I may as well have stayed in bed today."

I gave another knowing nod while I pondered my next pithy-yet-leading remark. Instead, I came up with the rather bland, "Yeah. Who'd have thought?" Good, I said to myself, just go with it.

"*Seriously*. And then those guys hanging around all afternoon?"

I nodded. What could I say?

Fortunately, he didn't wait for a comment. Have you ever noticed that if, when you're talking to someone you don't know well, you pretty much keep your mouth shut, they'll just blab on and on? And on. Wanting to fill up the empty space with their heated air. This seemed like a good tack now. To be honest, though, the fact that I was too nervous to speak for any length of time in a way that was perfectly normal is to be credited for what actually became a good course of action. "I'm sure at least some of them were cops," he said. "Some of 'em even looked like they might have been rent-a-cops." He was growing more animated as he spoke. And he clearly watched too much late-night television.

"You really think so?" Demure and ready to be convinced seemed to be the way to go.

"Sure," he answered knowledgeably. "All the signs were there. And who else would act like that? Did you see the way they were storming around as if they owned the place?"

"I…I didn't, actually," I said truthfully. "I was busy at my computer for most of the day." I didn't mention that my computer was an hour's drive away.

"Did you see *anything?* Like, no one I've spoken to has even seen the mysterious Ernest Billings. So I figure it must all have something to do with him."

"What else?"

"Exactly." He nodded as though I'd echoed his thoughts. And since I'd said precisely two words, I thought that was an interesting reaction. He was continuing. "I got the word to come up here in order to be addressed by the new chief. Then nothing, and then all of this." His gesture encompassed the building, and I took it to mean whatever foolishness was being cooked up by head office—a universally understood gesture. "A completely wasted day—even the doughnuts were lousy." Then another universally understood gesture— the late-arriving charm. "But I did get to meet a tall and striking blonde."

"I don't think we can say we've properly met." I stuck out my hand. "I'm Madison." Then silently cursed myself. Could I have thought of *anything* closer to Madeline? And why on earth had I thought it necessary to introduce myself, anyway? The answer was obvious even to me: I was stalling. And filling up the blank space with inane stuff and hoping he'd either get to the good stuff soon (although I was beginning to doubt he knew any good stuff), or provide cover that would get me inside. By now, though, I was figuring that with out-of-town sales people flitting around the office, there was a good chance no one would notice a sales-appropriate-dressed woman hanging around, as long as I stayed out of reception, which I *completely* intended to do.

"Steve," he stated. Of course. What else? "Steve Rundle."

He was looking at me expectantly, and I was suddenly blank. A part of me was already storming the gates; another part sensed that I'd better move quickly if I wanted to avoid a dinner invitation. And did I? I had to think about it for a second. Yes. I did.

If I were the betting type—and come to think of it, I am—at that moment I would have bet that if I were to make a move to go into the building, he would accompany me, thereby providing the cover I desired. I tried it on.

"I guess I'd better get going." I indicated the elegant zigzag building with my head. "Phone calls, you know."

"Yeah, I guess I should see what's up, as well," he said, stubbing out a Marlboro Light. "After you."

Too bad there's no profit in making bets with yourself.

My heart rose to my throat as we headed toward the door. This was it. I was imagining all sorts of high-tech nightmares by now: a single lowly retina scan (now who'd been watching too much late-night TV?) followed by the low thrum of sirens and the jangling of alarm bells, ending with me getting hauled off in handcuffs. "Renegade stockbroker attempts to infiltrate privately held company after the call of a halt to trading. Film at eleven."

What I was forgetting, and what all that late-night TV hadn't prepared me for, was that this was a company that made jam jars. And maybe jars for peanut butter. Nobody on TV does that. The companies in those shows are always deeply involved in making top secret nuclear systems for submarines and interesting stuff like that. No one ever sets movies or television shows in glass jar companies because there wouldn't be anything exciting going on. Certainly, little that would be top secret.

The side door that we entered was just a door. No high-tech stuff beyond a very formidable-looking lock, which wasn't locked. The door led to a nice, quiet little staircase that led to an unexceptional hallway. Steve looked as if he was headed right, so I opted to go left.

He stopped me before I could make good my escape. "Do you think they're still having the thing tonight?"

I must have looked as blank as I felt, because he went on, "You know, the Hyatt hail-the-chief thing."

"Geez, Steve." *Geez?* "I don't know. I haven't heard anything." Also the truth.

"Me, neither. Well, if they are, I'll see you there, okay?"

"Sounds good. And if they're not," I said, with a smile as bright and casual as I could muster, "I'm sure I'll see you around." And I headed down the hallway in what I hoped was the direction completely opposite to reception.

I followed the long hallway, still carrying my take-out bag—I'd finished the coffee while chatting with Steve—and trying to look nonchalant while I looked for a place to land. It was about five o'clock in the afternoon of an exceptional day for the company, so while some people were still beavering away in the offices I peered into as I walked by open doors, other offices were empty, while still others were occupied by two or more workers having the sort of urgently quiet chats that people have when the corporate ground beneath their feet has moved. My confidence soared.

In this moment—having just concluded a successful "interview" with an insider, and moving with easy confidence through an unfamiliar building—I felt as if I'd missed my calling. Suddenly I was Madeline Carter, girl detective on the case (though on the case of what I wasn't sure) and I promised myself more encounters like this one, just to get the old adrenaline pumping. I was, for the second time in one day, deliciously smug. And, like that earlier smugness, the feeling—unfortunately—wasn't permitted to last. Smug is definitely an area I need to target for self-improvement.

That smugness was challenged when two men and a woman came out of an office directly in my path—nowhere to run—and started heading down the hallway in my direction.

"So you haven't had any calls from the press yet?" the woman was saying.

"Not yet, not at all," said one of the men, and from the context and the voice, I thought it might be Hewitt, the PR flack I'd spoken to earlier. "We'll just have to hope that holds."

I mustered my courage to greet them with a nod, a smile and a bored expression as we passed in the hallway. I thought the first man looked at me piercingly, questioningly. For one tense moment I thought he was going to stop me, but he didn't, and in another minute they'd entered a different office and closed the door behind them. I felt like collapsing against the wall in relief, but I pulled myself together and kept going. This was hardly the moment to fall apart—that could come later, I told myself, once I was out of there. I kept moving.

The distant yet familiar beep-beep-beep of a microwave that's completed its mission came from farther up the hall. I could smell the odor of something souplike, and that, together with the beeping, gave my plan an immediate target. Some sort of lunchroom was not far ahead. I could stop there, appear engrossed in smearing cream cheese on my bagel and consuming it while fitting and listening in and planning my next move. I increased my pace.

As I'd known from the beeping, the lunchroom wasn't empty. And the moment I stepped inside the door, I saw something that my subconscious hadn't allowed me to contemplate as a possibility: the person removing a steaming cup from the microwave was wearing a mauve twinset. I started to back out the way I'd come, but either my determinedly casual entrance had alerted her or her preternaturally sharp and batlike senses had caught me on her sonar, because she looked up sharply, as an eagle might look at a mouse.

"You!" She probably didn't scream it, but that's how it seemed.

I backed up half a step.

"Don't even think about moving," she said as she went for the phone, never taking her eyes off me. It didn't take a lot of mental exercise to figure she was calling the much-hallybalooed security.

The lunchroom telephone was situated on a table deeper into the room, where munching workers could be conveniently disturbed while they grazed. It seems quite likely that my lilac-clad nemesis had made a quick calculation based on appearances—I could see I wasn't the only one who had done it—and decided that a thirty-something woman in a Prada suit was an unlikely candidate to flee. If that is, in fact, what she thought, she was wrong. While she entered the necessary extension numbers I did some quick calculations, wished I hadn't flunked calculus and had passed on philosophy altogether, collected myself and...bolted.

Though I had an almost unbearable urge to flee farther down the corridor I'd been following when I came upon the lunchroom, common sense prevailed, and I headed back the way I'd come, toward the things I knew: the little hallway, the smoking area and the safety of my nondescript car in the next block. I remember little of this flight beyond seeing a couple of curious eyes raise from desks as I headed down the hallway at breakneck speed. None of the publicly traded companies I know of have rules against running in hallways, but you never actually see anyone doing it. Even when things are superbusy, no one is ever in more of a hurry than what can be accomplished with a determined trot or a studied lurch or maybe even a casual gambol. I did none of these more dignified things. I *ran,* as they say, as if I were being pursued by the hounds of hell. Which I guess I was, if hellhounds ever wear mauve twinsets. I ran headlong, pell-mell and hell-bent-for-leather.

I had the presence of mind to collect myself just before I erupted out of the hallway into the outside world and the expected smoke cloud, in order to not draw attention to myself. I needn't have bothered; there was no one there. A good thing, because I'm sure I was wild haired and wild-eyed by then.

With no one to impress, I threw my temporary quasi-decorum out the window and my bagel on the ground, and ran for my car as quickly as my low-heeled pumps could carry me.

By the time I got to the car I was shaking, breathing hard, and had trouble finding my keys. It was difficult to keep it together long enough to beep open the doors, fire the engine and drive away. I kept expecting a band of rent-a-cops (what would a rent-a-cop even look like? I wondered) exploding out of the door behind me and, once they caught up with me, throwing me to the ground, handcuffing me and driving off with me to points that were unknown, but completely scary, anyway. Or, while I ran, a platoon of police cars—lights blazing—once again bearing down and.... From there the scenario looked pretty much like the first one, except this time there was a lot of blue polyester and static from police communication devices punctuating the air. Scary stuff, either way.

I drove around aimlessly for a while, trying to calm my nerves and determine my next move. It still wasn't time to meet Emily on La Cienega, so I did the only thing possible under the circumstances: I looked for the familiar green logo and the comfort of a well-made latte. And, yes, I'd had that coffee with Steve in the smoking area not long before, but it didn't count toward my caffeine total for the day. Not really. It only counts if you enjoy it, and I'd been too nervous to even taste that one.

As I parked near a Starbucks on Venice Boulevard— which I figured was too far away from Langton for them to find me, even if they bothered following me—I checked over my shoulder for signs of pursuit. It wasn't until I was settled in the cheerily familiar surround- ings—with mercifully soft jazz playing in the back- ground and a steaming cup of java clutched in my still-shaking hands—that I began to relax. I was being ridiculous, I began to see. After all, I was a stockholder. While it's not exactly smiled upon to waltz through an office back door unannounced, I also, strictly speaking, hadn't been doing anything illegal.

Except trespassing, a little voice whispered.

I ignored it and went on.

As an—admittedly quite new—shareholder, I had a right to know what was going on, didn't I? And if it in- volved not showing my driver's license and brandish- ing a bagel and more or less pretending to smoke, what of it? None of those activities were federal offenses, even if they took place on private property.

While I knew a lot of this rationalizing was worth

about as much as most rationalizing ever is, it made me feel better. And that, I guess, was worth something.

By the time I'd more or less talked myself around to *not* having reasons to be afraid, I actually wasn't, and I stopped looking over my shoulder. Fortunately, once I'd finished with all of that silliness, I still had enough hot beverage left in my cup—more than half—to contemplate what all of this adrenaline-raising had accomplished so far. Not much, I had to admit. In fact, with all of the running and schmoozing and pretending I'd done on this day, the handful of facts I had were the same ones with which I'd left the house, though some were now more sharply confirmed. They were (in no particular order):

1. The Langton Regional Group was a large company with many satellite offices.

2. LRG had a new CEO who happened to be my ex-boyfriend.

3. The new CEO hadn't shown up today and no one—at least outsiders and relatively unimportant (i.e. Steve Rundle) insiders—had any idea why.

4. If, as Sal had suggested, Ernie was missing, I hadn't disproved it.

5. LRG's receptionist probably didn't like me.

Oh, and one more:

6. There were people who sleuthed around for a living. I was not one of them, nor should I consider pursuing it in future.

In short, nothing. And, really, what had I expected? That I'd arrive on the scene and the whole place would collapse around me in an unruly heap of unburdening?

"Oh, Madeline! There you are. Now that you're here we can get to the business of straightening the world out about what's been going on. Have a seat and we'll tell you everything." And so on.

In fact, as the fortifying caffeine seeped into my bloodstream, I began seeing the venture as more and more silly. There could be any number of reasons Ernie hadn't turned up for work today. Just because Steve hadn't known about it...

What about the trading halt?

...didn't mean that everyone higher than him—a junior sales drone—knew exactly what was going on and...

And the rent-a-cops?

...even though Steve said he saw the rent-a-cops, I hadn't seen them. And it might just have been ill-dressed business dudes from some other company. That happens. Ernie might have been inking some new deal...

The day an internal company meeting and an evening blowout were planned?

...and it pushed everything else out of the way. Made it more important.

And so on. And here I felt I had to face facts, stuff I hadn't thought about before this instant. My life had changed a lot during the last few months. I'd had an awful, soul-shattering shock when Jack was killed, followed almost immediately by many changes so drastic, it was almost impossible to see where the two worlds joined. After having had such a high-pressure career, was it possible that my body was craving the adrenaline rushes that had come to me in New York on a daily basis? Never mind the market—in New York sometimes crossing a street could be pretty hairy. Was I somehow trying to compensate for my new, slower pace of life? I groaned inwardly at the thought. I'd have to get out more. And, I added, I'd have to curb myself from having further adventures like this. Maybe cycling or mountain climbing would be a better outlet for this type of energy.

While I mentally shopped for climbing shoes, I closed the door on the little voice that had called me to LRG in the first place. There might be smoke, but there didn't seem to be a fire, and even if there was, who was I to think I could put it out?

Eight

I don't believe there is a culture on earth that would be compelled to describe Emily as physically beautiful. She is neither heavy nor thin, but has a certain physical solidity about her that is not currently in vogue. Her features are equine, in a way: large, dark, liquid eyes, a full mouth and lots of big white teeth. I think her hair is beautiful, but she says it makes her crazy. It is dark and abundant and resists all of her well-intentioned attempts at domination; it springs out of hair clips and scrunchies and all types of elastic as though intent on having a life independent of the woman who grew it.

All of this combines in a way that you'd think would be entirely unappealing, yet when Emily smiles you just feel happier. Everyone does. And you can see it in the way they interact with her. She brightens things. And her world, not surprisingly, is a bright place. As a result, she has a lot of friends and there never seems to be any shortage of interested men in her immediate vicinity. It's why she's good at her job, I think. She can make things happen just with her presence and energy. And though she's still a first A.D., one day she'll be a director, just as she wants. It seems inevitable. She draws people to her and they are warmed by the proximity of this grace that is Emily.

I could feel that grace when the maître d' led me across the restaurant to our table. Emily was seated and nibbling corn chips and salsa and sipping a fresh-looking glass of red wine. The maître d' brought me to the table and announced me to her as though to a visiting princess. "Your companion has arrived, señorita," he said, seating me. "And have you found everything to your satisfaction thus far?"

"Perfect, Carlo," she said with a smile. "Thank you. Everything is perfect. As always."

That's the other thing Emily does that I can never believe: she remembers everyone's name and seemingly every bit of information about them that's been let loose around her. If she'd ever heard the name of Carlo the maître d's cat, she'd remember that, too.

The restaurant we'd chosen is about old-world decorum more than nachos. I imagine it to be the kind of Mexican restaurant where Spencer Tracey would have taken Katherine Hepburn back in the olden, olden, olden days. In fact, he probably did—I think it's been here that long. But it's big and dark and grand and opulent in an old-Hollywood sort of way, which is to say quite opulent indeed. The kind of place where the tablecloths are crisp and linen, and the serving staff all talk quietly and wear very soft shoes. I let Carlo seat me, and returned

Emily's smile. "You were right," I said, looking around. "This is an incredible place."

"What's up?" she replied, reminding me of something that I'd noted about her almost from the first: in addition to being upbeat and fun to be around, she's also sometimes eerily attuned to the moods of others. Another part of the aforementioned grace, and perhaps the budding director's intuition. Only right this second I wasn't in the mood for attunement or even unburdening.

"I wouldn't even know where to start. It's been a pretty odd day."

She nodded. "I can see *that* on your face." A waiter appeared and she ordered a glass of wine for me without any consultation. "Now tell me," she said when he'd gone away. And, much to my surprise, I did.

I told her all of it, and every time a waiter would stop by to take our order, she'd shoo him away with a polite and graceful hand movement, not wanting to interrupt my narrative. I began the story at the beginning, with bumping into Ernie and showers and sandwiches, to my conversation with Sal, the debacle with my mom, through to the pull that had brought me to Langton, my run-in with the receptionist, my chat with Steve Rundle and rechristening myself as Madison, right up to my flight from the area, sure for a while that I would be hunted down and apprehended.

After I'd finished, Emily didn't say anything for a minute. Just sat quietly as though thinking it all through and contemplating an appropriate response. At last she said softly, "You've had a busy day."

I grinned at that, maybe somewhat gratefully. Because, with a single line, she'd broken it all down into something digestible. She commiserated with me about my mother (since she has one, too, she understood), got me to give her more details about Ernie, asked for a description of Steve, and said she'd love to have been there for my run-in with the receptionist. And all of her questions seemed at least partly designed to make me feel less freaked out by the silliness I'd been getting up to this day, more comfortable with all of it as part of the past—recent, but still behind me. All of it, I'd discovered quickly, warmly and typically Emily. She followed this, though, with something less typical.

"So what about this Hyatt thing?"

At first I didn't even understand what she was talking about. *Hyatt. Thing. Hyatt thing.* The words didn't hold meaning. By the time I'd forced them to, she'd gone to another level. I could see it on her face. I don't know why I was so surprised. Already knowing her proclivity for crashing, I guess I should have seen it coming.

"Oh, Em. No. No, no, no."

"What do you mean, no? It's too perfect, don't you see?"

"But weren't you listening? Didn't you hear? I told you—the killer-receptionist-from-hell *saw* me, Em. She wanted to see my *driver's license*...." Even as I said it, it sounded lame.

"And how stupid is that? Anyway, she's not going to be there."

"She's not? You consulted the oracle?"

Emily didn't even bother looking miffed. "No oracle needed. You're just being theatrical and you know it." She made an airy motion with her hand. And she was calling *me* theatrical.

"I know it?"

"Of course you do. I know you've been doing this stock thing forever. And *you* know that I don't know the first thing about it." I nodded. She had me there. "Okay then," she continued, "since when do receptionists go to Hyatt-dos? They don't. Even I know that."

That was true. It was possible twinset might go, but not very likely. Nonetheless, I still didn't think showing up uninvited for a corporate bash was such a great idea. After all, I'd just spent most of a venti latte persuading myself that I'd been silly in pursuing any of this in the first place. I'd told Emily so. I told her again. That's when it hit me: never mind what I wanted, *she* wanted to go. From her perspective, I'd had a fun afternoon playing Nancy Drew and she wanted in. She is, after all, a Hollywood animal. And nothing makes her rise to a challenge like not being invited to a party that holds even the slightest promise. And, all right then— viewed in that light, with Emily in heavy persuasion mode, it actually could be fun.

"And, anyway, just in case, I have a friend in Santa Monica who's a makeup artist. He'll *completely* disguise your appearance." That's the other thing about Em—again, consider the business she's in. From the little I've discovered about Hollywood types, it doesn't matter if they're the "talent" or they work behind the camera or make sandwiches for the set. There's a reason they've aligned themselves with show business and not some other. That theater thing again. All of them love to pretend. They love the opportunity to be more or less or just somehow other than what they usually, normally, are.

Our new plan was put in place very quickly. I know we had an elegant if hurried dinner, though I couldn't tell you what we ate. Mine was sumptuous and beef-based and unlike anything I've ever heard described as Mexican food before. The few bites I had were delicious, and so I felt a little ashamed at just pushing everything around on my plate quite purposefully, but I was just too nervous to eat. Emily's food was similar, but sans beef—she's a vegetarian—and we dispensed with desserts or coffees and certainly after-dinner drinks. "There'll be time for all of that at the Hyatt," she told me wisely, as though we'd been planning it all along.

Then we roared off in Emily's SUV—a big, black, shiny beast of a thing whose only way of going forward is at a roar—to Santa Monica where her friend Brian lived.

Brian, Emily told me as we roared, worked on a lot of the same not-quite-schlock movies on which Emily made her living. She'd called him on her cell before we left the restaurant, told him an abridged version of our plan—which included my appearance change, but not why—and he'd said to come on over, it all sounded *too* fun.

And really, it was. While we were on our way to his house, Brian made his living room into a makeshift studio. I gathered from the conversation he and Emily quickly launched into that this was something that happened fairly often—playing dress-up at Brian's house. In addition to movie work, he also dressed a few minor—but, he hastened to add, not insignificant—stars for awards presentations and so on. I also surmised from the look of his nearly shaved pate, flawlessly trimmed eyebrows and long, pearlesent-tinted nails that our man Brian was a cross-dresser, or something rather like it.

Just as we settled in, the doorbell rang, and two of Brian's friends appeared bearing a bottle of wine. Robert was slender and dark and sharply effeminate, and I could barely see a trace of Carmen's masculinity at all. He—she?—was Asian, over six feet tall and completely willowy, with a complexion like a peach and an incredible mane of platinum hair. Like our host, these two looked as if they knew a lot more about women's evening wear than me or Emily, or both of us combined. Brian explained our mission to his friends as the wine was opened and poured all around, and the trio fairly crackled with excitement at the project before them. We were their willing canvases and it was apparent they liked the challenge.

Good, I thought. If you're going to have a makeover—and that was rapidly what this was turning into—who better to do it than guys who regularly transformed themselves into women? After all, if they could make themselves look like girls, what could they do for bona fide members of the female persuasion? I put myself into my team's hands and they went to work.

Brian unearthed a long, straight black wig for me—like Veronica Lake in a dark period—and a creamy, beaded sheath that he assured me was one of his more conservative dresses. It was beautiful—full length but with a slit almost to the crotch. It looked expensive, and not slutty, but definitely more suited to the Oscars than whatever do was doing at the Hyatt.

"It's an evening affair," Brian sniffed when I questioned him about the appropriateness of the dress. "It *will* be evening wear." Robert and Carmen nodded in agreement and lent assurances. It had all been said in tones that brooked no argument, and so, even though with the wig in place and the dress on I thought I looked more like a promiscuous Cleopatra than a corporate keener, I kept my mouth shut.

Emily was transformed, as well. Because she didn't need disguising, Brian had opted not to cover her hair. Instead he somehow miraculously pulled her unruly mop into a sleek and sophisticated chignon. He'd done her makeup expertly and lovingly, and Emily's look was entirely well-bred evening elegance. "I'm beautiful," she breathed when she gazed at herself in the mirror.

Brian looked gratified. "You are, darling Emily," he said to her quietly. "Never doubt it, *ma chère*. You always are."

He'd dressed her in a straight black skirt and a white blouse unbuttoned to a point daringly low, but with a high collar that framed her face. And he provided both of us with evening shawls that complimented our respective outfits, plus black evening shoes with mercifully moderate heels. From somewhere in his seemingly endless store of supplies, he even produced little evening bags. And everything was perfect. Everything fit perfectly and looked perfect. I could have shopped for a month and not found an ensemble that fit me so well. I imagined a room somewhere at the back of this house dedicated entirely to gorgeous evening clothes just like this in various sizes: from petite five footers to profes-

sional basketball players who were also closet queens.
It was an image to smile at, and I did.

"I'm too beautiful to operate a motor vehicle," Emily
proclaimed, and so we called a cab, which meant first
determining which Hyatt we were aiming at. A single
phone call confirmed Emily's guess: the event was
being held at the Hyatt Marina Del Rey in the Bette
Davis Ballroom, and was currently in full swing. And,
she was discreetly reminded, it was by invitation only.

"Of course it's at the Marina," Emily told me when
I asked how she'd been able to guess. "It's the closest
posh hotel to their office, and it would probably be
cheaper to hold an event there than somewhere downtown or strictly west side." An easy deduction to someone wise in the ways of L.A. party planning or crashing,
neither of which, obviously, were my fortes.

Brian, Robert and Carmen saw us cheerfully to the
door, with cries of, "Break their hearts, you lovely flowers!" and "Are you sure you don't want us to come?"
Which, on another day, to another function, would have
actually been pretty fun. I imagined some of the corporate events I'd been to in New York: the tightly buttoned
executives and their carefully coifed wives. We would
have made a stir arriving with Robert, Carmen and Brian
at an event like that. The thought tickled me and I resolved to make it happen sometime if I could.

Once the cab had deposited us at the hotel, Emily led
the way to the Bette Davis Ballroom. "Just trust me,"
she said conversationally as we moved through the
hotel. "And do what I do."

Though there was no uniformed guard posted in front

of the ballroom doors, there was someone sitting there waiting to check invitations: a young bell hop who looked properly bored at this assignment.

Emily held us back for a couple of minutes while the door was empty, then, as a flurry of people came out, she manipulated us into their midst. "Excuse me," she said to the bored attendant. "Can you direct us to the ladies' room?"

Once she had the requested directions, we were underway again, following them. I marveled at how effortlessly she'd pulled it all off. And, no, we weren't in yet. But we may as well have been. She'd angled her cleavage in such a way, and struck such a bold pose, there was no way the kid wouldn't remember that we'd come out of there a few minutes before, even though we actually hadn't. Brilliantly simple. There seemed to be no end to Emily's talents.

And I was right. When we got back to the "official checkpoint," the kid returned Emily's smile and pretty much waved us through. And me—I'd been so nervous about the actual getting-in part, I hadn't bothered to waste any nervosity on what we were going to do once we were there. Now that we were, it all washed over me in a big, unpleasant rush.

As far as ballrooms go, this wasn't a huge one. But it was L.A., not New York, I reminded myself. Not that I needed much reminding. One whole side of the room was open to the night and, beyond the bright lights and the balustrade, I got a sense of the Pacific Ocean whispering, beautiful and spectacular. It's so amazing when you can hear the view.

Perhaps three hundred people were involved in various levels of corporate-type schmoozing. There were round tables with the signs of dinner recently completed still upon them, while wait staff moved silently among them, removing the debris. Most of the party-goers were still at their tables, talking in their head-office-assigned clusters. Some were beginning to get up and mingle a bit or hook drinks from the servers who were circulating with trays intended for that purpose. And a few were heading out onto the aforementioned terrace. I was relieved to see that Brian and Robert and Carmen had been right: our attire was perfect (even if my dress was slit a bit more than I would have chosen). Everyone was dressed in what was clearly evening wear, and all of the women wore getups not that different from mine and Emily's. We didn't stand out.

"So what now?" I asked her, conceding to her superior knowledge of how crashers are supposed to act in order to not be detected as such.

"Do you see him?"

"Which him?"

"Your Ernie."

"Don't call him that," I said, while I scanned the room again, hopeful and apprehensive at once. "Nope. Not a sign." What would Ernie have said if he saw me here? I couldn't even imagine. And, of course, the other thing I'd noticed in my fast inspection was that there was no sign of sharp-eyed receptionists. I exhaled.

"Well..." She considered, duplicating my scan. "First we grab a drink, over there." She indicated a waiter circulating with a large tray. "Then, out to smokeland. You had success with that tactic earlier and I like the way it sounds. We can eavesdrop or bond with the locals while we inhale."

"I don't smoke," I reminded her.

She grinned. "Neither do I." And off we went to execute her short-term plan. She secured a glass of champagne—or at least, a glass of some champagnelike substance. I opted to be more conservative and held out for the white wine. If they're not in water, I can get somewhat suspicious of bubbles. Then we headed for the terrace, which proved to be every bit as beautiful as those open doors had suggested. You could smell the big, burly city that surrounded us on three sides. You could catch the odor of the ocean and all of its fishy promise. Inevitably—and for me inexplicably—the scent of flowers wafted to us from some unseen place, as they always seem to do in Los Angeles at night.

Dinner wasn't long past, so a number of people had made their way outdoors for their after-food smoke, or just because being out can sometimes be better than being in. I was guessing that, for a lot of the players— especially the more senior ones—it was turning into a pretty tense party. It would be difficult to keep up a celebratory mood when the reason you're celebrating has vanished into thin air. And if, as I suspected, some of these people knew more than they were saying, that would make things more difficult, not less.

The terrace was a relief, and it wasn't surprising to see a lot of youthful and less tense faces out there. Where inside there was a sort of smoglike cloud of not-quite-rightness over the proceedings, out here there were the happy sounds of people having fun: laughter, glasses tinkling and unstrained conversation. By unspoken consent, Emily and I maneuvered ourselves over to an open portion of balustrade and settled in to sip our drinks and see and hear what could be seen and heard.

I hadn't actually expected to recognize anyone, much less be recognized, so it surprised me, after about one and a half sips of wine and a single pass over the assembled revelers, to see a familiar face. It was even more surprising to see him looking back at me with probably the same look of mild surprise and pleasant recognition on his face. I shouldn't have been surprised: he belonged here. I didn't. But he was in evening dress—black tie and crisp white shirt and.... Well he looked amazing.

"You look amazing," Steve said as he approached, echoing my thoughts about him so neatly that for a second I thought I'd spoken them aloud. "The Cleo getup threw me for a minute, but it suits you. You're beautiful."

I am not beautiful. At least, I would never think of myself as such. I'm too tall, for one. I know my eyes are set too widely apart to allow me to be strictly beautiful. I think my neck is too long, like a blond giraffe. With effort, I can perhaps be elegant. I can work my way up to a look of sophistication. And, on the right day, at the right time of the month and in the right light, I think I can sometimes even lay claim to being striking. But beautiful? Not so much.

There are times when I suspect that I'm beautiful on the *inside*. Like when I cry at sad endings in movies, or I have a mad desire to rescue all of the world's abandoned kittens, or I read the newspaper and some colossal injustice makes me truly sad and embarrassed to be human. That's when I suspect myself of inner beauty. But then usually something happens—someone cuts me off on the freeway and I shout and give him the finger, or a stock goes down when it's supposed to go up and I feel like ripping someone's head off. Those times make me suspect even this internal beauty I would love to be able to lay claim to.

So Steve's compliment caught me off guard. And it was the oddest thing. You can hear compliments like that stacked on one another and not have them phase you. You know they're empty or said for personal gain (to get into your portfolio, your bed or both) or just because it's the thing that is said at a certain point, such as, "How are you today?" This didn't feel like that. It felt real and sincere and unexpected. And beneath Brian's expertly applied foundation, I could feel a blush creep up my shoulders and over my cheeks. It was an unpleasant sensation and I wanted it to go away.

I did the only thing I felt capable of doing under the circumstances: I filled the fluttery void with empty chatter. I may have a killer instinct for the trade, but I can go all gooshy at a single compliment.

"Steve Rundle," I said, "this is Emily Wright." They shook hands and exchanged pleasantries and, though I might have been oversensitive, I thought I heard the pause where I didn't explain Emily's connection with LRG. That was not something I was going to offer. Though when I found the courage to look more closely at Steve, and saw the way he was looking at me, I could tell it wasn't something he was going to press for. At the moment, shop was the last thing on his mind. Time to steer him back, on my terms.

"We got here late," I heard myself explaining. "Did we miss anything?"

Thankfully, Steve took the bait. "You know, you didn't. Except the expected round of rubber chicken." He made a face. "Not a peep about the Billings guy. And he still hasn't shown. Is that weird or what?"

"With all the maybe-police guys in Culver City today," I said, "you'd think something bigger than what appears to be happening is happening, wouldn't you? Maybe something to do with him. Billings."

Steve just shrugged. It was apparent that it wasn't that he didn't care, he just seemed to think it was something that maybe didn't have so much to do with him. Something that would resolve itself if he left it alone.

I tried again. "Do you think we should ask someone? Straight out, I mean?" As if. That was the last thing I could do at this point. But Steve might be pointed at the task.

"You're kidding, right?" He passed a glance to Emily that was clearly meant to say, Is she insane, or what? Not one to miss a cue, Emily rolled her eyes as though she'd never seen anyone so silly.

"It's just not the Langton way, is it?" he said.

"I guess not," I said. "But aren't you curious?"

He stood back on his heels, thoughtfully, as though considering. "Well, I guess on the one hand, I am. But really in a super broad way. The way I might wonder if the president will get back in at the next election. I mean, I'll read everything about it so I know what's going on, and I'll cast my vote when I'm supposed to, but if the dude I vote for doesn't get to work in that office, it won't really effect me much, either way, you know? That's how I feel about Billings. I'm going to have to go to work tomorrow whether he shows up or not—" he shrugged, tipped his glass to me "—so why sweat it?"

Here's what I was noticing while Steve spoke: the way his Adam's apple dipped and rose in his throat as the words found their way out. That his hands were strong and well-shaped. That his shoulders made themselves apparent through his evening jacket—I could tell it was him under there and not a lot of tailor-made buildup. I noticed that his chin was almost perfectly square—"lantern-jawed" was the phrase that sprang to mind—and that he was close but inexpertly shaved. And most of all, there was an earnestness and an honesty in his face and voice that drew me. Why, I wondered, had I seen none of this earlier today?

"Our share prices go up and down," he was saying. "Our management phases this way and that, but I work down in *Orange*, for crying out loud. None of this will effect me much one way or the other." He waved a hand in the direction of the ballroom. "Not as much, even," he said as he looked back into my eyes, "as seeing you again."

Emily cleared her throat. "Well, lookee me, my glass is dry," she chirped, obviously jumping onto the 'three's a crowd' bandwagon. "Off I go for a refill."

Steve stopped her. "No, I'll go. How about you, Madison?" It took me a second to focus on the unfamiliar name. "Would you like another?"

I nodded, passing him my glass and feeling oddly and unexpectedly…overwhelmed by him. By the depth of his eyes. And probably more importantly, the passion I could see rising there. Emily and I watched him go inside. And I watched his butt, simply because I suspected a comment would be coming immediately.

She didn't disappoint me. "Well, *he* works out."

"*Emily.*"

"Come on, you didn't notice? That boy sincerely has it going on." And then, as an afterthought, she said, "And he sincerely has it going on for you."

"But you said it, Em—he's a boy. Do I strike you as a cougar?"

"What's a decade between friends?" She leered. "And anyway, your age is the last thing on his mind. I'll bet he hasn't even noticed."

"*Whatever,* Emily. None of this has anything to do with why we're here. We should be doing something."

"We are doing something. We're *fraternizing*. It's cool." She favored me with a less leering smile. A warm Emily smile. I was relieved. "Seriously, though, Madeline, he's a charming, attractive guy, no matter where we found him. We'll see how this all turns out. After this, I think I might have to revise my manhunting strategies." She surreptitiously indicated a testosterone-laden trio on the opposite side of the terrace who were clearly checking us out. "You can come, too," she assured me. "This is fairly good huntin'." I must have looked exasperated, because she went on. "No, from now on we crash business functions, seriously. Think about it. All of these guys have jobs, and it's a fairly good bet they can read. That's a *lot* better starting point than most of the guys I've met at clubs."

Fortunately, I was spared having to come up with a reply because Steve returned with our drinks and a little tray of food he'd rustled up from somewhere. "In case you were hungry, because I know you missed the dinner."

Emily took her drink, downed a couple of canapés, then excused herself. "I should circulate," she said apologetically, while she looked challengingly into my eyes, daring me to say, But you don't *know* anyone. Which, of course, I couldn't. I could have excused myself to go with her, also muttering something about circulation, but I found I simply didn't want to. A decade's difference in age or not, I liked this guy. And it wasn't just that he'd brought me food—though the canapés hadn't hurt (you gotta like a guy who knows when you need feeding). Steve Rundle just exuded this basic niceness and small-town attractiveness that made me not want to put distance between us, and also made me forget why I was here.

Unintentionally, he reminded me.

"Tell me again what you do at Langton." He was probably just making conversation, filling the void left by Emily's departure, but it was a jolt.

"I don't think I did tell you."

"So tell me now." It wasn't probing. Just conversational. I told myself that while I tried to think of how to reply. But it's a lot easier to lie to someone you don't like or care about than someone you feel some sort of connection with. At that moment, when he started asking me stuff I didn't want to answer, I knew two things: I didn't want to lie to him, and there was just no way I could tell him the truth. I opted to do neither. I touched him gently on the arm. "Do you mind very much if we don't talk about work just now?"

He returned my touch, with a gentle hand on my bare shoulder and a smile. "Actually, I don't mind at all. In fact, why don't we leave work behind us for the evening? Do you want to walk in the marina?"

Did it surprise me that I did? But I found I wanted to. Very much. I told him so. "Let me just find Emily and tell her."

Emily was inside, seated amid a group of laughing matrons. Unsurprisingly, they were laughing at Emily's jokes. There's no place she's uncomfortable, no place she can't win over a crowd.

"He's asked me to go for a walk in the marina," I told her when I'd drawn her aside.

She smiled wickedly, though, thankfully, she didn't crow triumphantly, just said, "He's a nice guy."

"Well, I'm going for a walk with him, anyway." If I said it slightly defensively, Emily let it pass. "What about you?"

She pretended to look shocked. "You don't want me to come?"

"No, I just meant—"

"I *know* what you meant, Madeline. And I'll be fine. I'm actually having a very excellent time."

"Really? Have any of them asked what you do for the company?"

"Yeah. I just keeping telling them I'm here with my

friend Madison, and when they ask me what *you* do I just play stupid." She looked pleased with herself.

"No, you go off with Mr. Lovely Buns," she insisted, "and don't give me a second thought. I'm a big girl. If you don't show up by the time I want to leave, I'll catch my own cab." She shushed my objections, halfhearted though they may have been. "And I'll keep my ear to the ground. I have less at stake and less chance of recognition in this crowd. I might even hear something." And with that she gave me a quick hug and returned to her group without a backward glance.

Nine

The feeling that something was wrong—amiss, out of place—reached through my dreams and poked me awake. When I opened my eyes, it was confirmed. The clock on the bedside table said 7:30, which meant the markets had been open for an hour. But it wasn't just time's relationship to the markets. For starters, the clock I was looking at was unfamiliar. And I wasn't in my own little bed over Las Flores. For a second, I wasn't even sure exactly *where* I was. Then it came to me: in a hotel room in Marina Del Rey. The lack of light was why I hadn't wakened—that and plain old exhaustion—because the curtains were drawn. I don't have curtains in Las Flores. It's not a view you ever want to block.

More, I wasn't alone. Steve was there, beautiful in sleep. All hard angles and smooth planes. And I—and now it all came back to me—I felt wonderful. Energized. Beautiful. And torn.

What I wanted to do was snuggle back under the covers against this lovely man and let the incredible, if somewhat inexplicable, physical chemistry we had discovered we shared do its work.

What I did was slip very quietly out of bed and skulk around collecting my—or, to be more precise, Brian's—scattered clothing from around the room. And how was I going to wear this clothing now? A slinky beaded evening dress on the streets of West L.A. on a weekday morning? Lovely. And the wig? Forget it. In the bathroom I washed the sleep from my face and smoothed my hair as best I could with my fingers. Then I found a sack intended for laundry or shoe cleaning or something, and stuffed the wig in there. It obviously wasn't going to fit in my evening bag.

I started to leave, then thought better of it. How could I leave without some sort of acknowledgment? I found the obligatory hotel stationary in a bureau drawer and scrawled a fast—and quiet—note: "Steve…"

And then I hesitated. Now what?

"Thank you for everything."

Thank you? How lame was that?

"It was a very special evening. I'll remember it always."

Blech! Yet it felt true.

And I signed it with a simple "M" for "Madison" because I couldn't bring myself to write the whole fabricated name.

It *had* been. A special evening. And, for obvious reasons, I couldn't let it go any further. I wasn't at all who he thought I was. So, when I left the room, I let the door close very quietly behind me. And then I walked softly down the hall, feeling like a thief. Feeling as if I'd stolen something.

A cab took me back to where I'd left my car at the restaurant on La Cienega the previous night, and then I drove myself home, feeling spacey and unreal the whole way—forty-five minutes on the Santa Monica Freeway and then PCH, going against nasty morning traffic all heading into the city. Away from me.

At home, Tycho was excited and reproachful at once. It's a dual move that only dogs can do very well. I ignored the three dead lizards he'd lined up next to his bowl—I'd deal with them later. But I did replenish his water, which brought some slightly less reproachful tail wagging.

I noticed the message light flashing madly on my answering machine, but ignored it as I'd ignored the lizards. I knew who it was. Emily would be looking for a full report, and I'd give it to her, of course. Some version of it, anyway. But not just yet. Right now I needed to change out of last night's slinky clothes, have a long shower and pull on my usual work clothes: track pants and a T-shirt. "And, no, Tycho, no run today," I said to his delightedly reproachful face as I scratched under his chin. "Well, maybe later."

So, twenty-four hours later, here I was—back in the shower. Would I never learn? Bath people don't have to have those big, wet voids in their lives. If they want, they can take a cordless phone into the tub with them. It's possible to stay connected in a bath. Not so with water that tumbles from above.

But it's blissful. After fifteen minutes of hot, spiky needles of pressurized water slamming into your skin, it isn't possible to feel only half-alive. A shower wakes up even the sleepiest out-of-sorts parts of you, forces focus where a quarter hour before there was confusion. And it's nice to be that clean.

I padded around my apartment doing things as I dried off—a habit I'd picked up since moving to a warmer, moister climate. Plus living on a cliff just about guarantees total privacy. In Malibu it feels right to me to not wear clothes to do things that would have seemed unthinkable in New York.

I'd started a pot of coffee and was shuffling through my clothes, looking for my most comfortable track pants, when the phone rang. Even now there are some things I can't do undressed, and talking on the phone is one of them. (The other thing is eating hot food—I just find all of the possibilities too distressing.) I let the machine take it while I pulled on clothes, thinking I knew who it was and not sure if I was ready to take the call, anyway.

And I was right. Emily's voice began with a sigh. "Madeline. Shit." She sounded unpanicked. Resigned. "Where the hell are you? And why can't you carry a cell phone like a normal person? Well, I've left you all the details on the other messages and I'm not going to reblab them now but, as I guess you'll figure, I'm just talking on and on and on in the hope that if you're actually there and screening, you'll pick up the phone and—"

"Emily, I'm here. I just got out of the shower."

"So…are you completely freaked, or what?"

"Or what, actually." I smiled. "Well, pretty much the opposite, when I think about it."

There was dead silence for a moment. "Emily?" I said. "You still there?"

"Yeah, yeah. I'm here. I was just thinking about the meaning of the words you just said."

I think I must have actually pulled the phone away from my head and looked at it questioningly, just as they do on TV, before I moved it back in close and said, *"What?"*

"I guess what I mean is *how could you not be freaked*?"

"Jesus, Em. He was sweet and everything. And it was very nice, but I'm thirty-five years old. I have, you know, been down this road before."

Another silence. And then Emily's voice again. Ultrapatient this time, as though she were talking to a much-loved but slightly learning-deficient child. "Okay, Madeline. Have you listened to your messages yet?"

I was blank for a second, and then the blinking light caught my eye. Messages. "No, I haven't. I just walked in the door and hopped straight into the shower. I was going to call you right away and—"

"Never mind, Madeline. It's cool. Just…shit." That word again. "I dunno. I don't feel like explaining the whole thing again. Just listen to them and call me back, okay?"

"That's dorky, Em. Just tell me, already."

"But…"

"Come *on,* Emily. I'm just not in the mood."

She sighed, a resigned sound. "Where to start… Okay. Well, after you left, I spent most of the evening with these three really charming women. I think you saw me with them? Turns out they're all wives of executives—I don't think that company has any girl executives, do you?"

"Not so many, maybe. But equal opportunity employment is not why you left seventy-two thousand messages on my machine, right?"

"Anyway—" Emily ignored the barb "—we were drinking, laughing, you know, getting pretty chummy. I'm not sure who they thought I was, or maybe after a while they didn't care because...guess what?"

"I am not going to guess what." It was possible I didn't sound too friendly just then. I was tired and beginning to get annoyed. Emily didn't care.

"Well, it's all a big secret, but your old boyfriend has been kidnapped."

This woke me up. "Kidnapped? No way. Who kidnaps the CEO of a *glass* company?" But Sal's words came back to me: *not missing friendly*. Kidnapping would definitely qualify.

"Well, that's what Melissa and Cindy and Vera were saying." Melissa, Cindy and Vera were no doubt Emily's new buddies. "His wife reported that he left for work in the morning, but he never showed up. And it's not like Langton does any high tech or secret-y stuff. I asked."

I thought about what Emily had said. "But that's a big leap, Emily, from not showing up for work to kidnapping. How do they know he didn't just run away to Bolivia?"

"Bolivia?" she exclaimed.

"Or wherever. It was the first place that popped into my head."

"Bolivia was the first place that popped into your head?" she repeated, sounding incredulous.

"Will you forget Bolivia, already. I just meant, how do they know he didn't just take off with a mistress or something?"

"There was a note. Melissa's husband described it to her. The way she told it, the note looked just like the ones in the movies, made out of cutup magazine letters or something."

Which seemed weird to me. In the age of laser printers, who'd bother making an art project out of a ransom note? But I didn't think it was weird enough to comment on just now. There were too many levels of oddness to hone in on just one.

"What do they want?"

"The note didn't say! Just that they'd better keep it quiet and that someone would be contacted shortly. Or else."

"Or else what?"

"They didn't say that, either. Just—or else."

"That's odd, Emily. Don't ransom notes usually go to the family?"

She paused, thinking. "You know, you're right. And he hadn't even started with the company, so…that *is* weird. Do you think it means anything?"

I shrugged. "I don't know. It might, I guess. Or it might just mean they figured the company would be the most direct route. Or the most untraceable. When did they get the note?" I guessed they would have gotten it early West Coast time yesterday, about the time of the trading halt. If Ernie hadn't been missing they wouldn't have bothered with that. If it had been a nooner or a golf game or a meeting, there would have been no reason to stop the stock trading. But a kidnapping that might leak to the press at any time? For *that* you stop trading.

Emily confirmed my guess—the note had landed early the day before. "But here's something else I don't get. The wives club said the note instructed Langton to keep the kidnapping quiet, but it's all over the news this morning."

"Is the stock trading?"

"Geez, *you* don't know? You really did just get home, didn't you?"

"I told you I did. But is it? Trading, I mean."

"I don't know. I hadn't even gotten around to thinking about that part yet."

"I should go and check." I had a sudden burning desire to get off the phone and get on the computer. What the hell *would* the kidnapping of a shiny new CEO do for a company's stock price? The stock market is a fickle master. Depending on how the wind was blowing on Wall Street today, anything was possible.

"Wait, there's more."

"More what?" I asked distractedly, already booting my computer and preparing to download news releases.

"More. News. I don't even know how to tell you this next part. You sure you don't want to listen to your messages?"

"Emily," I said warningly.

"It's just too weird, Madeline. Oh hell, I'll just tell you. They have a suspect in the kidnapping. Photos and stuff. Someone they think might be part of, like, a group or something."

"Well, that figures. He's a pretty important guy. They

probably have a lot of people on it. That's a good thing, Emily."

"But it's *you*."

This barely registered. It just didn't make any sense. How could it be me? That's what I said: "How could it be me?"

"I guess it was your run-in with Miss Prissy Twinset. That's where it looked like the photos came from, anyway."

"They have *photos*?"

"Bad ones," Emily assured me. "Black-and-white. Like off a security camera, which is what I'm thinking it must have been."

"But you knew it was me."

"Sure, *I* knew. I'm not sure anyone else would recognize you, though."

"Like my mom?"

"I don't think it's exactly a CNN story, Madeline. Local news right now. What are you going to do?"

Do. That was the first instant it came to me: I had to do something. Society has expectations of you in situations like this. Like, if you see an old lady with packages, a poodle and a walker struggling across the street, you help her. And if you were implicated in the kidnapping of a CEO, you...

"Turn myself in?" The very thought of it floored me. Visions of a million reruns of *Law & Order* danced through my head: grimy cells, bad food and good cop, bad cop. Even as I said it, it didn't sound like a good idea. Emily agreed. She said so.

"I mean...you didn't do it, did you?"

"Emily!"

"Sorry. I had to ask. And they're not actually looking for, you know, *you*. Just someone who infiltrated the company headquarters yesterday. Someone who, well, happens to be you, but…"

"Oh, God."

"I know. It's kind of a mess, isn't it?"

The really weird part was I *felt* like I had made it all happen, even though, in actuality, I had just been thrashing around not accomplishing much of anything.

"Look, Em, I'm going to go and think about stuff. I need to digest it all. And, you know, maybe see if I can catch a glimpse of myself on television. Christ, this isn't how I wanted my fifteen minutes of fame."

Unaccountably, Emily giggled. I did, as well. Because, as perilous as the situation was if viewed from a certain angle, there were definitely humorous sides. Our giggles turned to laughter. And it helped. Actually, it helped a lot. Helped put things back into perspective. I *wasn't* a kidnapper. I was a lapsed stockbroker with more time on my hands than perhaps I'd previously realized. I got off the phone feeling a lot better. Calmer.

I walked over to my computer, preparing to do what I do. Emily's laughter—the laughter we'd shared—still rang in my mind, along with the ridiculousness of the whole situation…until a knock on the door stopped my heart.

The moment I heard the knock I *knew* it had to be the police. Who else could it be? I don't know a lot of people in L.A.—especially people who would drop by unannounced. My little guest house, as I've said, hangs under the deck of a large house and, collectively, they hang off a cliff. Even the most ardent Jehovah's Witness wouldn't make this trek without an invitation, and the last place a lost pizza boy would come ask for directions was at my door. And since we'd just gotten off the phone, I knew Emily was at her place in Huntington Beach, an hour away if traffic was good, so it couldn't be her.

My heart stopped. And the knock came again. More insistent. I resisted the urge to jump out the window—it's a long drop—and it didn't even occur to me to hide. They're three small rooms. Then I noticed that Tycho wasn't barking—his tail was wagging, which only meant...

"Madeline? Are you in there?"

It was Tyler. And the relief that washed over me was so large, I nearly passed out with it. The big relieved grin on my face faded when I saw the look on Tyler's. He looked wiped, as though he hadn't slept, and he was so pale he was gray.

"Tyler, what is it?" I didn't have to ask if something was wrong.

"Is she here, Madeline?" His voice sounded taut enough to break. "Tell me she's here."

I shook my head, not understanding. "Tasya?" I ventured.

His shoulders sagged with disappointment, but he came deeper into the guest house, plopping himself on one of my kitchen stools as his daughter did every time she came through the door. "No." He shook his head. "Not Tasya. Jennifer."

"Jennifer?"

"She didn't come home last night. And we noticed that you didn't, either, so we'd been hoping she was with you."

"Oh, Tyler, no. I'm sorry. But no, I haven't heard from her since..." I paused a beat, trying to recall the last time I'd talked to the teenager, then blanched guiltily when I remembered. "Yesterday. I saw her yesterday. Just before noon. She wanted to talk to me and I didn't have time right then. I'm so sorry."

"Not your fault," he said softly. "She tried to talk to me about that time, too. She got me on my cell. I was in a meeting, told her I'd call her back."

"But Tyler, maybe it's nothing. I mean, she's seventeen, right? There are a lot of places she could be without it being bad. Have you tried calling her friends?"

Tyler nodded. "I've tried any place I'd expect her to be."

"What about her mom?"

"Lena? God. No, that's a last resort. If she even gets wind that Jen's missing..." He let his words trail off as though even contemplating the scenario was too painful. "Maybe I wouldn't be this freaked if Jennifer was a different kind of kid. But she's always so good about letting me know where she is. In fact, she gives *me* shit when I don't show up when I'm supposed to."

"Listen, Tyler, it's not even noon yet. It must be hard not to worry, but give it a few hours. Maybe she'll turn up in the afternoon with a huge hangover and a good story."

He looked relieved, but only slightly. As if I was offering him the promise of a rope and he was opting to hang on. "It's good advice, Madeline. I know I can't call the police or anything until she's been missing for twenty-four hours, so I might as well cool my jets."

When the door closed behind Tyler, I sort of melted onto the couch and vegged for a minute, trying to get the leftover pounding of my heart under control. Everything seemed to be turning surreal and it wasn't even midday. I tried not to think about Jennifer for the moment. I'd meant it when I told Tyler to wait it out for the time being. Seventeen-year-olds can be as capricious as…well, anything. There is no metaphor equal to the task, for there is nothing as potentially capricious as a seventeen-year-old girl. I felt fairly confident that Jennifer would, as I'd told her father, turn up later in the day, tired and sorry and perhaps even with a story to tell.

Meanwhile, I told myself, I wasn't a kidnapper. I didn't even play one on TV. The fact that I'd been at Langton yesterday and been captured there on video didn't actually *mean* I was a suspect. Not really. Not me, Madeline Carter. Just some flickery black-and-white image of me as a possible someone. The police were probably clutching at straws and ol' Purple Twinset's reportage of our encounter the day before had likely been inflated beyond what had actually occurred.

Well, you did run away.

That voice again.

I flipped the television on in hope—or, more accurately, in fear—of seeing myself. Amid the wash of soap operas, game shows and reruns of old space series, there seemed little likelihood of this occurring before the noon news broadcasts. I left the set on when, finally, I got up to go to my computer.

That in itself was an odd feeling. Again, somewhat surreal: coming back to what was, for me, the most normal of acts and finding myself facing it with trepidation. I have made and lost big whacks—stacks!—of cash over the years with very little emotion attached to it beyond the most obvious. This whole Langton deal was turning into something quite different. Something that, for whatever reasons, had less and less to do with money. Which, as it turned out, was a good thing, because when I finally did get down to business, I got an unpleasant surprise.

"Four seventy-five!" I said it out loud, something that caused Tycho to pad over to see what was up. I was down a buck and a quarter. I didn't need a calculator to tell me that added up to thirty thousand dollars and change. I sighed. And admitted it—okay, part of it *was* still about money.

And then another thought occurred to me. "Oh, Mom." Again, I spoke aloud. Because this meant that, unless Roddy had miraculously managed to sell high this morning, if my mother was still holding LRG she was now down about twelve grand. I tried not to think about how many months' salary at the golf course that was. How many trips to Vegas (and Hawaii and Palm Springs and...). I tried not to feel responsible. But I did.

There are two very strong thoughts on what to do when you're down that big a chunk of cash with what's getting to be pretty close to a twenty percent dive that shows every sign of continuing to drop. Some guys I know sell all at the first sign of a serious dip. If it hits a ten percent decrease, they're out of Dodge. Me, I'm a little mixed. When it's other people's money? Absolutely: sell now. Because ten percent can turn into twenty can turn into thirty and so on. And when that happens with someone else's hard won cash, after a while you're having to make calls to Urbana (or Whittier or Tecumseh or Great Falls) and that's never pretty. "Well, yes. I understand that was your life savings and I'm terribly sorry about that. What's that? Why, yes. I do care. I care very much. However, the market does not. It eats people up and spits them out for breakfast if they're not watching every step and, quite often, even when they are. It does not care whose money it is. The market is a beast that feeds on virgins *and* the wise and well-prepared. I hope you don't have to eat dog food for the rest of your life, however I can't do anything about it, and the market still does not care."

No, not pretty. So, in cases like that—other people's money—the old ten percent rule pretty much rocks. But with *my* money? At sixteen percent and falling? And a more than thirty-thousand dollar drop? No, thank you. I wanted that money back. All of it. And bailing now would be kissing it goodbye. I set my jaw and held.

And now I noticed that the stock's sharp drop wasn't the only new wrinkle. The volume was to the moon. I checked LRG's price history—an at-a-glance record of the stock's high, low, opening and closing prices as well as daily volume. And the facts confirmed what Sal had told me yesterday. But it was a new day now and things were much worse.

When I'd made the initial purchase of LRG, the stock's daily average volume had been a couple of million shares, tops. The volume for today was fourteen million and it had been going great guns all day. I opened a screen that showed me the intraday trading graphs, indicating today's price and volumes. What I saw was even more disturbing was that it looked like two more big whacks of stock had been sold—one just after the bell and one an hour before close—from a single source. They had likely been market sells; in both cases, an order to sell five million shares in one big lump at whatever price the market would give it. And, of course, that had a disastrous effect on a conservative little stock like this one. The price had plummeted under the weight of filling two more big sell orders. With that kind of action going on, there was no way someone at that Exchange wouldn't notice and investigate if things looked fishy. But that seemed too iffy a possibility to bank on. And, it wouldn't help me now.

So, with the limited resources that were available, I did as much investigating as I could on my own. Although all this activity *could* mean that a couple of big investors got spooked when Ernie got snatched, it didn't seem likely. Anyone with that big a stake would know that selling at this particular time could be suicidal. (And if they didn't know, their broker should tell them!) Especially since Ernie hadn't even taken over yet when he'd disappeared. The kidnapping should not be affecting the stock price this greatly because, in reality, his being gone wouldn't affect the company's day-to-day operations yet.

Although there was no way I could be certain about it, my gut told me this wasn't an investor. As Sal had said about what he'd seen the day before, this looked like more short action. And, in this case, the short action combined with the current general weirdness around this stock was leading to what could very well turn into a death spiral—a downturn that, because down seems like a sure thing, invites further and further drops to, potentially, the very bottom of the market. It was an unappealing thought. Was there really *nothing* I could do to help avert it?

When I'm in heavy stock mode, as I am when carefully studying intradays, very little else can catch my attention. I get so fascinated running the numbers back and forth and following graphs and charts and reading press releases and news items that whole chunks of my life pass without my noticing. So it wasn't until I kicked back a little bit and scratched Tycho's soft ears and thought about perhaps eating something that the fullness of everything began to hit me: Ernie had been *kidnapped.*

Who kidnapped the new CEO of a glass company? Some sort of weird Save the Jars organization? It wouldn't be someone looking for money, would it? In L.A. there were a lot better pickings. Anything from high tech to high roller to high society: any kind of high profile if you were just looking for cash. Emily had mentioned a note. I wanted to know about it, wanted to know what was in it. And *why* did I want to know? Well, there was that thirty thousand bucks, for starters. There was—although this was a minimal point—my past connection with Ernie. And there was the fact that, for better or worse, I'd involved myself in this whole thing up to *here*. I had a stake now, on several levels.

And as though thinking about him had conjured him up, suddenly there was Ernie on the television screen. It was a still photo that looked as if they'd pulled it from some annual report. In the photo he looked older than I remembered him from college, but perhaps slightly younger than he had when I'd seen him at Club Z. I turned up the volume on the set.

The announcer was standing outside the building in Culver City I'd visited the day before. It looked just as it had when I'd seen it, though it had been sans news team then. Obviously, not much was going on, but it was a pretty building and, with the prettier news guy in front of it, the shot worked quite well.

"Though it's now been over twenty-four hours since Ernest Carmichael Billings was last seen, police have little to go on." The newscaster was continuing a story he'd started before I got to the volume control. "All they have is a note with minimal instructions and the image of a single suspect who infiltrated the Langton Group's head office in Culver City yesterday afternoon."

Then there I was. The pounding in my ears drowned out the droning of the announcer's voice. It was me. Okay, it was pretty grainy and the angle was sort of strange—from above. But *I* could tell it was me. I wasn't entirely sure that even my mother would know it, but I did.

Then my grainy visage was replaced by that of Ms. Mauve Twinset, although there was no sign of the twinset today.

"I was really quite frightened." *She* was frightened? "She had this crazy look in her eyes. I thought any second she would pull a gun out of her purse or something." Which of course brought a groan from me, because I had left my purse in the car while I was in there and *she* was the one that had been frightening.

Then the newscaster's head filled the screen again. Obviously, some paraphrasing was in order. "Ms. Farenholtz reported that, when she confronted the woman, the suspect fled—not once, but twice. Investigators continue to try to determine the woman's identity. For another aspect of this story, we join Cynthia Marlowe at the Sherbrook Hotel."

The image cut to a newscaster—presumably Cynthia Marlowe—in front of a toney-looking, low-slung building.

"Thanks, Malcolm," said Cynthia. "We're here in Beverly Hills where Mrs. Arianna Carmichael Billings is scheduled to attend a luncheon benefiting the Stop Hunger Foundation. There she is."

And the camera angle shifted to include the hotel's porte cochere, where Arianna was unfolding herself out of a Porsche. A Boxster. And it was the most amazing green. A slightly different shade and it would have been vile, poisonous. But this managed to look bright, and right and rich.

Cynthia Marlowe—presumably with her news crew in tow—headed off toward the car just as Ernie's wife got out and a parking attendant appeared to whisk the Boxster away.

"Mrs. Carmichael Billings!" Marlowe approached

her breathlessly. "We were hoping you'd comment on your husband's disappearance."

Slow news day, I thought. And, really, what I wanted to know was what the heck Ernie's wife was doing attending a benefit luncheon the day after her husband was kidnapped. Shouldn't she be off somewhere wringing her hands and crying? On the other hand, I know Ernie better than most. Maybe the wife was just relieved.

Then she was filling the screen. And it was the oddest sensation, because it wasn't something I'd noticed when I'd met her at Club Zanzibar. It wasn't that Arianna Carmichael Billings looked like me, exactly. But it was clear that we were cut from the same sort of cloth, or pulled from the same kind of mold. She was— and I say this with no attempt at false modesty, but merely in fact—she was far more beautiful than I am. And perhaps five years younger. But the similarities between us would have been obvious to anyone who saw us standing side by side.

I didn't for a second flatter myself in thinking that, in Arianna, Ernie had found a replacement for me. I'd never been that important to him. Rather, I realized what had been missing between us, as a couple. To Ernie, I'd probably never been anything more than the correct physical type. I had *looked* like the well-bred boarding school brat. And I'd known when we were together that the fact that my looks didn't really reflect my background was irksome for him. Hailing from rural Wisconsin himself—his family had been in the cheese business for three generations—he'd made no bones about making it known that he desired—*required*—a wife capable of opening the right kind of doors. The kind I clearly couldn't open. Of course, it had never been that serious between us. Though perhaps the fact that he was always looking for Ms. Right in all the wrong places got in the way. And here, finally, she was.

"There is not a great deal for me to comment on," Arianna told the camera in a controlled voice. "We're hoping for further word. And praying that whoever has him is treating him well." Though it was obvious Arianna was subtly trying to put distance between herself and the camera, Cynthia Marlowe wasn't quite done and, in typical reporter fashion, having gone in softly for the first quote, she now came in blazing for the close. By that time, from a reporter's perspective, there was nothing to lose. I didn't mind so much, this time, as it was a question I wanted an answer to, as well. I just hope if I'd asked it I would have looked less feral than Cynthia did now.

"Mrs. Billings, your husband was kidnapped twenty-four hours ago. Weren't you afraid it would seem odd and uncaring to attend a charity luncheon today?"

Arianna stopped inching toward the hotel and turned to face the camera fully. "It is *not* odd." I could see the controlled fury in her stance. "It's entirely the correct thing. My mother, Mrs. Nancy Enright, is the national chair for the Stop Hunger Foundation. I'm representing her today since I live in Los Angeles and she does not. This is an *exceptionally* worthy cause. And, frankly, preparation for it has provided me with a diversion from thinking about Ernest's plight. Good day," she said, as she stalked off regally.

I found myself silently cheering her, this new me (or was I the old her?) as the camera focused on the entirely unabashed-looking Cynthia Marlowe signing off, the hotel behind her, while Arianna Billings disappeared inside.

Before I really knew it was happening, a plan had formed and I was in action again, just as I had been the day before. For one thing, it felt like a better idea than sitting in front of my computer watching LRG go down.

I stopped at the house upstairs on my way out. "Jennifer told me she goes to school in Beverly Hills," I told Tyler at the door.

"Yeah, the Hestman School."

"I'm heading that way this afternoon. I thought I might stop and poke around a bit at the school on my way home. Talk to people, you know. That is, if you don't mind."

Tyler looked at me blankly for a moment before answering. "I'm frankly embarrassed I didn't think of it myself. And I can't now," he said regretfully, pointing behind him into the house. "I've got a script thing. But, yeah, if you're going that way, please. That would be so great. I'll call the school and tell them to give you every cooperation." He caught my hand, squeezed it. "Thank you, Madeline. Thank you so much."

Ten

I skipped the valet and parked a block from the hotel. I figured that if I was trying to fit in at a charity luncheon with the daughters of socialites, pulling up to the front door in a canyon-dusty Chevy—even a new one—was not the way to do it. Inside the hotel the heat of the day seemed a distant memory, not even a remote possibility. It didn't make you think of air conditioning so much as "climate control" of the sort that is flawless and imperceptible. Everyone has different needs in personal temperature. But at the Sherbrook Hotel, it seemed likely to be perfect for everyone.

A discreet sign in the lobby pointed me to the function I was hunting for. I trusted I looked the part: a crisp white blouse over a delicately patterned skirt with complementary heels. I headed to where the sign had indicated.

Thankfully, there was no one at the door of the banquet room to detain me. Without Emily to guide me, I hadn't been quite sure how I'd manage the crash, although I guessed this wasn't exactly a high security event. This was The Ladies Who Lunch to the max, and anyone who didn't belong here wouldn't even want to go. Except, of course, for me.

The banquet room held about thirty tables, each set for eight diners. Some of the place settings held name cards, I noticed, while every table had one or two unmarked spaces. Presumably this was so the organizers could do some last minute reshuffling, as well as have places for guests that hadn't signed up by the cutoff date, or whatever. Pretending to look for my name on a place card seemed like a good way of scoping the room while figuring out what my brilliant next move was going to be. The happy news was, it was beginning to look as if I might get a free lunch. My stomach growled most unbecomingly and, for the moment, it seemed like the hungry waiting to be fed was me. In that regard, however, the stars had not aligned on this day because my quarry found me before I could even begin to look for her.

I was leaning over tables, squinting at place cards—ostensibly looking for *my* name, but actually looking for hers—when there she was, right in front of me, extending one well-manicured hand and looking at me hard, as though she was trying to place me.

"Hello." She smiled. "I'm Arianna Carmichael Billings. Have we met?"

Her hand felt as cool and composed as she appeared, and when I'd straightened fully I realized that I was looking directly into her eyes. It's funny—you don't think about being tall until you meet another woman your own height.

"Madeline Carter," I said. "We met the other night at Club Zanzibar."

She gazed at me more closely once I'd said my name, making me suddenly conscious of the way my skirt was hanging and the way my blouse was tucked in. Did I have lipstick on my teeth? "Of course," she said finally. "Ernest's friend." I tried to gauge her tone, but gave up quickly. It wasn't giving anything away. "You're not a member of the foundation, are you?"

"No. I…I'm not," I admitted.

"Then why are you here?" The question was politely, even gently, stated, yet its directness caught me unawares. My professional life had not schooled me in the direct approach, yet I felt the need to return it here.

"I was hoping to have a word with you." As I said it, I thought how that might sound. Especially in light of the videotape of me at the office she may or may not have seen. Yet she didn't look alarmed. In fact, I realized suddenly, she looked intensely calm for a woman whose husband had recently been snatched and who was now being approached by an ex-girlfriend from his past.

"A word?" she prompted, looking as though she might be deciding something.

"Yes, it's…um, a little hard to explain." I indicated the people around us, meanwhile wondering exactly what it was I *would* explain if given the chance. While I wasn't sorry I'd come, I was also a little unsure of what, precisely, I was doing there.

She was studying me speculatively. "I would imagine it would be," she said finally, and I wondered if she had maybe seen the videotape of me, after all.

I tried again, matching her calm and level tone. "If I could have a few minutes of your time."

In the thirty seconds she took to consider my request, I thought I could see emotions warring not far beneath the surface. Or maybe I was just imagining how I would feel if I found myself in her carefully chosen shoes. I thought I saw curiosity followed quickly by fear. And then I decided I'd maybe just imagined it all, because—in the end—all I could see was resolution.

"That won't be possible, Ms. Carter," she said crisply, and I could tell she wasn't going to bother with an explanation. "And now, I have a luncheon to get under way. Do you have a ticket?" I shook my head. "Well then, it's two hundred dollars a plate." She smiled thinly. "But it's a very good cause. No? Then good day."

I lifted my hand, about to say something, but she'd already turned toward the door to meet a group of ladies who had just come noisily into the room. I was dismissed, that much was clear.

Another wasted trip. I left quietly, clearly ignored by Arianna Billings, wondering what to do next, although I knew that purchasing a lunch ticket wouldn't get me anything except closer to broke, even if it was a good cause. I stood waiting for the elevator when a familiar voice spoke close to my ear, just behind me.

"Excuse me, Miss Carter."

It was Arianna Billings, without the icy mask she'd been wearing just minutes before. She drew me out of the flow of women who were exiting the elevator, and spoke quietly and quickly.

"I've thought it over and I've had a change of heart.

I'd like to speak with you, hear what you have to say. But not now." She indicated the people heading toward the banquet room. "I've got my plate full." She gave a charming smile, as though discussing her next charity function. "Could we meet for coffee later?"

Coffee is my most major addiction, if you don't count the stock market. I seldom say no to it. We agreed to meet at three o'clock at a place she knew in Brentwood close to her home and not far from Jennifer's school. As I got on the elevator I felt a reluctant pang when incredible food scents wafted in from behind closed doors. My stomach, like my curiosity about Mrs. Carmichael Billings, would just have to wait.

I knew I had two hours before I had to meet with Arianna, and the most time I would possibly spend at Jenn's school would be an hour. With hunger threatening to overwhelm me, I opted to get some food inside me before I tackled anything new, and I headed—as new Angelenos tend to do—for the beach. Santa Monica, in this case, where there are about a million restaurants—or so it seems—within a few blocks, as well as interesting people to look at if you, like me, are dining alone.

I sat on the patio of a maniacally trendy little bistro on Main Street that nonetheless managed to produce a beautiful lunch for me. I munched happily on a "very colorful" salad and some ahi tuna, rare. I'd just finished eating when a trio of roller-blading guys caught my eye. It wasn't just the sweating *maleness* of them that interested me, though I admit it's what I noticed first. But there was something vaguely familiar about one of them, in particular. And they were practically upon me by the time I realized why. It was Steve.

I think the reason I haven't made room for a lot of men in my life is the fact that they can have such an unsettling effect on me. That is, the ones I like can, and I could never be bothered with the other kind. But realizing that, almost as if by magic and against all odds, Steve was right in front of me filled me with this pleasant warmth. And it's a slightly distressing feeling if you're used to keeping things controlled.

Seeing him there, suddenly, unexpectedly, I wasn't quite sure how to act—who to be—but the smile I broke into was warm. I was genuinely happy to see him again. The smile didn't last, though, as he stopped abruptly beside my chair. "I can't believe you didn't just bolt into the restaurant when you saw me," he said icily.

"What?" I was mystified.

"You guys go on," he said to his friends. "I'll catch up with you in a few minutes." I motioned to the chair opposite mine and he plunked into it angrily. "That was *so* cold."

"Cold," I repeated stupidly.

"Yeah. You. Are cold."

I thought about the night we'd spent. About the way our bodies had fit so naturally, like two parts of a whole coming together. I thought about moonlight on the water seeming to cascade through the hours we'd shared in his hotel room. And there had not been a great deal of sleep.

"Those," I said carefully, "are not the words I would have used," even though I vaguely recalled thinking that myself when I'd written the note. I hadn't *felt* cold. And I didn't now.

"Ah." There was a twinge of sarcasm in his voice. "What *would* you have said, then?"

I looked at him closely. On the surface he was mocking me somehow, but I didn't understand it. What I *did* understand was that I'd hurt him in a way I just couldn't see. In the face of all of this conflicting stuff, I opted to give him the truth.

"I don't know, Steve. You just said I was cold and I thought…I thought we had shared something really special." It sounded lame, but there it was. "And it felt very warm. To me."

"We did, Madison. We shared something special. Or I thought we did. Then I got up this morning and you were just…gone."

I was beginning to get a glimmer of understanding. But it was faint. "I left a note!"

"On hotel stationary. Not even signed. How cliché is that?"

"But…it was all there was to write on," I protested lamely.

"You could have woken me. Why didn't you wake me?"

Okay. That was a valid question. Why hadn't I? Even now, I wasn't entirely sure. "Oh, Steve…" I reached out to touch him, but he pulled back as though he'd been singed.

"Don't 'Oh, Steve' me. It was just a cold, shitty thing to do."

All I could do was shake my head in denial.

"It was. And that note—you didn't even leave a phone number. I thought your message was pretty clear."

"Oh, Steve." I'd said it again before I could stop myself. "It wasn't like that at all. It's just...it's just all sort of complicated."

"I get it." He wouldn't give up this injury so easily. "It's all a little too complicated for poor old Steve, huh? Like, for instance, just who the hell you are?"

This took me aback. For some reason I hadn't been expecting it.

"Yeah. I wanted to find you. To find out why you'd left. So even though I took the day off, I called Anderson in personnel today. I thought I might be able to talk him into giving me your phone number. Do you know what he told me?"

I shook my head, but I had a pretty good idea.

"We don't have anyone named Madison working for us in *any* of our offices. And you know what else?" This time I just kept quiet. I figured I knew where it was going. "He said that there had been someone at Langton yesterday afternoon possibly pretending to be an employee and possibly also a kidnapper. And I'm guessing that was you."

"No. I mean, I'm not a kidnapper. But yes, that was me and... Oh Steve, I *am* sorry. I can see how all of this must look to you, but..."

"Can you? Well, try this—I meet this woman who I think I have this incredible connection with, we end up in my hotel room having fantastic sex. It's like a fantasy, right? And...and I really thought we had something, you know, something going. Something...value added, maybe."

Value added? If I hadn't been so mortified, I would have laughed. Only a professional salesman would have put emotion in those terms.

"And then...well, what was I to you—Madison or whatever the hell your name really is—just a roll in the hay and a possible way into Langton?"

And I started to tell him no, that wasn't it. That wasn't it at *all*. Except it was, wasn't it? He'd hit it pretty much right on, if viewed from a certain angle. We'd shared a wonderful evening, and I hadn't thought of him all day, except this morning when I was relieved to get out of his room without waking him. And when I'd met him outside of Langton the day before, what *had* I been thinking of when I knew he was flirting with me? I'd been thinking about how to enter the building, then get away from him before he asked me out. And I had been thinking about a way to use him as cover, which I'd done. He was right. That was cold.

"Madeline," I said simply.

"What?"

"My name. It's Madeline."

"Really?"

"Yes. Honestly. I'm sorry, Steve. Truly. It's just... well, like I said, it's somewhat complicated. And nothing is what it seems, I guess." I held out my hand to him as though to someone I was meeting for the first time. "I really do like you, Steve. And I wish you'd give me the chance to explain." It was only as I said it that I realized this was true. I *did* like him. He was sweet and sincere and...nice.

He seemed to soften at my words—I could see it in

his eyes—as though he wanted to believe but was still nursing his injury. "You do?"

"Yes."

It surprised me when he ignored the hand and came to me, pulled me to my feet and embraced me—a big, puppyish hug. And then, through the hug, came the heat, and the hug turned into a kiss—deep and long and right there on the patio, me with my head tilted way up to accommodate the extra inches his Rollerblades added to his height. When he pulled back and looked down into my eyes, I realized for the first time that they were this really amazing shade of green. They were smiling at me now. The smile was nice. It warmed me.

He took the seat he'd abandoned, clasped my hand and looked at me intently. "So…go ahead," he said gently when we'd sat down. "Explain."

I could feel the air slide out of me in a whoosh. A sigh too long kept inside, a breath I hadn't realized I was holding. There was a part of me that wanted to unburden to him, then and there. But right at that second, it all just seemed—as I'd told him—incredibly complicated, like one of those Russian dolls you open to find another and then another and then another still. (Though the one I'd had when I was a kid only had three Russian dolls. How complicated is that?)

To be honest, I didn't even know where to begin. Not now, sitting at an outside restaurant while oblivious, self-centered Santa Monica rushed past us and the time when I was to meet Arianna Billings rushed toward me.

"I can't, Steve. Not right now." He didn't seem to

even try to hide the disappointment he felt. I suspected, also, that I'd failed some sort of test. "No, really, I have some things to do in Beverly Hills and Brentwood. But can we meet later?" He brightened instantly and I liked him even better for it. He was like water, sweet and clear.

"Sure. Where? When?"

"I don't know. Brentwood, okay? What about the Hamlet?" I named one of the few restaurants in that area whose location had stuck in my mind. "On San Vincente?"

"Sure," he agreed. "Say five o'clock?"

"Maybe make it five-thirty," I replied, checking my watch. "Just to be on the safe side."

He gave me a big, winning grin and a quick kiss that was as casual and comfortable as if we'd been seeing each other for a long time. Well, I reminded myself as I watched him blade away, lithe on his wheels, not *so* long; high school for him could only have been a few years ago. I chided myself for the thought as I made my way back to my car. And then I was concentrating on finding my way to Jennifer's school and thinking about meeting Arianna and, unexpectedly, I forgot all about Steve. Again.

Eleven

Finding the Hestman School was as difficult as anything I'd attempted since arriving in L.A. The place is so exclusive, it's practically invisible. You get the feeling that this is not an accident.

It's located on an early twentieth century estate in the most exclusive part of Bel Air. Driving through the wrought-iron gates and down the long, winding driveway felt more like visiting the home of some foreign dignitary than a high school. The only visible clues were the well-tended sports fields, which had once likely been well-tended gardens. Those and the parking area behind the building that housed the school. It was stuffed with enough twenty-first century horsepower to replace the gross national export of most small- to medium-size countries.

None of it was what I'd expected. I'd anticipated the type of building that I'd grown up thinking of as a high school: big, utilitarian and easily penetrated. I'd figured I'd pull up and maybe talk to lurking teenagers, ask if they'd seen Jennifer. One glance at the Hestman

School made me realize why Tyler had said he'd call the place and let them know I was coming. Anything else would have been like dropping by unannounced at the White House.

Nor was it the kind of school where you'd expect to find kids hanging around in clumps outside the building. The only teenagers I saw there looked very purposeful and directed. Hanging was clearly not encouraged.

I parked in the shadow of the largest Mercedes Benz I'd ever seen, and pointed myself at the front door.

The school was as well-appointed inside as out. Clearly, whatever astronomical tuition fees Tyler and other parents were paying was being well spent. Just the maintenance on the masoleum-proportioned old mansion-turned-school would have cost a fortune. Obviously, it was important that the studio moguls of tomorrow be surrounded by large quantities of Carerra marble, period furniture and art they couldn't possibly have any intention of understanding. I found the office easily and thought again of the White House— everything looked rare, expensive and slightly larger than life.

"I'm Madeline Carter," I told the man behind the desk in the office, who clearly did not care what my name was. "Jennifer Beckett's father was going to call and let you know I was coming."

"You're with the family?"

I nodded, knowing that probably didn't accurately describe my connection, but since the alternative seemed to be *against* the family, I let it pass.

"Fine. Dr. Alder has been expecting you. I'll let her know you've arrived."

Predictably, Dr. Alder's office would have shamed the president—that whole White House thing—but she herself was a surprise. A tall and striking brunette in her early forties, she was as warm and engaging as her receptionist was distant. I wondered if it was deliberate.

She didn't bother with small talk. As soon as I was seated across the desk from her, she said, "I got a message from Tyler Beckett that you would be dropping by. Since I've had an impossible time getting him on the telephone myself, I'm glad you've stopped by to talk about Jennifer."

This was a surprise. "Actually, that wasn't my intention. I'd hoped to just drop by here today and talk to some of her classmates and see if any of them know where she might be. Her father is quite worried about her, but—you know—she's seventeen. I'm sure there's some explanation. Maybe she and another friend—someone else from school—went shopping or something."

"Yet her father fears something more dire?"

"Jennifer didn't come home last night," I admitted, knowing this might be putting more of a spotlight on the kid than she'd want, but also wanting Dr. Alder to have a full understanding of the situation.

"I see." She pursed her lips slightly. "Yet your presence here indicates that this is not a usual occurrence?"

"That's right. Tyler—Jennifer's father, Mr. Beckett—says it's never happened before."

"Hmm. I'm not quite sure what to say to you, Ms. Carter." She watched me carefully as she spoke. "From what you've told me, I'm not sure you have all of the necessary information. What did you say your position was with the family?"

"I didn't."

Alder looked at me sharply. "All right then. That will limit my ability to be candid with you, but have it your way. There are some things that must be said. I've been unable to say them to Mr. Beckett directly—I'll trust you to tell him to call me. I've called Mr. Beckett on several occasions over the last few months and asked him to come and see me in order to discuss his daughter. I have never reached the man directly by telephone and my calls have not been returned." From the look she gave me it was clear people usually returned her calls. "And now things have gone very far."

I was more than curious; I had the sense that whatever Dr. Alder had to say needed hearing right now. It seemed to be my week for impersonation. "You asked about my connection to the family. I'm…I'm Jennifer's stepsister."

Dr. Alder pursed her lips again but didn't say anything. It's possible she doubted me. It's also possible she wanted the matter behind her.

"Then I can safely tell you that it has saddened me this term to find that Jennifer, formerly a first-class member of the Hestman community, has not been—how can I put this?—adequately pulling her oars."

I squinted at the woman, trying to understand.

"I can see I'll have to speak more plainly. Until the end of last term, Jennifer was a straight-A student who was well-liked, had a lot of friends and appeared to have the ability to map her future wherever she chose. She returned from winter break, however, a changed child." Here Alder began ticking Jennifer's crimes off on her fingers. "She was surly, disorganized, her grades slipped and she started cutting classes. That is, we *thought* she was cutting, but since we were unable to speak with her father, we were unable to confirm. I can see from your expression that all of this is a surprise to you, so I'll cut to the chase. Jennifer has missed an increasing amount of class time this term. As a result her grades have plummeted. Last week we didn't see her at all and, as a result of all of *that,* we expelled her yesterday."

"Expelled?" I repeated stupidly.

"That's correct. So while I'm sorry to hear she didn't come home last night, I also need to tell you that—as cold as this sounds—it is no longer my problem."

"Dr. Alder." I was shocked at everything she'd told me. "I'm not an expert on teenage girls but, from what you've said, Jennifer has been crying for help."

"The Hestman School is not a rehab center, Ms. Carter." She spread her hands apologetically. "I'm sorry, there's nothing more I can say. I had Bruce clean out Jennifer's locker while we were chatting. He'll give you her things on the way out."

Since our interview was clearly over—and I was cleanly in shock—I took the white plastic bag that Bruce handed me as I went past his desk, tossed it in the trunk and left the Hestman School as quickly as I could.

I felt so drained from my talk with Dr. Alder that all I felt like doing was driving home and talking to Tyler, but I'd told Arianna I'd meet her at three, and it was close to that time now.

Brentwood is where L.A. tries to be Connecticut and, clearly, where some of the students at the Hestman

School would spend part of their adulthood. The quiet shops, the tree-lined boulevards, the careful architecture—the enclave has an old money feel to it, not to mention a what-passes-for-old-money-in-Southern-California cachet. But Brentwood is pretty and a nice place to visit. It's superclean, the avenues are very wide and the stores and restaurants quiet and understated.

I got to the café a little early, which was good because I still had Dr. Alder and all she'd said very much on my mind. The café was over-the-top elegant, with ornate gold-framed mirrors and antique furniture set in casually comfortable corners. The front opened onto the street, all bright sunshine and plants. The back of the café, however, was dark enough that candlelight in midafternoon didn't look at all silly. The place looked quiet and inviting, and no one was sitting back there. I ordered a latte and found a table in the back. It would be a good place to talk privately.

Disconcertingly, when I went to add sugar to my coffee, a little heart was staring back at me from the foam. The barista noticed me notice and smiled. I smiled back, but I was thinking at least it wasn't a happy face. Sure, you pay more for your coffee, but the rent must be high and foam hearts don't come cheap.

I was having these completely dark thoughts about baristas who go to the trouble of disturbing perfectly good latte foam with sappy hearts, when Arianna Billings breezed into the café. At the front of the shop two young men were drinking coffee. As Arianna entered, their heads snapped around in an almost dangerous fashion, as did that of the male barista. And this was *Brentwood*. Beautiful women fall from trees here—or at least from the offices of extremely talented and well-paid plastic surgeons in this very neighborhood. But Arianna wasn't just beautiful, she had this incredible presence. And that breeze.

"Madeline," she said in her controlled voice, as she took a seat, "I'm sorry I'm late."

"You're not, actually. You're right on time. Sorry to start without you," I said, indicating my cup. "I felt the need."

"Not a problem," she replied, then ordered from the young male barista who was standing next to our table staring at her almost worshipfully. I noticed this with a sort of amusement because, though I had had to go to the counter for my coffee, Arianna apparently merited table service.

I pointed to the Boxster, gleaming out at the curb, the same one I'd seen on television that morning. "Your car is an amazing color. I love it. And I don't usually like green."

"Actually, it's chartreuse. It's my favorite shade. It wasn't one of the factory colors, they painted it to my specifications."

What does it mean when you can not only buy the most expensive car you can think of, but also have it tinted to match your personal palette? I'd been around money for a long time—and Chagall etchings don't come cheap—but Arianna was from a different world. One where your wedding shower got written up in *Town and Country* and summering at the Vineyard wasn't something you looked forward to, just something "to be gotten through, darling."

We made small talk for a few minutes while her coffee was being made. It was a strain, because we didn't have much in common. And neither of us seemed quite prepared to face straight on what we *did* have in common. Yet. And so we talked about the success of the luncheon—which, she said, had gone very well and raised a lot of money for a good cause. And we talked about the ineptitude of the press who had, she said, nonetheless given her a good in to plug her mother's pet charity. When her coffee came (she plowed the foam heart under without even a glance) she seemed to feel it was time to get down to business.

"Ernest has talked about you, you know."

"He has?" Even though she'd said it the other night, I was surprised.

"That's why your name was familiar when we met. And your face. I've seen pictures of you. In an album."

That surprised me, as well. I wracked my brain. "The rowing club parties?" It was the only possibility. Ernie had been a rower in college and I'd accompanied him to a few club functions early in our relationship. These were the only photos I imagined would still be around of the two of us; he would have had reasons other than me to keep them.

"He has special memories of you," she said, nodding. It was a pretty odd revelation, I thought, coming as it did from the wife of a kidnapped man to one of his ex-girlfriends.

I didn't say anything. There was no way I'd tell her I had fond memories of him. I didn't. Instead, I asked, "How long have you two been married?"

"Five years."

"Kids?"

"None." She cast her eyes down momentarily and I

couldn't read her. "Not yet, but we've been discussing it." Another sign of the void between us: in her world marriage was obligatory—part of the natural progression—and children a matter for negotiation. Me? I'd been married for about a minute early in my career, but stockbrokers make understandably terrible wives. It had been a disaster I didn't think I'd be repeating. And the idea of children—that is to say *my* having children—was, if not downright repellant, so absurd I couldn't get my mind around it. I mean, where would I put them? I barely had room for a borrowed dog.

Arianna watched me appraisingly for a while, sipping her coffee, nibbling her biscotti. Then she surprised me—she'd clearly had enough small talk. "Look, Madeline." Her voice was as calm and direct as when she'd been talking about her car and the luncheon. "I saw the videotapes on television this morning."

Candor continued to strike me as the way to go, despite my sudden terror that police cruisers were, even now, poised to descend on our quiet coffee klatch.

"I didn't have anything to do with the kidnapping."

"I know," Arianna said, looking away. "I know you didn't. That's why I wanted to talk to you."

These two sentences seemed oxymoronic to me—they canceled each other out. First, how did she know I hadn't had anything to do with it? From her perspective, you'd think I'd look like a pretty good candidate. Second, why would that make her want to talk to me? Then a light dawned. "You know something," I said. It was a statement, not a question.

She shrugged. An elegant gesture. "That's not important. What *is* important is what you know."

"Me? You already said you know I didn't kidnap him."

"That's not what I mean." she looked at me searchingly, as though deciding what she should say. Or how much. "Let's put it this way. Just between the two of us—and honestly—when was the last time you saw Ernest? Besides the other night."

I had to think for a minute because, although with Ernie it hadn't been a fizzle—more like a final eruption—it was long enough ago that it felt like ancient history. "It must be twelve, no, thirteen, years ago now. In May. Late May." Who am I kidding? That *is* ancient history.

"Thirteen years ago," she repeated needlessly. And though her tone sounded flat, uninflected, I could hear the disbelief in it.

"Yes. When we broke up. I haven't seen him since."

"I see." Her friendly—breezy—tone hadn't altered, and yet the temperature seemed to have dropped about ten degrees. "Thirteen years ago. And we just happen to run into you at a nightclub. And then you show up at his new office on the very day he happens to have been kidnapped. After more than a dozen years?"

It sounded thin, even to me. "Exactly. And you sound as though you doubt it. Though you didn't sound as though you doubted the fact that I had nothing to do with the kidnapping."

She met my eyes—a chilling blue gaze—and just looked at me. I couldn't quite gauge what she was looking for. An ally or an alibi? Someone reasonably unconnected to the situation to talk to? At length, she said, "I *know* you didn't have anything to do with kidnapping him. At least, I think I know. Because I think he did it himself."

Did it himself, my brain repeated stupidly. Did what himself? "Do you mean you think he kidnapped himself?"

She nodded.

"But why?"

"Why do you think, Madeline? Money."

I thought about Ernie's track record as a hard hitting CEO. And I looked at this beautiful woman across from me: the expensive manicure, the perfectly coifed hair, the designer clothes, the Boxster glinting at the curb outside the café. Miss Daughter-of-the-champion-of-feeding-the-hungry. She seemed *made* of money. I knew only too well, however, that looks can be deceiving. In more ways than one. And yet, what I knew about Ernie made me think there would be more.

"If what you're saying is true, it wouldn't just be about money, would it?"

She looked at me, but might as well have been looking through me. "Is anything ever just about money?" And then thoughtfully, as though aware of the contradiction, "Is anything ever about anything else?" She shrugged. "If you're asking if he needed money for anything, I'd say no. Not that I was aware of, anyway. Langton offered him a very good package to come out here, and he's done quite well by the companies he's worked for in the past." I knew all of this. And what I hadn't known, I'd surmised. I'd just thought that maybe there'd be something. What that something might be, I wasn't exactly sure.

"But you said you thought he was doing it for money."

"I did, yes. But I didn't mean because he *needed* money. No drug problem, no gambling debts—that I've ever been aware of—no actual need, if you follow what I'm saying."

"I think I do. What you're saying is he wants money…for the sake of money."

She nodded. Sighed. "To see who can make the biggest pile."

What Arianna was saying was so on target, so along the lines of what I'd been thinking, that I was somewhat suspicious. Though I wasn't exactly sure why. Despite the fact that I had once known her husband—in the biblical sense—I was a complete stranger to this woman. And I couldn't quite see her motivation for telling me as much as she had.

"Do you know where he is?" I asked.

She shook her head. "I don't know anything. Not really." She looked suddenly more vulnerable, as though she'd been at her best to catch me at something and, having failed, was letting her guard down, perhaps having determined it was unnecessary.

"Tell me what you do know," I said to her. And this suddenly seemed important. "Tell me why you think that."

This time she didn't hesitate very long before speaking. "We moved out here about a month ago, in anticipation of Ernest beginning to work with Langton. At first we'd thought I would stay in Connecticut and Ernest would commute. Then he talked me into coming out here with him. He said that it could be an adventure for us. Something different. So we rented a house here in Brentwood, thinking we'd wait to buy until after we got to know the city and what area we liked best, or whether we even liked it at all."

I listened carefully as she spoke and I heard the things she was saying, but I could tell there was a lot she wasn't saying, as well.

"Everything was fine—normal, for us—until about a week after we got out here. Then Ernie started acting strangely. Phone calls he'd have to take in the other room—something he never did before—and sudden dinner and lunch appointments. There was more and more stress on him and less and less time for...well, me.

"I could live with that. He's a busy man and I knew what I was getting into when I married him. But it got worse. On days that I'd thought we'd spend together, buying things for the house and getting settled in, he was spending more and more time away from home, even though he wasn't having to go to the office yet. And then I found this." She rummaged quickly in her purse—Hermès, I noted, and not the sort to brook much rummaging—and produced a business card, which she passed to me.

"Paul Westbrook," I read, "West Trade Financial." I struggled to keep my face neutral—not sure how much to give away. Because, of course, I knew that name. And seeing it in black and white, I felt something fall into place. Something indefinable at present, it was true, but it felt like a match of some kind. It was something I'd have to think about later.

The card was printed on inexpensive stock and heavily embossed—the type of embossing that's meant to look costly but seldom does. The address was in Woodland Hills.

"I did some checking." I must have covered my recognition of the name well enough because she didn't seem to have noticed. "It's a small, practically nonexistent investment firm in the San Fernando Valley. At first I couldn't imagine why Ernest would have anything to do with them. Then, after he disappeared, I found this." More Hermès rummaging, after which she produced an envelope which she passed to me and encouraged me to open.

I did. There were two carefully folded sheets of lined paper inside, like those torn out of a legal pad.

The first page was unmistakably Ernie's writing. Just seeing his careful handwriting in the dark blue ink he'd always favored carried me back the dozen years to our little off-campus apartment: notes on fridges, a birthday card, one extremely passionate letter avowing his undying affection (he'd been drunk). All of these things danced quickly through my head before I managed to focus on context.

There was a doodle of a mountain peak under a cloudy sky at one corner of the pad. It was funny to think of Ernie still doodling after all these years, but it also made it clear, to me, anyway, and likely to his wife, that he'd written the words and done the doodle while talking on the telephone.

There were only two words on the page in Ernie's clear hand. At the top, "Westbrook." And, near the bottom, "Arrowheart."

The way he'd situated the words made it look as though something should be between them. Or that he'd doodled them, parts of unfinished thoughts while he talked or listened.

The first word obviously related to the name on the card. "Who's Arrowheart?" I asked Arianna.

She shrugged elegantly again. "I have no idea. That's one of the reasons I wanted to show it to you. I thought it might have meaning."

I shook my head, even while I wracked my brain. But no, I was pretty sure I'd never heard of anyone—man or woman—named Arrowheart. I would have remembered. And she hadn't asked me about Westbrook, so I kept my mouth shut.

The second piece of paper looked as though it had come from the same pad as the first, but it would have been apparent to almost anyone—and certainly to me and Arianna—that it hadn't been written by Ernie.

"Ernie didn't write this," I said.

She shook her head. "The handwriting is unfamiliar to me."

Again the lined paper, but this time the message was even more cryptic. At first glance and to most people, it might have looked like something in code. Arianna watched me closely as I studied what was written on the paper in black ink:

22	25	26	27	28
6	5 1/2	4	3 1/2	3
-2	-10	-15	-15	+42

-179.5

+126

=53.50

The meaning was not instantly clear to me. Just apparently unrelated numbers that mostly didn't even add up. Not a calculation, then. But the way the second line was notated, it *could* refer to a stock price. And if the first line represented dates, then… My face must have registered something as the notation's meaning started to become clear—a widening of my eyes or just a look of sudden and shocked understanding. Arianna noticed right away.

"You see it, don't you." It wasn't a question.

I nodded. "I…I think so. Do you know what it is?"

"I think so, too." I must have looked questioningly at her because she added, "I have a financial background. It's how Ernest and I met."

"But it's crazy," I said. "It's beyond crazy. I can't imagine Ernie doing something like this. Can you?"

She shrugged again. "I don't know what to think anymore," she said softly. "I just wish he'd told me something. Anything." Now it was my turn to watch closely, to gauge the expressions flitting across her face and calculate their sincerity. Honestly, though, there wasn't much to see. Just that cool, clear profile. Arianna's was a face that didn't give much away.

"Did you show this to the police?"

She shook her head.

"Why?"

"If I'm correct and Ernest engineered this whole thing, well then, he's doing it for a reason, isn't he?"

I shrugged my shoulders. It was too big a mess to even contemplate engineering it.

"Well," she said, considering, "that's what I think. And then there's another thing—what if I'm wrong? And I told the police I suspected my husband of doing this? What if they stopped looking and something… something terrible happened? Then it would all be *my* fault." The well-bred control seemed to be slipping slightly. Arianna looked close to tears for a second. Then the cloud was gone, or I'd been wrong about it in the first place.

"But why are you telling me all of this then? Why bother talking to me at all?" I couldn't not ask.

"I thought about it a lot after I saw you earlier today. I had to stop at home to get these things, and I checked on you before our meeting. You're in this business—" she indicated the paper between us "—the business of stocks. Or you were. So I guess part of me wanted to know—to *know,* you understand—if you were involved on some level. That seemed important to me." I could understand that. All of it. It was Ernie we were talking about.

"When I first saw you," she continued, "I thought you might represent a missing piece. You know, an old girl-friend suddenly back on the scene. Quite a coincidence. Then, when Ernest was…missing, I thought…I thought maybe you were in on it. That maybe you knew things I didn't. But you don't, do you, Madeline? You don't know anything."

Since this summed things up even more neatly than I would have done—after all, I'd been the one driving all over West L.A. and dressing up and getting myself caught on incriminating video cameras—I had to smile, if somewhat ruefully. She was right—I didn't know anything.

"No," I agreed, "I don't know anything. And I haven't had any kind of contact with Ernie since we broke up."

"And I thought you'd know Ernest pretty well. You had a…a connection with him, and so you wouldn't wish him harm." Which made me wonder if we were talking about the same Ernie. But whatever. "Also, you were at Langton yesterday and you went out of your way to find me downtown today, so you have some kind of vested interest. You might not know anything now, but, for whatever reason, you want to. Is that correct?"

I nodded, if somewhat cautiously.

"Also, the fact that you're somewhat implicated makes you a good choice to tell. The police suspect, well, not you, but someone who matches your description. I thought it was unlikely you were on your way to the police. Am I right about that, too?"

And I could only nod because, of course, she was. I knew nothing about anything except that I'd managed to put myself in a potentially…embarrassing position. Going to the police was not high on my current list.

There were a few things I was burning to know, all around Ernie's actual disappearance. "Why do you think the note went to the office and not to you?"

Arianna looked stunned for a second, as though she hadn't thought about it before. "I…I don't know. But you're right—things like this usually go to the home, not the office, don't they?"

"That's what I was thinking. And the kidnappers haven't contacted you at all?"

She shook her head.

"Have the Langton people told you what the demands are?"

"No. That is, there haven't been any demands thus far. Which only confirms what I've said. If this—" she indicated the paper with the figures on it "—is truly his objective and it's the reason he's staged this whole thing, then he'd want all of the correspondence going through the place where there'd most likely be a press leak."

"He might even have leaked it to the press somehow himself," I said thoughtfully.

Arianna nodded. "That's precisely what I thought. And, if any of what I'm guessing is correct, the demands will appear right about the time the media interest begins to die down. Because that would build the pitch again."

"And so—" it was my turn to consult the paper on the table between us "—if what you and I are both thinking this means is true, the stock bottoms next Friday and Ernie buys back in. So, if it does all go that way, would that mean he's suddenly rescued or released on Wednesday?" It was a little scary—I was actually starting to see how it all fit together.

"Except maybe—" Arianna was studying her shoes carefully now "—the ransom note finally shows up in the next few days, the ransom gets paid and Ernest gets 'released.'"

I looked at her sharply. I hadn't thought about that part—that there was the potential to make an actual fortune by creating the LRG death spiral situation with the stocks, plus pocketing a handsome tip in the form of ransom money.

"Now I have a question for *you*," Arianna said. "I really don't understand why you suddenly reappeared at this time."

And that was the crux of the whole matter, wasn't it?

It had all been getting so convoluted, I could barely remember, myself. And then, of course, I did: something to do with a new life and a good tip and then the vision of my mom's stricken face. "It was the stock," I said clearing my throat. "At Club Zanzibar that night, Ernie told me to watch the stock. And I did. And..." Without my willing it, my voice dropped to a whisper. "And I bought."

"And then it dropped?"

I nodded.

Arianna studied me for a moment and I could see disbelief warring with the desire to accept what I'd said. "You really don't know anything?" she said. And I could tell that part of her wanted it to not be true.

I assured her that I didn't.

"Then where do you go from here?" she asked.

"Home, I guess. To be honest, I'm tired of thinking about the whole thing."

She agreed. "I just wish I could do the same. Forget about it, I mean. But Ernest..." She didn't finish, but I understood. If all that she'd said was true, her predicament was worse than mine. By a long shot.

Twelve

I followed Sunset down to the Pacific Coast Highway. Not the most direct route to Malibu, but it's interesting and peaceful in a perverse sort of way. A lot of people aren't crazy about driving in L.A. at the best of times, but I never mind it. All of those years of *not* driving in New York, I guess. I mean, back there, I never even *had* a car. I wouldn't have known what to do with one.

Sunset Boulevard is all it's ever been cracked up to be, and more. From the most crass and plastic aspects of Hollyweird, to practically pastoral (for L.A.) Brentwood, to the peaceful Pacific Palisades. The whole snaking route can be like a car show, where the lines of Benzes and Ferraris and Lexuses (Lexi?)—not to mention Porsches—are nothing short of decadent.

And that's when you understand it clearly, the fullness of this place. This ain't Great Falls, honey. This ain't Austin. And, sure, they also have sixty-thousand-dollar Toyotas in those places, but they're generally the exception, not the rule. Which is where the whole Hol-

lyweird thing stems from, I reckon. In Austin or Great
Falls or Bremerton or just about anyplace, if you have
a lot of money and you want to stand out from the
crowd, things are simple. You don't have to put a lot of
creativity into it. You grab the nearest Lexus, the newest BMW or the flashiest Chrysler and you're in business, turning heads. In West L.A. you have to go further
to be impressive. A lot further. A purple Rolls Royce
convertible might get a second look, but if it also has
antlers on the hood and a roll bar, heads will turn. The
fact that people might be laughing while their heads are
turning doesn't seem to phase some people.

If you're at all interested in the ultramobile one-upmanship that Angelenos love to practice at every opportunity, Sunset—the great serpentine length of it—is *the*
place to do it. Sometimes it's awful, sometimes it's awe-
some, but it's usually amusing.

Of course, this day my head was so full of what had
happened at the Hestman School and with what Arianna
had been telling me, I may as well have gone a different way. I'm capable of multitasking, so my driving was
fine, but I kept going over what Arianna had told me.
And one of the things I kept wondering was if she was
telling me the truth. I couldn't think of why she wouldn't
have been, but at the same time I had to wonder why she
had told me her whole tale to begin with. And why me?
Thinking about it made me uneasy. I wondered if I was
being set up. Or perhaps it was something as simple as
her hoping I would do some of the legwork for her. Or
it might be something…less appealing.

I had to admit that I liked Arianna. Aside from being

stunning (which I could forgive her, if I put some energy into it) she also seemed bright and open. Forthright. I'd wager that, under the right circumstances, she could even be vivacious.

But as sincerely as she'd imparted everything, some of what she'd said rang hollow, or at least a little off. She'd painted an attractive, believable picture: the happy—albeit insanely well-to-do—couple moving out from the East, looking forward to fixing up their little nest together and spending "quality" time before duties called. She had said Ernie called it an adventure. But I knew Ernie, or at least I'd known the Ernie he'd been thirteen years ago. *That* Ernie would have been as likely to pick tapestries for the foyer as…well, as he would have strapped on wax wings and flown to the sun. No Icarus, that Ernie. Solid, practical and always cognizant of the inside track.

Which led me to the other part of what she'd told me: that she believed he'd engineered the whole kidnapping. A fact that the neat columns of calculations—as precise as any ledger—seemed to confirm. Which kind of brought me back to the beginning again: why had she told me?

And then there was Paul Westbrook, someone I hadn't thought of in years. Ernie's shadow when we were at Harvard, his evil twin. It had been a joke between them, though; deciding just which one was the evil twin would have been quite a chore.

When Ernie and I were a couple, wherever he went, there was Paul. Increasingly, in the time I'd known them, they'd been two halves of the same whole. It hadn't been pretty, even from the sidelines.

The last few months had gotten more and more unbearable, until suddenly things weren't bearable at all anymore. I'd known that part of it had to do with Paul. For a lot of reasons, but mainly due to his presence in our lives and the way that Ernie and Paul were together.

Paul wasn't physically unattractive, yet from the beginning something about him repelled me. The wispy goatee he was always trying to cultivate; his neatly trimmed yet slightly greasy hair. But most of all, the way his cool blue gaze would never seem to look right at you when he spoke to you, fixing instead on a point just above your head or, in certain moods, on your chest. Being around him was always unpleasant for me.

I couldn't have put a name to what Paul and Ernie shared, though from the beginning it didn't seem healthy. On one level, it was like the classic competitive boys one-upmanship thing. But it was more, as well. And perhaps less. Small stuff at first, but rising—inevitably, it seemed—to higher levels. Ernie saying to Paul: "Professor Wannamakker is an asshole. I'd love to see someone take him out." And Paul flattens the tires of Wannamakker's car. Paul to Ernie: "I completely feel like getting stoned." And Ernie scores Paul some coke. Ernie to Paul: "The neighbor's cat is driving me crazy at night." And Paul kills the cat. This last one I didn't know for sure, but I had strong reasons to suspect it.

Paul had been at our place and Ernie was bitching about the cat. I was the one who found the cat—dead and stiffening—outside his owners' apartment door the next day.

"Paul killed the Johnsons' cat," I said to Ernie that night.

A smirk. "How'd you know?"

"I just know."

"Is the cat dead?"

"The cat is dead. I saw it myself today."

"That doesn't mean Paul poisoned it."

It took me a whole day to realize that Ernie was the only one who had mentioned poison in that conversation. And the cat had, indeed, been poisoned. I should have packed and left then, but I was young and stupid. Sometimes at that age you need someone to draw you a picture. That was still to come.

Paul had wanted me then; I'd always known that. And I hadn't found it flattering, even from the vantage point of my twenty-two years, when almost everything is flattering. Because I'd known that it wasn't so much me, Madeline Carter, that Paul wanted. It was me, Ernie Billing's girlfriend, that he desired. And for a while near the end of our relationship, Paul made it into a full-time campaign.

It finally happened at the end of finals week in our graduate year. There had been a party at Paul's frat house. I'd enjoyed myself for a while. I wasn't aware of drinking much, I know I didn't do any drugs, but in the morning I woke up in Paul's bed with Paul beside me, and both of us unclothed. We were naked and I was damp where there was no cause for dampness to be. My clothes, when I found them on Paul's floor, were damaged, as though they'd been ripped from me. I was aware of some bruises—nothing serious, but alarming nonetheless—on my back and arms and sides.

Unlike Steve, Paul didn't have the good sense to stay

sleeping while I got out of his room. I wish he had. But he woke up, saw my obvious discomfort. And he laughed.

"What is it like to have a real man, Maddy?" he asked, watching me from the bed as I collected my belongings as hurriedly as I could. The shirt I had been wearing was shredded, there was no way I could wear it in public, and I pawed through the mess, looking for something to cover myself with, ignoring Paul, trying to block him out. "I know you've been wanting me, baby. I've been seeing it in your eyes." He slithered up from the bed on his knees. I could see that his cock was hard. "Come here and give me more of what you gave me last night."

At twenty-two, most of us are not yet gifted with sleek tongues. Sometimes the words line up nicely in our minds, but they don't come out as elegantly as they should. That comes with practice, experience, years. I just know that, having found a T-shirt to pull over the fragments of my own blouse and skirt, and having secured my purse and only managing to find one shoe, I headed for the door, stopping only to scream at the top of my lungs, "You are an asshole, Paul Westbrook. I'll fucking hate you until the fucking day I die. And when I tell Ernie what you've done he is going to fucking kill you." As I ran out the door, all I could hear was Paul's laughter.

It was apparent to me, loathing him as I mostly always had, that there was no way I would have gone to bed with Paul of my own choice. I didn't even like the guy, and there was no amount of drink that would have made me want to sleep with him. Plus, I am by choice and nature a loyal person. I don't make commitments lightly or easily. When I do, I honor them. I was like that at fourteen and I'm like that now. And that was certainly my headspace when I was with Ernie. By then our relationship was no picnic, but it's simply not my style to sleep with my boyfriend's friends. Especially when I *loathe* them. And I loathed Paul, even before he raped me.

And, though courts of law can be wishy-washy about proving this kind of rape, there is no doubt in my mind that that is exactly what Paul did to me. I don't know for sure if he'd drugged me. But I know what was in my heart and the revulsion I'd always felt at the thought of Paul's touch.

In retrospect, all of this might have had a different ending if I'd done the right thing; instead of heading back—to my and Ernie's then home—bruised and emotionally bleeding, I should have gone to the police. Or, at the very least, some school counselor—campuses are always crawling with them, my tuition paying their salaries. Why didn't I? I felt violated. And maybe as low as I've ever felt in my life, before or since. But I was young and stupid. I wasn't even confident that what Paul had done was illegal, especially since I couldn't say for sure what he'd done.

So I went home. Luckily, I had a couple of dollars in my purse and caught the bus. Trudged up the stairs of our third story walk-up, focusing on what I'd say. How I'd explain things to Ernie and how angry he'd be. At Paul.

I knew the instant the door opened to my key that something was wrong. And then I heard the laughter from the bedroom—his low and lusty, hers high and sweet. I felt like running away, hiding. But I was home; there was no place to go. And curiosity was a component of my personality even then.

I didn't think a lot about what I was doing. Didn't hem or haw, just pushed through into the bedroom and stood there, mute until they became aware of me. And it was clear from the little I saw that *this* girl had not been raped. I knew her. I could never be positive, but I suspected Ernie made sure of that. She was teeny, yet voluptuous, bubbly and vivacious. Everything that, in my mind, I was not.

I expected—wanted—the classic television reaction. Ernie becoming aware of me and throwing the naked and exceedingly beautiful girl off of him, rushing to me, taking me in his arms and begging my forgiveness. I hope I would not have forgiven him, but it didn't matter. He did none of that.

"So how was it with Paul, baby?" He was naked, lying on his side, his leg entwined with the girl's, his hand stroking her thigh. "He always says he's hung. Was he hung like a pony?"

That was when I understood that Ernie had *known*. Had perhaps even helped make it happen. Maybe because Paul had wanted to, or maybe because Ernie himself had wanted the coast clear to be with the girl now sprawled on my bed.

For all the things I *didn't* do with the entire situation, I did one right thing: I got the hell out of there. For good. While Ernie watched, I grabbed a laundry bag and stuffed in everything of mine I could lay my hands on.

When the bag was full, I grabbed his wallet and relieved it of the fifty or so bucks it held. He didn't try to stop me. Maybe he'd ceased watching. I used the money to get as far from Cambridge as I could. When the money was gone, which wasn't very many hours later, I called my mother and sat in a Greyhound station waiting for the cash she wired to get to me. And then I went home.

Seattle is a long, long way from Boston by bus. When I think back on it, the trip seemed to take about a month, though in fact, it couldn't have been more than five days. But the miles soothed my soul. Soothed the part of me that Paul had violated. And the part that still couldn't believe that Ernie hadn't followed me. That, in fact, at any stop the Greyhound made, he'd be waiting for me when the doors opened and I went out to stretch my legs. I wouldn't have taken him back at that point, but I would have loved the chance to tell him so to his face. It didn't come up.

And that was the last time I'd seen Boston. Or Paul. Or Ernie. Until this week, that is. I didn't even go back for graduation. And my mom—whom I *did* tell every-thing to—backed me up by contacting the university and telling them I'd developed Talaxian flu or some-thing else really cool-sounding so that, ultimately, they just shipped my diploma out to me in Seattle. Which, inadvertently, was how I fell into the stock market. But that's a different story.

The Safeway sign at PCH brought me back to the present. It reminded me of the empty cupboards at home and that I was hungry again and should probably stop for provisions. I glanced at my watch as I pulled into the parking lot. It was six o'clock. And then I remembered.

"Shit." I said it aloud. And then I said it again as I turned my car around and headed for the exit in the direction that would take me back the way I'd come. "Shit." Because I'd told Steve I'd meet him at five-thirty. And I had a hunch he would have been on time.

Thirteen

Later, when I finally got home, it was like a replay of the morning. Tycho happy and reproachful—he'd spent the day without a run, without happy petting, without me—my answering machine blinking at me mindlessly, and the feeling of things not done, or done badly, nagging at the center of my gut. Part of this feeling, of course, was Steve. I'd finished meeting with Arianna in plenty of time to make it to the restaurant by five-thirty, as he and I had agreed. By the time I'd remembered and raced back there, he was gone, though the hostess had reported that a cheerful young man who fit his description had come in a little after five and grown slowly less cheerful until he'd left glowering—and apparently stood up—at six-fifteen.

"If he comes back, tell him I was here," I told her. She nodded her agreement, somehow managing to look skeptical and disapproving at the same time. Or so I thought. Not that it mattered. I'd told him I'd be there and that I'd explain things at five-thirty. I hadn't shown up. And we hadn't exchanged phone numbers. I simply had no way to reach him tonight.

I felt badly. And like I'd proven his earlier opinion of me to be correct. Maybe he was right; maybe I *was* using him. Could you use someone subconsciously? The thought made me feel hollow inside.

And then there was Jennifer and all I'd learned at the Hestman School. I quickly changed out of my quasi ladies-who-lunch duds, pulled on some track pants and a T-shirt, grabbed the bag Bruce had given me at the school and headed upstairs to talk to Tyler, something I wasn't looking forward to at all.

Tasya opened the kitchen door at my knock. She looked as drawn as her husband had earlier in the day.

"Have you heard from Jennifer?" I asked needlessly. The answer was written on her face.

"No. Not exactly." She called out to Tyler over her shoulder. "Madeline's here. Do you want her to come in?"

Tyler called back in the affirmative from somewhere deeper in the house, and Tasya indicated that I should follow her. As we left the Sub-Zero appliances behind us, I realized that I'd never seen any room besides the kitchen in Tasya and Tyler's part of the house. Usually I would have enjoyed this glimpse inside the real lifestyles of the rich and famous, but at that moment I had two things on my mind: Jennifer's whereabouts and the identity of the owner of the masculine voice I could hear that clearly wasn't Tyler's.

I followed Tasya into a large living room that looked, in some respects, like a grown-up version of mine. The view was the same, as well as the floor-to-ceiling windows, but opposite ends of the room were dominated by a fieldstone fireplace and a baby grand piano. The terra-cotta tile floors—the same as the ones in the kitchen and covering the decks—gleamed dully under my feet and, combined with large potted plants, gave the impression that indoors was outdoors and vice versa. It was a beautiful home. But I noticed it all in a peripheral way. What dominated my attention were two uniformed policemen standing in Tyler's living room. My first reaction was panic; they were here for me. I realized quickly, however, that they were there to talk about Jennifer.

When he saw me, Tyler broke off talking with the policemen and explained, "I wanted you here now in case you were able to turn up anything at the school. Were you?"

I shook my head. "She wasn't there."

I thought it would be better if I told Tyler what I'd learned at the school in private. After that, if he wanted the police to know, he could tell them himself. Also, I wanted to draw as little attention to myself as possible. While it didn't seem likely the cops would make the connection between Tyler Beckett's tenant and the person on the LRG surveillance video, I didn't feel like taking any chances.

Tyler indicated I should sit on the overstuffed sofa while he finished making the report on his missing daughter. I sat and tried to fade into the background as much as possible while examining my surroundings.

It was a good room. The setting was grand and many of the appointments were obviously expensive, but it looked like a place where people lived, not just a room to show to company. I focused on a photograph-covered wall near me, examining photos from Tyler and Tasya's wedding, some images of Tyler that had obviously been taken on the set of various films, plus photos of Jennifer—riding a horse, acting in a school play, at the beach with a woman unfamiliar to me who I took to be her mother.

"I have a bad feeling," Tyler said as soon as the police were gone. Tasya went to him, rubbing his shoulder while sitting on the edge of his chair. "A very bad feeling." He turned to me. "Nothing at the school, huh?"

"Well, they didn't know where she was. But they told me some stuff you should know."

Tyler and Tasya seemed ever more deflated as I relayed what Dr. Alder had told me—about Jennifer's increasing truancy, her slipping grades, the reported surliness and, finally, her expulsion the previous day.

"They said it started after the winter holiday?" Tasya asked finally.

I nodded and Tasya started to cry. "Tyler," she said, "I'm so sorry."

"C'mon, babe. It's not that." Tyler was now the comforter; Tasya the bereft.

"What is it?" I asked.

"Tasya and I were married last Christmas."

"There's something else, though," I said, finding myself reluctant to bring up the matter of Dr. Alder's unreturned phone calls.

And rightly so. Tyler exploded. "But that's ridiculous. I've always been so accessible for anything to do with Jen." Then he subsided, looking broken and adding quietly, "But we've been out of town a lot this year. And she's always been so strong. I thought I was past the point where I needed to worry about her. She took care of *me* after her mother and I split."

My own mother's voice came to me, how she had always said her children would never be too old to worry about. I understood the words more fully now.

"What about the boyfriend? Have you tried him?"

"What boyfriend?" They practically said it together.

It was inconceivable to me that they didn't know him. "I met him here. At your barbecue. A gangly looking redhead with a lot of product in his hair?"

They continued looking blank and I thought back carefully to what Jennifer had said to me about him. "That's what she called him—the 'boyfriend person.' Cody, I think his name was. No. Something even more nonsensical." A beat and then I remembered. "Corby."

Tyler and Tasya looked at each other in a way that told me plainly they'd never heard Corby's name before, and I wished there was some way I could change things, fix it so I wasn't the one who had to break that to them. I remembered the white bag. "And the school gave me this," I told them, handing it over.

They promised to let me know if they heard anything, and I saw myself out. The day, which had started in a strange hotel room at Marina Del Rey, was starting to take its toll.

The maniacally flashing red light on the answering machine caught my attention as I walked in the door. I groaned inwardly—I hadn't cleared it before I'd left in the morning, knowing that several of the messages were from Emily and, since she'd filled me in herself on the phone, there didn't seem a big reason to listen to them. I was even less interested now, but knew I couldn't just continue to let them pile up. And it was possible there'd be something on at least one of the messages I'd want to know.

I settled in to listen, out of habit taking up a position in my desk chair, poised to jot down notes and numbers. There was a message from my mother, time-stamped Monday evening about the hour, I figured, Emily and I were crashing the LRG party. Mom sounded deliberately neutral, asking how everything was going, as though we hadn't had several conversations earlier that day about the stock market. I made a note to call her later just to touch base. There were the expected messages from Emily, telling me all about things I now knew, but wedged between the Emily messages, time-stamped 2:45 a.m. Tuesday, was a message from Jennifer. Her voice sounded thin and worried and she spoke quietly, as though she were keeping her voice intentionally low.

"Hi, Madeline. It's me. Jennifer. I know it's the middle of the night, but please pick up the phone. I really, really have to talk to you. I can't...I can't leave a number, but I'm not at home." And then, as if she'd made a decision, "I'll try you again later."

I played the message back a couple of times, trying to squeeze information out of it, but there was nothing there. I could read things into it—perhaps fear, maybe apprehension—but I couldn't be sure about anything. There just wasn't enough information.

Then more messages from Emily, another from my mom and finally time-stamped just a few minutes before I'd gotten in the door, a message from Alex Montoya, asking if I'd care to join him for dinner sometime.

I played Jennifer's message another couple of times before I called Tyler. He would, I felt certain, want to hear it. The phone rang six times before his voice mail picked up. I started to leave a message, then reasoned that I'd just seen him a few minutes ago; they had to be there.

Tycho and I thundered up the stairs, but I could see before I knocked on Tyler and Tasya's door that no one was home. The house was in darkness and the kitchen door, when I turned the knob, was locked. I peered over the edge of the deck into the canyon. The rapidly falling twilight shrouded the details, but I could make out a car's taillights, moving quickly toward the beach. Tyler's Lexus? Maybe. But I couldn't worry about it now—I'd play Jennifer's message for him when I got the chance.

Back at the guest house, I thought about my day, about what I'd accomplished. At the same time, I tried to think about what I was *trying* to accomplish. Why was I even bothering? The stuff with Jennifer was obvious: the child had more or less adopted me on sight. If there was something I could do to help her, I knew I'd do it.

But the mess with the Langton Regional Group was another matter. Part of me just wanted to back away from LRG entirely—sell my stocks, take my loss and pretend I'd never even heard of Langton and that Ernie had never come back into my life. Ernie's own wife thought him capable of engineering a kidnapping in order to make a stock price fall. My whole involvement with Langton was a mess that showed every sign of getting messier.

Gallivanting around West L.A., I had missed the day's closing. I looked at my computer's blank screen, and thought about checking where the markets had ended up and having a look though my e-mail; there was likely to be quite a lot of it by now. But the events of a full day came rushing over me in a wave. I suddenly felt too tired to even think about doing anything but pulling off my clothes and crawling into bed. Which is what I did. And when I slept, I didn't dream at all.

Fourteen

The following morning it felt good to get up before the opening bell and take Tycho for a run through the hills. It's quiet at that time of the morning. And fresh and cool. The smell of eucalyptus followed us down the narrow roads and well-defined trails. I'd discovered an old orange grove at the end of our road, abandoned now because the house that used to be on the grounds had slid down the hill some years ago. Earthquake, mudslide or bad planning on the part of some long-forgotten architect, I didn't know. But I liked to go there and enjoy the overrun gardens and the shade and scent of the citrus trees, and think about what it must have been like when there was a house commanding that bit of earth. Tycho liked it, too. A chance to snuffle around and examine things of high interest to dogs. And, if I planned my run a certain way, it was about the right distance from home to wind down a bit and touch the earth before walking the final leg back. The run, the gardens and the walk relaxed me totally.

Then home and coffee made by my own hand, strong and good. Then to my computer.

Despite the trepidation I felt about what sorts of silliness LRG might get up to on this day, it didn't stem my excitement for the markets in the morning. This has been true throughout my career, no matter how badly I might have been doing the day before. I think it's the pure possibility that excites me. Because, within limits (at least, most of the time) *anything* can happen. From one day to the next, up can become down and down can become what you were wishing for before you went to sleep the night before. It's this merry-go-round of what-ifs that pushes me out of bed every morning. It's the promise that draws me. And all of those possibilities.

Even though I'd only set up my news feeds a week before, I was already deluged. Since most of it comes in the form of e-mail, I get a lot—two hundred or more pieces of electronic e-mail a day. It's pretty easy to get through, though. Not at all like getting two hundred letters from friends. I sort them all by date and then just whiz through them, quite often scanning headlines and not bothering to read the whole item unless it's about a stock I'm currently holding or one I'm thinking about buying.

This morning there were more than a day's worth because, with all of the running around I'd been doing, and my unexpected exhaustion the night before, I hadn't been spending as much time as I usually did clearing my mail. So today when I asked for my mail, over five hundred items came barreling down the pike at me. A little overwhelming, even for someone used to regular barrages. It was going to take me awhile to get through them all, and I settled in.

I hadn't gotten far into my scanning, though, when a return e-mail address caught my eye: feewaybill@lookforthis.com. Fee Waybill. Lead singer of The Tubes. And Ernie's college nickname. And since I don't actually *know* the lead singer of The Tubes personally— or even know if The Tubes still exist as an entity—that left exactly one person this could be from.

The subject line also grabbed my eye, a salutation that included the pet name Ernie had called *me* during our time together: Pooky. I'd always hated it. I think he must have thought it sounded posh, something you'd call a girl-friend who summered at the Vineyard. Someone who pal'd around with girls called Bunny and CJ. Someone who wasn't me. Seeing those names now, in the context of an e-mail, was oddly chilling. Like a hand reaching out of the grave from the past I thought I'd buried a long time ago. My own hands weren't steady as I read the message.

From: feewaybill@lookforthis.com
To: madln@aol.com
Subject: Hello Pooky
The reason for the nicknames should be obvious: easy identification. I trust you get it.
I've gotten wind of some poking. You need to stop. Alternatives could be unhealthy. All is under control. I promise to explain soon and perhaps I can even make it worth your while.
Your,
Fee

I sat and read and then reread the message. And then I didn't read it, just sat there hoping that the words on the screen would somehow seep into my brain and make sense. There was little doubt in my mind that it was from Ernie. The madlin address was an old one—my first e-mail address. He must have taken the chance that I'd kept it active—which I had. It forwarded to the e-mail address I use most often, saving me from having to check the numerous e-mail accounts I've set up and moved on from over the years. For his part, anyone could set up a lookforthis.com account in about a minute. And it was free and completely untraceable. Lacking other possibilities, this really had to be Ernie.

He'd said: *I trust you get it.* And I did. I *had.* But it was phrased in such a way that, if I hadn't kept the address and someone else had gotten the e-mail, it would make absolutely no sense and would likely have been trashed as yet another piece of spam. But if I got it, I'd have no doubt who it was from. It was a warning. *Alternatives could be unhealthy.* A warning and a promise. And those things— especially served up together—probably had the opposite effect on me than he'd hoped. They made me mad.

I've gotten wind of some poking. Which could mean a lot of things but, really, boiled down to only one— someone had told him I'd been at Langton the other day, which meant he had contact with at least one person inside the company. Or—and this seemed entirely likely—he'd seen the same news report that Emily and I had and recognized me, and was now warning me off. He was right, though, poking pretty much summed up what I'd been doing.

He'd written that he could possibly "make it worth my while" to stay out of this. So he thought he could, what? Bribe me? I found myself seething and, even as I told myself to breathe and let it go, I knew what was fueling *this* fire. Here was Ernie, thirteen years later, still being coldly controlling. Still thinking he could pull my strings and make me dance. And with the LRG dance he was currently involved in, he was completely raining on my parade.

I hit Reply and began a message.

Dear Ernie,

Then thought about that and settled on

Ernie

Then decided even *that* was too friendly and opted for no salutation at all. Which left me with a blank message because I couldn't think how to respond. Though various expletives flitted through my brain there was little to be accomplished by any of that. And without expletives, there was nothing I could think to say. At least, not right this minute. I put it aside and moved on to other tasks that would divert my attention from Fee Waybill. Today, however, everything seemed related.

Looking over my portfolio did nothing to help my mood. LRG opened slightly above what it had closed at the day before. It rallied briefly and then another large whack of LRG shares—a market sell, no doubt— started pushing the stock price down again: $4.25.

$4.18. $4.27. $4.16, and so on. I stopped watching. It was too painful. I was too mad.

"Son of a bitch." I said it aloud, but quietly. Tycho thumped his tail. Cocked his head. It hadn't sounded angry, but he couldn't quite place the tone.

Last night, in defeated exhaustion, I'd determined to sell my LRG shares at a loss and wash my hands of the whole thing. Now rested, refreshed and awash with re-kindled old resentments I hadn't even realized I'd hung on to, things didn't look the same.

Alternatives could be unhealthy. All is under control.

"Jerk!"

Jerk in so many ways, too. Never mind that his mach-inations had upset my personal apple cart. If he really *had* kidnapped himself in order to make the stock of the com-pany he had been newly employed by go *down,* he didn't have even a quarter of the intelligence I'd always given him credit for. I'd known he thought he was a force unto him-self—above things like the laws and moral imperatives that other people function under—but there were lines. And this… This sincerely crossed all of them.

I thought about the calculations on the paper Arianna had found. If she and I were interpreting it right, we were talking about over forty million dollars for a week or so of being "kidnapped." There weren't a lot of ways to make that kind of money.

And then what? What could possibly be next? Would he be miraculously recovered somehow? In some splashy manner that made headlines and caused the stock to go up? Was that what he was planning? And when? What had the paper Arianna showed me forecast as the low point? I thought about it. *Three* bucks? And if that happened, I'd be down fifty percent. Or about seventy thousand if I converted all those figures into a dollar amount, which didn't seem prudent for my mental health at the moment.

And then something Alex Montoya had said at Tyler's party popped into my head. I could see Alex sitting forward intently, wineglass in hand, talking to me with great passion about his work. Thinking about it now, I could almost feel gears clicking into place. What if Ernie was a psychopath? The quest for new highs, the lack of conscience and morals—all of it added up. I still had the concept of the eater of human flesh flitting around my brain, and I figured Ernie was into Kobi beef and grilled chicken rather than anything more exotic. But kidnapping?

And I knew that Ernie couldn't be doing this by himself. He'd need someone unattached to him professionally to be doing the actual selling and buying of the securities. Since stock transactions are entirely traceable, if that invisible someone had a leg up on the shady side of trading and maybe didn't have a lot to lose, so much the better. All of this added up quite neatly to Ernie's Harvard toady, Paul Westbrook. Someone I wouldn't have thought of at all had his name not come up in my conversation with Arianna.

I let my mind go for a minute, tried to free it of my own conceptions and just associate with facts. Alex had said that psychopaths used people up. But what if Paul had always proved useful? What if—and the more I thought about it, the more sense it made—what if Paul had always had a hand in Ernie's success? The shadow. Knowing both of them well didn't make me discount this theory.

Knowing who was likely doing the actual paper moving didn't make much difference to me. It was Ernie who was doing the manipulation and Ernie who was, in my professional estimation, culpable. What he was up to was so beyond insider trading, I hesitated to even call it that. He was deliberately manipulating the stock he was—by virtue of having been made Langton's CEO— responsible for. And he was manipulating it in a way that might have a long-term negative effect on the company, its share price and its value. And if word got out, it could even affect the overall market, especially in the environment of corporate suspicion that had been growing since the demise of the bull.

It was becoming clear to me that, while concerns over my own financial involvement in this were valid and growing larger with each drop of the share price, I had a moral obligation to do something. Just what that something might be was less clear.

If Ernie had been a broker or a dealer, my course would have been clear. The National Association of Securities Dealers moves swiftly and mercilessly against infractors. It has to; there's so much at stake. However, Ernie wouldn't be a member—he wasn't a dealer. And in this situation, he wasn't a trader, either. The Securities Regulation Division functions on the state level, but LRG was a nationally traded security, even though the company was based in California. I might be able to go to the SEC, but with what? A report of a scrap of paper of unknown authorship with potentially meaningless numbers, an untraceable and slightly encoded e-mail, and the suspicions of a wife who I was pretty sure would deny everything, including our meeting, if what she'd told me was taken public? And then there was me on that security tape and the suspicions that had given birth to. No. With what I had to go on, the SEC was not a possibility. I needed something more.

Even though I knew my motives were impure—I wanted information, not just the suave doctor's company—I returned Alex's call just after 9:00 a.m., figuring he'd be in the office by now. I was right, though he surprised me by answering the phone himself—the number on the card he'd given me was his direct line.

"Hi, Dr. Montoya, this is Madeline Carter. We met at Tyler Beckett's house the other night."

"Call me Alex, Madeline. And of course I remember you. In fact, I left a message for you last night."

He sounded pleased to hear from me and we scheduled dinner for seven o'clock that evening, at a seafood place along the coast near Pacific Palisades, between Malibu and Santa Monica.

By nine-thirty I figured Tyler and Tasya would be up and around. I wanted to know if there had been any updates about Jennifer overnight, plus I wanted them to hear the message she'd left for me.

Tyler seemed cagey when I asked him where they'd gotten to the night before. This surprised me, because he'd seemed so forthright about everything before.

"Uh, you know. Had some errands to run."

We were in the kitchen, Tyler sitting on a stool at the

counter watching Tasya work. When he said it I noted that Tasya, madly chopping onions on a cutting board near the sink, looked up at him with one eyebrow raised, but didn't say anything.

"What are you making?" I asked Tasya, more to fill the void I felt in the room than because I actually wanted to know.

"Soup, I think. Yes, soup. I feel like cutting something." I thought it a good thing she was focusing on vegetables and not something softer. And when next I looked she seemed to be pulverizing large clumps of parsley and had a pile of carrots at her elbow ready for massacre. It was going to be a very finely cut soup.

"One of the reasons I came up here was to tell you guys I got a message from Jennifer a couple of days ago. On my answering machine. But I didn't clear it until last night." Tyler had looked at me hopefully when I started speaking, then looked disappointed when he realized the message was a couple of days old. "Sorry, Tyler. I didn't want it to sound more hopeful than it was, but there was no other way to say it. And she doesn't say much on the message. But I thought you'd want to hear it anyway." I pulled the tape out of my pocket, then Tasya and I followed Tyler to his home office, Tasya wiping her hands on a dish towel as she went.

Under other circumstances I would have loved the chance to look around Tyler's office. The wall directly behind his desk was covered with awards and photos of him and other famous people, and there was other sorts of Hollywood memorabilia on his desk and nearby shelves. But today Jennifer was foremost on all of our minds.

Tyler rummaged in his desk for a second before he came up with a tape recorder. Without a word he pushed the tape into the device and pressed Play.

I'd queued the tape up just before Jennifer's message, so we first heard the time stamp, then Jennifer's voice floated into the room. "Hi, Madeline. It's me. Jennifer. I know it's the middle of the night, but please pick up the phone. I really, really have to talk to you. I can't... I can't leave a number but I'm not at home. I'll try you again later."

"Did it say 2:45 a.m. Tuesday?"

I nodded, and Tyler, sitting behind his desk, put his head into his hands as though it needed holding together. "About thirty-six hours ago." It was a statement and there was so much left unsaid. And simply nothing I could add.

"For God's sake, Tyler," Tasya said from the doorway behind me. "Look at her, she's as worried as we are. Tell her. Maybe she'll have an idea."

I looked up expectantly. "Tell me what?"

Ignoring my question, Tyler seemed to be considering his wife's words. Finally he looked at her and said, "What the hell, right?" She shrugged, raising her hands helplessly.

"All right." Then to me, "Last night we didn't have any errand. Right after you left here I got a call. It was an automated voice—I couldn't interact with it—saying there was a package for me at the bottom of the hill. That I was to look under the mailbox by the store at PCH and there'd be something taped to it. I knew it had something to do with Jen. Tasya and I raced down there and this is all there was." He placed an envelope in front of me, and when I hesitated, he said, "Go ahead. Open it."

Fearing what was inside, I found I didn't want to touch the crumpled manilla envelope at all. But Tasya and Tyler were watching me expectantly.

The envelope itself looked as though it had been through the wringer, almost literally. It was scuffed up and even torn in spots. The label had clearly been printed on an ink-jet machine because watermarks had caused the ink to smear slightly. There were no stamps and no return address. "Was it this damaged looking when you picked it up?"

"It looked exactly like that, which doesn't make any sense to me. It didn't even have to go through the mail."

"And it was taped under the mailbox?"

Tyler nodded. "Just where the phone call said it would be."

I pulled the envelope toward me gently and pulled the flap back. There were three things inside: a photo, a letter and a sandwich bag containing a hank of hair.

I picked up the sandwich bag carefully and looked at the hair through the clear plastic. Tyler answered my unasked question. "It's hers. I'm about ninety-five percent sure."

The photo was clearly Jennifer. It was a Polaroid and she looked frightened, though undamaged, and was holding a copy of the *L.A. Times* with yesterday's date showing clearly. Behind her you could see a pale, blank wall, a window with the blinds closed, an electrical outlet—it could have been taken anywhere.

The ransom note looked to be straight out of a bad

kidnapping movie, like a kid's art project gone horribly wrong. The letters that made up the words were cut from magazines and pasted on a heavy piece of paper. Even the message itself was crude.

YouR dAUghter hAS beeN KIDnappED. IF yoU wANt TO see HEr aLIVe in THis LiFE DO NOT cALL tHe PolIcE. AWAiT FUrThER iNSTRuC-tIONS oR tHe KID dIEs GROtEsQUely.

As soon as I saw it, something twigged. There was something familiar here I couldn't quite put my finger on.

"Did you call the police?"

Tyler shook his head. "And it's killing me. All my senses are telling me to call them. There are all kinds of clues there. Prints and stuff, you know. Maybe they could find whoever has her." He looked me in the eye then, and I blinked at the raw and naked pain I saw there. "But they said they'd kill her, Madeline. How can I take that chance?"

For Tyler it was rock and hard place time: he could jump in either direction, but the view wasn't going to get any better. And I couldn't begin to imagine what I'd do in his place.

"And you haven't heard anything since?"

He shook his head again. "Nothing." He indicated the phone. "And I've been glued to this thing ever since. I figure if I just bide my time, they'll contact me again and come up with a sum. I've got money, Madeline. And I can get my hands on more if it's not enough. I just wish they'd contact me. I hate all this sitting here. Waiting."

And then, more quietly, "and I just pray to God they don't hurt her."

And then the reason for the familiarity hit me: the message looked just as Emily had described the one sent to Langton—letters cut from magazines, crude, like a ransom note on a television show. It wasn't that I thought the two disappearances were connected, except maybe in one way.

"Tyler," I said, not really knowing how to bring it up, "considering what they told me at school, is it, you know, possible that Jennifer might have arranged this herself?"

He looked at me, first startled, then with an anger that seemed to grow. "Are you suggesting that my only child might be playing some sort of horrible game with me?"

I wouldn't have put it that way, but… "It's a possibility, Tyler. She's seventeen. She was kicked out of school the day before she disappeared. I'm sorry but, yes, I guess that's exactly what I'm suggesting."

"Tyler, stop it," said Tasya. "What Madeline is saying is very possible, and you know it. Jennifer has been so angry lately. It's not Madeline's fault, she's only pointing out another possibility. We must keep our minds open."

His anger seemed to flare out, like a candle extinguished. "I'm sorry, Madeline. It *is* a possibility. I guess, at this stage, I *hope* it's a possibility. Here's the problem, though—it doesn't change anything on my end. Not unless I know. I have to proceed as though she's in the utmost danger. I *have* to."

I hated leaving them, but there was nothing more I

could contribute. I asked them to let me know if they heard anything and especially if they thought of anything I could do to help, though I couldn't imagine what that might be.

Though the weather was warm enough, my apartment felt bleak. I kept thinking of Jennifer's message and what it might have meant. More importantly, what might be different if I'd been home and able to answer. What if. It made me think of Jack. I looked at the time: eleven. It would be two o'clock in the afternoon in New Jersey. There was a good chance Sarah would be home, preparing to go pick the kids up from school.

She sounded delighted and slightly amazed to hear from me.

"I'm only on the other end of the country, Sarah. Not the moon," I chided her.

"I know. It's just odd. I was thinking about you so hard this afternoon—it's like I called you telepathically. And you answered!"

I laughed. For all the talk of telepathy, it was good to hear her grounded voice.

"How are you getting along?"

She hesitated. "You know, I cope. You just do one day at a time. Some days are better than others. You?"

"Oh, Sarah, I don't even know where to begin. Remember when I told you I hoped to find a quieter lifestyle? A simpler pace?"

"Sure."

"It hasn't happened. I don't even know if I can tell you all that has." Then, before I could even think about it, I did. I told her everything that had happened since I moved to L.A.

"God, babe, you would have done better moving to Brooklyn or Queens. It sounds pretty hairy out there."

"It does, doesn't it? It's starting to feel like…" I hesitated. This wasn't a thought I'd even articulated to myself before. "Like stuff is following me, or something."

"Oh, pish, Carter. That's just silly and you know it." I did, but it made me feel better hearing it from her. And being called Carter. That was a New York name. A work name. It made me feel more like my old self: in charge and in control. "Sometimes things just happen. Coincidence. Sometimes they're good coincidences. Sometimes they're not. You know."

Though she couldn't see me, I nodded. She was right.

"But tell me again the name of the old boyfriend you ran into."

"Ernie. Ernest Carmichael Billings. Why?"

"Dunno. It twigged something. I'll have to think about it, but I'll let you know if I remember what it is I've forgotten. Meanwhile, are you ever going to come back here to visit? The kids would love to see you."

We chatted for a while. Rose had lost another tooth, Nigel was doing better in math. "They seem so okay, Madeline. I know that should make me happy and it does—it does, really—but sometimes I want them to be more broken. Like me. And sometimes I'm afraid they've forgotten Jack altogether."

"It's okay to feel that way, Sarah. Whatever you feel is okay. But kids are superresilient. Think about yourself as a kid. We bounced back from whatever was thrown at us. It's harder when you're an adult, I think." My voice cracked a bit. "When it's your whole life. Oh, shit, I'm sorry...."

"No, no, Madeline. You're right." I could hear she was crying softly. And I realized something: we get better at anything we do a lot of. With practice. Sarah could now cry and carry on a conversation while doing it. She'd had practice since Jack died. "It's good to hear all of this. Out loud. From a friend."

After I got off the phone, I remembered a saying I'd liked in college, though in retrospect, at the time I didn't have a clue what it meant. *Wherever you go, there you are.* Here I was, twenty-five hundred miles away from the place that had been my home for more than a quarter of my life, and I was still dealing with what I'd left behind. Plus now I had a whole new set of problems.

I gave myself half an hour to wallow in self-pity, self-recriminations and self-loathing before I hit the shower. I knew myself—if I gave into it completely, it would overcome me, as it had in New York after Jack died. The only thing I knew that would save me was motion. I felt like a shark: if I stopped moving, I'd die.

Fifteen

I kept moving. At four o'clock, knowing I had three hours before meeting Alex for dinner, and the restaurant was only a half hour drive away, I left the house, dressed in black slacks, a sleek, black tank top and boots. This would do for dinner and whatever else happened in between.

My destination was unclear, but I had an idea. I'd noticed several surf shops between Las Flores and downtown Malibu proper. It stood to reason that surfing instructors would frequent surfing shops, though everything I knew about that world would fit onto the head of an Advil.

Walking into a shop called Da Kine reminded me of when I'd moved to New York and ventured into Saks for the first time. Then I'd felt underdressed, underaged and underfinanced. Da Kine gave me the same feeling at a different volume: now I felt overdressed, overaged and fully alien, as though stepping onto a different planet for the first time.

The guy behind the counter was cut, half-dressed, and

wore his blond dreadlocks like a badge of honor. He looked as if he could get a bit part in a surfing movie. I decided this was a good starting point for a conversation.

"Say," I said, amusing myself. "Didn't I see you in a surf movie?"

He smiled. "Which one?"

"Which one were you in?"

He laughed, a vaguely stoned sound. "All of them. You casting something?"

I thought about the lie I could tell, then thought better of it. I'd been on the West Coast less than a month and even if I technically did live in a famous director's house, I still didn't know much about the film industry. Now Emily, on the other hand…

"No. I'm looking for an instructor. Named Corby."

I saw the suspicion flare up like the hood of a cobra. "Why?"

"I…I want lessons." This admission brought no less suspicion.

He looked me up and down, then came closer, putting his hands on me as though we were dancing. The top of his head came roughly to my shoulder, and I could smell the product in his hair—coconut and fruit.

"I could give you lessons," he said softly, bending his head to kiss the exposed skin of my upper arm.

His movement shocked me, but didn't rock me, though I knew it should have. Despite the disparity in our height, ages and personal grooming habits, I felt myself begin to move to his rhythm, felt myself strangely aroused by his blatant and ridiculous come-on, and perhaps by some raw sexuality housed in his surf-taut body.

Whatever the case, I knew it wasn't what I was there for, nor was it something I actually wanted, no matter what my body was currently telling me.

I took a step back, almost upsetting a display composed of brilliantly colored latex bikinis. "I don't think so."

He crossed his arms over his chest and stood where he was. "I can teach you better than Corby ever could." He cocked his head to one side, like a dog listening for something he wants to hear. "A *lot* better than Corby."

"You know him, then?"

"Yeah, I know him. This isn't his turf, though." He took a step toward me, and when I took one back, he laughed, but not unkindly. "You'll find him at The Curl." He pointed north up Pacific Coast Highway. "But when he lets you down, I'm here."

It wasn't until I was back in my car, driving farther up the coast, that the flicker of a possibility occurred to me. I looked at my Kate Spade bag, my Balenciaga boots and Kors pants and top—all leftovers from my New York trading life—and realized that, in the context of Malibu in the afternoon, specifically in a surf shop, there might be various types of lessons that a well-dressed, an *expensively* dressed, woman might be looking for, especially one over thirty. I felt color rise to my cheeks, but pressed on. At least I'd had the good sense to turn him down.

The Curl was near Zuma Beach, and clearly different turf. Da Kine had been in a strip mall between a scuba diving shop and one that sold ice cream. The Curl stood alone. Inside I was greeted by the same smell of new latex and wax and the same lackadaisical looks from the sales staff. And they certainly didn't seem as though they believed in dressing for success.

Since I knew that a surf instructor named Corby was associated with this spot, I decided to dispense with the subterfuge. "Do you know where I could find Corby?" I asked the bikini-clad salesgirl, whose one concession to dressing for the office seemed to be a pair of Sanuck sandals.

"Naw. But hang on." She shouted toward the back of the shop, "Hey, Piston!"

A lanky-haired guy popped his head around a doorway. "Mmm?"

"Corby?"

I deduced that surf-type people didn't believe in wasting a lot of words, possibly a necessary trait on the ocean when the surf is crashing in your ears, though it didn't do much for communication on land.

Piston looked me up and down, then up again, then looked at the surf chick and shrugged his shoulders. "Not today," he said, then disappeared again.

"He come in here most days?"

"Most," she said, as though she really didn't care.

"Look, I really need to get hold of him. I'm…I'm casting a movie and I think…well, never mind. I should really speak to him directly."

The girl suddenly looked a lot more interested. "A surf movie?" Wow, three words at once.

"I really shouldn't say but…" I looked at her blond hair "…is that your natural color?"

She nodded enthusiastically and I felt suddenly bad

that I wasn't really a casting director. I could tell her hopes were rising by the second.

"Well, listen, after I've had a chance to talk to Corby, we'll see where we are, okay?"

She nodded enthusiastically. "Okay. Leave me your number. He usually stops in here every couple of days. When I see him, I'll tell him to call you."

"Excellent," I said, jotting down Emily's name and home phone number. "Thanks."

"Should I give you my number?"

"No, we'll be in touch." And I beat it back to my car.

The first phone booth I saw was at the Malibu Center Mall. When I called, Emily wasn't home, so I left her a message. "Hey, Emily, I hope you don't mind but I've taken your name and phone number in vain. I gave it to someone who might have a reason to recognize my number and I don't want them knowing it's me who's trying to get in touch with them. Confused? You should be. I'll explain better when I talk to you. For now, though, if anyone you don't know calls about being in a surfing movie, try to tell them you're not there and take a message, okay? Thanks. And I owe you, obviously. See ya."

I went back to my car and just sat there for a few minutes and thought about things. Assessed. Was any of this a good idea? Was it traceable? Would it endanger Jennifer? I decided that it wasn't and wouldn't. I didn't have any options, and in any case, it was already done. I couldn't take it back.

I looked at my watch. Five-thirty. Still an hour before I had to head to the Palisades, and I didn't feel like going home in between. I looked around at the mall and could see that coffee was a possibility. I took myself off to where I knew a latte was waiting for me.

I got to the restaurant a little early, before Alex did, which was fine. It gave me time to look around. It was one of those charming places with a fish in the logo, a stuffed marlin over the bar and lots of things with swordfish on the menu. It's a place where you know the food won't be terribly good and the prices will be astronomical but no one cares because you're really there for the view.

This one had all of that, plus practically no light and a lot of candles, meant obviously to be an expensive, seaside, *romantic* place for dinner. Despite a latent hint of touristy, the room had a very real warmth, and I felt comfortable waiting for Alex at the corner-window table he'd reserved for us, watching the gulls play over the darkened water.

When he arrived I was quickly reminded of the old-world quality that had attracted me to him in the first place. He owned a courtliness that I'd seldom experienced in a man. It would have surprised me if, had we gone for a ride in a car together, he wouldn't have rushed to my side first to open the door. He just had that air about him.

He smiled when he saw me. "And you are punctual, too," he said. "There is much that is refreshing about you, Madeline Carter." When he took my hand, I half expected him to kiss it, and couldn't decide whether or not I was disappointed to find it merely firmly shaken.

Dinner was better than I'd expected, something Alex remarked on, saying that he came here often for that very reason. This surprised me since, being a raw-food vegetarian, it didn't seem to me that he ate much that couldn't have been purchased at a vegetable market and prepared for table with a good scrub. He seemed to delight, however, in the enjoyment I took in my seared scallops in a wasabi sauce with risotto served plain, Milanese style.

"Amazing," I said when he asked how it was, though it would have been clear I was enjoying it. "Will you please have a scallop? Or a bite of risotto? I feel like a complete animal here wolfing down this wonderful food while you watch me, eating your raw corn relish or whatever that is you're having."

"Raw corn risotto. Which, of course, isn't a risotto at all, since it's made with no rice and is almost entirely composed of practically uncooked corn. But they must call it something smashing to justify these prices." He smiled. "But I love it. I enjoy it. And it's good for me."

I pointed to the bottle of pinot gris we were sharing and said, "What about that? Surely that can't be raw-food-vegetarian approved?"

He shrugged in an entirely continental way. "I eat as I do for my health and to increase the enjoyment of my life. But food without wine? That would reduce my joy sufficiently that it would shorten my life." He smiled. "That's how I see it, anyway. That's my story and I'm sticking to it."

We laughed. It was easy to laugh with Alex and he seemed dedicated to making me laugh as much as possible, so it was difficult to steer him to talking about his work. But I persevered. There was a great deal I wanted to know.

"I've been thinking so much about what you were talking about the other night. The subject of your work."

"Corporate psychopaths." He nodded.

"Yes. What you said made me think of someone I used to know. Someone who perhaps fits your description."

He wagged a gentle but accusing finger at me. "You be careful with that, my dear. It's something I hear a lot. And while many people—especially ex-husbands, it would appear—can seem to exhibit psychopathic behavior, the label doesn't fit everywhere it's applied. It's very specific. And, truly, my colleagues are correct, some of the behaviors I described to you *can* be ascribed to other causes. Some of them even medical. But the true psychopath can best be identified by his utter lack of remorse. And people say that—'Oh, he was remorseless.' But to see it on a clinical level is quite different. Remorse—conscience, call it what you will—is simply not a factor of the psychopath's makeup."

"So how would you tell?" I paused, thinking. "How would *I* tell?"

"You'd bring your psychopath to me—" he smiled "—or someone like me. A professional. It's not the sort of thing for armchair, or amateur, diagnosis."

"But let's say I wanted to make an amateur diagnosis. From a distance. One that would have no impact on the person in question's life. What would I look for?"

"We're being hypothetical, yes?"

I nodded.

Alex looked thoughtful for a moment, as though debating if he should answer at all, and then about what might be useful to me. But it was obviously a topic close to his heart, and he didn't have to dig very far. "Okay, hypothetically then. Is this person a corporate type or of the more common criminal class? It's salient because, while there are commonalties, there are differences, as well."

"Definitely corporate," I said without hesitation.

"Right, then this person would most likely give the appearance of being—and would in fact be—highly intelligent and strongly capable. There would probably be a glibness about him, a slyness. The kind of person who can get into a scrape, but can always get out. Beneath the surface would be a sexual promiscuity, one that would probably be at least a factor in the succession of relationships your psychopath would have.

"The other factor is the boredom. Since psychopaths are easily bored by many aspects of their lives, this manifests itself both in the promiscuity and in the way they conduct their business. There must always be bigger and better thrills. And the psychopath finds people valuable, but not as you or I might. To him, it is always about how can this person help me, aid me, make my life better? And once that usefulness has been extracted, it's on to the next one. You see how many of these things tie into each other?"

I nodded. I could see exactly. "What you're describing is a monster, capable of anything," I said flatly.

Alex sighed. Nodded. "In many cases, I'm afraid you're right."

Sixteen

Inexplicably, I dreamed of Arianna. She was standing in a field, keeping something hidden from me. "You'll never find her," she finally shouted. And I knew she was talking about Jennifer. I woke up with a start and a shout, and Tycho rushed over to me to see what the problem was.

I'd forgotten he was there. "Don't you have a home?" I asked him. He just wagged his tail.

Thinking about Arianna reminded me of the other paper she'd shown me. And *Arrowheart*. A name or word that was completely unfamiliar, yet I felt as though it should twig *something*. I lay back in my little nest and toyed with the word in my head. Arrow. Arrowroot. Heart of Arrow. Was it a name? A company? A place? A product? A car? Finally I couldn't stand it anymore and, even though it was only 4:00 a.m., I swung out of bed and booted my computer.

And then I did a Google search: *arrowheart*. Just like that, the single word.

There were *lots* of references. Inns on the East Coast. Something about bridges in Madison County. A very worthwhile-sounding program that had to do with telling stories to young offenders and people in prison. I scanned on, occasionally following a link, until I came to one dealing with the history of the Big Bear, California, area. And there, on a badly designed Web page that looked as though it had been lost in cyberspace since 1998, I found something that made sense. Amid reams of text scattered with bad photos, it mentioned Camp Arrowheart, built by the YMCA in the mid-1920s about fifty miles from Lake Arrowhead, where "thousands of Southern California children came to learn about clean and healthy living over the next seven decades."

In 1995, the camp had been abandoned, and infrequent attempts to revive it in one form or another had either failed financially or not gotten past whatever local approval needed to be secured. It had been, at least according to the tired-looking Web page, unused since that time.

I pulled out the map of Southern California that I keep in my desk to help me know where I am in relation to anything people mention to me. And I could see that if I were to drive from the spot where I currently sat (which I had circled when I first got the apartment, the desk and the map, in order to keep track of myself) to Lake Arrowhead, I'd be heading about a hundred miles southeast.

A plan was starting to form, and this time I was fully on top of it.

Orange County was south, not east, but bits of it

were pretty close to the route someone would have to take if driving to Lake Arrowhead. I left the map out and went back to my computer, bringing up the Langton corporate information once again. And, just as Steve had said, the LRG sales and manufacturing office was based in Orange County—in Brea, not far from La Habra. Back to the map.

From the looks of things, Brea was only slightly south of the most direct route to Arrowhead. I thought about this for a while. I knew that if I drove all the way down to Camp Arrowheart, it was most likely I'd find exactly what the Web page had told me: a Y camp that had been abandoned for the better part of a decade. But I had never been that far south before, and a trip to the mountains sounded like more fun than staying here and brooding. And if, as I suspected, Ernie had jotted down the word *Arrowheart* because that's where he was planning on holing up during his kidnapping, then what a bonus—I'd have a fun day trip *and* find out what the hell was going on.

It was true that, in his e-note to me, Ernie had included a warning: *Alternatives could be unhealthy.* But this *had* to be a bluff, didn't it? I couldn't imagine corporate Ernie posing an actual threat to me, except maybe financial, and how much worse could that get? And what was he going to do? Sue me? I didn't think so. Anyway, if I brought Tycho along, the dog would get a day in the mountains while providing some canine protection should I need it. Especially from lizards. But he'd be company on the drive, if nothing else.

Brea on my flight plan either on the way down or on

the way back tied the whole thing together. I'd stop at Langton and somehow track Steve down and apologize, and try to make things up to him. That idea appealed to me more than I knew it probably should have.

I slid on khaki shorts, a white V-necked T and hiking boots, plus I brought a sweater. Mountains, I knew, could be cold. Tycho and I were under way in less than an hour. Heading down PCH again, I felt truly happy for the first time in days. I felt powerful and optimistic and, most of all, I felt like I was doing something. In retrospect, I guess I also felt a little smug. Again. Why didn't I know better?

Seventeen

At Tyler's party, between networking with Emily and chatting quietly with Alex, I'd talked to this guy, Ned or Ted or Fred. Some kind of "ed" name, anyway. He was a favored key grip or camera guy or some other behind-the-scenes person. He was a rarity: a native Angeleno. He'd told me he'd been born in Hancock Park—I remember that part—and that he now lived in one of the beach communities, though which one slipped my mind. Obviously, he didn't make a strong impression on me overall, but I do remember one thing he told me. It was about his first trip to the redwood forest, when he was thirteen. He said he'd never been out of the city much before that, but driving through the forest in the back of the family sedan he was completely struck with awe. More importantly, he was suspicious. Suspicious of the forest. He told me he'd thought that the huge, majestic trees that lined both sides of the road were a facade. That if his father had stopped the car and his family had piled out and walked into the woods, after a few hundred feet the trees would thin and they'd be in a residential neighborhood. That there would be paved streets and high schools and strip malls.

"How could you think that?" I asked. A recently transplanted New Yorker who, nonetheless, had been born in Seattle, the official home of gorgeous trees, I couldn't understand such thought. And when he told me that, when the family had stopped for afternoon coffee and cherry pie at a roadside diner, he'd slipped alone into the trees and walked and walked and walked, believing that, at any second, they would thin out and he'd find what he expected, I laughed aloud. But to him it was the *trees* that were unnatural. That and the peace and solitude that forests engender. And at the time he told me, this wasn't something I could get my mind around.

When you live in Malibu and maybe shop in Santa Monica, you're not seeing L.A. Both touch the ocean, and whatever place the ocean touches tends to have its own kind of peace: a wilderness of water. Even my infrequent forays into other parts of West L.A. and downtown didn't give me a sense of what Ned/Fred/Ted had told me. Maybe a taste, nothing more. But driving, driving, driving anywhere—except north from Malibu—to get out of L.A., you begin to understand.

Looking at a map gives you a hint, but it really is only a hint. Los Angeles, Commerce, Bell, Cudahy, Downey, Norwalk, La Habra…you see them first as names on a map and, if you're from Washington State, or a lot of other places, you think in terms of what you know: that between each place there'll be some type of physical relief. City followed by a thinning of humanity when you reach the outskirts, followed by at least a brief lull that includes some green and maybe even the occasional cow.

In L.A., things are different. You can't really go west, of course, because you'd end up in the Pacific. And if you go north, you get clear pretty quickly because then you're in Ventura County and almost anyone will tell you that doesn't count. But in any other direction, you can drive for a long way and never get the feeling that you've left something behind and started something new. The mileage boards will tell you so, and you'll see signs saying Welcome to Bellflower, Welcome to Alhambra whizz past, but nothing will give you the visual respite that a Pacific Northwesterner needs to tell her she's left one city and started into another. It gets a little eerie, after a while. Like something from *The Twilight Zone.*

So sitting on Tyler's deck with a drink in my hand, a breeze tickling the eucalyptus trees and the ocean within visual range, I couldn't begin to relate to Fred/Ted/Ned's story. But today, with Tycho panting happily in the back seat, I got a good taste. You feel like it will go on forever, the desert of asphalt, the sea of car lots, the forest of industrial buildings. That you'll never see another tree or lake or stream. I began to feel as claustrophobic as Ned/Fred/Ted had probably felt in the back seat of the family car, though in reverse.

That was why, at first, I wrote off my sightings of the burgundy Honda Accord as my own paranoia. All of those towns. All of that asphalt. The fact that I could have sworn I'd seen that Accord several times between

Santa Monica and Brea seemed to me not even a matter for consideration. It's not like seeing a purple Bentley. To get to Brea I followed the Santa Monica Freeway—Highway 10—to the 60 East to the 57 South to the Imperial Highway and finally to 90. That's a lot of traversing. My last Honda sighting was on the Imperial Highway, and then I was ankle deep in negotiations for which Brea exit to take, and I forgot all about the burgundy car.

There was no hint to announce Brea—no grass, no trees and certainly no happy cows. Just, suddenly, there you were in a city named for tar that is now home to a lot of corporations. Including, of course, the Langton sales office.

I didn't feel nervous today. I had a plan that I was conscious of. And I wasn't trying to do any infiltrating, only intercepting. I *could* have just called Steve and asked him to meet me somewhere, but I knew it wouldn't have the same impact. I could see how hurt he'd been by my skulking out of his hotel room that morning in the marina. Plus there'd been the whole potential kidnapper thing. Then I'd stood him up in Brentwood. Since I'd been more or less going his way—well, less, but now here I was—it just felt like the right thing to do to try and surprise him. And now that I was thinking about him, I realized I'd like to be able to make him smile—at me—again.

I didn't pull into the lot, just parked Tycho in the next block in the shade of a couple of palms. I rolled the windows down so the dog would have air, but not enough so he could squeeze out if the thought occurred to him.

Not far from the loading dock, I found what I was looking for: a picnic table with a metal bucket on it. Close inspection revealed I was right on target. The bucket was filled with sand and the sand was filled with butts.

I'd come prepared. I sat down at the picnic table, pulled a book out of my bag and settled in to wait. I figured that, since this was a sales office and a manufacturing plant, a peaceable looking woman reading in the smoking area would not cause any raised eyebrows. People from sales would think I belonged in the plant somewhere. People from the plant would think I was from sales and it was casual Friday or some damn thing. I'd give it an hour. If Steve didn't show, I'd go find a telephone and get him out here the old-fashioned way. If he wouldn't see me, well…at least I'd be able to say that I'd visited Brea.

I didn't have long to wait. After about twenty minutes of reading, and just as the book was finally getting interesting, I saw him see me. And I also saw him decide what to do about it.

I was pretty pleased with myself for thinking up this surprise visit. I had stood him up. I'd eventually gotten to the restaurant, but he had no way of knowing that. He'd already been somewhat hurt about everything when I last saw him. I know if our situations had been reversed and, after all of that, he'd called me, I would probably have hung up. But a surprise visit that's extremely out of the other person's way? That makes up for some stuff. And I could tell by the look on his face— flattered yet still slightly hanging on to injury—that he felt that way, too.

"I just missed you," I told him as he approached. I closed my book, but continued sitting at the picnic table. "Yesterday. The waitress told me. At the restaurant. I'm sorry."

"What are you doing here?"

"Apologizing. I felt badly about missing you. But I had no way of getting hold of you."

"You want to go for a walk?" he said, indicating approaching smokers. I was relieved. Walking would mean talking and talking meant that, as I suspected, he wasn't going to stay mad.

I smiled at him. "I don't know, Steve. Last time we went for a walk, things got out of hand."

He smiled back. "I'll behave this time. I have to get back to work pretty soon, you know."

"Okay. Walk me back to my car."

And he did. And he thought Tycho was an "extremely cool dog." Tycho smiled at that (though he smiles at everything). Steve and I didn't talk about anything—he had smoking and then working to do—except that he accepted my apology and we swapped phone numbers. I told him I'd call him later and then Tycho and I were back on the road.

I found my heart was lighter. I liked the reflection I saw in Steve's smile. I was still smiling myself when, at the place where Highway 90 joins up with 57 North, I spotted the burgundy Honda again. This time I knew I couldn't just write it off. Though the car had never been close enough for me to see the driver's face, the basic human-shaped bulk of the person behind the wheel was beginning to look familiar. I was still willing to be wrong, though. In fact, I was kind of expecting and hoping for it. I kept telling myself, "This is Southern California. Do you know how many burgundy Hondas are probably just in this little grid of the map alone?" I couldn't even guess, but I knew it would be a lot. Plus I knew if it *was* the same car—both before and after I'd made a nearly hour-long stop at Brea—then the only explanation would be that someone was following me. In a Honda. I couldn't begin to ponder who might be doing so. It frightened me just to think about it.

Simply going along blithely didn't seem like a good idea. I had to do something that would, if nothing else, tell me if I was right or wrong. Even though I hadn't been planning on stopping at Redlands, I deliberately cut over two lanes to take the Orange Street exit that the sign said led to downtown. And then I watched my rearview mirror as carefully as I could without colliding with oncoming traffic.

As I turned onto Brookside Drive I was chiding myself for getting jumpy. How goofy could I get? All this cloak and dagger stuff was getting to me. I'd pulled into the parking lot of the Redlands Mall in order to turn the car around and see if I could figure out how to get the hell back on the freeway when I saw the familiar flash of burgundy and my heart sank again.

I pulled into an open spot near a mall entrance and just sat in the car, trying to calm myself and think about what to do. Obviously, my original plan was out. Driving into the wilderness with some unknown person following me did not seem like a good idea. Likewise, just cruising unconcernedly home didn't sound particularly

appealing, either. The great unknown represented by
the Honda was too...unknown.

In my side mirror I could see the Honda pull into a
spot a good six aisles and ten cars behind me. Like me,
the driver did not get out of the car. Okay, that did it.
Someone was definitely following me. Watching me.

Even in big cities, we tend to go through most of our
lives feeling pretty anonymous, fairly isolated. In a
Manhattan condo with, literally, millions of people
around you, it's possible to feel completely alone. It's
some sort of mental island we create to keep from losing our minds at our proximity to everyone else. These
are things we don't even have to think about—our an-
onymity in a crowd—and I certainly never had, until
now. The loss of it was unnerving. In fact, it felt downright creepy.

This time, when I got out of the car, I left the windows open only slightly. I wanted Tycho to be able to
breathe, but I didn't want anyone getting into the car,
either. So I took precautions. Then, without looking
around at all, I headed for the mall entrance.

Inside, I scouted around for an exit that would take
me out another way, one that would bring me up behind
my would-be follower. I asked myself if I was really
thinking of getting the jump on the Honda guy and I decided that I was. A public place like a mall seemed the
perfect place to do whatever I was thinking about doing.
Better, anyway, than the wilderness or the Malibu hills,
where there might be no one around to rescue me if rescue was required.

As soon as I got within sight of the Honda, I pulled

a pen and paper out of my bag and jotted down the license plate number. I wasn't quite sure what I hoped to accomplish with that, but it seemed like the proper first step. And, anyway, it gave me something to do while I thought about my next move.

With that bit of business out of the way, I moved in what I thought was a stealthy manner toward the car. The driver's seat was in a normal position and the headrest blocked my view of the driver, but I reasoned that he probably couldn't see me, either. And, in any case, his eyes would likely be fixed on the door I'd entered, and he wouldn't have expected me to circle back so quickly.

My instincts—not the ones that keep me moving forward in the market, but the ones that keep animals made of meat from becoming lunch—were urging me to flee, get the hell out of Dodge or at least make for the nearest pay phone and call the cavalry. I didn't listen. Instead, I let my feet propel me to the side of the car, ready to confront the person that I was now sure had been following me at least since Santa Monica, maybe even from Malibu.

I got to the driver's door, turned and…found it empty. I scanned the parking lot quickly; it was full of people, but none looked as though they belonged to the Honda. Before I was even aware of it, my hand snaked out and, very authoritatively, tried the door. Almost as soon as I touched the door handle, all thoughts of anything were driven from my mind by the raucous sound of the Honda's alarm bleating painfully to everyone within shouting distance. I took an involuntary step back and collided with something soft. I turned quickly and found it was a large woman with a bemused expression on her face currently messing with her keys, pushing buttons and, apparently, trying to turn her alarm off.

"Just what were you trying to do?" she asked calmly when the air was quiet again. Her British accent sounded cultured to me—a complete contradiction to her appearance, which was not.

I shrugged a little helplessly. It was a pretty good question.

"Well, if you've completed your attempt at stealing my car, perhaps it's time for you to keep moving. Or do I have to call the police?"

By then I'd gained some perspective. "Maybe calling the police would be a good idea. And you can explain to them why you're following me." I was proud of myself. I sounded a lot calmer than I felt.

She sighed. Obviously the car thief thing had been a weak gambit in case I really didn't know she'd been tailing me. She sighed again. "I'm not having a terribly good day."

"*You're* not? Sheesh…try being on this end of it. Now why the hell are you following me?" I was rapidly feeling more brave. She was large and rumpled and tired-looking. Hardly a physical threat.

"That would be telling, wouldn't it?" In certain circumstances, it might have been taken as a humorous comment, but her tone was not too cheery.

"That's the idea. Telling. You did a really crummy job following me. I saw you. A lot. I don't know much about this, but I don't think I'm supposed to be able to know. You lose the advantage, following someone, if you spoil the surprise. Now the surprise is spoiled, anyway. So…go ahead. Tell me. Why are you following me?"

Another sigh. Her plump face screwed up in concern. Then, "I really can't afford to lose another job this week. It's not like affluent clients fall from trees, you know."

"You're not with the police?"

She rolled her eyes, as though what I'd stated was so obvious it didn't warrant an answer. She indicated her somewhat seedy attire, her worse-for-wear Honda. "Do I look like official law enforcement to you?"

"I guess not. But I don't have much experience. I just can't imagine why anyone would follow me." This was only half-true. A week ago it would have been completely true. In the last few days, though, I'd given several people motivation to follow me. I just wasn't sure which one would do so. "If not police, then what?"

"I'm a private investigator."

"Cool," I said, and meant it—I'd never met a real life P.I. before, though I hadn't imagined one would look like this woman. I had thought that a private dick would be lithe, or at least in relatively good physical shape, from all the running around and catching crooks that you'd imagine go with the territory. This private eye seemed as though she'd have trouble stuffing herself into a booth at McDonald's and would get out of breath in the process. And running down a crook? Forget it. I'm hardly a marathoner, but on foot I could have lost her in half a block. She looked out of shape *and* down on her luck. This last gave me an idea.

"What do you get paid?" I asked her. "For this, I mean." I indicated the car.

"I'm receiving five hundred dollars per day for this job," she said quickly. She could see where this was leading.

I considered. And suddenly I was feeling better, less afraid. I was on familiar ground. "Okay, then, how about I give you a hundred and fifty and you tell me why you were following me and then stop."

"I can't do *that*." She donned a shocked expression, but I could see I had her attention. "There's such a thing as professional ethics, you know."

"I'm sure," I said agreeably. "But look, the jig is up. You can't very well follow me anymore now that I know you're doing so. It would be useless. And I'm not doing anything very interesting, I promise. You could just tell whoever that you followed me here and then I went home, or you lost me, or whatever you want to tell them."

"That wouldn't be honest! I have my license to consider, you know."

"Well, it wouldn't be exactly lying, would it? You *did* follow me here, and I found you out." I shrugged. "Saying you lost me might just be a bit neater, if you see what I mean."

She didn't say anything, but I could see that she saw exactly what I meant.

"It's not like I'm going to contradict you. I just want to know who is so curious about me that they'd hire someone to follow me. And it's not like I'm a criminal or anything. I'm not married, I'm not having an affair, I'm just so completely not up to anything that would make me worth following." I gave another shrug. "So your conscience would be clear."

"But my license…" she said again, though I could see she was weakening.

"Like I said, *I'm* not going to tell anyone. So if you don't…"

"Make it two-fifty. I could have gotten another half day, or more for following you tomorrow."

We went inside the mall and I left her at the food fair while I went to find an ATM so I could give her cash. I didn't bother asking if she'd take plastic or a check. I found her overlapping a mushroom-shaped plastic chair while munching on a side of fries doused in ketchup. I plunked myself down on the mushroom opposite her, forked over half the money and said, "So spill."

She looked around theatrically while she pocketed the cash. Making sure the watcher wasn't being watched? I would have been amused if I wasn't so freaked out and annoyed.

"It was someone called Mrs. Billings."

"Arianna?" I said, somewhat incredulously. And it wasn't just that she'd had me followed—she had been at the top of my suspect list, anyway—just that high-rent Arianna would hire this obviously low-rent private investigator. "How do you know her?"

"Give me the rest of my money," the woman demanded, wiping grease from her chin with a napkin that had already done similar work. I guess she was eager to make sure I didn't bolt with the other half of her dough.

"Sure, but just tell me, how do you know her?"

"I don't," she said as I watched her make my money disappear into her purse. "She called me Thursday afternoon. Gave me the address of a coffee place in Brentwood. Told me to go there and wait outside. Said there would be two blondes coming out of the coffee place together. The one that *didn't* get into the Porsche parked outside would be you." Arianna had told me she'd stopped at home before she met with me that day. She'd said it was to check on me and to get the papers she'd shown me. What she hadn't told me was that she had hired a private detective at the same time.

"But how did she know to call *you*?"

She shrugged. "Probably called my ad in the Yellow Pages. I think she liked my name. Clients like her generally do."

I looked at her, trying to imagine. "Why? What's your name?"

"Anne Rand," she told me, forking over a card. "See? No *Y*, but it sounds the same."

Anne Rand. I stopped myself from laughing out loud, but it was hard.

Her french fries were finished and so, apparently was our business. Anne Rand was pushing herself to her feet.

"Listen, Ms. Rand, before you go, why were you following me? What did Mrs. Billings hope you'd see?"

She looked at me, then at her purse, and seemed to come to a decision. Perhaps she figured she hadn't given the greatest value for two hundred and fifty clams. She didn't settle herself back down, but perched awkwardly where she was, a feat that was only possible through the sheer largesse of her bulk and the sturdiness of the plastic mushroom.

"Well, as you'd imagine, she didn't go into great detail. I guess a sort of need-to-know basis, right?" I nodded. "I assumed it was a husband matter. People who introduce themselves as 'Mrs.' then pay with a credit card in the name of the 'Mr.' are generally looking to find out what the other woman is up to." I snorted, and Anne held up a hand. "Well, it's the commonest sort of thing I get hired for, as you can well imagine."

I had trouble imagining anyone hiring her for anything, but whatever. "Did she tell you anything about why she wanted me followed?"

"No. I was just to keep a log and check in with her at the end of each day."

"You mean it wasn't just today?"

"No, I told you, she had me eyeball you as you left the café the other day. I've been around pretty much ever since."

I had a vision of her perched in her Honda at the top of the cliff, keeping an eye on Tyler's driveway.

"That was two days ago. You mean you were watching me at home in Malibu? You were there that whole time?"

"Pretty much. I have a friend I work with sometimes who spelled me for a few hours here and there. So I went home once, ate, showered, you know. But mostly I was there." She grinned. "I didn't want to have to give up too much of my fee."

I felt violated, somehow. Exposed. I thought about what she might have seen me do. Not much, when I considered. Then I thought of something else.

"You've been watching me pretty much ever since I met Arianna—Mrs. Billings—in Brentwood?"

Rand nodded.

"Did you happen to see a kid—a teenage girl—leave the house at a funny hour?"

She nodded again and crossed her arms over her chest, saying nothing.

I got the point. "What's it going to cost me?"

She considered. "Another two-fifty?"

"Two," I countered.

"Done."

I looked at her. She looked at me. "You're waiting for the money," I said finally.

"That's correct."

I sighed. "Wait here."

When I got back she was sitting down properly again, a plate of teriyaki chicken and rice in front of her. It looked like a lot of my money was going to go for food.

"Okay..." I said, plunking myself down opposite her. "I've got the money."

She held out her left hand, palm up, while not breaking her stride eating. I put five twenties into it and held the other five within view. She rolled her eyes but started to talk.

"Now, the times won't be perfectly accurate because I didn't take notes on this stuff because, since it wasn't you, it didn't matter to my report." She looked at me and I nodded. "The first night I was out there, about three o'clock in the morning a van pulled up, and a girl got out. Went in the house."

I stopped her. "Like a delivery van?" Jennifer drove an SUV.

"Well, yes and no. It wasn't marked for deliveries or anything. And it had a pretty distinctive paint job and funny cutout windows. Like what we would have called a shaggin' waggin' back in my day."

Not wanting to hear her Woodstock stories, I moved her on. "Anything else?"

"Sure. About fifteen minutes later, the girl came back, carrying a little pack, you know, like for school?"

"A backpack."

"Right. Looked quite full, too. She gets in the van—passenger side—and drives away."

"Did you see what she looked like?"

"Not really. It was dark. Slender, that's for sure. And long dark hair. And she moved like a kid. You know, like a youngster."

"Who was driving the van?"

Anne held our her other hand—she'd finished eating by now—and looked at me expectantly.

"Oh, all *right*," I said, and gave her the rest of the money.

"I don't know who was driving." She shrugged, pocketing my cash. "It was too dark to see."

I didn't say anything, just looked at her. She smiled. "I like you. You're a smart cookie. I piss you off, but you don't shoot your mouth off, make me mad. The van, it was green-gold, kinda pretty. And—" she started rummaging in a voluminous bag "—I got the plate."

"I thought you said you weren't taking notes."

She smiled, obviously pleased that, despite the fact

that I'd caught her on the freeway, she could still take credit for some stealth. "I was bored. And I *always* get a plate. Just in case."

After we left the mall, I waited around long enough to see Ms. Rand stuff herself back into her car and head toward the freeway, then I found a phone booth. Tyler wasn't home. I was going to leave voice mail, then thought better of it. Taken alone, what Anne had told me really didn't add much to what we already knew. And, though it was interesting, taken out of context in a voice mail message it might give Tyler false hope. Plus explaining why a private detective had been watching me in the first place was more than I felt like tackling in a one-way conversation.

Tycho and I poked around the parking lot for a bit while I pondered things further—I figured he needed emptying—and I wasted time making sure Anne was well and truly gone. When we were both empty and then refilled—cool water, all round—we got back on the road.

Once I was driving, I thought again of the private detective. I imagined Arianna pouring over the Yellow Pages, trying to find an investigator on extremely short notice—one who was available. I could just see her making the literary connection in her mind, then hearing the cultured voice on the phone and thinking, Sure, she'll get the job done. Never suspecting the reality of this particular Rand.

"Anne Rand," I said aloud as I drove. And then I laughed. Hired to watch one person, inadvertently getting information on another. Sometimes it's just such a funny old world.

Eighteen

Camp Arrowheart turned out to be tougher to find than even the Hestman School had been. It had looked pretty simple, but that was only because my map hadn't reflected unpaved mountain roads. In real life, things twisted when they'd merely looked curved, they were rocky when I'd expected them to be paved. And the camp itself was nowhere near where I'd thought it would be. Sure, fifty miles from Lake Arrowhead, but as the crow flies. As the Chevy bounces, it was an hour and a half. Tycho and I fell out of the car with joy when we found the overgrown entrance to Camp Arrowheart. And both of us found private places in the undergrowth to relieve our driving buildup. I think we both felt lighter when we reunited.

I'd planned to leave the car at the road and sort of skulk, sort of wander toward camp even before I'd gotten a peek at the drive, but that peek clinched things. The track that led to the camp wasn't precisely grown over, but my car was less than a month old and my experience as a driver wasn't much richer than that. I didn't want to risk getting stuck or scraping some important bits. Plus, even though part of me was certain that this whole exercise was a wild-goose chase, another part was sure this particular driveway would lead to an outraged Ernie asking me what the hell I was doing there. Not giving too much warning of my approach seemed like a good idea.

Tycho, of course, refused to respect the top secret nature of our mission. He thought this was heaven. The way he was acting, our trip to the wilderness was probably some sort of doggie fantasy come to life. He ran around like crazy, snuffling at new and wonderful smells and peeing on everything growing as if he were shouting "Mine! Mine! Mine!"

As we trudged up the track that I assumed led to the camp, I tried to think like a Girl Guide in order to tell if the road had been recently used or not. Trouble is, I never was a Girl Guide and the tree-lined road held no hints for me—just a couple of twin depressions with grass growing on either side and between them.

It was beautiful country that would have done Ed/Ted/Ned's soul good. There was no way you could trudge and trudge and trudge along here in the deepening wilderness—evergreens towering and forest scents freshening—without feeling your heart lighten. I imagined him falling on his knees and shouting, "I believe!" The dense quiet—filled with bird and bug calls, the occasional animal noises and the sounds various vegetation makes when in its natural habitat (creaks, groans, rustles)—reassured you if required. There was no way anyone could think they'd come over the next rise and find a 7-Eleven.

After what seemed like quite a long trudge, perhaps a half mile, I could begin to make out the shapes of buildings ahead of us in the distance. I took them to be various lodges and cabins. The closer I got, the less occupied everything appeared. At a distance the camp looked like a rustic beacon of humanity. As I approached, I could begin to see hints of things as they were: a shutter missing here, a window boarded over there, a chimney at a funny angle, an overgrown tennis court, the fence surrounding it sagging sadly. All of these things collectively sent a message of loss. I could almost sense the spirits of children running by me in Y T-shirts, little voices raised in the mindless hilarity of childhood. I felt sad and, to be honest, a little frightened.

If a tree falls in the forest, does anybody hear? This was like that, with a twist. The camp was being reclaimed by the forest and it didn't feel right to listen. There were no cars, abandoned or otherwise, to be seen, and I had a strong suspicion that no one was here, but that didn't make me feel any easier.

I called Tycho to me quietly. His softly padding presence beside me was reassuring if not particularly threatening. Another living soul, he kept me company. Companion dog. The classic canine occupation since time out of mind. I understood better now and stopped to scratch his head appreciatively, noticing how he watched me carefully with his liquid amber eyes.

"Good boy," I said softly. And we walked on, exploring the perimeter of Camp Arrowheart while I worked up my courage to have a peek inside the buildings.

We skirted around a deep swimming pool, empty but for a thick covering of green sludge at the bottom, and entered what might have once been a counselors' meeting house, or maybe even a lifeguard's office or storage for sporting equipment. It was hard now to tell—everything that gives a room context had been stripped from it, leaving the mildewing walls bare, the room devoid of any clues about what sort of human goings-on might have happened here. But it was a good starting point. Finding the small hut completely empty gave me the courage to try some of the bigger buildings. A few other cabins and what might have once been a small lodge—a big fieldstone fireplace at one end was my clue here—didn't show signs of recent human occupation. As we entered the largest of the lodges I was starting to breathe easier. I hadn't seen anything thus far that indicated recent signs of either human or ghostly life.

The big lodge looked as though it had also been the cookhouse. We passed through a pantry and into what had clearly been the kitchen. I guessed that the best of the cooking equipment had been salvaged, but the remnants of a big industrial kitchen could still be seen. The place looked as though it would have been capable of serving hundreds of meals at every sitting.

It was as we moved from the kitchen into the main lodge area—a big empty room with a large center hearth and doors to what I took to be smaller rooms to my left and right—that I noticed Tycho was behaving oddly. He was moving very carefully, his ears at full attention and his nose snuffling anxiously.

"What is it, boy?" I asked in a low voice.

As if in answer, he padded cautiously toward the exit. I felt like the doomed heroine in one of those stupid horror movies—where the girl is in her bedroom or maybe the bath and she hears a funny noise, or her dog starts acting funny, and she's scared but she goes to see what it is, anyway. And all the time you're sitting at home watching it on the late-late-late show simply because there's nothing else on, and you're screaming at the television, "Don't do it! Go back to bed! Better still, get the hell out of there while you still can!" But she never listens, just keeps right on tripping into the mouth of danger while you can do nothing but sit there and say, "If that were me…"

And now it *was* me. As strong as any gut feeling that ever told me to sell or buy a stock, every part of my sharply honed instincts were now screaming, *Never mind what's out there. Don't go through that door. You don't need to know. It doesn't matter. Just get back to your car.*

If my car had been right outside, maybe I would have gone for it. But if danger truly *was* lurking on the other side of the door, there was no way I'd make it back to my car, anyway. And if what was out there was so scary it made me scream, no one would ever hear.

I told myself to get a grip. There was *nothing* out there besides a rodent or maybe a coyote. And then I heard something that I couldn't write off as sounds created by Mother Nature. It was a human voice. Not right outside the door, but not far away, either. Definitely within the camp's immediate vicinity. And then I heard another, different voice. This one softer—pleading?— but no closer to where I was.

"Tycho, heel," I murmured, pointing to that part of my anatomy. The last thing I wanted was the occasionally boisterous canine to go romping up to whatever humans were out there. I told myself that there was nothing odd about people being here. This was beautiful country. Hikers probably came this way all the time.

But it hadn't sounded like hikers, and my instincts told me that it wasn't. I thought about my car, my safe little automotive haven, too far down the road for me to get there quickly. Still, I thought, if we went back the way we had come, and made a big circle around where I felt whatever human activity was coming from, there seemed a good chance we'd get back to the car undetected. And suddenly the undetected part seemed important.

We retraced our steps, Tycho seeming to understand that he needed to stay close and quiet, back through the main lodge, past the smaller lodge, the cabins we'd walked through not long before, past the pool and the tennis court. Relief flooded through me like a live thing when we made the cover of the trees that followed the track into camp, but we weren't clear quite yet. I hadn't heard the voices again, so maybe it *had* been hikers, after all. And then I saw a flash of white. Focusing even as I ducked behind a little stand of trees and made sure all of Tycho was out of sight, I could make out a human male, in business dress, heading in my direction. Could he see me? I didn't think so. But then another man—

this one in garb suitable to the terrain—appeared, and I understood. The first man, the well-dressed one, was in flight. He was heading, naturally enough, for the road out of camp, which, unfortunately, was exactly where I was standing.

I pulled Tycho deeper into the trees. I felt my panic rise when he tried to resist me. Putting a hand on his chest and one on his back, thinking to quiet him, I was almost surprised when he responded as I wished. Though I'd never be sure if it was due to that physical restraint or the bushel of quieting energy I sent his way. Whatever the case, on some canine level he seemed to understand the urgency of the situation, perhaps not so surprising when you think about how dogs in the wild spend their time.

By now the men were closer than they had been, and I could hear their words.

"Jesus, asshole. Stop. You don't really think I'd kill you?"

"Why wouldn't you?" This was the running man. The one in the suit. His voice was ragged from his exertions, but I recognized it instantly. "Why would I think you wouldn't?"

"Come on, we're way past games. If I'd wanted to kill you, I would have done it back there."

And now I realized I recognized the second voice, as well. Incredulity forced me to lift my head, carefully, to see if I could get a glimpse of him. And I could, but barely, and with the sun against me I couldn't quite be sure. It could be him. But then again, it had been a long time since I'd seen Paul Westbrook, and at this distance, it might just be someone who looked and sounded like him.

But who also has a connection to Ernie?

That little voice again, though I didn't stop to think about it. Ernie—if it *was* Ernie, and I was pretty sure it was—was moving directly toward me. And he hadn't seen me…yet. But I was also fairly sure that if I moved very far in either direction, one of the two would spot me. And then I caught a break.

"Okay, man. Look, you win." It was the chasing guy—Paul? "You're right, okay? Let's talk about it. Maybe things *have* gotten a little out of hand."

The first man hesitated, then stopped and turned toward his pursuer. "You mean it?"

"Sure. I'd been thinking that myself. C'mon, let's go back inside and talk this through." As if to illustrate his sincerity, he turned around and headed toward the camp without a backward glance. Ernie hesitated. For a second he seemed to look directly at me. Though I knew he couldn't possibly see me, I pulled still farther back behind the tree. Finally he sighed, as though resigning himself to something, turned around and followed the first man.

I held my position, flattened against the back of a tree and, cursing the whim that had made me don a white shirt in the morning, I watched their progress while I waited for both men to get themselves out of sight, which would, of course, mean I was out of *their* sight, which would leave the coast clear for me and Tycho to scurry back to the road.

It didn't happen. I watched while Ernie trotted across the camp toward the man I was pretty sure was Paul. They were out of earshot again, but I could see them clearly—they were less than a hundred feet from where I crouched. I couldn't see their expressions or make out their words, but I saw when Paul turned and held something in front of him, and his stance and the way he held the object was familiar. I flashed quickly on Jack— *What can I do you for?*—the gun in the shooter's hand, Jack on the floor.

Now, in the San Bernardino forest, I could see Ernie take a few steps back, as though he'd run again if he had the chance. He didn't get it. The distance between us warped the sound, so I heard the shot at the same time Ernie's legs just seemed to give out beneath him, and he fell. The undergrowth prevented me from seeing the spot where he'd gone down, but he *did* go down. I saw it as clearly as I could see the tips of Tycho's ears.

Time is a funny thing. When you're a kid, a month can seem like a year, especially if the month is September and it means you have to go back to school after a summer that has been endless. When you're an adult with a regular job, that same month can whizz by in a moment, regardless of season. Intellectually, I know I hesitated behind my tree for only a minute, maybe two, my hand resting on the reassuring dome of Tycho's head. But in that relatively small speck of time I tried hard to process what I had just seen and, more importantly, what I should do about it.

My feet moved me forward before I'd even fully considered my actions. Someone was hurt, needed my help; I didn't think much beyond that. I wasn't aware of doing anything either noisy or more visible than what I'd been doing previously, and had moved only a few feet away from cover when I saw Paul's head jerk up, his gaze scan the area and light on me.

I saw him hesitate—perhaps processing what might be represented by this visual aberration—then raise his weapon in my direction. I heard a shot, and then another, but I had no way of gauging if the bullets were landing close to me or not because by that time I was in full flight, not worrying too much about direction, only that I put distance between myself and the man pointing a firearm at me.

Tycho and I stopped in the protection of a little copse of trees and strewn boulders so I could catch my breath. I crouched behind a rock, my hand on the smooth surface grounding me, and listened as well as I could over my ragged breathing and Tycho's panting. Had we lost him? And then the crunch of feet on dry wood forced us into motion again. It might have been a deer, I knew, but it might just as easily have been a man, and taking chances at this point didn't seem like a good idea.

It took me awhile to understand how completely in the wilderness we were. It's not as if you could loop around and run into a goat farm or, as Ned/Ted/Fred had anticipated, a 7-Eleven, though I would have loved *that* right now. The camp was situated in the San Bernardino National Forest. Sure, there were bound to be roads and highways and probably even farms or ranches out there someplace, but in the deep silence of the forest, with the mountains all around me and what was very probably a crazy man somewhere behind me, it was easy to believe in the total wilderness I saw in every direction.

Getting back to my car was the only type of safety I dared think about.

And so I ran. I ran as though my life depended on it, for by this point, and after what I'd just seen, it seemed very likely that it did.

I was in unfamiliar terrain. Without the old camp road to follow there were no markers, and I just hoped I was running in the right direction and that, before very long, I'd come across the road and could, from there, find the way back to my car.

Every now and then, when I encountered a particularly large boulder or well-positioned stand of trees, I'd scrunch down to catch my breath and listen carefully. Was that the crunch of a branch? A shout? A shot? No? Maybe? Then off we'd go again.

I wasn't sure how long or how far we ran, but after a while, with our shadows lengthening, the trees thinning and the road still not in sight, I began to suspect that I had fled in the wrong direction. This realization didn't concern me as much as I would have thought. I was *alive*. Alive and running toward all of the possibilities represented by that fact. What was behind me was a less attractive option. Lost and moving was preferable to the fate to which I'd seen Ernie fall.

Hoping we were no longer being pursued, but knowing I had to figure out where we were, I stood on a boulder and tried to get my bearings. Being perched up there made me regret again that I'd passed on the whole Girl Guide thing, because nothing I saw made any sense to me. All the more because this wasn't wilderness as I'd come to know it in the Pacific Northwest, where trees are trees and mountains are formidable.

Where we were now was arid and mountainous. The dense trees that had hugged the camp had given way to scraggly, low-lying scrub and huge rocks. To make matters worse, we'd been running hard for most of the last hour and hadn't passed anything that resembled potable water. Harder on the canine than me, sure, but I was starting to think about it, too. Poor Tycho's tongue was practically dragging on the ground, and I hated to see bits of dirt and plant material clinging to it. We were okay for the moment, but we wouldn't be able to go on like this indefinitely. I had no feeling for where we were, and though I had a hunch there would be towns between here and Las Vegas, the very possibility of running until we hit the desert filled me with dread.

There was no choice. I just kept leading us on and hoping like hell we weren't going in circles like the poor saps in movies always tend to do. As we moved, I kept peeking over my shoulder, partly to see that the scenery behind us was staying the same but growing more distant, and partly to check if anyone was following.

Another hour and the terrain became even more rugged and the ground began to slope upward more sharply. We were climbing. Gently, but we were definitely heading to higher altitudes. I didn't dare stop to wonder if up was a good idea. I knew what was behind us: a whole lot of nothing with a gun-toting killer at the end. And going up at least meant that we hadn't passed this way before. We were bound to come upon something or someone sooner or later.

Just as I was about to give in to despair, we came upon something hopeful. At first, and from the distance, I thought it was some kind of luxury home perched at the top of the highest mountain in the vicinity. As unlikely as it seemed to find a structure like that way out here, I still thought it would be a good thing.

As we got closer, I began to be able to make out the building's details, and could see it wasn't a house. It was some kind of ranger station or forest outlook. A man-made crow's nest the size of a small house, perched on stilts, commanding a view of the forest on all sides. I was so relieved I felt like crying.

Once I was reasonably sure that it was, in fact, some sort of government-built forest lookout—not just a mirage brought on by hours of wandering and a lack of water—I took my sweater from around my waist and waved it frantically over my head. If someone was watching, it seemed it would be a much better idea to try and get their attention and maybe grab a lift up there rather than walking the rest of the way. After a while with no response, though, I stopped and just kept walking. The waving sweater had produced no results and I'd started to feel sharply ridiculous, like I was trying to hail a cab on Fifth Avenue. I tried not to think about what it meant that no one had responded to my frantic waving. Where there was a human structure, there would be probably be humans, or at least a telephone or other communication device.

Just trudge.

My step grew lighter as the ranger station grew nearer. It was still a long way off, but the closer I got, the more detail I could see, and I thought the various aerials and satellite dishes I could now make out were a good sign. Not some derelict abandoned in the 1960s, then—something I hadn't even allowed myself to consider until it was no longer a possibility—but a modern outpost where there would be people and a telephone and water.

The last few hundred yards were the worst. Some lookout, I thought, if they couldn't even see a lone woman and a dog coming toward them from miles and miles and miles away. Until I had to scale the rocks that looked distressingly like cliffs that led to the peak where the station actually sat, I kept hoping that some ranger—on a white charger? or, more likely, an SUV emblazoned with a forestry service logo—would come barreling down the hill and give us a lift back to his remote post. When this didn't happen, I plunged ahead, keeping myself going—up, up, up—with thoughts of the water cooler that likely dominated one corner, right next to the telephone, across from the bathroom and so on.

Tycho, for his part, followed valiantly wherever I led, though occasionally I'd swear I caught an incredulous glance, saying, *This is the craziest walk I've ever been on.* And, of course, he was right. Crazy didn't even begin to cover it.

Finally, we scaled the clifflike face—Tycho hopping and dodging lithely, putting all of his practice hunting lizards on the Malibu cliffs to good use; me pulling myself from boulder to boulder, ever upward—until we stood at the foot of the outlook. Attaining our goal made me feel more ridiculous than I'd ever thought possible, and even more out of my element.

From what I now saw, the cliff was on one side only—the side we'd come from. Murphy's Law. On the side directly opposite was a meadow sloping gently away from us, cut through by a paved road that ended where I stood, at the outpost's gangly legs. All we'd had to do to avoid that climb, I could see, was skirt the cliff face by a couple of hundred yards, and we would have hit the road. A Girl Guide, I knew, would have thought of that in an instant. But me? I'd just gone ever forward and up.

All of this—road, ranger station, meadow, relative civilization—was the good news. The bad news I could see with my own eyes: there was nothing remotely resembling a motor vehicle in sight. And, though I hoped that meant that the rangers worked in pairs and one had gone for a pizza, I doubted it. I just wasn't having that kind of day.

Although one approached the ranger station—outlook, outpost or whatever it was—via a very lockable metal stairway, the gates were open and unlocked. A steel platform at the top of the stairs formed an outlook veranda on all sides of the station itself. I gazed out at the darkening landscape, toward what I thought was Camp Arrowheart. If anyone was following me, I couldn't see them: the world out there looked peaceful. And empty.

The door to the station was closed. I knocked and, when no one answered, tried the door. "Please don't be locked. Please don't be locked." I said it out loud, a sort of prayer that I had no real hope of having answered. When I tried it, though, the doorknob turned in my hand and the door swung open. Tycho followed me inside. Things were definitely looking up.

The station was all one room and I could see at a glance that no one was there. The smell of coffee permeated the place and I caught the odors of good electronics and slightly musty wood. The water cooler was there, just about where I'd hoped it would be. And more. A Porta Potti sheltered behind a makeshift screen. A coffee mug stood on a windowsill and, when I checked, I could see the dregs of a fresh cup in the bottom. Someone had been here quite recently, looking out at the forest. Though they apparently hadn't seen me.

I stood at the window and looked back in the direction of Camp Arrowheart. Nothing but trees and rocks... No gun-toting madmen in sight at all. I resumed my examination of what I was now sure was a forest lookout.

There was a lot of stuff—mostly machines whose uses were alien to me, but I didn't care. Everything I needed was here, including a rotary dial phone that looked like it had been sitting there since the 1950s. I put a coffee mug of water down for Tycho and then poured one for myself. By the time I'd half finished mine, Tycho was looking at me for more, so I refilled his.

I'd just put Tycho's cup down for a third time and was trying to remember how to use a rotary phone when I heard a vehicle approaching fast. I thought about hiding, but a second glance around confirmed what I had already seen: it was a single room. No place to hide. Even the screen around the Porta Potti wouldn't provide much protection, especially with all of Tycho's breathing. Then there was the sound of rubber on metal and I knew someone was coming up the stairs. I suddenly wished I'd used the phone *before* gorging myself on water.

What would it be like to die out here? Who would ever know? These were the thoughts I was having as the door was flung open by a casually dressed man about my own age with a box in his hand. Miraculously, pizza. I could smell it.

He was clearly startled to see me standing there. And me? I felt like Goldilocks being discovered by a fairly gentle looking bear.

"The…the door was open," I said awkwardly.

"I usually don't lock it if I'm not going to be away long. No one comes here this time of day." He indicated the box, looking slightly embarrassed. "But I got hungry."

"Pizza in the wilderness." I must have said it with some wonderment because he chuckled.

"Naw, we're only five, maybe ten miles from Running Springs." A light seemed to dawn as he said this, and he took in my appearance, which couldn't, by that point, have been pretty. I'd pulled my hair up during the heat of the day, and limp portions of it had escaped its confines. My face was streaked with sweat, my knees and arms were scuffed and scraped from close encounters with rocks, and I'd snagged my T-shirt on an especially uncooperative and prickly bush. Nothing revealing, but it would have contributed to what had become a fairly scary ensemble.

"I got lost," I offered by way of explanation. "I

walked here—well, ran here—from over there." I pointed out the window, back the way I'd come. "From Camp Arrowheart."

He looked as though he didn't fully believe me. "Do you know how far that is?"

I nodded. "Far. Very far."

He drew me toward a desk, pulled out a map. "Look." He pointed at a green blip. "That's Arrowheart." Then he drew his finger across an ever lightening stretch of pale green nothingness, finally resting on a blip so pale green it was almost gray. "And here's us, Command Peak Tower. That's…let's see…six miles, I guess. Give or take. Not *so* far, from the sound of it, but not the most hospitable country. Not that way. Why'd you do that?"

"I got lost," I repeated. "And I think someone was chasing me." My voice grew quiet with the weight of what I'd seen. "I think I saw someone killed. At Arrowheart. And I think someone saw me. And I wanted to run and get help. I thought I was going back to my car, but…after a while I knew I was lost. And I just kept going."

"At Arrowheart? There's nothing there. It's been closed for years."

"Yes, I know. But please, call someone. I saw a shooting. Hours ago now," I said regretfully. It was probably too late to do anything about it, even if there had been time when it first happened. "Five hours ago, maybe a little more."

I was relieved when he put down his pizza and crossed to the phone. "I think Arrowheart is in Yucaipa's jurisdiction." Whatever, I thought, just get on the horn. "I'll see what they say."

Then to whoever answered his call, he said, "Yeah, this is Morgan Dunsford at Command Peak Tower. No, sir, I'm a volunteer fire lookout." Not a very good one, I thought. The forest could have gone up in flames while he went for his pizza. "I have a woman here claims she walked across from Arrowheart." Claims? "Claims someone was chasing her and that she saw someone shot. No, sir, I don't know that. Let me ask her."

He turned to me and said, "They want to know was the person chasing you the same one as got shot?"

I looked at him stupidly for a moment. "No. Different people. One shot. One chasing. He shot at me, too."

Dunsford turned back to the phone and the exchange went on for a while in that vein. Judging from his side of the conversation, I could tell that this particular wilderness wasn't exactly a hotbed of violent crime.

"Well," he said to me as he hung up, "they're sending someone out there to have a look-see."

I gazed at him expectantly and I guess he could tell I was waiting for something more, because he went on. "Well, they'll call us when they know something, I guess. Likely they'll want to get a statement or something from you, but Deputy Ganner didn't say."

"You have a car, right, Morgan?"

He looked at me suspiciously. "Sure," he admitted.

"Please, can you take me there?"

"I'm not so sure that would be a good idea, miss." I saw his eyes slide over the pizza box longingly.

"Listen, I have to get back to my car, anyway. If the cops don't want us around, I'll just get out of the way. My car is there. You can bring the pizza and eat it on the way."

He finally, if somewhat reluctantly, agreed to take me back to Camp Arrowheart, though not before he'd checked back in with the sheriff's station and made sure it was okay. As he was getting off the phone for the second time, I saw his eyes scan the horizon and stop. He gave a low whistle and pointed.

"Looks like there might be something to what you said."

I followed the motion of his hand and his eyes and I saw it, as well. Smoke. Blacker near the base, near the earth. A gray wisp farther up.

"Arrowheart?" I asked.

He just nodded as he applied himself, once again, to the phone. Clearly there were things expected of a fire lookout when fire was actually spotted. With the phone calls made, he grabbed his long-neglected pizza and we headed for the door. I noticed as he left that, this time, he locked up behind himself.

Morgan had a pickup truck and Tycho was forced to ride in the back ("My wife's allergic") which the dog actually seemed to think was pretty fun once I'd showed him where to sit. He noticed right away that he could stick his head over the side and smell all the good fast-moving forest smells while barely moving his head.

It turned out that Camp Arrowheart was a lot farther via road than it had been the way I'd come, cross-country. Five or six excruciating miles on foot, twenty comfortable miles in a car or truck. Though I wasn't complaining.

Morgan ate his pizza happily while we drove, and I helped him with a bit of it. There's nothing like an unexpected hike and a brush with death, I'd found, to help you work up an appetite. As we drove, Morgan explained that the outlooks in San Bernardino National Forest were no longer staffed by the forestry service. In fact, they functioned mainly as educational tourist attractions, keeping seasonal hours and maintained by volunteers who, like him, committed a certain number of hours each month to help forest visitors look for fires.

"That's why I wasn't in when you got there. We close at five. But my wife's visiting her sister up at Barstow and I thought I'd just have me a little pizza and watch the forest." He looked embarrassed. "Please, miss, do me a favor?"

"Sure," I said.

"Don't tell anyone I wasn't there when you arrived? Or that it was unlocked? I wasn't gone so long and I really didn't think anyone would come...."

"Sure," I repeated. "Anyway, who would I tell?" And I thought about the few minutes I'd been there alone at the lookout before he came back. The feeling of finding sanctuary and the exquisite taste of the water. It had been the most wonderful feeling of rescue, despite the fact that no one was there.

The only way I recognized Camp Arrowheart in the dark was the sight of my car still parked at the side of the road where I'd left it. This seemed miraculous in itself, as though it should have moved or been somehow damaged. Altered. But it sat there reflecting Morgan's headlights, benignly awaiting my return.

I pointed out the camp entrance to Morgan and we bumped along up it. I was glad he had a four-wheel drive. I wouldn't have wanted to attempt the walk in the dark, even accompanied.

We could smell something amiss before we arrived—the unmistakable odor of roasting wood. The place itself was transformed from the quiet ghost camp I'd visited in the afternoon and was alive with emergency vehicles and the men and women who service them: firefighters, sheriff cars, even an ambulance stood by, unneeded for the moment, but—I imagined—on the scene just in case.

The big lodge I'd walked through with Tycho earlier, the one with the kitchen and the big fireplace, was in flames. As Morgan and I pulled up, we could see that the fire was blazing madly, the firefighters just settling in. And it looked as though it had been burning for a while—there was little left to distinguish the building aside from its placement. By the light of the vapor lamps in the back of two of the sheriff's trucks, you could see that a chimney still stood, as well as some of the outer walls, but most of the place was gone.

I imagined that the wood that had been used to build this place some eighty years before wouldn't have taken much encouragement to go up in flames. And it was clear to me without asking or even looking very far that this fire *had* been encouraged. After what I'd seen happen here this afternoon, it seemed like too much of a coincidence that the place would have self-ignited.

While the firefighters were dealing with the blaze, sheriff's deputies were busy with other things. We could see four or six people in uniforms with able-looking flashlights scouting the perimeters of the area and checking through the smaller buildings. Securing the scene. As Morgan and I approached, a couple of them broke off their search and came toward us.

"You Dunsford?" one of the officers asked. They were Mutt and Jeff: one tall and lanky, the other short and with a look about him that said he loved doughnuts.

"Yeah," Morgan said. "This is Madeline Carter. She's the one says she saw what she saw."

"Have you found anything?" I asked.

The doughnut guy seemed to look at me for the first time. "Naw. But it's dark, don't think we'll find anything tonight." He addressed his partner. "Riley, get her statement, all right? And keep the dog in the truck." Tycho had just jumped down. "We don't want him messin' up a crime scene."

"Do you want me to show you where it was I saw the shooting?"

"Like I said, I don't think we'll find anything tonight. But I guess, since you're here, it couldn't hurt to know. Just, we can't get too close." He indicated the firefighters hard at work. "But you can show us the vicinity. Point, you know."

I couldn't, of course, be precise in showing them. It was, as doughnut man pointed out repeatedly, quite dark, even with the vapor lights and the dying flames. In any case, what I'd seen had been from a distance. They assured me that, if there was anything to find, they'd spot it in the morning.

The statement-taking was about as precise as the search seemed to be. It struck me that Riley kept forgetting to ask for pertinent details, so I filled him in as well as I could, but better than if he'd been left to his own devices.

"Do you guys believe me at all?" I asked at one point.

Riley looked surprised. "Sure. Why not? I mean, there's no body, there's no blood, the place is on fire and, from what Morgan says, you *walked* clean across to Command Peak when there was a perfectly good road to follow, but—hey—what's not to believe?" He said all of this without a trace of irony. It was the only thing that kept me from wanting to hit him.

I told him everything, or as much of everything as I knew. I gave him names, drew what relationships for them I could. And apparently Emily had been right: news of the Langton-related kidnapping hadn't been broadcast very far out of L.A. because Riley looked blank when I mentioned the connection, though he jotted what I said down in his notebook.

As he was finishing taking my statement, doughnut man rejoined us.

"Did you remember to ask what kind of car she drives?" he said, as though I wasn't standing right there.

"I drive a Chevrolet Malibu."

"What color?"

"Silver." I pointed to where I thought the road was, though, as I've proved, my sense of direction isn't always impeccable. "You probably saw it. You would have driven right past it to get in here. Why?"

Doughnut man hesitated for a second as though debating whether this was something he should mention or not. Then he shrugged, obviously having decided it didn't matter. "One of our guys, heading to the office, reported they saw a sports car in this area this afternoon. Would have been around one or two, right around the time you said this all happened. He said he wouldn't have even noticed, but it was a pretty special car. And a little different for up here."

I didn't have to ask; I volunteered. "Don't tell me, it was a chartreuse Porsche Boxster."

"Naw, but close. It was a Porsche all right. But it was green. Snot green."

Nineteen

Emily was amazed to see me standing on her doorstep. As much, I guess, by my disheveled state as by the actuality of me being there. Dropping in unannounced is *so* not an L.A. thing—there's just too much distance between places to make it really practical. Yet here I was.

"You look like shit," she said cheerfully as she invited me in. "I can't even believe it. I should take a picture. Cool, collected Madeline Carter looking like she's just gotten back from safari...and the lions won."

"Would you believe I was in the neighborhood and just thought I'd drop by?"

"Somehow, I would. But where the hell have you two been?" she asked, including Tycho in the conversation. His staying in the car at this point had seemed entirely out of the question. He needed a break as much as I did.

"In the San Bernardino National Forest," I answered blithely. "And look, I completely want to fill you in, but can I just be the guest from hell for half an hour and grab a shower? I gotta tell you, I feel a *lot* worse than I look."

"Not possible, doll. You look like hell. But, yeah, shower away. My bathrobe is on the back of the door. Use it if you want and we can *burn* your clothes. You and supermutt eaten in the last four or five days?"

"I had some truly awful pizza a few hours ago. Tycho got none. If you're offering, we're eating."

Emily has a massaging showerhead. A lot of images from that day—and even that week—are blurry, but that shower stands out in sharp and perfect relief: a lovely little island in an impossible storm. When I rejoined her in the living room, wrapped in her fluffy white bathrobe, I felt nearly human again.

Like mine, Em's apartment is not large. Both of us have sacrificed space in order to have view. However, where my vantage over Las Flores is a distant sort of overview, Emily's relationship with the Pacific is more intimate. Her place is at beach level and, even at night when you can't see much of anything, you can hear the waves.

While I was in the shower, Emily's living room had become an oasis. She'd gotten some incense burning and classical music was being beamed to us from the stereo. Somebody's requiem for something, I think. Soothing.

I settled into a comfy, deep green armchair almost large enough to be a love seat. Emily sat on the sofa with the coffee table between us laden with four kinds of cheeses nestled happily on a plate surrounded by two kinds of grapes. On another plate, she had placed slices of apple, mango and avocado. A third held vegetarian paté and good European crackers. Plus there was tea and two highball glasses with about a half inch of amber liquid in each.

"Scotch," she said, noticing my interest. "Single malt. Ballvenie. You looked like you could use it. I gave Tycho some cat food while you were in the shower. Now sit. Enjoy. And tell me what the hell is going on. And I mean now. Around mouthfuls. You have to pay for this kind of service, you know."

So, once again, I unburdened myself to my new friend. And once again she sat and listened, stopping me only occasionally with a clarifying question. A lot, I realized, had happened in a couple of days.

"You should have taken me," she said reproachfully when I was done.

"I should have. You're right. But weren't you on set?" I hoped she had been. It frankly hadn't occurred to me to involve her still further than she already was.

"You're right," she said, nodding. "I was on set. Still, you sound like you had a *lot* more fun than I did."

"Fun?"

"Sarcasm," she said, holding up one hand as though to ward me off. "Sorry. Kidding. So you seriously think you saw Ernie get whacked?"

"Whacked?"

"You know, shot, killed, murdered."

"I know what it means. It just sounded sort of odd coming out of your head. Sounds like movie talk." I smiled, thinking that, all things considered, Emily was entitled to movie talk. "But, yeah. I think it was Ernie. And I think he…got whacked."

"But the wife thought he cooked the whole scheme up?"

"Yeah." I'd forgotten that until now. Emily was right.

What I'd seen put things in a whole different light. "Looks like she was wrong." And then, what about her car? And it *had* to have been her car. How many chartreuse Porsches could be running around that neck of the woods? My money said not a lot. "Or maybe partly wrong? I don't know anymore. And here I still am, stumbling into all of this stuff. What the hell do I think I'm doing? Playing detective? And then I get *lost*. What if Ernie *is* dead? And what if he died because I didn't get there soon enough?"

"Christ, girl, don't beat yourself up about that. I mean, there might be things in here you can beat yourself up over…"

"Thanks."

"…but that's not one of them. What happened would have happened if you were there or not. From what you've said, it didn't happen *because* you were there, but in spite of it. Do you see what I'm getting at?"

I did. But still. "If I'd been a little quicker…"

"C'mon, Madeline. You know that's just goofy. A man with a gun. And you. There's *nothing* you could have done without endangering yourself." Which I thought was fairly perceptive of Emily, not that that's surprising. But I hadn't even mentioned feeling somewhat guilty that I hadn't rushed into the fray and somehow pulled ol' Ernie out. Maybe I hadn't even really admitted it to myself. Yet there it was, just as Emily had laid it out. And she was right, of course. But still.

I told Emily I wanted to check in with Tyler to tell him where his dog was and talk to him about what Anne Rand had told me, plus clear my own telephone messages. I'd been gone all day and hadn't given a single thought to the market. And no withdrawal.

Tyler had news of his own and didn't wait for mine. "We got another note, Madeline. This afternoon."

"That's wonderful, Tyler." Then I hesitated. "Is that wonderful?"

"I hope so. They're asking for money this time."

"How much?"

"That's the weird part—ten grand."

Ten thousand dollars wasn't very much money. The barbecue last week had probably cost him more than that.

"What do you have to do?"

"Just take the cash down to the mailbox at the bottom of the hill tomorrow night at 11:00 p.m. Tape it on, like they've been doing. And there'll be a letter taped to the box telling me where I can go and pick her up."

"That's not good."

"That's what I thought. Because it's not like an exchange or anything. So they might grab the money and not give me Jennifer. But, like you said, it's not much money. I have to take the chance."

I hung up the phone without telling him any of my news: about Anne Rand or about maybe finding boyfriend person. With the latter, I was afraid that he might go down to the surf shop himself, do some yelling and blow any chance I had of contacting the kid. And the stuff with Rand seemed too complex for the moment, involving as it did the necessity for explaining why a P.I. had been watching me at the house.

I got off the phone feeling positive, though. To me it looked more and more like Jennifer was pulling the strings on this one. With extorting ten thousand dollars from her father, maybe she was getting close to resolving it. The two of them could worry about the discipline problems that obviously entailed. I didn't put the situation out of my mind, but at the moment, it didn't look like there was a lot I could do.

My machine let me know I had four messages.

Mechanical voice: "Six-thirty. Pee, Emm."

Hiya, sweetie. I wanted to let you know I was sorry about the other day.

Mom. I hadn't called her back.

You've told me often enough how you feel about things. And I understand it. Really, I do. Even if it didn't seem like it. But listen, kitten, part of it is just a mom's pride, believe that. I know you're the best stockbroker in the world—I tell everyone that, too. And it doesn't seem right that the best stockbroker in the world can't broker her mom's stocks, if you get what I'm saying.

Even though I'm not a broker anymore.

Oh, I know you say you're not a broker anymore, dear, but no matter what, I know how these things work. I mean, a doctor can quit being a doctor, but he can still save lives, if you know what I mean and I'll bet you do.

Anyway, despite all of this rambling…

And my mom can *ramble.*

…I just wanted to tell you that I do understand and I do love you and I know everything will turn out for the very best.

Oh, Mom, if you could see the day I've had.

Seattle is lovely, though it's been a bit wet.

This was a news flash?

I was at Nordstrom today and bought this really lovely, sky-blue jacket with very careful fur trim. I bought it for me, but it made me think of you.

As ridiculous as that sounds, there was something very warm and homelike about this statement. For a second it made me smile. And it made me miss my mom. Isn't it goofy how the oddest things can do that?

Well, it's dinnertime and I'd hoped to catch you, but I think your not being home this time of night is maybe a good thing. I hope you tell me about him. Call soon!

Mothers. The slightest fluctuation of my estrogen levels and Mom is on the alert. If I'm out after 9:00 p.m. she starts phrasing my wedding invitations and planning my trousseau *and* a layette. Dinnertime away and she's at least hopeful. And while none of that is strictly true, it's probably not far off, either.

Mechanical voice: "Six-forty-five. Pee, Emm."

Hey, Madeline. Your voice on the machine sounds really good. Sounds just like you.

Steve. I'd never heard his voice on the phone before, but I liked the sound of it. Somehow deep and vulnerable all at once. Yummy.

It's possible that you're going to think this call is incredibly pathetic. I've decided to risk it. I've been home from work exactly half an hour and I keep thinking about you, so I thought I'd call. Well, you're not there but maybe when you do get there, you can call me.

There was a hesitation, then:

I thought it was nice you came by the office today. Sweet. Thanks. Bye.

Not pathetic. No. *Charming,* that was the word. He was

charming. So why was it that I kept, in one way or another, avoiding him? Strange. I'd have to think about it.

Mechanical voice: "Seven-oh-five. Pee, Emm."

Hello, Madeline, this is Alex Montoya. Dinner last night was lovely. I enjoyed your company very much.

I shot Emily a glance. "It's raining men."

Did her ears perk up? "What?"

"I'll tell you later."

I had hoped we might dine again tomorrow evening. Saturday. Please call me at your convenience.

His accent was perfectly charming. *He* was perfectly charming.

I called Steve. He answered on the first ring.

"Yello."

"Hi Steve. It's Madeline. From Langton today…"

"I *know* who you are." I could hear the smile in his voice.

My voice smiled back. "I'm glad."

"What are you doing right this second?"

"I'm at my friend Emily's house in Huntington Beach. I had a sweaty day, so I just grabbed a shower and we've been sitting here having snacks and blabbing and drinking good Scotch so, of course, that made me think of calling you."

"You're seriously in Huntington Beach?"

"Yeah. Why?"

"Because I'm only a couple of beaches away. I live in Laguna." Which made sense. I'd completely forgotten that, like Brea, Huntington Beach is in Orange County.

He seemed to expect some kind of response to this, so I said, "Oh, cool."

"Yeah, very. So what are you guys up to tonight?"

"Well, actually, I'm pretty tired. I ended up having an exceedingly busy day." Talk about understatement. "And I guess we thought we'd just blab for a while longer and I'd crash here."

"Now don't even *think* about putting me off again, Madeline. It's not happening, you hear?" He was cheery, but firm. "Look, we'll do something low-key. Is Emily the girl who was with you the other night?"

Emily is thirty-eight. "She's the one."

"Cool. My roommate is home tonight, too. We were just wondering what to do with ourselves and now we'll have plans. The four of us can go out to dinner."

I looked at the clock in the living room. "Steve, it's *nine-thirty*. Everything will be closed."

"Are you kidding? You're at the beach. Things are just getting warmed up."

"I'll have to ask Emily," I said doubtfully. "Hang on." Then, while shaking my head no, I addressed her. "Steve wants to know if we want to have dinner with him and his roommate. They're in Laguna."

I am *such* an idiot sometimes. I mean, of course she saw me shaking my head. But she said, "What's his roommate's name?"

Which I didn't have to translate, because Steve heard. "Tristan Kelly. Tell her he's a writer."

This was becoming too high school. I parroted what Steve had said, adding—to both of them now—"I don't have anything here to wear."

I got replies in stereo. "Emily will lend you something" and "I'll find you something." So I was pretty much outvoted. No one really seemed to care that I was extremely tired and had had a very hard day. In fact, when I'd hung up, having agreed that the two of us would meet Steve and Tristan at a little restaurant not far from Emily's place, she assured me that getting out and having a bit of fun was "precisely what I needed" and that it would "do me the world of good." Which she and I both knew translated to: "Steve is extremely hot so there's a good chance his roommate will be hot, and there's no way you're screwing up this perfectly good opportunity."

And understand this: high school isn't just for sixteen-year-olds. At least, not the social aspects. Given the right associations and the right set of circumstances, any woman—regardless of age—can turn into the sort of mindless, giggling party animal she was just post puberty. I've seen my mom get together with some of her school friends—this more than four decades after they'd left school. And, man, was that embarrassing. So with Emily running around blabbing about makeup and what to wear and "I hope he's cute," pretty soon, tired or not, I got into the spirit.

Even though Emily's closet was not nearly as well stocked as Brian's appeared to have been, she pulled happy little sundresses—the kind that look cute but don't need to be precisely the right size to work—out of her closet for both of us. We *were* staying at the beach, we reasoned, we could look beachy if we wanted. And even though my feet were bigger than Emily's, she had one pair of sandals that didn't look ridiculous on me and wouldn't hurt, provided I wasn't forced to walk too far.

We left Tycho with another can of Em's cat's food, lots more water, instructions not to eat Puss Puss and we were off.

I've always tried to make it a point not to date men who are prettier than I am. It just keeps things simpler. With Steve, I knew, I was on the point of throwing that rule out.

The guys were already at the restaurant when we got there, and Steve looked exceptionally fine. In a faintly ridiculous Hawaiian shirt, khaki shorts and sandals, he appeared tan and lean. I'm not someone who undresses men with her eyes, but in Steve's case—since I'd actually seen him in that condition, and quite recently, when I thought about it—I made an exception. From the expression on his face when he saw me, I thought he might be doing the same. Our eyes met over a mutual blush, which would be cute if you weren't the one inside it.

I could tell right away that Emily liked Tristan, which was sort of a fun bonus. We sat at a round table for four, boy, girl, boy, girl. Tristan and Emily looked like a couple from the first moment. I wondered what I had set in motion. It turned out he was a screenwriter working on projects of about the same magnitude as Emily's, which was to say no one was throwing Oscars at either of them quite yet. And they'd worked with some of the same people, so they had tons in common. He was maybe thirty-three or thirty-four, but looked older, so the whole age thing seemed less heinous than the difference between Steve and me. Anyway, what with the related lines of work, the people and places in common and the fairly genuine spark that could probably be seen from the other side of the room, before very long Steve and I might as well have been alone, because Tristan and Emily sure were.

"I knew this was a good idea," Steve said, indicating the two of them with his glass of cabernet shiraz and a satisfied grin. "In fact, when I met Emily at the Hyatt, I thought of Tris."

"He seems nice."

"Yeah, he's a good guy. You know, both of us are kind of past the place in our lives where you have to have a roommate, but we get along so well we thought we'd keep it going until there was some reason not to." He hesitated, then said, "I've just been realizing, I know next to nothing about you. Which, when you think about it, seems pretty strange."

"I guess. I don't know much about you, either."

"It's true, but I have a feeling there's less to know." I thought for a second he was talking about my vastly deeper reserves of experience due to my age. But, of course, he was not. "After all, you're the one continually shrouded in mystery."

"I guess it must seem that way," I admitted. "But, really, it's only this week that's made me mysterious. Honest. And then, in some ways, only as things relate to you." I knew that sounded cryptic, but I was tired, the wine was good, the company sweet. "And I know I promised you the whole story, but not tonight, okay Steve? As it is, I think I might have a tough time keeping my face out of my soup."

"Okay. Agreed. Tonight is not for explanations. Despite our shared history and our present company, tonight can be our first date. So let's play first date. Tell me the things that aren't mysterious about Madeline Carter."

And so I did. I told him about growing up in Seattle and falling in love with the stock market and New York, and how I'd finally wound up on the sunny coast. He told me about coming of age in Idaho and moving to L.A. at nineteen to study at the Guitar Institute—he'd wanted to be a bass player—and how he'd wound up at USC studying business, instead. "Because of a girl," he told me, straight-faced, and I almost, but not quite, believed him. "I needed an MBA to impress a girl."

"Did it work?"

"Naw. Took too long. In the end she left me for a drummer."

We had a nice evening. The four of us left the restaurant at—oh, I don't know, a million o'clock or so—and went back to Emily's place, got Tycho and took him for a walk. The beach, of course, but he needed to be emptied. And then the guys walked us home and said a sweet and chaste good-night. As Steve had promised, it truly had been like a first date.

After they'd left I was subjected to a full half hour of "Tristan said this," and "Tristan did that," before Emily finally conceded that the day was sufficiently full and I could now go peacefully off to slumberland on the sofa.

It felt as though I had barely gotten to sleep when a telephone woke me up. I propped myself up on one elbow in time to see Emily tiptoe into her office, where she didn't pick up the phone. I could hear a masculine voice while Emily screened but still didn't pick up. She popped her head out after a couple of minutes. "Madeline, you up?" I nodded sleepily. "Come here. I think you should hear this."

It was a youthful male voice. "Hey, um, this is Corby Frye. Stacey at The Curl told me to call you. You can get me at..." He left a number and I recognized the Malibu exchange. "I'm not here all the time but the machine will be on."

Emily and I looked at each other. "I know it's not particularly telling," she said, "but I thought you'd want to hear the voice."

I nodded. "And it's two o'clock in the morning. Who leaves messages at 2:00 a.m.?"

Emily shrugged. "Surfer dudes, I guess. A'it?"

"I guess. So now what do I do?"

"You think it's possible he's involved?" Emily looked thoughtful.

"Sure. But it's possible he's not, too. But if Jennifer *was* behind it herself, it would make sense she'd have her boyfriend involved or that he'd at least know where she was."

"But I just don't get it, Madeline. Jennifer seems like such a nice kid. And we really did have fun at the movies that time."

"Yeah, we did. But it's not about us. It's about her dad, I think. And Tasya."

"One of those classic cries for attention?" Emily shook her head. "I just don't buy it. This is pretty extreme."

"For you and me, maybe. But in this world..." I shrugged. "Think about it. Your whole life is around making movies since you were a kid. And sometimes what you want and need is bumped back or overlooked because of something that is, essentially, make-believe. And then your parents split up and, not long after, your dad goes to Ibiza to make a movie, and comes back with a beautiful new wife young enough to be your sister."

"Ibiza?" Emily echoed.

"Yeah, I know. See, it's sort of bizarre. And if all of that is your reality, maybe you do some weird things for attention."

"Or," Emily said thoughtfully, "for money."

"Money? They have lots of money."

Emily shook her head. "No. He has lots of money. She's a kid. She probably gets an allowance or something. And remember," Emily said excitedly, warming to her theory, "she told us she wants to go to acting school but that Tyler was against it. Maybe she knew she was getting kicked out of school and it moved her personal deadline up."

"But ten grand." I shook my head. "Where would that get you?"

"From her perspective, remember, it would get you to New York."

We were both quiet for a couple of beats, thinking our own thoughts. Finally, I said, "I think I have a plan."

"Uh-oh."

"I don't even think it's dangerous. Tyler said he has to make his cash drop tomorrow night at eleven. I want you to call boyfriend person first thing in the morning and tell him you want to audition him for a role in a surfer movie you're doing."

"Pre-screen," Emily said matter-of-factly.

"Pardon?"

"For commercial roles, the first meeting is called an audition. For film work it's a pre-screen."

I looked at Emily steadily for a moment, trying to determine if she was kidding or not. She wasn't.

"Well, actually," she said thoughtfully, continuing the thread, "for a pre-screen there has to be sides." I was still looking at her. "You know. Sides of dialogue. Some kind of little script, even if it's short. And we won't have that."

I looked at her levelly. "I don't think it matters."

"Well, it should be accurate, you know. What I tell him should be right."

"Whatever. Just call him, okay? We're talking about a surfing instructor. If you tell him to meet you at a car wash in Reseda he'll be there, as long as he knows it's something to do with his being in a movie."

Emily nodded, resigned. But I knew that, whatever she ended up telling him, it would probably be something technically correct. "Why me?"

"Well, it won't make much difference which of us calls, but you know movie lingo. Like all this pre-screen, side business, for instance. If he asks you something tricky, you'll know how to answer it."

"True. Okay, where is this fictional pre-screen going to take place?"

"Malibu Center Mall. The coffee place there."

"Auditions don't work that way. Or pre-screens. They never take place in public like that."

"Do you think he'd want to take the chance?"

"Good point," Emily said. "Am I actually going to audition him for something? Because I can, you know. I've been through that process before."

"No," I said thoughtfully, riffing as I went along, "because you're not going to go. Neither am I. He's going to be stood up. Then when he storms off home in a huff, I'm going to follow him."

"And you think that's where Jennifer will be?"

"Sure," I said, with more confidence than I felt at that moment. "He's a surfer. I don't think it'll be a sophisticated operation."

"But then what? Do we just storm in and grab her?"

"We?"

Emily looked surprised. "Sure. I'm coming."

I gazed at her, not saying anything.

"Duh! I'm *coming*."

"Okay," I said finally. "Actually, that could be good. With two of us, one could run in and divert him, while the other goes in and grabs Jennifer."

"Do you think we should call the police or anything?" Emily asked suddenly, as though she'd just thought of it.

"Oh, probably."

"But we're not going to, are we?"

"I don't think so."

When Emily and I finally quit yakking and I got back to sleep, I dreamed of Paul. Paul Westbrook. A blood red dream. Not of him chasing me through the wilds of the San Bernardino Forest, but Paul as I'd last seen him, in college: on his knees on the bed, his face contorted with cruel laughter.

I woke in the half dark that is the best that Huntington Beach, at the beach, can provide. The dream didn't wake me, but Tycho's big wet tongue on my face did. He was doing his Tycho-best to comfort me. I must have cried out.

"S'okay, boy. I'm okay. Go back to sleep." He snuffled my face closely as though reassuring himself I was, in fact, all right, then padded back to the position he'd taken up on a small rug between me and the door. I think he was asleep as soon as he tucked his nose under his tail. I wasn't so lucky.

Paul Westbrook. I hadn't expected to see him again. Ever. And certainly not in such weird circumstances. Though I wasn't a hundred percent sure it had been him, in my heart there was little doubt. Like when you see a stranger—in a mall or at a restaurant—and you think could that be so and so? You doubt it and, inevitably, it turns out not to be them at all. But when you *do* recognize someone, you might still doubt, but on another level you're sure from the first moment. That's how I felt about this Paul sighting. I didn't want it to be, yet it was.

I had little doubt that the Paul Westbrook on the business card Arianna had shown me was the Paul I'd known. And the significance of that name in Arianna's—and formerly Ernie's—possession was now fairly clear. Paul had been a part of this all along. I felt I should have known that. Time passes, you change and you think everyone around you has changed, as well. And in this case, it looked like they had. But the thing between Paul and Ernie seemed to have deepened, not been outgrown.

Just seeing Paul again had brought back a lot of things that I thought I'd buried pretty efficiently. Paul and Ernie. Ernie and Paul. In the quiet of the early morning hours, with a little sleep behind me, things were beginning to make sense. And then there was Anne Rand. What had *that* been about? I knew I had to see Arianna. And that meant I had to find her. But first, there were some things I needed to do.

I looked at the clock. Six-thirty. Too early to call the sheriff's office to discover what they'd found back at Camp Arrowheart. That would have to wait until later. But early meant that traffic would be light and I could probably make it home in under an hour. I pulled Emily's sundress and sandals back on, balled up my crusty clothes and stuffed them into a plastic shopping bag I found under the sink (only half kidding when I thought I should probably just go ahead and burn them), left a note thanking Emily for her shelter, clothes and friendship, and reminding her to call me as soon as she'd talked to Corby. And then, with a single and predictable stop at Starbucks for a latte to go, Tycho and I were back on the road.

Twenty

I was surprised to see the FedEx package stuffed into my door when I came home. I flipped it over as I unlocked the place: the sender was listed as S. Shoenberger, Lawrenceville, New Jersey. Sarah.

I couldn't imagine what she might be sending me, but I wanted to steel myself before I ripped the package open, anticipating something that would make me sob. Pictures, maybe, of me and Jackson. Or even a nice portrait of Jack. Or Jack and Sarah.

I plopped the unopened FedEx pack in the middle of the living room floor and circled it uneasily while I went about getting myself together: putting my forest-stained clothes from the day before into the laundry basket, getting the coffee machine ready for the day. When I got out of the shower, fresh-brewed coffee perfuming the air, the FedEx pack glinted at me evilly from where I'd left it.

"Oh, this is stupid," I said aloud. Tycho thumped his tail, mutely agreeing. I hunkered down next to the package, ripped it open, then sat staring at the contents. I knew what I was looking at, but not why Sarah would be sending it to me.

Then a note in her neat, schoolteachery handwriting caught my eye. Her tone was formal, but I understood that.

Dear Madeline,

I can imagine that this package will come as a surprise to you. When you mentioned the name on the phone, it was unexpected, and even then I couldn't be sure. It seemed like too much of a coincidence to believe. I had to go and check.

And now you have everything in your hand. Jackson's "weekend project," as he liked to call it. You'll see he had his eye on your old friend for quite some time. You'll note from the clippings I've added (the most recent ones) that he might even have indirectly had a hand in what happened to Jack.

Madeline, this was Jackson's pet project for so long, I almost couldn't stand to let it go. But it sounds like it will be more useful to you than the emotional flaying is doing for me.

I hope you're well. Come see us soon. Failing that you might have the three of us land on your doorstep one day soon. We'll make you take us to Disneyland.

Love…

Sarah

Jackson's pet project floored me. A regular FedEx envelope filled almost to bursting with company stats, newspaper and magazine clippings and SEC filings. These last were the most interesting, mainly SEC exemptions that several of the companies Ernie had been involved with had applied for and mostly gotten. Exemptions that had been draped in innocent language that, if viewed a certain way, might have had far-reaching effects for the companies involved and their shareholders.

From the look of the paperwork that spilled out of that FedEx package, Jackson had been following Ernie's career and the trades related to it for at least the past five years and, from the type of stuff he'd been collecting, he'd been doing it in order to prepare a case for the SEC.

I knew I hadn't mentioned Ernie to Jack for years, almost a decade. When the two of us had started at Merriwether Bailey we'd both been so young and my Ernie wounds were still relatively fresh. I thought Jack had forgotten all about it, the way you forget someone else's bad headache. I touched the papers again, almost reverently, feeling Jack in the sharp edge of every page.

"He didn't forget," I said softly, realizing there were tears on my cheeks. I don't even know when I'd started crying.

I could tell the items that Sarah had contributed, because they'd been added after Jackson's death. One was a photocopy of Jackson's killer's final account statement with Merriwether Bailey—I could only guess how Sarah had gotten her hands on *that*—and it indicated a huge loss on Salt Spring Technologies, the company I knew Ernie had been CEO of about two jobs ago. While SST was rising, the shooter had Jackson buy a huge whack of shares on his behalf, against Jack's advice.

When the stock had started to flag, Jackson had told him again to sell, but the client had him buy still more. I'd probably never know how Jackson had managed to connect Ernie to these shaky deals; the press hadn't thus far. But it stood to reason that if Jack had, there were likely others who had, as well. That alone might have been a good enough reason for Ernie to want to make himself disappear.

With shards of Jackson's handwriting and signs of his deep interest all around me, I could feel his presence very strongly. It was as if he was in the room. I could almost hear his voice: *We'll get him, Carter.* I whispered it back to him now: "We'll get him, Jack."

Along with being a fairly complete dossier on at least the top end of Ernest Carmichael Billings's shady dealings, Jack's files presented me with possibilities for connections that I'd previously missed.

I'd been looking at what was apparent, and supposing I had the whole picture. Jack's files made me think about Paul and Ernie, how they'd been when I'd known both of them well. Over this I juxtaposed the snippet of conversation I'd heard between them yesterday. It felt like a metaphor. What I'd heard wasn't real, just as it was quite possible that what could be seen from the surface over the years between college and now wasn't what had been happening at all. Layers of deception. Shades of gray. Sleight of hand and weight of air and nothing is what it seems.

Here's what could be seen on the surface: Paul and Ernie graduate. Paul goes away and does whatever it is he was supposed to have been doing but—and here's the salient bit—he does it separate from Ernie. Ernie grows up to become this savvy business dude who saves poor little struggling companies. Boys grow up. After a while you outgrow each other, go separate ways, lead your life. That's what's *supposed* to happen.

But I had a sudden sense—call it gut, intuition, whatever you want—that, when it came to these guys, what the world saw didn't reflect anything real at all.

In support of the material I now had from Jack via Sarah, I did a Web search on Ernie. Fortunately, his name was not Bill Smith or I would have been out of luck. But there are simply not a lot of Ernest Carmichael Billingses running around out there. Every search response I got was relevant. And, with the exception of a few society notices announcing his wedding, engagement and the death of his father-in-law, they were all about his various daring and impressive business exploits. I jotted down the names of the companies as they came up, and downloaded whatever data I could find on his techniques as a savior. Then, armed with dates, I went to my market data and started plugging stuff in and—with Jackson's research filling in a few holes—piecing things together.

As I had expected, the surface data looked good. Without exception, Ernie had brought each company he signed on with greater glory and faster returns. All lined up, though, it seemed weird. The first company had been just a couple of years after our graduation. Too early, really, for him to be brought in as a superstar, but there it was.

Publicly traded, the company made outboard motors

and lawnmowers, and their paper was in such bad shape when Ernie came on board that they were in danger of being delisted. Then some virtuoso management shuffling, a sharp eye here, a well-placed kick there, and within six months their papers were pristine, the stock exchange was smiling at them again and Ernie's face was getting plastered in minor business rags as the wunderkind of the turnaround.

That was on the surface, what you saw at a casual, even careful, glance. But the market data showed a different story. I noted that, without exception, trading volumes went up almost as soon as Ernie took over the CEO's chair. Most of this new volume didn't show up as insider action—that is, trades made by officers of the companies in question and filed with EDGAR, the Securities and Exchange Commission's Electronic Data Gathering, Analysis and Retrieval system—which meant that, one way or another, the new volume was coming from outside of the company.

Within three months, the company's price-earnings ratio had gone supernova. That ratio divides a publicly traded company's market price over earnings per share and indicates a security's market price in relation to its earnings. It tends to be a pretty good indicator of what lies in store for the stock price's immediate future. After only four months with Ernie at the helm of this little company, the security was trading at a very impressive five times trailing earnings. At the end of the year, with the company looking much happier, at least on paper, he had replaced himself as CEO and resigned to take another post. Where the same thing happened again. Only this time faster, with results even more out of synch with the company's financials. And once again, the business press chose not to notice this. Instead, they plastered Ernie's face on ever more impressive articles and magazine covers. Wunderkind. Golden Boy.

All pretty on paper, but if you looked very carefully and took a couple of artful leaps you could draw a different conclusion, just as Jack had.

To really manipulate the market, you'd need a talented and connected outside person. One that the rest of the world wouldn't necessarily associate you with. That was what Jack couldn't have known, if he'd suspected it. Even Ernie and Paul having been at university together wouldn't be enough of a connection. It was Harvard. I'd graduated with a lot of people I was sure I'd never seen before, as had Paul and Ernie. There was nothing post-university that I could find to connect the two of them to each other.

What *was* easy to track was the meteoric corporate rise of Ernest Carmichael Billings. And, as the years went by, the corporate recoveries he was responsible for got increasingly more dramatic and took ever shorter periods of time.

Understandably, before very long Ernie was a hot property, and articles about him started blabbing about all the companies that were trying to snag him. After a decade of this, and with a lot of experience under his belt and a great record, he could pick and choose whom he worked for. At that point he could, I'm sure, have worked anywhere in the world he wanted to. He would have had offers from all over the U.S. and there would have been companies in Hong Kong and Montreal and Leeds and *everywhere* competing for a year or so of his time. They would have been big high-techs and resources and brand-name electronics. And, out of all comers, he chose a glass manufacturer based in Culver City, California. The math of all of that really wasn't very good. It was practically nonsensical.

The more I thought about it, ran the numbers, looked at the old clippings and Jack's research and put everything together, the more I started thinking that Ernie, and most likely Paul, had decided on Langton because it could represent the big piñata. A company so lame, so badly managed, so undervalued and so out of the mainstream that it was ripe for their biggest, most outrageous and richest scam yet. They'd short-sell the shit out of it, arrange a high-profile kidnapping of the CEO. And, yes, the more I thought about it, the more sense it made—they'd even arrange for a witness—me—to see that CEO killed. Just thinking about what that little piece of news would do to the stock price Monday morning made my head hurt.

So Ernie, I decided, wasn't dead. Just hiding out someplace new. Waiting to reap the rewards of his ill-gained labor. I wasn't sure how they'd arranged to have me there to see their little show, but by now I was pretty sure there must have been blanks in the gun, both when Ernie was "shot" and when Paul took a shot at me. Which would, of course, let me off the hook for allowing him to die in front of me, but my guilt was just replaced with anger. I was so confident that I was right, I would have put money on it. Ernie was not dead. He was alive. I could feel it in my bones and, certainly, in my gut.

The ringing of the telephone stopped the spiral of my thoughts.

"The cock crows at noon. The sun shines on the elevator shaft."

"Emily."

"*Da*. I've got ze microfilm." Her Russian accent was really quite terrible.

"I take it you got hold of Corby."

"*Da*, he ees expecting to be auditioned at high noon."

I checked my watch; it was nine-thirty now. "Perfect. You want to meet me up here, or at the bottom of the hill?"

"Your place, please. I want to see the teeny guest house I've heard so much about."

"Done. See you when you get here."

Being on the telephone reminded me that I had yet to return Alex's call. And, with everything I'd been thinking about relating to Jackson's package, I felt a sudden urge to speak with him. I dug out his office number and dialed it quickly, before I could change my mind.

"Hi, Alex," I said when he again answered his own phone. "It's Madeline Carter."

"Madeline! It's lovely to hear from you. I enjoyed our dinner the other night very much."

I flushed a little at that. His interest in me was so obviously romantic. And, while I liked him well enough, and under other circumstances might even have been interested, my attention had been…diverted.

"I did, too. Sorry not to return your call sooner, Alex. I've been so preoccupied with a…with a business matter that I've not been good about returning social calls this week. Forgive me."

"But of course," he said instantly, and I had to smile. That old-world charm and courtliness was practically irresistible. Which wasn't why I was phoning him.

"To be honest, Alex, this call isn't entirely to return your call, either. It's the business matter I was just referring to. And I guess I mentioned it the other night, as well." I took a deep breath before I went on. Just say it, Madeline. "I've become embroiled in something rather ugly—criminal, I think—involving an old…school friend of mine and a company he has recently been made CEO of and— How can I put this…?" Because it suddenly all sounded so ridiculous, out loud and hanging on the telephone line between us. Preposterous, really. And what did I think Alex could do? And yet…

"You think this person is a corporate psychopath?" Alex asked. And he didn't sound skeptical or annoyed or anything. Which gave me the courage to continue.

"I do. And, actually, from what you've said and from…things that have been happening, I'm pretty sure about it. Except one thing I wanted you to clarify, if you could, that would be helpful to me."

"If I can, Madeline, I will."

"Well, the other night you mentioned a 'career arc' that is not unusual in psychopaths. You said they might start with small things and then work their way up."

"It is, I think, because of the boredom," he said, as though I'd caught up with him in midlecture. "When a thing is done—accomplished, as it were—it's no longer interesting to revisit. For the psychopath that seems to be true of people as well as activities, substances and so on."

"But is it true also for corporate psychopaths? Or does it manifest itself in different ways?"

"How do you mean?"

"Well, you talked about the psychopath starting with stealing from the corner store, then maybe stealing a bike as a teenager and then graduating to larger ticket items. But a *corporate* psychopath would have a different career arc, don't you agree?"

"I do, but go on. It sounds as though you have a hypothesis. Let's hear it."

"Well, I think it's all about environment. Accessibility." I thought of some of the stories Ernie had told me when we were first together, during our honeymoon period when we were just getting acquainted. Stuff that I'd maybe thought was cute at the time, with the blinders of new love upon me. "Maybe he'd start out by cheating at Monopoly or stealing the money from his brother's piggy bank. Then maybe move up to manipulating his paper route for his own profit, taking money from his mother's purse, cheating on high school exams, that sort of thing."

"All of this is possible," Alex agreed. "But none of it conclusive."

"But what I'm thinking is this—all that truly separates the corporate psychopath from the other kind is opportunity. Advantage. Perhaps intelligence, but also education. But the regular, everyday psychopath mostly gets put out of circulation. You said you thought prison psychopath populations were as high as twenty-five percent."

"That's right."

"But is that just because corporate psychopaths behave in a manner that's acceptable in their environment? Acceptable and maybe even encouraged? Is it not even possible that, to get to the top at a lot of big companies, it's almost *necessary* to display that type of behavior?"

"This is something I've noted as well. There is even a theory that psychopathy as found in certain individuals is a genetic influence, one that is perhaps there to help ensure that individual's survival."

"Please, Alex. I don't even wanna hear that."

He laughed. "Science is full of things none of us want to hear, Madeline."

"I see what you're getting at, though. But the career arc, Alex. On the surface, it sounds as if your average jail-bound psychopath is more dangerous than the corporate kind. That the corporate ones will do ruthless stuff for advancement, maybe have crummy marriages and terrible personal lives, but the really awful stuff is left for other, commoner psychopaths. But that's not true, is it?"

"No, it's not."

"In fact, Alex, I'm thinking the opposite may be true. That because he is more cunning, more versed in the way the world works and perhaps more practiced, the corporate psychopath could potentially be even more dangerous than the noncorporate kind. Because he's smart and educated. I think—and this is why I'm calling—that sort of corporate psychopath would be capable of…well, anything. Do you agree?"

"And we're still really talking hypothetically, aren't we, Madeline?" Alex asked, with the professional caution of one who knows his way around the mysteries of the ivory tower.

"Sure. Yes. Of course."

"Well then, I'd have to say yes. I agree. The corporate psychopath is capable of—as you say—anything at all."

Twenty-One

I had to find Arianna. When we'd met, I couldn't imagine why I'd want to call her, so I'd given her my phone number and not asked for hers. Between that and the forgetting-phone-numbers-with-Steve fiasco, I knew this was yet another personal flaw that was going to require work.

Now I *needed* to talk to Arianna, and I had absolutely no way of getting in touch with her. And then I remembered a billboard across from the café where I'd met with her. And then the back of a bus bench. A raven-haired woman, beautiful in a carefully preserved kind of way. I couldn't think of her name or the company she'd been with, but I had a feeling she'd be The One.

First things first, though. Emily and I had a date with a surfer, sort of. At exactly ten-thirty, Tycho chuffed when he heard a knock at the door.

"Open!" I called from the bedroom.

Then Emily's voice. "Is that a good idea?"

"Please—" I popped my head out and indicated she

should take a stool "—don't start with me on that one. I've heard it all before."

Being reminded of that made me think of Jennifer and what we were about to do.

"Are we crazy?" I asked Emily as I joined her in the living room. "Is this a crazy thing we're contemplating?"

"Of course." She laughed. I could see the signs of the short night on her face, but she looked excited at the prospect of the adventure before us. "And that's why I'm here—to keep you from bailing. And you're here to keep me from bailing. But the two of us together can do this, no sweat." If she was the least bit apprehensive, she didn't show any signs of it. I supposed I probably looked the same: calm and resolved.

We both took our cars to the Malibu Center Mall and parked within sight of the entrance to the café with fifteen minutes to spare. My car was closer, and Emily joined me for our vigil.

We saw the green-gold van pull into the parking lot. If I needed further confirmation, I checked the plate number on the van against the one Anne Rand had given me in Redlands. A match. There could be no doubt this was Corby's van.

"There he is!" Emily said needlessly.

"Oh, shit," I said as we watched him cruise for a parking spot. "Jennifer's with him." This wasn't something we'd expected. "What if she goes in with him?"

"She won't," Emily said. "This is supposed to be an audition, remember? He'll leave her in the car."

Emily was right. Corby parked the van on the other side of the lot. We could see him give Jennifer a quick kiss, and then practically skip into the coffee place. He was excited.

"Okay, change of plans. Em, you're going to have to go in and keep him there for a while."

"What if he remembers me from Tyler's party?" She sounded slightly panicked.

"It won't matter. It was mostly film people, anyway. You could even say you scouted him there."

"What are you going to do?"

"I'm not sure yet," I said. And I wasn't. "Just go. If I'm not here when you come out, meet me back at my place."

I watched Emily go inside, counted to ten while trusting she'd get Corby out of view of the window if he was anywhere near, then left my car.

Reasoning that Jennifer wouldn't be looking out the rearview mirror, I skirted around the lot so that I approached the van from behind. I could hear the bass line of a noxious rock tune bleeding from inside the vehicle and, when I got close enough, I saw that the passenger door was unlocked.

Because of the music, stealth wasn't required. I was quiet, anyway. With my hand on the door handle, I counted to ten silently—one, two, three…—as much to calm my nerves as anything. At ten, I opened the door and snaked out my arm, grabbing hold of Jennifer's wrist while simultaneously bringing myself around to face her. After all this, I didn't want her running away.

"Madeline?" She looked terrible. Wasted. Bedraggled. And, I was relieved to note, in no condition to fight me.

"Come on," I said, hauling her out of the van.

She followed me docilely enough at first. "Where we goin'?" she asked as I led her across the parking lot.

"Home," I managed to answer, moving her steadily towards my car.

"I'm not going home," she said, shedding the docility like a sweater and twisting away from me. The change in attitude—from compliant to wildcat—took me by surprise, and I felt her dry, slender wrist slip out of my clammy grip.

"Jennifer!" I cried as she headed across the parking lot toward the coffee place, toward Corby. If she heard me, she gave no sign.

It's funny how time compresses in urgent moments. From the instant Jennifer slipped out of my grasp until I tackled her near the entrance to the café could only have been about twenty or thirty seconds, but so much happened in that time.

I was running full out when Jennifer narrowly missed being hit by a would-be shopper cruising too fast looking for a parking space. Jennifer wasn't watching where she was going and jumped practically into the path of a white Audi TT. The driver had the top down and screamed, "Crazy bitch!" even as he hit the brakes.

The sound of the car and the adrenaline-mad driver caused Jennifer to hesitate for a couple of seconds. Not very long, but it was enough. As she pulled herself back into a running position, her eyes wide as she looked around like a wild horse in the path of a predator, I launched myself at her, both of us scraping our knees on the concrete walkway.

I have about five inches and at least twenty pounds on Jennifer. Once I grabbed her, I knew she wasn't going to get away from me again. We tussled a bit, but I pulled her arm behind her back in a half nelson and began forcing her to her feet with the upward pressure. My concern was twofold at this point—to get her away from the café before boyfriend person came back out, while not breaking the girl's arm. The funny thing was, I knew in that instant that I *would* have broken her arm to prevent her getting away from me again. I think she knew it, too, because the struggle seemed to go right out of her.

"Is everything all right?" The woman's voice was cultured, soft. She had come out of the flower shop we'd landed in front of, and her well-made features showed two clear emotions: fear and genuine concern.

"Call the police!" Jennifer screeched. "This crazy bitch is trying to kidnap me!"

The woman looked from Jennifer's wild, hyper-dilated eyes to mine with obvious concern. "Sorry to bother you, madam," I said, trying to sound as controlled as possible. "The girl is my daughter. She's been running with a very bad crowd and I'm just trying to get her home." I didn't wait for a reply to either my words or Jennifer's blue screams of denial, but started half dragging, half pushing her across the parking lot toward my car. The woman followed us for a bit.

"Can I help?" she asked, obviously believing me.

"Yes, please. Can you open the back door of that silver car right ahead of us?"

Once I was behind the wheel I activated the childproof locks in the back. I wondered how I was going to manage driving with a deranged teenage animal in the back seat, but I needn't have worried—the fight seemed to go out of her as soon as the doors were locked. A few beats later Jennifer slumped into a beaten heap. I looked over my shoulder at her. Was she trying to con me? But no, I could see she'd passed out.

I backed out of my spot and drove past the café, honking to get Emily's attention, wanting her to know that—with the exception of a few bad moments—plan A had actually worked and we were under way.

And then I headed for home.

We managed to get up the canyon without mishap, but once I'd parked I realized there was no way the semicomatose girl could manage the cliff stairs alone, and I didn't want to leave her while I ran and got Tyler. It was while I sat on the hood of my car waiting for Emily, one eye constantly on Jennifer still in the back seat, that my hands started to shake. And I didn't mind. Some type of delayed shock. Better delayed, I thought, than at the scene.

Emily showed up after about ten minutes, and between us, we managed to shift Jennifer from the car, down the stairs, to Tyler's front door. Tasya looked at us wide-eyed, not quite comprehending, calling for Tyler while she ushered us in.

"Madeline! Jennifer! Oh, my God." Tyler swept the teenager into his arms.

She woke slightly at the movement. "Daddy?"

"What's wrong with her?" Tyler demanded. Tasya put a hand on his arm.

"I'm not sure. Drugs, I think. Though I don't know what kind or...or if they were self-administered or given to her to keep her docile."

"What happened?"

"Tyler," Tasya interjected. "Not now. There's plenty of time for that later. Let's see to Jennifer first, please."

"Does she need a doctor?" Tyler demanded of me.

But Tasya answered. "No. Look at her." She had pulled open one of Jennifer's eyes and checked the pupil's dilation. She opened the girl's mouth and looked at her tongue and the color of her gums. She managed all of this with the quiet, competent air of someone who knew exactly what she was doing. I realized that there was more to Tasya—and her background—than met the eye. "She needs to sleep. Please, put her in her room, let me see to her." All of Tasya's attention was focused on Jennifer; for the moment Tyler had ceased to exist. "Please, Tyler. No more standing." There wasn't room for argument in her tone. "Take her now."

Emily and I hovered around the foyer until, after a very few minutes, Tyler came back and motioned for us to follow him into the kitchen. He called a GP friend of his who said he'd make a house call in half an hour. Then, while he put water on for tea, Tyler looked me in the eye and said, "You want to tell me what the hell is going on?"

"It's sort of a long story," I started, lamely.

He indicated for us to sit on stools at the big kitchen island. "We've got time."

Emily and I sat, and I told Tyler about tracking Corby down and arranging to meet him in Malibu.

"You told him you were auditioning him for a movie?" Tyler asked incredulously. "Where did that come from?"

"Air, kinda. Plus, when I went to these surf places, it seemed like a preoccupation—being in movies."

"What were you guys thinking? Do you have any idea how dangerous this could have been? To you and to Jennifer?"

We nodded, both of us feeling like chastened schoolgirls. "I think, really, we just wanted to see if Corby was involved and maybe see if we could find out where he had her or if he knew where she was."

Emily spoke for the first time. "We were completely blown away when she turned up in the van with him."

"And then you just grabbed her?" Tyler fumed.

"Pretty much," I said, nodding.

Though, for a few minutes, he'd looked ready to kill someone, with a single sigh Tyler seemed to give in to whatever he was feeling. Part relief, I thought. And part defeat. He dropped his head in his hands. "What the hell was it all about? Do you think she did it? The kidnapping stuff? Or was it all the kid?"

"I'm not sure," I said. "Maybe it was all just some stupid prank. You're going to need to talk to Jennifer. Later. But even if she had nothing to do with it..." I knew I was approaching shaky ground, so I moved with caution "...there's been stuff going on with her. With you and Tasya. Stuff that's maybe just beginning to manifest itself in weird ways."

Tyler's shoulders kind of slumped at that. "I know. I just wish I knew what the hell to do."

"Just love her, Tyler," Tasya said as she entered the room, coming up behind her husband and putting her hands on his shoulders. "I know you do, but I think she needs to see it more. The way, perhaps, things were before I arrived."

"Oh, Tasya. No." Tyler started to protest, but she shushed him.

"I'm not going anywhere, Tyler." She smiled. "But she is your baby. And no matter what, she won't be with us in this house forever. She'll have her own life sometime. Maybe soon. Right now she needs more of you," Tasya said firmly. "Perhaps more than you were able to give her before. It's not too late, my love. But it will be if you don't act soon. I can see it."

Motioning to Emily that we should go, I told Tyler and Tasya that I'd be out all afternoon, but that I was anxious to hear how Jennifer was and that I'd love to be able to come by and see her later.

Tyler assured me he'd call me later in the day. "And come by anytime, Madeline. You, too, Emily. Don't even knock."

"Do you think that Corby kidnapped her?" Emily asked when we were back at the guest house.

I shook my head. "Not so much, really. At least, however it ended up, I think she started it."

"God, Madeline. When I was that age, I thought acting out was cutting a class to see a movie with my friends. Not staging a kidnapping so I could go to acting school."

"You think she did it." It wasn't a question.

"I guess. Don't you?"

I shrugged. "What I think doesn't matter. I know I like her, Emily. I think she's a good kid who is troubled right now. But I think they're good enough people—" I pointed at the ceiling, toward Tyler and Tasya's part of the house "—that they can get her through it. Though some professional help probably wouldn't be out of order, either."

"Look, I gotta go," Emily said, getting up and collecting her bag. "I was supposed to be on set an hour ago." She grinned. "I have a good excuse, though. Let's talk later, okay? I want to hear how it goes with the kid." I nodded in agreement—so did I.

When Emily was gone I sat and collected my thoughts for a minute. Two self-kidnappings in one week was more than I could handle. In Jennifer's case, it had been for attention. With Ernie it was definitely more complicated. Or was it? I had to find Arianna.

I showered, wincing when the hot water met my raw knees. Afterward I dressed carefully—the Prada again. I needed to look like a well-heeled matron. Anyway, long pants would cover the road rash I'd acquired skidding after Jennifer.

Outside the Brentwood café where I'd met Mrs. Billings, the billboard was where I'd remembered. Thankfully, it hadn't been plastered over. And there was the name: Beverly Marston, Brentwood's Number One Realtor Since 1997. Despite the Anne Rand debacle, it stood to reason that if she *had* used a Realtor to find the home she'd told me she and Ernie had rented, Arianna would have secured the services of the very best one.

I used a pay phone to call Ms. Marston. I was in luck;

she was in her office doing some paperwork. If I wanted to buzz on over, she told me, she had the time to discuss my needs.

On the stairs on the way up to her office, I belatedly remembered the naked condition of the third finger of my left hand. I wear my grandmother's engagement ring on the center finger of my right hand—a talisman. She gave it to me when I moved to New York; she had remarried and had a shiny new ring from her shiny new husband. Secretly I thought she wanted me to wear the ring because she hoped it would magically attract some keeper I'd actually keep. So far it hadn't worked, but I wear it because it's simple and lovely and it's a part of her I know was dear to her. At least until she met Henry.

Anyway, on the stairs, I worked this ring off my right hand and transferred it to the ring finger on my left. It was loose, of course, and not actually a wedding ring, but with the stone turned inwards, it could do in a pinch.

In person, Ms. Marston looked perhaps ten years younger than her photo had indicated. Such can be the case with photos shot to make the subject look more beautiful and glamourous. They do both of those things, but often at the price of youth. Something in the preservative chemicals of the makeup. In person, she was an average looking fifty rather than the beautiful sixty the photo had led me to expect.

We sat on either side of the Queen Anne desk in her exquisitely appointed office. A notebook and a Waterford fountain pen were ready on the desk beside her. As we spoke, every so often she paused to scratch my answers—or her interpretations of them—down for future reference.

"You're looking for a new home?" she said once we'd gotten introductions out of the way.

"That's right. My husband has just taken a job out here." I watched her face carefully while I spoke. "He's heading up a local company. Based in Culver City. We've decided to rent in Brentwood while we get to know the area. We'll decide where to buy later on."

Scratch, scratch, scratch. "Where do you live now?"

"Connecticut," I said, remembering what Arianna had told me. "And we'll keep the house out there, of course. But for now, we need something rather special. We both like our privacy and…" What would Arianna want in a home? "And something with a good address and in a neighborhood that's not too crowded."

Scratch. Scratch. "Children?" she asked.

"Not yet, but at sometime, perhaps."

Scratch. "Do you work also, Mrs. Carter?"

"No, no. Not anymore. I have my charities. My… interests."

She regarded me thoughtfully for a few moments. "You know, it's uncanny. I rented a house to a couple just a few weeks ago with very similar needs."

I suppressed the urge to punch my first into the air and shout, Yes! Instead, I forced a bored look onto my face and said, "Oh, really?"

It was her turn to look closely at me. "Yes. You know, you even look very much like her. Like the woman of the couple, I mean."

"And you rented them my house, I suppose?" I said it with a careless laugh. I was leading, but would she follow?

"Yes, I suppose I did. It's a splendid place, on Oakmont Drive. Do you know that area?"

I shook my head. "I don't know Brentwood that well. But I like what I've seen. It seems quite pleasant. Just what we're looking for."

"Oh, from your description, Brentwood is *exactly* where you and your husband will want to be. If you have time, perhaps I can take you out there for a peek? We won't be able to go in, just drive by. But it will give me a better idea of what you're looking for, help me hone in on the type of place you and your husband might like."

This was more than I had been fishing for. A guided *tour* to Arianna's house. I had been hoping she'd say the street name, which would at least make my haystack a little smaller. And she had: Oakmont Drive. But now she was actually going to take me there. I was very pleased with myself. Realtors, like brokers, are hungry creatures. Promise them food and they'll take you anywhere. I settled myself into call-me-Bev's dove gray Mercedes S600 and enjoyed my tour of Brentwood Heights.

The Carmichael Billings house was set well back from the street in an old Brentwood neighborhood.

"It's not an ostentatious place at all," Bev said. "Which is why I wanted you to see it. It wouldn't be everyone's cup of Darjeeling." She looked pleased with her joke. I smiled thinly. "And it's just five bedrooms and the teensiest little pool. Some people looking in this price range want something more…impressive. But it really is one of the better neighborhoods. That seemed important to the people I told you about, so…I thought it might be to you, as well."

I assured her that it was just what I was looking for, and though she insisted on taking me past several other places on a circuitous route back to the office, I told her that the first one was exactly what I wanted and the others wouldn't do at all. She promised me she'd put together a list of things to show me and would call me in a few days.

I pulled into the driveway on Oakmont without much apprehension. Arianna had been forthcoming enough with me and open enough to chatting that I didn't think she'd mind my dropping by like this, though it amused me somewhat that it had been easier to find out where she lived than getting her phone number would have been. And she was the one who'd sicced a private investigator on *me*. I didn't think I'd call her on it—I'd told Anne Rand I wouldn't, for one thing—but it did sort of mean Arianna owed me.

I wanted to talk to her for two reasons: Why had her car been spotted near Camp Arrowheart the day before? And had she had any type of contact with Ernie? *If* she'd tell me that, of course. But the fact that Ernie and Paul had staged their little "murder" made me think that whatever was going down was now happening fast.

When she answered the door, Arianna stood looking at me for a moment as though trying to place me. She appeared slightly disoriented. Looked, in fact, as though she'd been crying.

"It's me. Madeline Carter. From the café the other day."

"Of course, Madeline. Pardon me, it's just that…just that…" she seemed close to coming apart. "Oh, come in, please."

She led me poolside. "I feel the need to be outside. I hope you don't mind," she said, so I followed.

As Bev had said, the pool *was* teeny, but it was also completely charming. It was a deep green, rather than blue, and looked to be quite deep. A diving pool, then. Deeper than allowable for modern day pools, but in the 1950s—when it appeared as though the house had been built—it wasn't unheard of to dig twelve-foot-deep swimming pools. The small size, the color and the proximity of a little palm grove gave the pool area a grottolike feeling. It seemed a relaxing spot to sit and read a book or just contemplate life. Arianna, however, didn't look as though she was in a contemplative mood. In fact, in the unforgiving daylight, she looked drawn and pale.

There was no small talk today. She cleared her throat. In her current state, it seemed to be a calming effort. Some sort of preparation. I could see that it was costing her to stay glued. She didn't waste time on preamble. "Ernest is…Ernest is dead."

This floored me. I'd been so convinced of my theories, the possibility of them being wrong hadn't actually occurred to me. It just hadn't fit. And yet…

"How do you know?"

"A sheriff called me. Told me. And he said… He said…" I could see her struggling for composure. Winning. But it was training that got her there. *Breeding* they would have said in another era. "I have to go there." Her voice slipped to a whisper. "Identify him."

"San Bernardino?" I asked.

She looked at me sharply. "How did you know?"

I sighed. "Long story. Maybe it's not for right now. But it started with the note you showed me. Arrowheart."

"Yes, the note. I remembered that, as well." Her sentences were short, choppy. As though saying these things aloud was causing her great effort. "Yesterday. I got a call. A man. It was frightening and, when I think about it, he didn't really tell me anything, except he gave me an address. I was to be there at one o'clock yesterday afternoon. At Camp Arrowheart. And when I heard the name, I made the connection. I knew it had something to do with Ernest."

One o'clock, I figured, was probably about the time I went stumbling off into the land of the lost. Which meant that whatever I saw hadn't been staged for me at all. It was Arianna they'd intended to lure there as a witness. I had just once more blithely stumbled in. But wait, I thought. She had said that Ernie was dead. They'd found the body. So what did that do to my staged theory?

"So you went there, at one?"

She shook her head. "Well, I *drove* up there, but then I got frightened. The driveway was in disrepair. So I knew I'd have to walk in, and since I didn't know what, or who, was up there, I just got scared. I—I sat in the car for a while, and then I came home." Her voice got very quiet and her head dropped even lower. This was obviously what she'd been thinking about when I arrived. "What if I *had* gone, Madeline? Maybe that's why I was supposed to go. Maybe I was meant to save him."

I thought of Ernie as I'd known him: self-centered, manipulative, egocentric. Maybe he'd changed. Maybe, to inspire the sadness I could now see in this woman—his *widow*, I corrected myself—I'd misjudged everything very badly. .

"You loved him very much, didn't you?"

She pulled her head up and her gaze met mine. And her expression was full, but I couldn't read it. "He was my husband," was all she said.

It took me awhile to realize that didn't exactly answer my question.

I offered to drive Arianna down to San Bernardino. It had occurred to me that she hadn't been in Southern California very long and probably didn't know many people. Asking someone you'd met at a society luncheon to accompany you to view your husband's last mortal remains just wouldn't be...done. And viewing your husband's body seemed to me to be something you wouldn't want to do alone. Plus I found that, despite everything, I was coming to like Arianna. Her quiet dignity combined with her forthright manner and a very real intelligence had won me over. And the P.I.? As icky as it had made me feel, I wasn't so sure I wouldn't have done something similar in Arianna's place. Anyway, I wasn't busy and, to be honest, I wanted to see how it all played out.

Arianna was mostly quiet on the drive down and I let her be. She would, I reasoned, have a lot on her mind. I knew what I was thinking: how would I be if this was me? I knew she was calmer than I would have been, but that was just part of who she was. Calm. Cool. Somewhat distant. And you don't hook up with a guy anticipating that someday you'll have to view his mortal remains. It's just never a part of any plan.

"After our meeting on Thursday," she said when we'd been driving for a while, her voice only slightly punctuating the soft quiet inside the car, "I...well, I had my doubts about you."

I risked a quick glance at her profile. She looked as though she were choosing her words with care.

"I guess I kind of had my doubts about you, too. Pretty natural, under the circumstances."

"Yes, but I...I did something about it."

I shot her a questioning glance.

"I hired a private detective. To follow you."

"You did." It was a statement. I hoped she didn't notice. "Why?"

"I didn't fully believe what you told me—that you hadn't seen Ernie in all that time."

"And you believe me now?"

She smiled then. It wasn't a big smile, but it touched her eyes. "To be honest, Madeline, I'm not completely sure. Just at some point between then and now it ceased to matter as much."

I thought about this for a while. Oddly, and at some level, it made sense.

"Well, for what it's worth, Arianna, I haven't been in touch with him at all. I've had no reason to, for one thing. We travel in different circles. Also, it ended badly between us. Very badly."

"Tell me."

I thought about it for a minute, but it didn't seem appropriate. It would amount to dumping on her now apparently deceased husband. Which seemed *so* not cool. I told her as much—fewer words, same sentiment. "I don't think this is the time, Arianna. Or the day. Sorry. But, trust me, there were no lines of communication left open between us. Anyway," I added, "it was all so very long ago. None of it matters anymore." That's what I said to her, but I was thinking about Alex Montoya's words and wondering if what I was saying now was entirely true. Maybe it all mattered. Very much.

In any case, Arianna let it rest and we traveled in silence for a while longer.

After a few miles more, I remembered the posh accent, the rumpled housedress, the ambling, overfed gait. "So how do you go about finding a private detective, anyway? The recommendation of friends? What?"

Arianna looked vaguely embarrassed at the question. "No. I…couldn't think of anyone to ask." She wrinkled her nose. "Too sordid. Too much fodder for the rumor mill. I loathe that sort of thing. I looked in the phone book until I found one I thought I could trust."

"What happens then? I really have no idea. A meeting, money exchanging hands?"

"Well, I don't know if there's a usual way. I never felt the need for one before just a few days ago. But I hired her over the telephone and paid her the same way, by credit card."

Funny, I would never have thought that P.I.s were hired on the phone and paid that way, as well. It made it sound like phone sex—1-900-dial-a-dick, or something.

"Didn't you think that was chancy? I mean, how did you know you could depend on her?"

Arianna shrugged. "It was a chancy idea, I guess. And it wasn't like it was a *lot* of money. Just three hundred dollars for the day."

Three hundred? Rand had told me five. So the extra two-fifty had been practically another whole day for her. And then Arianna had told me about everything voluntarily. I seethed for about forty-five seconds, then gave it up. That P.I. had looked hungry. That is, she'd looked as if she was telling the truth when she said rich clients don't fall into her hands every day. She could probably use the money. I let it go with a sigh.

"I paid the private investigator with one of Ernest's credit cards." Her smile was slightly evil, as evil as I'd seen it yet, anyway. I liked her for it. "I thought it was certainly an expense *he* should handle, even if he's not around. Executive decision."

"So, what'd you find out?"

"Things that should make me even more suspicious of you," she said cautiously.

"Like what?" I was genuinely surprised.

"Well, like you were at the Langton sales office yesterday, for starters." Arianna's tone was even.

I was embarrassed; I'd forgotten this bit. Or rather, I'd been so focused on Steve, I'd forgotten that he worked for Langton. "I can imagine how that might have looked. But it was an…unrelated matter."

I could feel Arianna looking at me closely for a minute. "She told me that you met with someone. He walked back to your car with you and you exchanged notes."

"Phone numbers," I said, remembering. "He's someone I met at a Langton function I attended the day before you and I met for coffee. I can see how it must look to you."

"Well, the private investigator took pictures of the two of you." She had? How creepy was that? "And yesterday afternoon she told me who he was—a minor sales employee, no obvious links to Ernie or you, so…it seems possible you're telling the truth."

She said this so smugly, I bridled. We already know about my war on smugness. "Oh, it seems possible, does it?"

She shot me a glance. "It does. I don't know why you're sounding so offended, Madeline. I did what I felt I had to do under the circumstances. What I do or think shouldn't make any difference to you in the long term. It won't affect anything. I did it for me."

I still didn't like it, but I tried to put myself in her shoes—since that actually involved imagining myself married to Ernie, it was hard—and figured that, had it been me, I would possibly have done the same thing. Scratch that. The way things were going, it was more likely I would have followed her myself.

"And the private investigator said she lost you on the freeway near Redlands. But it seemed to me from her description of where she lost track of you, that you were very possibly headed to the same place I was supposed to go yesterday. That camp."

"The camp you went to, but didn't get out of your car?" She nodded.

"Which," I added, "put us on the road at about the same time yesterday."

She sensed where I was going and rushed in ahead of me. "Yes, but I didn't know any of that—any of the things about where you'd been—until yesterday evening. And then...then the sheriff called me this morning and told me about Ernie."

"But then, with all of that evidence, why on earth did you let me drive you down here? With the stuff you've told me—about what I was doing, where I was going—I think I would have at least partly thought I did it." I stopped to consider this jumble of words, then kept going. I could see she knew what I meant. "Weren't you at least a bit afraid of me? I would have been."

"Madeline, if it were just facts, I guess I would have been. But I know you didn't kill Ernie." She spread her hand in front of her face. "I know it like I have five fingers, and I've never thought about explaining that, either." Then she really surprised me. "No, Madeline, you and I are going to San Bernardino together to make sure the son of a bitch is dead. And he's not, is he? You don't think so any more than I do. But we'll play this out."

She sat back in her seat, as though this last admission had exhausted her. For a while, I thought about things to ask her—questions and theories and beliefs. But I left it alone and retreated into my own thoughts and interpretations about what she'd said. We traveled the rest of the way to San Bernardino in companionable silence. What she'd said had proved once and for all that, regardless of our differences, we were sisters under the skin.

Twenty-Two

It's possible there's a reason that morgues must always be located in the nether regions of the buildings that house them. If so, I don't know what it is. We followed a sheriff into the bowels of the San Bernardino Hospital, beginning our downward journey in an elevator that smelled of sterilized cleanliness masking the odors of illness and despair, then trekking down mostly empty corridors where the sounds of our shoes seemed impossibly loud in the stillness. Every step we took seemed to carry us farther from life and sunlight and air. The deeper into the earth we penetrated, the more I could feel it closing in above me. After a while, I had to remind myself to breathe.

Arianna had been given directions to the hospital and, when we got there, I offered to wait in the car, but she asked me to come in with her. Actually, she insisted. "We're going to see this thing through, Madeline. You and I. Someone is dead in there, and I have a terrible feeling it's not Ernie." Which was a cryptic enough statement that I chewed on it for a few seconds before I followed her out of the car.

The sheriff, a nice fiftysomething man with a quiet and serious demeanor, was waiting for us. I hadn't seen him before, so, thankfully, he took no notice of me. Since Arianna and I are similar in build and coloring, anyway, he probably assumed I was her sister or some other relative.

"I have to warn you," he said when we'd completed our underworld journey and stood outside the morgue's viewing area, "this might be upsetting for you. The body is in…imperfect condition. I wouldn't put you through this if it weren't absolutely necessary, but as it is, Mr. Billings is not recognizable to the casual eye."

Arianna and I exchanged a glance. What could that mean? I think we both imagined horrors beyond the most horrible. What we imagined, however, didn't even come close.

The body was wheeled, covered, into a small viewing area. A window separated us from the corpse, but it was close, anyway. Too close. I could hear Arianna's sharp intake of breath when an orderly moved the sheet away. I put a hand on her elbow in what I hoped was a comforting gesture, bracing myself to catch her should she fall.

We could see that the corpse had been severely and curiously burned. It looked as though his head, legs and arms had been cooked: that simple. Roasted like a Sunday chicken. There was no hair and not a lot of skin left on his head, and we could see where the flesh on his cheek had, literally, been cooked away. The same was true for his hands and arms, legs and feet. They were purplish, blistered and completely unrecognizable.

I knew it was ridiculous, but right then I would have sworn that, along with the dead chemical smell always found in hospital-type places, I could taste charcoal in the air, right through the glass between us. It was like a campfire, but without the pleasant connotations. I shuddered.

Where the body wasn't burned, it was ruined. And it was difficult to tell what was fire damage and what had come from other sources. There appeared to be wounds across the neck, chest and torso. From bullets. I saw again the glint of silver in Paul's hand the day before. I averted my head for a moment. Closed my eyes, wishing I was anywhere but here.

"Mrs. Billings, is it him?" The sheriff's voice was quiet but insistent.

"I…I believe so. It's difficult to tell."

I studied her closely, looking for some sign. *I* could see it wasn't Ernie, but no one was asking me, so I kept my mouth shut. What I saw while I watched her, though, was a transformation. She went from looking like the suitably subdued new widow to…what? I couldn't tell, but I saw her sort of blanch, saw her pallor heighten, and caught a throb begin at the base of her throat.

I followed her glance; she seemed to be looking very carefully at the corpse's left thigh. And there, in a spot miraculously saved from ruination, I saw it, too. A mole, vaguely heart-shaped and about the size of my own thumbnail. Not a mole I recognized. Not Ernie, if there'd been any doubt. But then, why this new layer of despair? And why wasn't she saying anything?

"Mrs. Billings, I can imagine this is difficult for you, but if you could give me a positive identification, one way or the other, it would be very helpful to us here."

She hesitated a minute, obviously fighting for control and, perhaps, for guidance. Then she murmured, "It's…it's him. I'm quite sure."

As the three of us made our way back to the surface, I asked the sheriff what had happened to Ernie. I hardly recognized my own voice as I spoke.

He looked at Arianna before answering. She nodded and the sheriff replied in a gentle voice, "We found him in a burned out lodge at an abandoned YMCA camp about a hundred miles from here. There will be an autopsy…sorry, Mrs. Billings." Arianna nodded an acknowledgment at his consideration. "But, as you'll have observed, there is some question about the cause of death. He's badly burned, but death appears to have been from gunshot wounds. And we had a witness report from someone who says they saw a person shot at that location yesterday."

"How did you know it was him?" I heard myself asking.

"His wallet was on him, all his ID—driver's license, credit cards." He shot a cautious glance at Arianna, saw she was holding up, and continued. "When we ran his name, we found a match in missing persons, and it all seemed to fit pretty well. All we had to do then was bring Mrs. Billings in for a positive ID."

"But there'll be DNA testing, right?" Arianna asked, her voice weak. Not surprisingly so, all things considered. But I wondered.

He replaced his hat while answering—a studied gesture, as though he was weighing how to answer. "Wouldn't think so, really. We don't do that as a matter of course, not down here. Not when there's no question about the victim's identity. And everything here seems to add up pretty much."

"Parts of him," I observed cautiously, "seem more seriously burned than others."

The sheriff hesitated again, noted Arianna watching him intently for an answer. "There'll be an investigation so, really, I don't know how much I should say."

We'd reached the hospital's admitting area. We were not far from sunshine. But for the moment, we stood in the wretched recycled hospital air, the pale green walls giving Arianna's face a ghostly glow. She was visibly fighting tears. "Please, sir," she said plaintively, and if I hadn't suspected how much acting was involved, my heart would have gone out to her. "You have some idea. And it would…it would be soothing to me to know."

"Well…" He ran his fingers through his hair. Grieving widows were obviously not his specialty. "…I don't know how soothing it will be, but right now we suspect that some of the burns you saw in there—particularly on the hands, feet and face—were done intentionally, before the fire, to obscure his identity. Maybe whoever did it hoped we'd take the body to be a drifter or a hiker and not think it was Mr. Billings at all. Since the…since Mr. Billings was a victim of kidnapping, we think the perpetrators probably wanted people to think he was still alive so that they could get their money. I guess they didn't count on our witness. And, because of that witness, our men got to the scene in time to put the blaze out before it did more damage to…to your husband's…remains."

I was ready to tell the sheriff who I was—that I was the witness—and mention Paul's involvement, as well, but Arianna started speaking rapidly—maniacally?— before I had a chance.

"Sheriff, thank you for your time," she said. "I think you'll understand that I have a need to get out-of-doors right now." She was already in motion. "You know how to contact me should you have further questions."

He let us go more quickly and easily than I would have imagined. I figured that the thought of a beautiful widow blowing her cookies on the cold linoleum floor made him more tractable than he might have been. We were outside in minutes.

The sunlight on our heads felt like tonic. It also felt impossible after the cold, metallic sterility of the morgue, a sterility that had been offset only by that sickly sweet burnt wood smell I still thought I'd imagined, though I was no longer completely sure. Now sun, newly watered grass and, from somewhere nearby, flowers. What had gone before might have been a dream.

The hospital was part of a large civic complex. We walked for a bit, each full of our own thoughts, until we came to a bench surrounded by green grass and flowers. Arianna indicated she'd like to sit, and so we did.

"That's not Ernie," I said without preamble.

She shook her head, no. But it was a sad, resigned no. Her husband was not dead. She had not told the police. And she looked more upset than when we'd arrived. "How did you know?" she asked.

"That guy is circumcised. Ernie isn't…well, wasn't."

"I noticed that, too."

"Why didn't you say anything?"

"I'm…I'm not sure, Madeline. I nearly did. But then…then I realized something else. Something that showed me how much bigger all of this is than I'd thought." She looked at me intently, as though willing me to understand. "There's more here than you see, Madeline. More here than I do, as well. And I keep thinking that, if we just let it play out, maybe it will go away."

"You don't really think that."

She nodded. "I do."

I suddenly understood something. "That wasn't Ernie in there, but I get the feeling you knew who it was."

Her reaction surprised me. I had expected denial, or maybe a cornered shiftiness around the issue. What she did, though, was put her head in her hands and sob. And not delicate little Wellesley sobs, either, but gut-wrenching silent wails that came from some deeply hurt place. I was mystified, but you couldn't witness this and not know she wasn't acting anymore. This was real. She was, in her careful way, completely devastated. I looked around. There was no one within earshot, and anyone watching from a distance—like the sheriff, say—would be seeing an understandably distraught widow who had just been forced to view the charred remains of her beloved husband.

"His name was Marcus." She whispered it like a prayer. Like a benediction. "Marcus Hayles."

I thought of her reaction to the mole on the thigh. "You knew him well."

Arianna nodded through sobs. "Very well. And now I think—I *have* to think—that nothing was as it seemed." She looked directly into my eyes, almost a plea. "You see, Ernest didn't know about Marcus. There was no way he could have known. And yet…" She indicated the building we'd come from, lying peaceful and white in the sunshine, giving no hints about what we'd seen inside. Marcus Hayles. Arianna's lover, because what else could all of this mean?

"But if he didn't know, then how…?"

"That's just it! And when I think about it now, it was all too perfect. Even the way I met Marcus, the way…the way we came together."

"Tell me, Arianna." Yes, I wanted to know. But I felt part of me *had* to know, as well.

"When I was coming out here, to California to meet Ernest, I met Marcus on the plane. He made me laugh, Madeline. He made me laugh the way Ernest had when I first met him. He even looked a bit like Ernest—the same coloring, the same height and build." Her voice broke, perhaps thinking of what both of those things might mean.

I could see Arianna struggling for control. I sat there with her and waited. Somewhere nearby a sprinkler started, and the wet, rhythmic sound of it was slightly soothing. The scent of flowers and things growing wafted to us. Birdsong rippled through the air.

"Ernest had said he couldn't meet me at the airport that first day. He had meetings. I'd have to find my own way to Brentwood. That wasn't unusual. I'd take a cab. But Marcus and I had enjoyed such a nice chat on the plane and he offered to give me a ride home—to my new home, which should have been Ernest's job! He was so charming, Marcus was. So…irresistible.

"I'd never had an affair before, but we practically started it on that very first day. Marcus seemed so *smitten* by me. And I think that affected me more deeply than anything. No one had felt that way about me for so long. No one had shown me that I was beautiful." I looked at her lovely face but I could see she wasn't acting now. "No one had made me feel as though I mattered. Not for a long time." Her voice slid to a whisper. "And then Marcus. I loved him. I thought he loved me."

"But you said Ernie didn't know about Marcus."

Her head snapped back up, a glint in her eye. "Don't you see? That's what's so frightening. What if Ernie did that, too?" she hissed. "What if he gave Marcus to me, knowing that he would take him away." She seemed to be warming to her theory, working it out even as she spoke. "What if Ernie selected him for me?" Her voice broke. "Sent him to me. Maybe…maybe even paid him to be with me, just so he could take him away? Take him away and use him in his own place. Like this."

What Arianna was suggesting was horrible. Beyond belief. Yet it fit with the things I'd been theorizing earlier. And it fit with what Alex Montoya had said: that the corporate psychopath—and I'd gone beyond the point of wondering if Ernie fit the description—was capable of anything. Even this.

Previously, I wouldn't have thought Ernie capable of premeditated murder, not really. Maybe if, as I had supposed yesterday, maybe if you were to get in his way. But to find a man physically similar to himself and then manipulate the situation in this incredibly twisted way— was that even possible? I'd underestimated him. Again.

"And then there's Paul." I was hardly aware that I'd said it aloud.

"Paul?"

"Westbrook. The business card." She just looked at me questioningly. "The name really doesn't mean anything to you?"

She shook her head. "Just the card. Should it?"

And so I told her everything I knew and even everything I *thought* I knew. And the things I'd learned from Arianna today just made my theories seem all the more likely.

"Wait then," she said after a while. "What you're suggesting is that Ernest and this Westbrook person were manipulating things—together—all along."

"In a sense." I nodded. "Yes. Though when I think about it now, I believe it must always have been Ernie who was the manipulator, the puppeteer, almost. And that he's probably been using Paul as keenly as he's ever used anyone. Including us. Maybe Paul just stayed useful to him longer." And, being the sycophant that he was, he'd probably made sure he stayed useful, as well.

"I find it inconceivable that I wouldn't have known about Paul. About him being such an important part of Ernie's life." She paused as though thinking this through, then said more forcefully, "I *would* have known."

I spoke softly to her. Gently. "Think about what you're saying. We're talking about someone that you suspect put you together with a lover he had every intention of killing at some point." I thought of Alex again. "I think your husband is capable of anything."

"But it's done now, isn't it, Madeline?" Her voice was pleading. Hopeful. "It's done. Finished. There's nothing more that *we* can do."

I watched her carefully before I answered, yet there was no manipulation in her eyes. Just hope. She wanted me to agree with her. She wanted to be right. But she wasn't right. At some level she had to have known it.

"Arianna, he's out of control. *They're* out of control. Someone has to stop them. And, between us, you and I seem to hold all of the keys, all of the things that put these pieces together. That's why we have to go find that sheriff again and tell him everything we know. The police have to be involved in this. If we don't tell them, Paul and Ernie are going to get away."

You don't know—not really—the condition of your

moral fiber until something like this happens. I hadn't had the opportunity to check mine in a long while, so it really surprised me how badly I now wanted this thing done. It would no longer be enough for the stock price to ooze back up and for things to get more or less back to normal. I thought of Arianna's poor cooked lover. I thought about me trekking through the forest in a panic after watching what had been merely a display. And distraught pensioners in Urbana? They had *nothing* on this. I wanted Ernie and Paul behind bars—forever if possible—and if my hand was partly responsible for their apprehension, so much the better.

I guess, though, that if Arianna was doing her own moral fiber check at this point, she saw something different. "It would be better," she said in a surprisingly calm voice, "for me, anyway, if they did get away. As long as they got far away and never came back."

I was mystified by this for a moment. I studied her closely and she suddenly looked very young to me. Young and vulnerable. And I thought about what all of this would mean to her. The way things stood, the way Ernie had set things up, she would be the beautiful, bereaved widow of one of the most interesting businessmen in the country. A businessman who'd died tragically, more or less, in the line of duty. A hero, almost.

However, if the truth was what she and I suspected, and that truth became known, she would be a social pariah, at least for a while. The wife of a disgraced, and likely imprisoned, con man. I could imagine the Hamptons rippling with whispers already. And it would all come out:

the markets he'd manipulated, the companies he'd "helped." The fiscal fallout alone would be tremendous.

And I thought about the burned corpse we'd come down here to identify. Arianna's lover. He represented both a promise and a threat from Ernie. Marcus's body had been disfigured in a way that would make him difficult to identify. If Arianna left it alone, agreed that, yes, this was her husband, there was a good chance that Marcus would be buried as Ernie, which meant the real Ernie would have to disappear. Forever. So the promise: don't say anything and you'll never hear from me again. The threat was also in that horribly disfigured corpse. It said as clearly as anything, "Look what I am capable of. *Anything*. Silence is the best course."

I reached over. Smoothed Arianna's hair as a mother would a child's. Then I pulled her, gently, to her feet. She didn't resist. "I know it would be better, Arianna. But we have all the missing pieces, you and I. We have to tell them what we know. We *have* to."

She studied her hands, tears streaming quietly down her cheeks, and said, "I know."

And when we turned together, we did so with resolve. We both knew there were things that had to be set in motion.

I don't think the sheriff ever really knew what hit him. One minute he thought he had a resolution: the kidnapped CEO of a corporation found dead in his jurisdiction. A door closed, a case wrapped up. The next minute he had nothing but questions, plus a potential

John Doe on one of his slabs. While we talked to him you could see a rough day getting rougher. I felt a little sorry for the guy.

"Why didn't you tell me any of this before?" He glared at Arianna accusingly.

"We weren't sure." I cut through the glare. "And what we've been telling you must sound so outlandish, we felt we had to be certain." One way or another, it was the truth.

"You're right about one thing—it certainly *is* outlandish." The hat was back off, and he ran his fingers agitatedly through his hair. "But if what you're suggesting is true—and I'm not ready to concede that it is— but *if* it is, it seems very likely that your husband and his compatriot are no longer in my jurisdiction." What he didn't say was, "Why the hell didn't you take this to the LAPD and make it *their* problem?"

"That's true," I said. "But once we felt we knew what was going on, we thought we'd best go to the authorities right away. And we were here," I pointed out. "So that was you."

More hair raking. "What a mess. I'm not even sure where to start. I'll contact LAPD right away, of course. But, again, if what you say is true, we don't even know where the hell the two of them might have gotten to."

I started to agree, but Arianna surprised me again, saying in a quiet voice, "I…I think I may know where they've gone." Both of our heads turned toward her. "Ernest took up flying recently. He said it calmed his nerves. Eased his stress."

"Does he have a plane?" I asked.

"No. But he has access to them. At Santa Monica Airport."

The sheriff looked pleased for the first time. It was a good expression on him. I thought he should wear it more often. "I would suspect, then, that that's just where he'd go."

I was not in a position to see things play out. Not really; not up close. There are things in life you need to know, other things you don't care to find out. Truthfully, this situation was neither of the above. Not that it mattered. Sometimes resolution comes whether you're looking for it or not.

Twenty-Three

It's very warm here. The water, like the sky, is very blue. Sometimes, from a distance and when the sun hits it at just the right angle, the sand looks like ice. When Steve first suggested Ensenada, I thought he was kidding. To a Pacific Northwesterner who'd come to L.A. by way of the East Coast, Ensenada, Mexico, sounded incredibly exotic, not to mention unbelievably expensive, something I'm really not into right now, all things considered.

"No, it'll be fun. *And* cheap," he assured me. It was only about a four-hour drive, he said. He had the use of a friend's seaside *casita*. The little house usually got rented out by the week to rich Americans for astronomical amounts of money, but there'd been a last minute cancellation that had resulted in a call to Steve: did he want it for two weeks, at a rock bottom rent-it-or-it'll-be-empty rate? Steve said yes. And then he called me.

I've decided I like Ensenada. I could stay here a long time; it almost makes even Malibu look like the rat race.

Yesterday we went horseback riding on the beach—I
felt like we were in a movie—and then we went to Hus-
songs Cantina for dinner and drinks and to commiser-
ate with each other about our sore rear ends from all the
riding. I think Steve was a little more sore than I was,
which we determined probably had something to do
with the fact that boys generally have less fatty padding
on their posteriors. Not that mine is huge, but it's not as
bony as his.

Today we haven't done anything. At all. Well, nothing that could appropriately be included on a postcard
to my mother. We rolled out of bed around one in the
afternoon, Steve scrambled us some eggs for breakfast—I made the coffee—and then we worked off our
breakfast by sitting in the hot tub.

After our grueling whirlpool-sitting, Steve said he
was going into town on an errand. He was all mysterious, said there was something he had to get. He came
back with an emery board and three different shades of
nail polish. He plunked me into a lounge chair on the
terrace, gave me a pedicure and then painted my toenails. Painted is an understatement. When he was finished, each nail looked as though it had a leopard pelt.
Ten little masterpieces. Very strange and strangely relaxing. Steve looked pleased with himself. "I've always
wanted to do that." He smiled, admiring his work.

"You are *too* weird," I told him, but I was smiling.
And my nails look amazing. I wish Emily was here just
so I could show them off. Maybe I can take a picture.

I love Ensenada. One of those things I didn't know
I needed until I was here. I haven't even missed the mar-

kets. Though, with most of my money tied up in LRG stock for the foreseeable future, there's really not a lot I can do right now. I've made a couple of phone calls since we've been here. Scanned a couple of newspapers. Now that all the shit has hit and the business writers have had a party with LRG, the stock is beginning to recover, but it's going to take awhile for it to even get back to where it was.

Steve has been helping with that, indirectly. It's funny how things work out. While the coast guard was fishing Ernie out of the waters off Baja—not far from where I am now, when I think about it—Steve was doing what he does. That Thursday, he signed the biggest contract of his career. Even as we cavort in sunny waters just a few steps from the little house, Langton's factories are gearing up to produce all of the jars for Doctor Gelkii's International Jams and Jellies. And I mean all of them. The Sultry Single Malt Marmalade from Scotland, the Sassy Saskatoon Berry Jam from Canada, the Luscious Lemon Curd from England and the Grab your Grape Wine Jellies from Napa. And others, all with names too ridiculous to remember.

Closing the sale meant a bonus for Steve and, the sale coming as it did at a critical time in the company's history, Langton agreed when he asked for a couple of weeks off. I'd seen the Langton news release come down the pipe about an hour before Steve called me: Langton Regional Group Closes Doctor Gelkii's Deal Worth $18.9 Million.

Since all of the recent news around Langton had been doom, gloom and scandal—and the stock had been appropriately rocked—closing this deal at that moment meant a lot to the company. And it was reflected in a happy and immediate little hike in the share price, despite the fact that, while the ink was drying on the Doctor Gelkii's contract, the newspapers were beginning to choke with stories about the CEO who never got to the office.

For a couple of minutes it looked as if Ernie had gotten away. Later on, when I lined up all the dates and times and did a little figuring, I realized that about when Arianna and I were driving down to San Bernardino to view what turned out to be her lover's body, Ernie and Paul were taking off from Santa Monica Airport in a chartered plane. It surprised me that he could file a flight plan and everything without it alerting anyone, but it turns out that when you've been kidnapped and are in the process of being pronounced dead, it's just not the same as when you're plain old wanted by the police. I guess people don't generally check to see if you're still among the living. Go figure.

They had chartered a Piper Arrow Retractable in Paul's name at Santa Monica Airport and filed a flight plan indicating Las Vegas as their destination. Of course, they never made Vegas, but, it later turned out, they left the plane at Fallbrook Community Airpark, a field so small they don't even sell fuel. The whole plane/Vegas thing must have been a smokescreen to put off anyone who happened to be looking in their direction.

Ernie and Paul had a car waiting at Fallbrook, which they drove to a marina in San Diego, where a boat had been purchased in Paul's name two months before. The money had probably come from Ernie, one way or the other, but it didn't show up on paper that way and, in the long run, it turned out the paper trail was all that mattered.

The boat was a thirty-seven-foot Sea Ray Sundancer. There's been speculation in the news about why it was *that* boat and not something bigger, which they could certainly have afforded, especially if everything had gone as planned. Which it didn't. The *Times* reporter suggested that, since the Sundancer is a "handy little boat"—that's the way she said it, although to most of us it would be considered a small yacht—it could be piloted easily by only one person without a crew, and was small enough to not attract attention in most marinas. But the boat had been equipped with digital satellite and all sorts of high-tech equipment. Paul *could* have completed his trades from that boat quite easily. They had e-mailed a couple of crime reporters anonymously, telling them about Ernie's "demise" in San Bernardino—it had to have been them; no one else would have known to do it. The pair of them would have been counting on the news of Ernie's death to rock the stock price just a little lower, then, before anyone could get organized enough to start DNA-testing Marcus's body, the two of them, safely at sea or in some southern port, could start buying LRG stock, covering their positions and, basically, completing their deal. So they *could* have done all of that from the boat. They just didn't get the chance.

San Diego in general, but the area where the marinas are in particular, is close enough to Mexican waters to throw stones into. Paul and Ernie—or perhaps Paul alone—would have taken trips in the boat to get a feel for how easily an American-registered yacht could pass into Mexican waters. On those test runs it would have been ridiculously easy. Rich Americans are welcome in that part of Mexico, and their boats ferry them to various marinas and resorts on the Pacific with a sort of carte blanche. Boat owners spend big bucks; it kind of goes with the territory.

But those test runs would probably have been during the day, maybe even on the weekend. Rich American yachters don't try to slink out of port in the middle of the night. When they do, the authorities surmise that said boat owners are up to no good, and in the waters between the U.S. and Mexico, there's plenty of no good that boaters can get up to. Because of this, the watchers are sophisticated and experienced. While you might think you're running in and out of various ports undetected, there are forces on both sides of the border keeping their eyes on you. Or maybe, for Paul and Ernie, it was just plain bad luck.

It was actually a U.S. Coast Guard vessel that flagged them down; they hadn't even gotten out of American waters. I can imagine it: "Prepare to be boarded." Here everything gets a little hazy, but you can picture these two—this particular two—high on adrenaline feeling *this* close to pulling off the biggest score, the master score, of their lives. The score to, literally, end all scores. And everything is in place. Everything has been going like clockwork, just as planned. And then, in a heartbeat, the jig is up. Ernie, of course, was supposed to be dead. But Paul, as far as the two of them could tell, wasn't wanted by anyone. There was nothing that they knew about to connect them to each other. Whatever their thinking was, Ernie hit the water, or was pushed. It was night, they would have figured he could float around in his life jacket or cling to the dark side of the boat until the heat had cleared off. Or maybe Paul suddenly got tired of playing second string to a showy hitter.

What neither of them could have anticipated was me. If, as they'd supposed, Arianna had seen the "killing" at Camp Arrowheart as they'd intended, she would have just reported that the guy doing the shooting was a man of medium height and medium build, average enough looking to be unfindable outside of a police lineup. Possibly not even then. But since Arianna and I had gone to the police and given them everything we had, the authorities knew they were looking for Paul, as well. And they also figured that, when they found Paul, Ernie wouldn't be far away.

So the coast guard secured the boat, right there in the water. I can visualize the scene: Paul, a picture of innocence and thinking no one even knew his name, forking over identification. The coast guard running his ID and finding Paul was anything but the vacationing executive he was pretending to be.

They took Paul into custody, and then they searched the boat, no doubt looking for Ernie. But they found other stuff of interest, including Paul's laptop so jam-packed full of evidence, he would no doubt have thrown it overboard with Ernie if he'd had even the slightest inkling that their encounter with the coast guard would be anything other than a routine check.

Among other incriminating bits of computer evidence, when the electronic investigators got their hands on that laptop, they found passwords and log-on information for no less than ten different trading accounts under as many different names, none of them traceable to either Paul or Ernie. They also found e-mail from Marcus Hayles, now deceased. It was an ambiguous note, slightly encoded, but it seemed to be asking for more money for services not specified. Another couple of pegs fell into place.

When the coast guard apprehended Paul, he didn't mention his partner in the water. He probably would have been hoping that, somehow, Ernie would manage to slip away. Even with one of them in jail, if the other was free, there would be a chance to complete the trades and cash in on their Langton scam. And even if the accounts got blocked, Ernie had access to the kind of money that can buy a lot of happiness when it comes to lawyers and just generally smoothing out legal stuff.

The coast guard towed the boat back into port, secured the vessel and handed Paul over to the police. Still nothing was said about Ernie and, in fact, the earliest news reports didn't mention him, either.

Arianna had a couple of bad days around Ernie's disappearance. She was completely freaked that he'd show up at their house in the middle of the night, and from her perspective, he wasn't her husband anymore. In her mind, he'd turned into some kind of monster. I couldn't blame her.

She could have stayed at a hotel, but it just seemed right to invite her to stay at my place. I seriously don't have room for houseguests, but we borrowed a futon from Tyler and turned it into a three-day slumber party. I think it was healing for both of us. Not that surprisingly, and with everything considered, we discovered that we had a lot in common. Secret sisters, in a sense, both having survived a close encounter with, as Alex Montoya would have said, a corporate psychopath.

A vacationing family in a charter boat fished Ernie out of the water three days later, still floating in his life jacket. The coroner's report said he didn't drown, but had been killed by a "sharp blow to his skull" as would happen, for instance, if you were floating around in the water at night very carefully, very stealthily, and a coast guard vessel—or maybe even your own boat—suddenly moved quickly, or you were lifted against another boat's wake, hit with a blunt object and jettisoned overboard or…. Well, we'll never really know and speculation is pointless. Ernie was dead. I mean, this time he was *really* dead. They didn't even dick around with visual identification this time, but went straight to DNA testing.

Arianna said she felt oddly empty, but that it was time for her to head back to Brentwood and figure out how to fill up the rest of her life. I couldn't blame her. There was a sudden and unexpected hole where her husband was supposed to be, even though, truly, that had happened long before he got himself dead.

Aside from the things that I had told the sheriff in San Bernardino—and how relevant was any of that, when you thought about it?—there was nothing to suggest Ernie had been involved in the whole kidnap/short-sell/murder scenario in any way except as a victim. The FedEx pack Sarah sent me burns with its own weight in the file drawer in my desk. The material Jackson accumulated would be a damning cap on everything, would cast its own kind of shadow. I think about it sometimes, about what it would mean, how it would change things. But ruining a dead man's reputation would do nothing but hurt his widow, and maybe even make things easier on Paul. I don't want any part of either of those scenarios.

Of course, as soon as he heard they'd found the body, Paul tried to pin everything on Ernie—who, as a dead person, couldn't defend himself—but there was simply no corroboration from anywhere. The two of them had done that good a job covering their tracks.

The newspapers have been enjoying that aspect of the story, as well. All of a sudden, Ernie is the deceased hero CEO who "lost his life attempting to escape from his captor, a man who had been jealous of Billings since they were together at Harvard."

And, no, I didn't almost lose my lunch when I read that. Because it doesn't really matter anymore. In some regards, it's better this way. For one thing, Wall Street just doesn't need another insider scandal—this one would be even juicier than the guy who used company money to buy an eight thousand dollar toilet-paper-roll holder. Also, since the trading damage—all that manipulative short-selling—had come from *outside* of the company, Langton's damage control is somewhat easier than it would have been if Ernie's involvement had come to light. And since that will ultimately result in the stock price recovering more quickly, I'm all for that. And I know my mom would certainly feel the same way.

It would all have been different if Ernie had lived. I

would have happily done everything I could to bury him then. But he's dead and, like I said before, dead is dead. He's already buried.

I would have thought that, with all that's happened, I would have been glad that Ernie was gone. Relieved. And I won't lie—part of me *is* relieved. He got very scary, there at the end. But another part of me is surprisingly sad. Maybe not so sad for the Ernie he became, but perhaps the one he *could* have been had he taken different roads, made other choices. It's hard not to grieve a little bit for that Ernie.

That Wednesday when we knew he was dead, and Arianna went home, I called Steve and he drove up to Malibu. He brought a pizza and I opened a bottle of wine and we sat out on the deck together and I finally told him everything—*everything*—while the sun set over the Pacific. It felt good—cleansing—to be able to spill it all at his feet in a big messy heap. I realized I was crying about the same time as I realized he was cupping the back of my head in one hand, very gently. A reassuring gesture, and somehow an intimate one. And I hadn't even known I wanted to, needed to, cry.

We were still sitting there like that when Jennifer, Tyler and Tasya came back from some family outing. We heard them before we saw them, shared laughter announcing their arrival like some joyous wave. My tears were gone by then and they smiled when they saw us. I caught Jennifer's approving gaze as I introduced them all to Steve.

Jennifer looks so healthy now, though it's only been a short time. It seems to me she glows with some internal light that wasn't there before. Finding love can do that. It doesn't matter that the love she's found was there for her all along. That kind of love doesn't do you any good if you don't know how to access it. It's like having a key but not knowing what door it opens.

She's seeing a psychologist, getting regular Reiki treatments, and Tasya said she'd signed her up for some kind of aromatherapy empowerment workshop. Being the kind of skeptic I am, I guess I figure the real power in all of that is discovering how loved and cared about she is. These crazy film people that she's forced to call her family, as self-involved as they can be, will go to any lengths, no matter how whacko, to help her put herself back together again. Don't kid yourself, there's power in that, too.

Just as importantly, I think, Jennifer has found some things inside herself that she thought she'd lost and some others she never knew she had. She's reconnected with her father and has discovered that Tasya is an ally and a friend, not the enemy and rival she had feared.

After the doctor had examined Jennifer and announced that all she needed was to sleep it off, Tyler went raging down to The Curl to have a talk with Corby. Tasya said Tyler came back deflated and looking ten years older. Corby had told him he had nothing to do with any of it. He said he didn't even know anything about a kidnapping, just that Jennifer was having trouble at home. "He told me," Tyler said, his voice quiet but edged with pain, "that Jennifer had said her father didn't care what happened to her. What did I do to make her feel that way?"

I told Tyler that, at some level, it doesn't really matter. The paths we take to get places can be even or convoluted, but in the end it makes no difference. As long as we get where we're intended to go. And Tasya has put her foot down—Jennifer has to work very hard now to make up for the schooling she'd lost but, provided she finishes the year with adequate marks at a new school, Tasya has insisted Tyler help Jennifer with her goal to become an actress. Her first year of study will be in L.A., and provided that all goes according to plan, she can go to New York the following year. Tasya confided in me that this will give them another whole year with Jennifer, to make sure she's stable and strong and ready for such a big step. But, from Jennifer's perspective, she'll get the chance to make her dreams come true. And Tyler and Tasya will watch her do it, from very close by.

The night of the wine and pizza, Steve didn't share my bed. To be honest, after he left I was somewhat disappointed that he didn't even try. Later, in Ensenada, where the bed has become a place where we spend a lot of time, he told me it wasn't that he didn't think about it that night.

"I thought about it a lot, in fact. But I would have felt like such a shit that night, Madeline, taking advantage of the vulnerable girl in my arms." And then he smiled. "And anyway, I knew there'd be ample opportunity if I bided my time."

I'm not in love with Steve. I love him—who wouldn't love a guy who painted your toenails?—but I can't imagine sharing my life with him. With anyone, for that matter. Not just now. But right this minute, with the prospect of another moonlit evening on the terrace, another walk in the surf, another chat over breakfast, I can't think of any place I'd rather be. For the moment, that's enough.

New York Times Bestselling Author
Rosemary Rogers brings you a sensual tale
of dark secrets and forbidden passion

ROSEMARY ROGERS

Wild child Madison Westcott detests convention and has no
desire to marry. After scandalizing herself in a coming-out
ball in London, Madison is whisked away to the family's
lush Jamaican plantation by her wealthy aunt and the dark,
mysterious Jefford Harris, for whom Madison soon feels a
powerful attraction she is desperate to deny. But not even
the passion of their one forbidden night can protect them
from an unexpected danger that threatens the unspoken
love between them—and their very lives....

Jewel of My Heart

"Her novels are filled with adventure, excitement and,
always, wildly tempestuous romance."
—*Fort Worth Star-Telegram*

*Available the first week of December 2004,
wherever paperbacks are sold!*